John Dryden

Stanzas on the Death of Oliver Cromwell

John Dryden

Stanzas on the Death of Oliver Cromwell

ISBN/EAN: 9783337024000

Printed in Europe, USA, Canada, Australia, Japan

Cover: Foto ©Andreas Hilbeck / pixelio.de

More available books at **www.hansebooks.com**

ENGLISH CLASSICS

DRYDEN

CHRISTIE

London

HENRY FROWDE

OXFORD UNIVERSITY PRESS WAREHOUSE

7 PATERNOSTER ROW

Clarendon Press Series

DRYDEN

STANZAS ON THE DEATH OF OLIVER CROMWELL
ASTRÆA REDUX; ANNUS MIRABILIS
ABSALOM AND ACHITOPHEL
RELIGIO LAICI; THE HIND AND THE PANTHER

EDITED BY

W. D. CHRISTIE, M.A., C.B.

Trinity College, Cambridge

THIRD EDITION

Oxford

AT THE CLARENDON PRESS

M DCCC LXXXIII

PREFACE TO THE FIRST EDITION.

THE Editor of this volume has published within the last twelvemonth an edition of Dryden's Poems,—one of Messrs. Macmillan's Globe Series,—with a carefully revised text, the result of a labour of some duration. The Globe edition of Dryden's Poems contains more than a hundred corrections of the text as presented in Sir Walter Scott's edition, or that of Mr. Robert Bell in his series of the English Poets. In the portion of Dryden's Poems published in this volume the text is the same as that of the Globe edition; and there are some forty corrections within the compass of these Poems. The Notes to this volume contain a suggestion of one new correction which I have not embodied in the text, not feeling absolutely sure about it; but I think it probable that the words *Caledonian* and *Caledon,* which have come down to us from Dryden in ' The Hind and the Panther' (Part I. line 14, and Part III. line 3), were intended by him to be *Calydonian* and *Calydon.*

The Biography prefixed to this volume is of necessity in much part a repetition of the longer Memoir at the beginning of the Globe edition. Since the publication of the latter I have satisfied myself by additional information obtained from Trinity College, Cambridge, that the story of Dryden's continued residence at Cambridge till 1657 is a mistake, and that he ceased to reside there in 1654 or early in 1655.

W. D. C.

32 Dorset Square, London,
    February 1871.

In this second edition I have been able to make an interesting addition to the note at p. xvi. as to Dryden at Trinity College.

W. D. C.

October, 1873.

CONTENTS.

THE HIND AND THE PANTHER. A POEM
IN THREE PARTS.

BIOGRAPHICAL INTRODUCTION.

THE poetry and authorship of Dryden cover a period of
more than half a century. His first poem was written in
youth, within a few months after the execution of Charles the
First, and his last a few days before death, within not many
months of the death of William the Third and the accession
of Anne to the throne. 'Glorious John Dryden,' or 'Glorious
John,' as Sir Walter Scott christened him, is the great literary
figure of the forty years that follow the Restoration. Dryden
was born only fifteen years, and his first poem was written only
thirty-three years, after the death of Shakespeare. It is strange
to find Dryden deliberately writing in 1672 that the English
language had been so changed since Shakespeare wrote, that
any one then reading his plays, or Fletcher's, or Jonson's,
and comparing them with what had been written since the
Restoration, would see the change 'almost in every line[a].'
There are frequent careless statements and hasty generaliza-
tions in Dryden's critical dissertations, which were mostly
composed rapidly for particular occasions, and there may be
exaggeration in this assertion, but it probably contains more
truth than exaggeration. Milton, born eight years before
Shakespeare's death, was Dryden's senior by twenty-three

---

[a] Defence of the Epilogue to the Second Part of 'The Conquest of
Granada.'

years, and 'Paradise Lost' was published in 1669, the year
before that in which Dryden received the appointment of
poet laureate, succeeding Davenant, the author of 'Gondibert,' and Dryden's co-operator in a versified abridgment
and debasement of 'Paradise Lost.' Milton died in 1674,
unhonoured by the multitude, when Dryden was at the height
of his dramatic popularity, and is spoken of as 'the good
and famous poet' by the cultivated Evelyn [b]. A quarter
of a century later Dryden had a splendid public funeral.
Cowley, who was Dryden's superior in the imaginative faculty,
and who, like Dryden after him, had had a fame unjustly
superior to Milton's during his life, had died in 1667. The
poetry of Cowley had been a favourite reading of Dryden's
youth. He speaks of Cowley, in several passages of his prose
writings, with the respect due to a master, and says on
one occasion that his authority is 'almost sacred' to him [c].
Before the end of the seventeenth century, the popularity of
Cowley had disappeared [d], and no traces of the influence of
his metaphysical style are to be discovered in any of Dryden's
poems later than the 'Annus Mirabilis' of 1666. Denham
and Waller, two poets of humbler order, had, while Dryden
was young, produced smooth and harmonious poems, and
contributed to the improvement of verse; and it remained
for Dryden to advance this work, and bring metrical harmony to perfection in his own poems, and, during forty years
after the Restoration, of various writing in prose and in
verse, to give precision and purity and new wealth and capa-
bility to the English language.

---

[b] Evelyn's Diary, June 27, 1674.

[c] Essay on Heroic Plays, prefixed to the First Part of 'The Conquest
of Granada.'

[d] In the Preface to the 'Fables,' written in 1699, Dryden wrote of
Cowley: 'Though he must always be thought a great poet, he is no
longer esteemed a good writer; and for ten impressions which his works
have had in so many successive years, yet at present a hundred books
are scarcely purchased once a twelvemonth; for, as my last Lord
Rochester said, though somewhat profanely, "Not being of God, he
could not stand."'

John Dryden was born on the 9th of August, 1631[e], at
Aldwincle, a village in Northamptonshire, which was also the
birthplace of the Church historian, Thomas Fuller. Both
his parents belonged to Northamptonshire families of distinction. His father, Erasmus Dryden, the third son of Sir
Erasmus Dryden, Baronet, of Canons Ashby, was a Justice of
the Peace for Northamptonshire. The Drydens were all
Puritans and Commonwealthmen. Sir Erasmus Dryden, who
died in 1632, the year after the birth of his celebrated
grandson, was sent to prison, but a few years before his
death in old age, for refusing to pay loan-money to Charles
the First. To this event Dryden refers in his Epistle to his
cousin John Driden of Chesterton[f], Member for Hunting-
donshire, whose public spirit he compares with their common
grandfather's :—

> ' Such was your generous grandsire, free to grant
>   In Parliaments that weighed their Prince's want,
>   But so tenacious of the common cause
>   As not to lend the king against his laws;
>   And in a loathsome dungeon doomed to lie,
>   In bonds retained his birthright liberty,
>   And shamed oppression till it set him free.'

The old man was liberated on the eve of the general election
for Charles the First's third Parliament in 1628. Sir John

---

[e] The year of Dryden's birth is incorrectly given as 1632 in the inscription on the monument in Westminster Abbey.

[f] Malone and some other biographers have said much about the
spelling of Dryden's name, and represented that he early in life deliberately changed the spelling from *Driden* to *Dryden;* and Malone has made
a statement, which appears to be totally without authority, that the poet
gave offence to his uncle, Sir John, by this change of spelling. The
spelling of names was very variable in Dryden's time, and I believe
there is nothing more than accident in the variations of spelling of his
name: *Dryden*, *Driden*, and also *Dreyden* and *Dreydon* occur. Dryden's
name is spelt *Driden* on title-pages of his works after the Restoration,
and in one instance ('Astræa Redux') as late as 1688. I follow other
biographers and editors in preserving the spelling *Driden* for the name of
his cousin John, to whom he addressed the beautiful poetical epistle, on
account of convenience of distinction.

Dryden, successor to Sir Erasmus, and Dryden's uncle, inherited the Puritan zeal. Dryden's mother was Mary, daughter of the Reverend Henry Pickering, rector of Aldwincle All Saints from 1597 till his death in 1637. The Pickerings were near neighbours of the Drydens, and the two families were connected by marriage before the union of the poet's parents, a daughter of Sir Erasmus Dryden having married Sir John Pickering, Knight, the elder brother of the rector of Aldwincle. Sir Gilbert Pickering, the son and successor of Sir John, was thus doubly related to Dryden. Sir Gilbert, having been made a baronet by Charles the First, became a Cromwellite, and held high office during the Protectorate; he was Chamberlain to Oliver Cromwell, and High Steward of Westminster, and one of the so-called peers of Cromwell's second Chamber of 1658, and afterwards one of Richard Cromwell's chief advisers.

The marriage of Erasmus Dryden and Mary Pickering took place on the 21st of October 1630, in the church of Pilton, a village near Aldwincle. The poet was their first child, the eldest of a family of fourteen. A room in the parsonage-house at Aldwincle All Saints is shown as his birthplace. This tradition, which has been maintained uninterruptedly from Dryden's time till now, is unsupported by positive evidence, but as it necessitates only the probable supposition that his mother was on a visit to her parents at the time of the birth of her first child, there is no reason for not accepting it.

Of the early life of Dryden very little is known. His father possessed a small property at Blakesley in the neighbourhood of Canons Ashby, the seat of the Drydens, and of Tichmarch the seat of the Pickerings. A monument erected in Tichmarch church to his memory, by his cousin Mrs. Creed, has an inscription which boasts that 'he was bred and had his first learning here.' But the best part of his education was obtained at Westminster, under Dr. Busby. He entered the school as a King's Scholar, but in what year is not known. He retained through life a pleasant remembrance of his Westminster days, and a great respect for Dr.

Busby, to whom in 1693 he dedicated his translation of the
Fifth Satire of Persius. He says in the Dedication that he
had received from Dr. Busby 'the first and truest taste of
Persius.' Two of his sons were educated at Westminster
under the same head-master, Dr. Busby. He remembered
to the last, but without resentment, Dr. Busby's floggings.
In one of his latest letters, written in 1699 to Charles
Montagu, Chancellor of the Exchequer, when sending for
his inspection some poems before publication, he speaks of
having corrected and re-corrected them, and he says, 'I am
now in fear that I have purged them out of their spirit, as
our Master Busby used to whip a boy so long till he made
him a confirmed blockhead.' Charles Montagu had been
educated at Westminster, but he was thirty years younger
than Dryden, and might have been at the school with Dryden's
sons.

In 1650 Dryden left Westminster with a scholarship, for
Trinity College, Cambridge. In 1649 he had written his
first poem, which gave little promise of the smoothness and
harmony of versification to which he afterwards attained.
Lord Hastings, the subject of it, the eldest son of the Earl
of Huntingdon, had been educated at Westminster, and his
rare attainments had raised among his friends high hopes of
future eminence. When these hopes were destroyed by his
untimely death from small pox, when he was just of age, in
1649, the event was lamented in as many as thirty-three
elegies by different authors, which were collected and published in 1650 by Richard Brome, with the title of 'Lacrymæ
Musarum, the Tears of the Muses; exprest in Elegies
written by divers Persons of nobility and worth upon the
death of Henry Lord Hastings, only son of the Right Honourable Ferdinando Earl of Huntingdon, heir-general of the
high-born Prince George, Duke of Clarence, brother to King
Edward the Fourth 8.' Among the contributors to this volume
were three who were already known as poets, and whose

---

8 Sir Walter Scott, who had not seen this little volume, erroneously
gives ninety-eight as the number of the elegies.

fame has survived them, Denham, Herrick, and Andrew
Marvel. Dryden's second known poem, a short complimentary address prefixed to a little volume of sacred poetry
by John Hoddesden, a friend and schoolfellow, was probably
written at the beginning of Dryden's residence at Cambridge. Hoddesden's little volume bore the title 'Sion and
Parnassus,' and was published in 1650.

Dryden was entered at Trinity College, Cambridge, on
the 18th of May, 1650; he matriculated July 16, and
was elected a scholar of the college on the Westminster
foundation, October 2, 1650. He took his degree of Bachelor
of Arts in January 1654. Beyond these dates very little is
known of his college life. With the exception of a single
passage in his life of Plutarch, where he mentions having
read that author in the library of Trinity College, Cambridge,
and adds that to that foundation he gratefully acknowledges
the debt of a great part of his education, there is no mention
of his Cambridge days in his writings; and this silence has
created an impression that in after life he regarded Cambridge
with aversion. Some lines in one of his Oxford Prologues,
written in 1681, have seemed further proof of such a feeling—

> 'Oxford to him a dearer name shall be
> Than his own mother university;
> Thebes did his green unknowing youth engage,
> He chooses Athens in his riper age.'

But these lines prove nothing, being probably prompted by
no other motive than the desire of the moment to please an
Oxford audience. A passage in a letter from Dryden to
Wilmot Earl of Rochester, written in 1675, in which he
sends him copies of a Prologue and Epilogue for Oxford,
composed on another occasion, shows that all he wrote for
Oxford may not be sincere. He tells Rochester that the pieces
were approved, 'and by the event your lordship will judge
how easy 'tis to pass anything upon an University, and what
gross flattery the learned will endure.'

But Dryden's life at Cambridge had not passed always
pleasantly. In the second year of his residence at Trinity,

statutes of the University, any one possessed of any estate, annuity, or certain income for life amounting to 26*l.* 13*s.* 4*d.* was required to pay 6*l.* 6*s.* 4*d.* in addition to the ordinary fees for any degree; and those for the M.A. degree for one not a fellow would be as much. Dryden, with his small income of forty pounds, might naturally be unwilling to incur this expense. It is possible also that Dryden's premature departure from Cambridge without fellowship or degree may have been caused by a disagreeable incident, such as he is taunted with by Shadwell—

> 'At Cambridge first your scurrilous vein began,
> Where saucily you traduced a nobleman,
> Who for that crime traduced you on the head,
> And you had been expelled had you not fled[1].'

The scurrility of Shadwell is anything but perfect authority, but there must have been some foundation for the taunt of these malicious lines.

A degree of Master of Arts was conferred on Dryden by the Archbishop of Canterbury in 1668, on the recommendation of King Charles the Second, when he had made himself known as an author, and had acquired the King's favour by political poems and plays suited to his taste.

There is no information about Dryden's life after his leaving Cambridge till he appeared as an author in London on the occasion of Oliver Cromwell's death. It has always hitherto been said that he began to reside in London about the middle of 1657; but this was probably a part of the story that he continued to reside till 1657 at Cambridge. It is not impossible that he went to London earlier than has been hitherto supposed; and it is quite possible that he may have gone there later. He was probably aided by his relative, Sir Gilbert Pickering, at the beginning of his life in London, and he may have gone thither soon after his father's death to profit by Sir Gilbert's friendship. High in Cromwell's favour, a member of his Privy Council, and Chamberlain of his household, he was in a position to render

---

[1] 'The Medal of John Bayes.'

valuable assistance to his clever young cousin. Shadwell, after taunting Dryden with discreditable flight from Cambridge, next holds him up to scorn as clerk to Sir Gilbert—

> ' The next step of advancement you began,
>> Was being clerk to Noll's Lord Chamberlain,
>> A sequestrator and Committee man [k].'

It is not improbable that Sir Gilbert employed him as his secretary.

Oliver Cromwell died on the 3rd of September, 1658; and Dryden, now in his twenty-seventh year, wrote a poem in honour of his memory. Since he had written the verses to John Hoddesden in 1650, being then an undergraduate at Cambridge, he had written no poetry that is known, and the ' Heroic Stanzas ' to the memory of the Protector is his first poem of any importance. This poem was published with two others on the same subject by Waller and Sprat. It is written in quatrain stanzas, and ·is very superior to Dryden's two earlier efforts. When the ' Heroic Stanzas ' appeared, Richard Cromwell seemed to be firmly established as his father's successor, and Dryden celebrated the peaceful security which the able and vigorous government of the Protector had bequeathed to his country. .

> ' No civil broils have since his death arose,
>> But faction now by habit does obey ;
> And wars have that respect for his repose
>> As winds for halcyons when they breed at sea.
>
> His ashes in a peaceful urn shall rest ;
>> His name a great example stands to show
> How strangely high endeavours may be blessed
>> Where piety and valour jointly go.'

This tranquillity was of short duration. On the meeting of Parliament in January 1659 it was evident that Richard Cromwell was unable to rule, and in less than eighteen months after the publication of the ' Heroic Stanzas ' Charles the Second was restored.

---

[k] Malone strangely thinks that the last line may apply to Dryden himself, but it is clearly intended for Sir Gilbert Pickering.

Sir Gilbert Pickering, who had been closely and conspicuously connected with both the Protectors, and who had sat as one of the judges at the trial of Charles the First, though not when sentence was given, was lucky to escape with life and with most of his property. He was made incapable of all office, and became a private and powerless man. Dryden, having lost this serviceable benefactor, and not being disposed to sacrifice all advancement to political consistency, became a warm Royalist, and now endeavoured, by zealously espousing the cause of the restored King, to blot out all recollection of his praises of the Protector. 'Astræa Redux,' a poem written in celebration of the return of the King, was published before the end of the year, and was quickly followed by two other poems in. like strain, a 'Panegyric' addressed to the King on his coronation, and an address to the Lord Chancellor Clarendon, on New Year's Day, 1662. These poems doubtless brought presents of money. Some complimentary verses, addressed by Dryden to Sir Robert Howard, were published in 1660, in the beginning of a volume of Howard's poems, the first of which was a panegyric on the restored King, and the last a panegyric on Monk, his chief restorer. Sir Robert Howard was a younger son of the Earl of Berkshire, who had been constant, with all his family, to the cause of royalty, and had impoverished himself in the cause. Henry Herringman was at this time the fashionable publisher, and published both for Howard and Dryden. Shadwell proceeds, in his vituperative biography, to taunt Dryden with drudgery for Herringman, and with living on Howard.

> 'He turned a journeyman to a bookseller,
> Wrote prefaces to books for meat and drink,
> And, as he paid, he would both write and think;
> Then, by the assistance of a noble knight,
> Thou hadst plenty, ease, and liberty to write:
> First like a gentleman he made thee live,
> And on his bounty thou didst amply thrive[1].'

---

[1] 'The Medal of John Bayes.'

Theatrical representations, which the austerity of the Puritans had proscribed during the Commonwealth, were now revived, and Dryden immediately turned to play-writing and made it a source of income. After the Restoration, two theatres, and only two, were licensed, one called the King's, which was under the management of Thomas Killigrew, the court wit and a dramatic writer, and the other, the Duke of York's, under the poet laureate, Sir William Davenant. Dryden's first play, 'The Wild Gallant,' was produced at the King's Theatre, in February 1663. It was not successful, and he attributed the failure to his boldness 'in beginning with comedy, which is the most difficult part of dramatic poetry.' A tragi-comedy, 'The Rival Ladies,' brought out in the same year, was better received. Pepys, who had pronounced 'The Wild Gallant' 'so poor a thing as ever he saw in his life,' thought this 'a very innocent and most pretty witty play [m].' The plots of both plays are extravagantly improbable, and coarseness and indecency appear in both. But they pleased the court, perhaps rather on account of than in spite of their demerits; and even the unpopular 'Wild Gallant' was specially favoured by Lady Castlemaine, and her royal lover caused it to be several times performed at court. Dryden next assisted Sir Robert Howard in the composition of a tragedy, 'The Indian Queen,' which was acted with great success at the King's Theatre, in January 1664.

Before 'The Indian Queen' was brought out on the stage, Howard and Dryden had become brothers-in-law. Dryden was married to Lady Elizabeth Howard on the 1st of December 1663. This was not a happy marriage. Lady Elizabeth was a woman of violent temper, and had apparently no sympathy with her husband's literary pursuits. Dryden has been taunted by some of the virulent foes of his later life with having been hectored into this marriage by the lady's brothers in order to save her reputation; and there is reason to believe that her conduct before marriage was not

---

[m] Diary, February 23, 1663, and August 4, 1664.

irreproachable. If this were so, happiness could hardly be expected.

The success of 'The Indian Queen' encouraged Dryden to bring out in the following year, 1665, a sequel, under the title of 'The Indian Emperor,' and that play was a great success and much advanced Dryden's fame. 'The Indian Emperor' was published in 1667, with a dedication to the young and beautiful Duchess of Monmouth, the 'charming Annabel' of 'Absalom and Achitophel,' who was an early patroness of Dryden, and whom in his later years he called his 'first and best patroness[a].' 'The Rival Ladies' had been published with a dedication to the Earl of Orrery, a dramatic writer. 'The Wild Gallant' was not published till 1669, when the fame otherwise acquired by Dryden helped to recommend it to favour. He revived 'The Wild Gallant' on the stage in 1667.

In the summer of 1665 the Plague broke out in London, and all who could do so fled to the country. Dryden retired to Charlton, in Wiltshire, the seat of his father-in-law, Lord Berkshire, and he remained there for the greater part of eighteen months. During this period of retreat he wrote the 'Annus Mirabilis,' the 'Essay on Dramatic Poesy,' and the comedy of 'Secret Love, or the Maiden Queen.'

The 'Annus Mirabilis,' a poem celebrating the events of the year 1665–6, and describing the war with Holland, the Plague, and the Great Fire of London, was published in 1667, with a dedication to the Metropolis, and a long preface addressed to Sir Robert Howard. This poem is written in the quatrain stanzas in which Dryden had sung the praises of Oliver Cromwell eight years before. In the preface he says, 'I have chosen to write my poem in quatrain stanzas of four alternate rhymes, because I have ever judged them more noble and of greater dignity both for sound and numbers than any other verse in use among us.' The minute knowledge of naval matters displayed in the poem was acquired

---

[a] Dedication of 'King Arthur,' to the Marquis of Halifax, 1691.

it appears, for the occasion and under some difficulties. 'For my own part,' he says, 'if I had little knowledge of the sea, yet I have thought it no shame to learn, and if I have made some mistakes, it is only, as you can bear me witness, because I have wanted opportunity to correct them, the whole poem being first written and now sent you from a place where I have not so much as the converse of any seaman.' In this poem Dryden's skill and force of language is first strikingly remarkable. Some parts of it, and especially the description of the Fire of London, are very fine.

Dryden's next publication was the 'Essay on Dramatic Poesy,' also written during his long residence at Charlton: this was published in 1668. A subject treated of in this essay was the use of rhyme in tragedies, which was now the fashion, and favoured by the King. Dryden had praised rhymed tragedies in his dedication to the Earl of Orrery, of the 'Rival Ladies,' published in 1664. In the following year Sir Robert Howard published a collection of plays, with a preface, in which, though he had himself done tragedy in rhyme, he severely criticised Dryden's doctrine. In the 'Essay on Dramatic Poesy,' Dryden vindicated his views. The essay was in the form of a conversation between four persons, Eugenius, Lisideius, Crites, and Neander; and under these names were respectively veiled Lord Buckhurst (afterwards Earl of Dorset), Sir Charles Sedley, Sir Robert Howard, and Dryden himself. Neander maintained the cause of rhyme in tragedies, and Crites argued on the other side with inferior force. This led to a literary controversy with Howard, which produced for a time some ill-feeling between the brothers-in-law, but the estrangement did not last long.

During the ravages of the Plague and Fire the playhouses had been closed. They were re-opened towards the close of 1666, and in the following March 'Secret Love, or the Maiden Queen,' the play which Dryden had written at Charlton, was brought out at the King's Theatre. It was a great success. Pepys, who was present on the first night, commends 'the regularity of it and the strain of wit,' and is quite enthusiastic in his praises of Nell Gwyn, in the part of

Florimel °. The play was published in the following year, with a preface, in which Dryden states that Charles had 'graced' the successful comedy 'with the title of his play.' Another comedy, 'Sir Martin Mar-all,' was brought out in the autumn of 1667 at the Duke's House. This was an adaptation of Molière's play, 'L'Étourdi,' which had been translated by the Duke of Newcastle; and when it appeared on the stage, Pepys tells us that the general opinion was that it was a 'play by the Lord Duke of Newcastle, and corrected by Dryden.' Dryden afterwards published himself as author, and we may take for granted that the authorship was really his. 'The Tempest, or the Enchanted Island,' produced at the Duke's Theatre in November, 1667, was an adaptation by Dryden and Davenant of Shakespeare's Tempest. The new play was nothing more nor less than a debasement of Shakespeare's, and Dryden doubtless knew well its inferiority. In the prologue he paid a fine tribute to the genius of Shakespeare. These are the opening lines :—

> 'As when a tree's cut down, the secret root,
>   Lives underground, and thence new branches shoot,
>   So from old Shakespeare's honoured dust this day
>   Springs up and buds a new reviving play:
>   Shakespeare, who, taught by none, did first impart
>   To Fletcher wit, to labouring Jonson art;
>   He, monarch-like, gave these his subjects law,
>   And is that Nature which they paint and draw.'

And in the same prologue he says—

> 'But Shakespeare's magic could not copied be;
>   Within that circle none durst walk but he.'

Again—

> 'But Shakespeare's power is sacred as a king's.'

Dryden and Davenant's 'Tempest' was published by Dryden in 1668, Davenant having died in the interval : and in the preface Dryden mentions that Davenant had taught him to venerate Shakespeare.

° Diary, March 2, 1667.

If Dryden's mutilation of the Tempest seems inconsistent with his reverence for Shakespeare, it must be borne
in mind that Dryden wrote for money, that to adapt took
less time than to create, and that the audiences for which he
wrote neglected Shakespeare's plays and applauded Dryden's.

> 'Those who have best succeeded on the stage
> Have still conformed their genius to their age P.'

The year 1667 had been one of great dramatic success for
Dryden. The 'Maiden Queen,' 'Sir Martin Mar-all,' and
'The Tempest' had all been well received, and his first play,
'The Wild Gallant,' unsuccessful when it first appeared, had
been revived with some success.

Until now the profits derived by Dryden from his plays
had come from the third night's representation, which custom
made the author's benefit, from the prices received from his
publisher, from presents in return for dedications, and probably also from a retaining fee from the King's company, to
which all his plays were given. A successful 'third night' of
a play would probably at this time bring Dryden forty or at
most fifty guineas, and the price of the copyright of one of
his plays would now be but a trifle. Thus, for 'Cleomenes,'
one of his latest plays, he is known to have received thirty
guineas, and no more; and this was probably the highest
price he ever got. He is said never to have received, in his
days of greatest fame, more than a hundred guineas for third
night and copyright together. There had been no dedication
to his last three published plays, the 'Maiden Queen,' 'Sir
Martin Mar-all,' and 'The Tempest.' But henceforth his
plays were always dedicated to some noble patron, who, according to the custom of the time, sent a present of money
in return for the compliment. To recount Dryden's noble
patrons is a necessary part of his biography. 'What I pretend by this dedication,' he said in 1691, in dedicating 'King
Arthur' to George Savile Lord Halifax, 'is an honour which
I do myself to posterity by acquainting them that I have been
conversant with the first persons of the age in which I lived.'

P Dryden's Epilogue to the Second Part of 'The Conquest of Granada.'

After the production of 'The Tempest' he entered into a contract with the King's company, by which he bound himself to produce three plays a year, in return for a share and a quarter of the profits of the theatre, all which were divided into twelve shares and a quarter. Under this arrangement Dryden received from 1667 to 1672 a yearly income of from 300*l.* to 400*l.* a year. The King's Theatre was burnt down in 1672, and the losses of the company then reduced Dryden's share of profits to about 200*l.* a year. His reciprocal duty, to write three plays a year, was never fulfilled; but the company appear to have behaved always generously to him and not to have mulcted him for his shortcomings.

Under this new contract two comedies, 'An Evening's Love, or the Mock Astrologer,' an adaptation of the younger Corneille's 'Feint Astrologue,' and 'Ladies à la Mode,' were produced in 1668. 'An Evening's Love' was not very successful. Evelyn went to see it, and was 'afflicted to see how the stage was degenerated and polluted by the licentious times[q].' The criticism of Samuel Pepys is very similar, and Herringman, the publisher, told Pepys that Dryden himself considered it but a fifth-rate play[r]. Of 'Ladies à la Mode,' Pepys, from whom alone we have knowledge of it, says that it was a translation from the French, and that it was 'so mean a thing as when they came to say it would be acted again, both he that said it, Beeson, and the pit fell a laughing, there being this day not a quarter of the pit full.' It was never acted again, and Dryden never published it[s].

Dryden's mother died in 1670. He was an affectionate son, and there are indeed none but pleasant indications of his relations with members of his family. The first of some little bequests in the will of the mother, who had little to leave, is a silver tankard and her wedding-ring to her son, now so famous. 'I give and bequeath to my beloved son, John Dryden, a silver tankard marked with J. D., and a gold

---

q Evelyn's Diary, June 19, 1668.

r Pepys' Diary, June 20 and 22, 1668.

s Ibid. September 15, 1668.

ring, which was my wedding-ring. And it is my will that after the decease of my dear son, John Dryden, his eldest son, Charles Dryden, should have the ring as a gift from his grandmother, Mary Dryden.' On the death of his mother, Dryden came into possession of the whole of the little Blakesley estate, and the addition thus made to his income was not more than 20*l.* a year: but his income at this time, derived from various sources, from his estate, his salary and his brain-work, probably amounted to about 700*l.* a year.

Three tragedies in heroic verse, 'Tyrannic Love, or the Royal Martyr,' and 'Almanzor and Almahide, or the Conquest of Granada,' in two parts, each being a separate play, appeared in 1669 and 1670, and added greatly to Dryden's fame. 'Tyrannic Love' was dedicated to the Duke of Monmouth, and 'The Conquest of Granada' to the Duke of York. In August 1670 he received a substantial mark of royal favour. The two appointments of Poet Laureate and Historiographer Royal, which had been vacant, the one since the death of Sir William Davenant in 1668, the other since the death of James Howell in 1666, were conferred upon Dryden, with a salary of 200*l.* a year and arrears from Midsummer 1668; and an annual butt of canary wine from the King's cellars was added to the salary.

In December 1671 'The Rehearsal,' a farce the preparation of which had for some ten years occupied the second George Villiers, Duke of Buckingham, and in which he is said to have had assistance from the author of 'Hudibras' and others, was brought out at the King's Theatre. The object of this farce was to ridicule the rhymed tragedies of the Restoration. The farce had been begun some time before the death of the former poet laureate, Davenant, and he had been the original hero, but Davenant dying before the farce was finished, Dryden, his successor in the laureateship, was caricatured in his stead as the poet 'Bayes.' It is said that the Duke of Buckingham himself drilled the actor, Lacey, to whom the part of 'Bayes' was allotted, to imitate Dryden's manner[t]. The piece had a great success, and its fame endures;

---

[t] Spence's Anecdotes (Villiers, Duke of Buckingham).

the name of Bayes stuck to Dryden through life. Dryden
bore this attack in silence, claiming credit in later years
for a forbearance which was probably prompted by prudence,
for Buckingham was at the time a leading minister and in
great favour with the King [u].

During the year 1671 Dryden produced no play. In
January 1672 the King's Theatre in Drury Lane was burnt
down, and the company removed to a house in Lincoln's Inn
Fields. The impoverished circumstances of the company,
which directly affected himself, probably stimulated Dryden
to exertion, and in this year he produced two new comedies,
'Marriage à la Mode,' which was very successful, and 'The
Assignation, or Love in a Nunnery,' which was condemned.
'Amboyna, or the Cruelties of the Dutch to the English
Merchants,' was Dryden's next production. England and
France were now jointly engaged in war against Holland, and
the tragedy of 'Amboyna' was written for the purpose of
inflaming national feeling against the Dutch. This is one of
Dryden's worst plays. It was written, he says, 'in haste, but
with an English heart.' This eager advocate of the Dutch
war of 1672 afterwards reviled and persecuted Shaftesbury
for having promoted it. 'Amboyna' was dedicated to Lord
Clifford, Shaftesbury's colleague in what is called the Cabal
Ministry, who was a private friend and zealous patron of
Dryden. 'Marriage à la Mode' had been dedicated to
Wilmot Earl of Rochester, who later became Dryden's
virulent enemy, but of whom he now said, addressing him,
'You have not only been careful of my reputation, but of my
fortune,' and 'I have found the effects of your protection in
all my concernments.' 'The Assignation' was dedicated to the
witty and dissolute Sir Charles Sedley.

---

[u] There is a severe and vigorous poem on the Duke of Buckingham
printed in the collection called ' State Poems,' which some have ascribed
to Dryden, but probably wrongly. The slow composition of ' The Rehearsal' is there alluded to :

 ' I come to his farce, which must needs be well done,
  For Troy was not longer before it was won,
  Since 'tis more than ten years since this farce was begun.'

'The State of Innocence,' a transformation of 'Paradise Lost' into an opera, and intended for the stage but never acted, was Dryden's literary work of the year 1674. Aubrey relates that Dryden called on Milton to ask permission to versify his poem, and was dryly told by the blind old man that he might 'tag his verses' if he pleased. 'Paradise Lost' had been published five years before, and had not excited enthusiasm. But Dryden had taken a just measure of the poem, and in the preface of his own 'State of Innocence' he declared it to be 'undoubtedly one of the greatest, most noble, and sublime poems which either this age or nation has produced.' Shortly after the publication of 'The State of Innocence' Milton died, on the 8th of November, 1674. Dryden's well-known lines on Milton were written fourteen years later, to be printed under his portrait prefixed to an edition of 'Paradise Lost,' published by subscription in 1695 by Jacob Tonson.

> 'Three poets in three distant ages born
> Greece, Italy, and England did adorn.
> The first in loftiness of thought surpassed,
> The next in majesty, in both the last.
> The force of nature could no farther go:
> To make a third she joined the former two.'

In the prologue of 'Aurengzebe, or the Great Mogul,' a tragedy produced in 1675, Dryden informed his audience that he had grown tired of rhyme in tragedy and generally dissatisfied with play-writing. Having begun by speaking disparagingly of the play, but, as he said, 'out of no feigned modesty,' he proceeds in this prologue :—

> '‘Not that it's worse than what before he writ,
> But he has now another taste of wit:
> And to confess a truth, though out of time,
> Grows weary of his long-loved mistress, Rhyme.
> Passion's too fierce to be in fetters bound,
> And Nature flies him like enchanted ground.
> What verse can do he has performed in this,
> Which he presumes the most correct of his;

> But spite of all his pride, a secret shame
> Invades his breast at Shakespeare's sacred name:
> Awed when he hears his godlike Roman rage,
> He in a just despair would quit the stage;
> And to an age less polished, more unskilled
> Does with disdain the foremost honours yield.
> As with the greater dead he dares not strive,
> He would not match his verse with those who live.
> Let him retire betwixt two ages cast,
> The first of this and hindmost of the last.'

Dryden had now for some time wished to apply himself to the composition of an epic poem: but for this leisure was necessary, and play-writing gave him bread. He explains himself on this subject in the dedication of 'Aurengzebe,' to Sheffield Earl of Mulgrave. He had had an opportunity, through Mulgrave's good offices, of speaking both with the King and the Duke of York of his desire to devote himself to the production of a national epic poem, and he now asked Mulgrave to remind the King of his ambition. Several years later, in 1693, in his 'Discourse on Satire,' addressed to the Earl of Dorset, he mentions two subjects which he had thought of; one was the conquest of Spain by Edward the Black Prince, and the other King Arthur conquering the Saxons. Dryden's wishes were not gratified by the King. No office was given him which relieved him from the necessity of writing for subsistence. It is however possible that the King may now have granted him the pension of 100*l*. a year in addition to the salaried offices of Poet Laureate and Historiographer Royal, which it has been lately ascertained that he obtained during the reign of Charles II; but the date of the grant of the pension is not known [x].

Dryden's next play did not appear for two years after;

---

[x] This pension from Charles was first made known by the publication by Mr. R. Bell in 1854 of a treasury warrant of 1684 for payment of arrears; and Mr. P. Cunningham has since published a treasury warrant for payment of a quarter due January 5, 1679. (Johnson's 'Lives of the Poets,' Cunningham's edition, vol. i. p. 334, note.)

it was 'All for Love, or the World Well Lost,' the story
of Antony and Cleopatra, and it was produced at the King's
Theatre in the winter of 1677-8. To the preparation of
this tragedy Dryden had devoted more time and labour
than usual, and he considered it his best play. 'All for Love'
had great success, and the company gave Dryden the benefit of
the third night, to which the terms of his contract did not
entitle him. This act of generosity appears to have been ill
requited by Dryden; his next play 'Œdipus,' written in
conjunction with Nathaniel Lee, was given to the Duke's
company and brought out at the rival theatre. This was
regarded by the King's company as a breach of contract, with
the aggravation of ingratitude. He had never fulfilled his
engagement to write three plays a year, and indeed had produced on an average less than one a year. The King's company
now complained to the Earl of Arlington, the Lord Chamberlain, of Dryden's proceeding as a violation of contract; but
there is no sign of their having obtained redress ⁷. Dryden
now broke with the King's Theatre, or the King's Theatre
with him, and his subsequent plays came out at the rival
house. 'The Kind Keeper, or Limberham,' a very coarse
comedy, followed 'Œdipus,' and gave such offence that, after
it had been three times acted, Dryden withdrew it. In April
1679, he produced with indifferent success 'Troilus and Cressida,' an adaptation of Shakespeare's play. 'All for Love,' on
its publication, was dedicated to the Earl of Danby, then the
chief Minister; 'Limberham,' to Lord Vaughan, a literary
nobleman, and 'Troilus and Cressida,' to the Earl of Sunderland, a rising politician and future leading minister.

As Dryden was returning to his house in Long Acre through
Rose Alley, Drury Lane, on the night of the 18th of
December, 1679, he was fallen upon and severely beaten by a
gang of ruffians. There appears to be little doubt that the

---

⁷ Almost all our information as to Dryden's partnership in the King's
Theatre is derived from this memorial of complaint addressed to the
Lord Chamberlain, which is printed in Malone's Life of Dryden, p. 73.

instigator of this cowardly attack was Wilmot Earl of Rochester, who conceived Dryden to be the author of a poem in
circulation, an Essay on Satire, in which he was severely
attacked. Sheffield Earl of Mulgrave, afterwards Marquis
of Normanby and Duke of Buckinghamshire, is now known
to have been the author of the poem; but at the time a
belief seems to have prevailed that Dryden had written it.
It is not impossible that Dryden may have seen the poem
before it was put in circulation and given it some revision.
Yet it is difficult to believe that Dryden, who was dependent
on the King's pleasure for 300*l.* a year of his income, would
have been so imprudent as to make himself in any way respon-
sible for a poem in which the King also was severely assailed.
It is more likely that the great intimacy which existed at this
period between Dryden and Mulgrave is the sole origin of the
suspicion. Mulgrave positively asserted in a note in a later
edition of the poem that Dryden was entirely innocent of the
authorship. In a poem of Rochester's, published the year
before, Dryden had been freely and unpleasantly criticised,
and Rochester may have expected retaliation and been
prone to conclude that Mulgrave's attack on him came from
Dryden. These are Rochester's lines in his 'Allusion to
the Tenth Satire of the First Book of Horace,' published in
1673.

> 'Well, sir, 'tis granted, I said Dryden's rhymes
> Were stol'n, unequal, nay, dull many times.
> What foolish patron is there found of his
> So blindly partial to deny me this?
> But that his plays, embroidered up and down
> With wit and learning, justly pleased the town,
> In the same paper I as freely own.
> Yet having this allowed, the heavy mass
> That stuffs up his loose volumes must not pass.'

A publicly advertised offer of a reward of fifty pounds for
the discovery of the offenders failed to furnish any clue to
the author of this dastardly assault. This Rose Alley assault
became the theme of many taunts from Dryden's bitter

adversaries after he threw himself into political controversies[z].

One of Dryden's most successful plays was the 'Spanish Friar, or the Double Discovery,' a satire on the Roman Catholic priesthood, produced at the Duke's Theatre in 1681, at a time when popular feeling was strongly excited against the Papists, and when the question of the day was the exclusion of the Duke of York from the succession because he was a Roman Catholic.

Dryden's pecuniary resources about this time had become much crippled. Through the poverty of the Treasury, his salary and pension were not paid, and in May 1684 there was a four years' accumulation of arrears. After the production of the 'Spanish Friar,' Dryden turned from play-writing to political satire. His famous political poem 'Absalom and Achitophel' was published in November 1681. The subject of the poem, Shaftesbury and Monmouth, is said to have been suggested by the King himself. Monmouth, the Absalom of the poem, for whom his father, Charles, had always a tender affection, is treated through the poem with great delicacy, but Shaftesbury, who is Achitophel, is truculently and unscrupulously assailed. Together with Shaftesbury, Buckingham, who was now one of the great Protestant opposition to the court, is described in Dryden's happiest vein, under the name of Zimri.

Shaftesbury had been lying in the Tower under a charge of high treason since July 2, 1681, and Dryden's poem was published a very few days before his trial, probably with the deliberate object of inflaming public opinion against him and helping to obtain a condemnation. The poem was published on November 17; on November 24 the bill of indictment

---

[z] One of these is worth quoting to illustrate the old pronunciation of *aches* as a word of two syllables as late as 1680—

'Thus needy Bayes, his Rose Street aches past.'

'The Protestant Satire.'

Dryden himself pronounced the word in the same manner in his first poem, the 'Elegy on Lord Hastings,' written in 1649. *Aches* rhymes with *catches* in 'Hudibras,' Part II. Canto ii. l. 456; and see also Part III. Canto ii. l. 407 of 'Hudibras.'

against Shaftesbury went before a London grand jury, and was thrown out. The decision was received by the people of London with acclamations, and a medal was struck by his friends in commemoration of his triumph. The sale of 'Absalom and Achitophel' was so rapid that a second edition appeared within a month. The medal celebrating Shaftesbury's escape from his persecutors furnished Dryden with a subject and a name for a new political satire, which was even more fierce against Shaftesbury than its predecessor. 'The Medal' was brought out in March 1682. This poem, as well as 'Absalom and Achitophel,' was published anonymously, but there was no doubt as to the authorship of either poem; and Dryden's opponents were quick to produce answers, all more remarkable for virulence than literary merit. 'The Medal of John Bayes,' by Shadwell, especially roused Dryden's anger. Shadwell and he had formerly been on friendly terms, and Dryden had written in 1678 a prologue to Shadwell's play, 'The True Widow.' They probably now quarrelled only on political grounds. There was now great fury between the partisans of the Duke of York and those of the Duke of Monmouth, and at this period arose the divisions and the names of Whig and Tory. Dryden was with the Tories, and Shadwell with Shaftesbury, Monmouth, and the Whigs. 'The Medal of John Bayes' provoked Dryden to write a new satire, 'Mac Flecknoe,' in which Shadwell is represented as the poetical heir of Flecknoe, an inferior poet and voluminous author, who had died some five years before. 'Mac Flecknoe' was published in October 1682. In the following month a second part of 'Absalom and Achitophel' appeared. Of this poem only a small portion was by Dryden; the bulk of the poem being the production of Nahum Tate, who afterwards translated the Psalms into verse, and became in time poet laureate. Dryden contributed two hundred lines, and he perhaps revised the whole of Tate's work.

Dryden now passed from politics to theology, and produced 'Religio Laici,' a clear and argumentative exposition in harmonious verse, of the Protestant faith. The merits of this poem are happily, and without exaggeration, described

by Dryden's friend and brother-poet, Lord Roscommon, in
some lines of commendation which were prefixed to the
poem on its publication :—

> ' Let free impartial men from Dryden learn
>   Mysterious secrets of a high concern,
>   And weighty truths, solid convincing sense,
>   Explained by unaffected eloquence.'

A drama, the 'Duke of Guise,' a joint work of Dryden and
Nathaniel Lee, was brought out in December 1682. The two
rival theatres had now found it necessary to combine, and
this was the first new play brought out by the united company. In the prologue Dryden announced the play to be a
parallel :—

> ' Our play's a parallel; the Holy League
>   Begot our covenant; Guisards got the Whig.'

In spite of Dryden's zealous championship of the court,
his salary remained unpaid, and his pecuniary distress was
great. In a letter to Laurence Hyde, Earl of Rochester,
a Commissioner of the Treasury, probably written in the
latter part of 1683, he prays for the payment of the arrears
of his salary, amounting to about 1300*l.*, and asks also for
some small appointment. He says in this letter, ' I have
three sons growing to man's estate; I breed them all up to
learning, beyond my fortune; but they are too hopeful to
be neglected, though I want.' Of these sons, Charles, the
eldest, born in 1665 or 1666, entered Trinity College, Cambridge, as a Westminster Scholar, in June 1683; the second,
John, born 1667 or 1668, was now at Westminster; and the
youngest, Erasmus Henry, born in May 1669, had been admitted to the Charterhouse by the nomination of the King
in February 1683. It was probably in consequence of Dryden's
appeal to Rochester that an Exchequer warrant for the payment of half a year's salary and a quarter's pension was issued
on the 6th of May, 1684; and there is reason to believe that
in time all arrears were paid to him. He received also in
December 1683 the appointment of Collector of Customs
in London, which may have been a profitable one.

Various literary labours occupied the poet at this time.   In
1683 he contributed a life and a preface to a new translation
of Plutarch by various hands, and he translated, by order of the
King, Maimbourg's 'History of the League.'   In 1684 and
1685 he published successively two volumes of poetical Miscellanies, containing, with some poems by other authors,
translations of his own from Virgil, Horace, and Ovid.   To
the second volume his eldest son was a contributor.

On the 5th of February, 1685, Charles the Second died, and
the crown passed to his brother James.   Before the King's
death Dryden had written an opera, 'Albion and Albanius,' to
celebrate the triumph of the court party over the opposition;
this had not yet been publicly acted, but it had been several
times rehearsed at court with approval. 'Albion and Albanius'
was published after James's accession.   But before this publication Dryden produced an ode to the memory of Charles
under the title of 'Threnodia Augustalis,' in which both
Charles and James were extravagantly lauded.

As, on the restoration of Charles the Second, Dryden, to
win royal favour, had broken away from all the associations
of his youth, and had appeared without delay as the eager
champion of monarchy, so now, when a declared Roman
Catholic was seated on the throne, and to be a Roman
Catholic seemed the best way to advancement, he was soon
convinced that it was right to be a Roman Catholic.   Before
his conversion James had continued him in the posts of Poet
Laureate and Historiographer Royal; and shortly after it,
in March 1686, the additional pension of 100*l.* a year, which
had been granted him by Charles, was renewed by letters
patent.   Lord Macaulay, who has represented this pension
granted by James as the reward of Dryden's conversion,
wrote before it was known to be merely a renewal of an
old pension granted to Dryden by his predecessor, and he
has certainly exaggerated its effects in producing that conversion; but it would be difficult to prove that Lord Macaulay
has been unjust in ascribing Dryden's change of religion to
interested motives[a].

---

[a] History of England, vol. ii. p. 96.

During the greater part of the year 1686 Dryden was engaged in writing 'The Hind and the Panther,' an elaborate defence in verse of his new religion. This poem is in the form of a dialogue between a milkwhite Hind, representing the Church of Rome, and a Panther, representing the Church of England; and the Hind has of course the best of the discussion. The author of 'Religio Laici' and of 'The Spanish Friar,' could not bring himself to treat the Church to which he so lately belonged with entire disrespect; and the Panther is described as

> ' sure the noblest next the Hind,
> And fairest creature of the spotted kind;
> Oh, could her inborn stains be washed away,
> She were too good to be a beast of prey!
> How can I praise or blame, and not offend,
> Or how divide the frailty from the friend?
> Her faults and virtues lie so mixed, that she
> Nor wholly stands condemned nor wholly free.'

The various dissenting bodies are introduced into the poem under the names of different animals. This, the most imaginative and the longest of Dryden's poems, was published in April 1687.

Dryden's first ode for St. Cecilia's day was written in November 1687, at the request of a musical society formed four years before the celebration of the feast of St. Cecilia, the guardian saint of music [b].

On June 10, 1688, the Queen gave birth to a son, an event which was hailed with joy by all the friends of the Court, while the Protestant party declared the child an imposture. The birth of the Prince was celebrated by Dryden in a poem entitled 'Britannia Rediviva,' which was very hastily composed, and is one of his least successful efforts.

There was a very short interval between the birth of

---

[b] A perfect text of so celebrated a poem is of much literary importance. The editors have generally substituted *uprooted* for Dryden's better word *unrooted* in the line

> ' 'And trees unrooted left their place.'

This is one of very many similar corrections in the Globe edition of Dryden's Poems.

James's unfortunate heir and the Revolution, which drove
James into exile, placed William and Mary on the throne, and
destroyed Dryden's prospects of advancement. His newly-
adopted religion made it impossible for him to take the oaths
required of all holders of office, and to recant now would
have been at once indecent and unprofitable. [His offices of
Poet Laureate and Historiographer Royal, his place in the
Customs, and his pension of 100*l.* a year, were now all lost
by him.] It was stated by Prior, and has been often repeated
on his authority, that the Earl of Dorset, who was now
appointed Lord Chamberlain, made the poet an allowance
from his own purse equivalent ·to the official salary he had
lost. This is a mistake; but there is no doubt that Dorset
at different times made Dryden handsome presents of money,
and the poet, in his 'Discourse on Satire,' dedicated to Dorset
in 1693, gratefully acknowledges his generosity. Sheffield,
Earl of Mulgrave, was also bountiful to him in his reduced
circumstances.

In his fallen fortunes Dryden turned once more to the
drama. In 1690 he produced two plays. The first was a
tragedy called 'Don Sebastian.' Though one of his best
dramas, it was not very successful, and Dryden attributed the
failure of it to its length, or in his own language, to his
having exceeded 'the proper compass of a play.' A comedy,
'Amphitryon,' produced in the same year, had better success. At the time of Charles the Second's death Dryden was
engaged in writing, as a sequel to 'Albion and Albanius,' an
opera, 'King Arthur, or the British Worthy.' This work,
much altered to suit the altered times, was now brought out
with great success. About the representation of his next
play there was some difficulty. The story of 'Cleomenes,
King of Sparta,' was of an exiled king seeking protection at
a foreign court. King William was absent in Holland, and
Mary, the Regent, feeling that the play was disagreeably
suggestive of her father's position at St. Germains, objected
to its being acted. Her objections were, however, overcome
by Dryden's friends, and 'Cleomenes' was produced in May
1692.

Dryden had been seized with a severe fit of illness while hastening to finish 'Cleomenes,' and he was compelled to call in the aid of a young friend, Southerne, to finish it for him. Southerne, Dryden's junior by twenty-eight years, had acquired sudden celebrity by his first play, 'The Loyal Brother, or the Persian Prince,' produced in 1682, when he was only twenty-three. It had been brought on the stage with a prologue and epilogue by Dryden; and Dryden again had written the prologue for Southerne's second play, 'The Disappointment, or the Mother in Fashion,' which had also been a success. A check came to Southerne's success in. 1692, shortly after Dryden had honoured him by seeking his assistance for 'Cleomenes.' His fourth play, the 'Wives' Excuse,' was not well received on the stage, and Dryden now consoled his young friend by some lines of condolence and compliment. He ascribed the want of success to the story and the absence of a favourite actor :—

> ' Yet those who blame thy tale commend thy wit,
> So Terence plotted, but so Terence writ.
> Like his, thy thoughts are true, thy language clean,
> Even lewdness is made moral in thy scene.
> The hearers may for want of Nokes repine,
> But rest secure, the readers will be thine.
> Nor was thy laboured drama damned or hissed,
> But with a kind civility dismissed.'

One more play, 'Love Triumphant, or Nature will Prevail,' was produced by Dryden in the beginning of 1694, and he relinquished play-writing. 'Love Triumphant' was a failure. A letter written by one who was evidently a bitter enemy of Dryden, and who calls him 'huffing Dryden,' says that the play was 'damned by the universal cry of the town.'

'Don Sebastian' was dedicated to the Earl of Leicester, elder brother of Algernon Sydney; 'Amphitryon' to Sir William Leveson Gower of Trentham; 'King Arthur' to George Saville, Marquis of Halifax; 'Cleomenes' to Lawrence Hyde, Earl of Rochester, son of the Lord Chancellor Clarendon, and uncle to Queen Mary; and 'Love Triumphant' to the Earl of Salisbury. These were all friends of the Revolution, and of William and Mary's government, who, Dryden is careful to say in each of his dedications, had continued kind to him in his adversity. He endeavoured, he says, 'to pitch on such men only as have been pleased to own me in this ruin of my small fortune, who, though they are of a contrary opinion themselves, yet blame me not for adhering to a lost cause and judging for myself, what I cannot choose but judge, so long as I am a patient sufferer and no disturber of the government.' To Lord Leicester, whose mansion was near his own residence in Gerrard Street, Dryden writes that 'his best prospect is on the garden of Leicester House,' and that its owner has more than once offered him his patronage, 'to reconcile him to a world of which his misfortunes have made him weary.' And in the last of these dedications, written in 1694, and addressed to the Earl of Salisbury, to whom he says that his wife was related, he writes, 'You have been pleased to take a particular notice of me even in this lowness of my fortunes, to which I have voluntarily reduced myself, and of which I have no reason to be ashamed.' Dryden held himself proudly in his enforced change of circumstances. King William's government could not favour him, even if there were the disposition to do so. His Toryism and his many gibes at the Dutch might have been, and probably would have been, generously forgiven; but he could not recant his new Roman Catholic religion and conform to the tests required for office. In his poem 'Eleonora,' written in 1691, in honour of the memory of the Countess of Abingdon, for which he received a very handsome pecuniary reward of five hundred guineas from the Earl, he speaks of himself as one

> 'Who, not by cares or wants of age deprest,
> Stems a wild deluge with a dauntless breast.'

Dryden had in 1692 produced, with aid from others, a translation of the Satires of Juvenal and Persius, to which he prefixed a 'Discourse on Satire,' addressed to the Earl of Dorset. Among those who aided him were his two elder sons, John and Charles. Dryden himself translated the first, third, sixth, tenth, and sixteenth Satires of Juvenal, and the whole of Persius. Dryden also wrote a life of Polybius for a translation by Sir Henry Shere, given to the world in 1692. A third volume of 'Miscellanies' was published, under Dryden's editorship, in 1693, and a fourth in 1694. In the last volume appeared Dryden's translation of the fourth Georgic of Virgil, and his poem addressed to Sir Godfrey Kneller. This poem has been always reprinted in an imperfect state; the omitted passages are restored in the lately-published Globe edition. One of the omitted passages, immediately following an allusion to the first pair in Eden, is of autobiographical interest:—

> 'Forgive the allusion; 'twas not meant to bite,
> But Satire will have room, where'er I write.'

There is in this poem an admirable description of a perfect portrait :—

> 'Likeness is ever there, but still the best,
> Like proper thoughts in lofty language drest.'

Dryden's new friendship with Southerne has been mentioned. Through Southerne he became acquainted with another young dramatist, Congreve, who was also early famous. Congreve's first play, 'The Old Bachelor,' was brought out in 1693; Dryden had seen it in manuscript, and declared that he never saw such a good play, and he aided to adapt it for the stage. Congreve was at this time but twenty-three years old. A second play was produced by him within a twelvemonth, 'The Double Dealer,' which did not attain the brilliant success that had attended Congreve's first effort. Dryden, who the year before had consoled Southerne under a similar disappointment, now addressed to Congreve a poem, which was prefixed to 'The Double Dealer' when published. The poem is headed, 'To my dear friend, Mr. Congreve.' He anticipates in this poem a brilliant future for Congreve, designates him as the fittest of living writers for the laureate-ship which he himself had lost, and ends in well-known beautiful lines by bequeathing to Congreve the care of his own reputation :—

'In him all beauties of this age we see,
  Etherege his courtship, Southern's purity,
  The satire, wit, and strength of Wycherly.
  All this in blooming youth you have achieved,
  Nor are your foiled contemporaries grieved ;
  So much the sweetness of your manners move,
  We cannot envy you, because we love.

    .   .   .   .   .

  Oh that your brows my laurel had sustained !
  Well had I been deposed, if you had reigned.

    .   .   .   .   .

  Yet this I prophesy,—Thou shalt be seen,
  Though with some short parenthesis between,
  High on the throne of wit, and seated there,
  Not mine—that's little—but thy laurel wear.
  Thy first attempt an early promise made;
  That early promise this has more than paid.

    .   .   .   .   .

  Already I am worn with cares and age,
  And just abandoning the ungrateful stage;
  Unprofitably kept at Heaven's expense,
  I live a rent-charge on His providence.
  But you, whom every Grace and Muse adorn,
  Whom I foresee to better fortune born,
  Be kind to my remains ; and oh, defend,
  Against your judgment, your departed friend.
  Let not the insulting foe my fame pursue,
  But shade those laurels which descend to you:
  And take for tribute what these lines express,
  You merit more, nor could my love do less.'

An air of insincerity is given to the prophecy of the laurel
for Congreve by a similar compliment addressed a few years
later to another young dramatist, George Granville, who was
rich and of noble family, and became afterwards Secretary
of State and a peer, with the title of Lord Lansdowne, and
who was a beneficent friend of Dryden in his last years. A
poem addressed to Mr. Granville in 1690, 'on his excellent
tragedy, called "Heroic Love,"' contains these lines :—

  'But since 'tis Nature's law in love and wit,
    That youth should reign, and withering age submit,

> With less regret those laurels I resign,
> Which, dying on my brows, revive on thine.
>
> Thine be the laurel then: thy blooming age
> Can best, if any can, support the stage [c].'

Dryden renounced the drama in 1694, in order to devote himself to the translation of Virgil, a work which occupied him almost exclusively for the next three years. The translation was published by subscription in 1697, and it was a success both pecuniarily and in respect of fame. Writing to his sons a few months after the publication, he says, 'My Virgil succeeds in the world beyond its desert or my reputation,' and he goes on to say that the profits might have been more had his conscience allowed him to comply with the wish of his publisher Tonson, and dedicate the work to the King. The publisher had been so bent on gaining his point in this matter that he caused the engraving of Æneas to be altered into some likeness of William, in the hope that Dryden might relent at the last moment. But this wily stratagem failed, and Dryden's Virgil appeared with three separate dedications; of the Pastorals to Lord Clifford, the son of his early patron, the Lord Treasurer; of the Georgics to the Earl of Chesterfield; and of the Æneid, to his old and kind friend Mulgrave, now Marquis of Normanby. The Virgil was published by subscription. There were two sets of subscribers: one of five guineas each, and the other of two guineas. There were 102 of the first class, and 250 of the second. The profit to Dryden was twelve or thirteen hundred pounds. It is extremely difficult to arrive at a definite notion of the exact arrangements between Dryden and Tonson as to profits, and Malone and other biographers have expended much ingenuity

---

[c] George Powel, one of the principal actors at Drury Lane Theatre, irritated by taunts at the Drury Lane company in Dryden's poem to Granville, twitted Dryden with his giving to Granville laurels which he had given away before, both to Congreve and Southerne. (Preface to 'The Fatal Discovery, or Love in Ruins,' 1698, quoted by Malone, vol. i. part i. p. 311.)

in discussion and conjecture on this subject [d]. The poet's relations with his publisher during the progress of his translation and of the printing of Virgil were anything but pleasant. Several of Dryden's letters of this period which have been preserved abound in complaints and accusations against Tonson. At one time he has thoughts of leaving him, but upon trial he finds that 'all of his trade are sharpers, and he not more than others.' He accuses him of paying him in clipped and in bad money, and on one occasion he sends him by Tonson's messenger three insulting lines of poetry, with a message, 'Tell the dog that he who wrote these lines can write more.' Tonson must have been startled by this beginning of a portrait of him :—

> 'With leering looks, bull-faced, and freckled fair,
> With two left legs, and Judas-coloured hair,
> And frowsy pores that taint the ambient air [e].'

Dryden is said to have begun his translation of Virgil at the house of his cousin John Driden of Chesterton, and there

---

[d] From a positive statement made by one of Dryden's biographers, the Rev. John Mitford, in Pickering's Aldine edition of Dryden's Poems, published in 1832, there should be in existence an agreement dated June 15, 1694, between Dryden and Tonson, attested by Congreve as one of the witnesses: but Mr. Mitford does not say where the agreement is to be seen, and he makes his statement without giving any authority. Mr. Mitford says that by this agreement Dryden was to receive for the Virgil 200*l*., to be paid at stated intervals, and a hundred copies of the work on large paper, Tonson to pay all expenses, and have the proceeds of the sale of the small paper copies. But this statement of the case is not consistent with many passages of Dryden's letters on the subject, of 1695, 1696, and 1697, which are printed by Malone and Scott. Dryden's letters, however, are not sufficient to enable us to arrive at certainty as to his arrangements with his publisher. The subject is discussed in Malone's Life, in the Rev. Mr. Hooper's, prefixed to the recent reprint of the Aldine edition, and in the Memoir of the Globe edition.

[e] These three lines are introduced into a poem called 'Faction Displayed,' ascribed to Mr. Shippen, published after Dryden's death, and are there quoted as Dryden's description of Tonson, who figures in this poem as Bibliopolo. Pope called Tonson 'left-legged Jacob' in the Dunciad, and referred in a note to Dryden's 'two left legs.' This story therefore is well authenticated.

to have written the first lines with a diamond on a window-pane. Some part of the work was done at Denham Court in Buckinghamshire, the seat of Sir William Bowyer, an old Cambridge friend; and the Seventh Book of the Æneid was translated at Burleigh, the house of the Earl of Exeter, in Northamptonshire. Dr. Knightly Chetwode supplied the Life of Virgil and the Preface to the Pastorals, and Addison wrote the arguments of the books and an Essay on the Georgics. Among those who recommended the work to the public by poetical addresses of compliment printed in the front were George Granville the dramatist, the future Lord Lansdowne, and Henry St. John, the future celebrated Lord Bolingbroke.

Amid general congratulation and eulogy, the publication of Virgil called forth some enemies and detractors. The most elaborate attack on the translation came from a Norfolk clergyman, the Rev. Luke Milbourne, neither whose criticism nor whose name would be remembered but for Dryden's having pilloried him in some of his subsequent writings[f]. The most famous of Dryden's detractors was a younger kinsman, the celebrated Jonathan Swift[g], who never forgetting, it is said, a discouraging opinion on some of his early poetry privately given him by Dryden, whose advice he had asked,

---

[f] Dryden on two occasions couples Milbourne with Sir Richard Blackmore, the doctor, who attacked his plays: in the Epistle to John Driden, where Blackmore is Maurus,—

'Wouldst thou be soon dispatched and perish whole,
    Trust Maurus with thy life and Milbourne with thy soul;'

and in the preface to the ' Fables,' where he lashes Milbourne unsparingly, and after replying to Jeremy Collier with some respect, he ends with a general defiance: 'As for the rest of those who have written against me, they are such scoundrels that they deserve not the least notice to be taken of them. Blackmore and Milbourne are only distinguished from the crowd by being remembered to their infamy.'

[g] The relationship between Dryden and Swift has not been clearly ascertained; but Malone conjectured, with much probability, that Swift's grandmother, wife of Thomas Swift, vicar of Goodrich in Herefordshire, was daughter to a brother of Sir Erasmus Dryden, John Dryden's grandfather. The lady had a brother, Jonathan Dryden, a clergyman; whence Swift's Christian name.

has sneered at the work and its trio of dedications in his witty 'Battle of the Books.' The story is told that Swift, about the year 1692, sent Dryden several Pindaric odes for perusal, and to obtain his advice as to publication, and that Dryden returned them, saying, 'Cousin Swift, you will never be a poet.'

Swift was always ready to sneer at his cousin Dryden. The translation of Virgil is alluded to disrespectfully in the dedication of 'The Tale of a Tub.' Some lines of Swift's ridicule Will's and his cousin's prefaces :—

> ' Put on the critic's brow and sit
> At Will's, the puny judge of wit.
>
> . . . .
>
> Read all the prefaces of Dryden,
> For these our critics much confide in ;
> Though·merely writ at first for filling
> To raise the volume's price a shilling.

While Dryden was engaged in translating Virgil, he published a translation of Du Fresnoy's Latin poem on the Art of Painting, to which he prefixed an essay, entitled 'Parallel of Poetry and Painting.' He wrote also in this period a Life of Lucian for a translation of Lucian's works, which was being prepared by Mr. Moyle, Sir Henry Shere, and other gentlemen, and which was not published till after Dryden's death. Dryden's great ode, Alexander's Feast, his second ode for St. Cecilia's day, was written very soon after the completion of the Virgil, and was sung at the feast of St. Cecilia, November 22, 1697. It is stated by Derrick, on somewhat doubtful authority, that Dryden received forty pounds for the use of this ode on that day. It is likely that he received a gratuity from the Society for which he composed it ; but on the other hand, Dryden wrote in September to his sons at Rome, after he had undertaken to produce this ode for November,—'This is troublesome, and no way beneficial ; but I could not deny the stewards who came in a body to my house to desire that kindness, one of them being Mr. Bridgman, whose parents are your mother's friends.'

Dryden's three sons were now at Rome; the two elder had gone there in the end of 1692, and the youngest followed them. They were favoured by the Pope, Innocent the Twelfth, who made the eldest his Chamberlain, gave some other office in his household to the second, and made the third an officer of his Guards. A comedy written by Dryden's second son, John, 'The Husband his Own Cuckold,' was brought out at the theatre in Lincoln's Inn Fields in 1696, with a prologue by Congreve and an epilogue by Dryden the father. Dryden wrote also a preface for the play when published, in which he gave his opinion that his son's comedy had been surpassed by only two living writers, his friends Southerne and Congreve, and ended characteristically, 'Farewell, reader; if you are a father, you will forgive me; if not, you will when you are a father.' Sir Robert Howard had taken great interest in his nephew's play, and had helped to adapt it for the stage: the play was dedicated to him, and the father's and uncle's encouragement was happily indicated by a motto from Virgil—

'Et pater Aeneas et avunculus excitat Hector.'

Sir Robert Howard, Dryden's brother-in-law, with whom in earlier life he had had a literary controversy and a quarrel, was now his friend and benefactor, and Dryden mentions in one of his letters to his sons an intention to refashion for the stage a play by Sir Robert, 'The Conquest of China by the Tartars,' with an expectation of receiving a hundred pounds for the work.

The publication of Jeremy Collier's famous work on 'The Immorality and Profaneness of the English Stage,' is unfortunately connected with Dryden's biography. Dryden was a prominent offender and deservedly a special object of attack. Collier's work appeared in March 1698. In June Dryden refers to it, in some lines addressed to Motteux on his play 'Beauty in Distress.' Collier was a clergyman, and Dryden, whether Protestant or Roman Catholic, had always attacked all clergies. He affected to consider Collier's anger against himself as inspired by his attacks on Collier's brotherhood, and, while confessing faultiness, suggested that his antagonist exaggerated offence and spread mischief. He docs not name Collier, but he replies to 'the Muses' foes,'

> ' But when to common sense they give the lie
> And turn distorted words to blasphemy,
> They give the scandal; and the wise discern
> Their glosses teach an age too apt to learn.
> What I have loosely or profanely writ
> Let them to fires, their due desert, commit.
> Nor, when accused by me, let them complain—
> Their faults and not their function I arraign.'

And then in beautiful lines he claims for the drama participation with the pulpit in moral instruction:

> ' But let us first reform, and then so live
> That we may teach our teachers to forgive;
> Our desk be placed below their lofty chairs,
> Ours be the practice, as the precept theirs.
> The moral part at least we may divide,
> Humility reward, and punish pride;
> Ambition, interest, avarice accuse:
> These are the province of the tragic muse.'

There was moderation in this reply, and if Dryden had stopped here, posterity might have accepted his confession and apology. But in his very last composition, his epilogue for a representation for his own benefit, written within a few weeks before his death, he treats Collier's rebukes in another tone, throws the blame of his immoral writings on the court of Charles the Second, and on the brink of the grave jests on·virtue and vice:

> ' Perhaps the parson stretched a point too far,
> When with our theatres he waged a war.
> He tells you that this very moral age
> Received the first infection from the stage;
> But, sure a banished court, with lewdness fraught,
> The seeds of open vice returning brought.
>
> .   .   .   .
>
> The poets, who must live by courts or starve,
> Were proud so good a government to serve;

> And mixing with buffoons and pimps profane,
> Tainted the stage for some small snip of gain.
>
> .   .   .   .   .   .
>
> The sin was of our native growth, 'tis true;
> The scandal of the sin was wholly new,
> Misses there were, but modestly concealed;
> Whitehall the naked Venus first revealed,
> Who standing, as at Cyprus, in her shrine,
> The strumpet was adored with rites divine.'

Towards the end of 1698 Dryden began his 'Fables,' or translations from Chaucer and Boccaccio, which were published only a few months before his death, in a folio volume entitled, 'Tales, Ancient and Modern, Translated into Verse from Homer, Ovid, Boccaccio and Chaucer; with Original Poems.' While engaged on this work, Dryden entertained hopes of obtaining some favour from the government, chiefly through the good offices of his friend and connexion Charles Montagu, the Chancellor of the Exchequer. He sent to Montagu for perusal some of the poems designed for this last of his publications, and he rather pressingly solicited his patronage. But his hopes were disappointed, and shortly after he writes to his cousin Mrs. Steward despondingly: 'The court rather speaks kindly of me than does anything for me, though they promise largely.' And again, 'I doubt I am in no condition of having a kindness done me, having the Chancellor for my enemy.' The Lord Chancellor whom he suspected of hindering his advancement was the great Lord Somers.

. The 'Fables' were published in November 1699, and Dryden had the gratification of seeing this, his last work, well received. The epistle to his cousin John Driden appeared for the first time in this volume, and Dryden thought this poem 'the best of the whole'; and it is an excellent poem.

Dryden's health had now been failing for some time. In the preface to the 'Fables,' published in November 1699, he speaks of himself as a cripple in his limbs, and alludes to interruptions in his work from 'various intervals of sickness.' But he congratulates himself on being as vigorous as ever in the faculties of his mind, and says that he intends, if longer life and moderate health be granted to him, to translate the whole of Homer. This design was not accomplished. During the winter of 1699–1700 his infirmities increased. He had been long a martyr to gout and gravel. In December the appearance of erysipelas in his legs added to his sufferings, and during the months of March and April he was mostly confined to his house by gout. At last mortification set in on one of his legs, and amputation of the limb was recommended as the only possible means of averting death, but this operation Dryden refused to submit to, and on the 1st of May 1700 he expired at his house in Gerrard Street. At the time of his death he was within three months of completing his sixty-ninth year. His body was embalmed, and lay in state for several days at the College of Physicians. Thence it was removed on May 13, and carried with great pomp and with all the honours of a public funeral to Westminster Abbey, to be buried in Poet's Corner beside the graves of Chaucer and Cowley.

There appears to be no doubt that Lord Jefferies, son of the Lord Chancellor Jefferies of bad repute, was principally instrumental in securing for Dryden the honour of a public funeral; and the Earl of Dorset, and Charles Montagu, who is said to have offered in the first instance to pay the expenses of a private interment, doubtless zealously seconded the proposal of Jefferies. Garth, a poet of no mean skill, and President of the College of Physicians, placed the College building at the disposal of Dryden's friends, and he delivered a Latin oration before the body left the College. Thence some fifty carriages, filled with distinguished friends, followed the hearse to Westminster Abbey. Among these would be some who had been friends from early days, and who for the greater part of half a century had watched his literary career— Dorset, Mulgrave (now Marquis of Normanby), Sir Charles Sedley, and Samuel Pepys; and other younger men, distinguished in literature, wit and politics, who had been attracted to him by his fame and by their literary sympathies —Charles Montagu, already a leading statesman, Laurence Hyde Earl of Rochester, son of the Lord Chancellor Clarendon, Southerne, Congreve, Wycherly, Vanbrugh,

d

Creech, the translator of Lucretius, Walsh, an accomplished man of letters, who was afterwards prominent among Pope's friends, Sir Godfrey Kneller the painter, Betterton the actor, and the young St. John, destined to a fame brilliant but irregular under the title of Lord Bolingbroke.

It was expected that Montagu and Dorset would erect a monument to Dryden in Westminster Abbey, but this expectation was not realized; and it was not till twenty years after his death that a monument was placed over his grave. This was done in 1720 by his old friend Mulgrave, now Duke of Buckinghamshire, who died a few months after he had discharged this duty to friendship and public desert. Two years later another monument to the poet and his family was erected in the church of Tichmarsh, in Northamptonshire, by his cousin, Mrs. Creed, who describes Dryden, in the elaborate inscription, as 'the celebrated poet and laureat of his time,' and proceeds to say that 'his bright parts and learn- . ing are best seen in his own excellent writings on various subjects: we boast that he was bred and had his first learning here, where he has often made us happy by his kind visits and most delightful conversation.'

Dryden died without a will. He had little to leave beyond the small estate at Blakesley, which he had received from his father, and probably some small landed property which he had acquired in Wiltshire through his marriage. The expenses of his mode of living and of his family had never, in his most prosperous days, been below his income, and of late years he had had great difficulty, even with kind aid from many friends, in meeting his expenses. Lady Elizabeth Dryden, the widow, survived her husband for several years. Soon after his death she became insane, and she continued so till her death in 1714. The three sons all died before their mother. The eldest, Charles, was drowned in the Thames, near Datchet, in August 1704; John, the second son, had died at Rome, in January 1701; and Erasmus Henry, the youngest, died in December 1710, a few months after he had succeeded to the family baronetcy on the death of his cousin, Sir John Dryden.

In person Dryden was short and stout, with a ruddy face. Pope, who when a boy saw Dryden once in his old age, describes him as plump and fresh-coloured, with a down look. His hair is said by an enemy to have inclined to red[h], but it early became gray, and he wore it long and flowing. He had a large mole on one of his cheeks. His eyes were far apart. In a poem on a portrait of him, written by a friend in 1700, his eye is called 'sleepy.' His expressive face, without being regularly handsome, was winning. He says of himself in one of his early writings, not meaning probably all that is said, ' My conversation is slow and dull, my humour saturnine and reserved; in short, I am none of those who endeavour to break jests in company or make repartees[i].' An adversary took him at his word, and has made him say,—

> ' Nor wine nor love could ever make me gay,
> To writing bred, I knew not what to say.'[k]

But if his conversation was not brilliant, it was agreeable among friends of congenial spirits, and he was a favourite companion. We learn from Pope, through Spence, how Dryden's days were generally passed. He lived for many years before his death in Gerrard Street, Soho, where he died. The room in which he sat and wrote was on the ground floor, looking into the street. He spent his mornings in writing, dined early with his family, and after dinner went to Will's coffee-house in Russell Street, where he spent the evening. 'It was Dryden,' says Pope, 'who made Will's coffee-house the great resort for the wits of his time[l].' At Will's Dryden was, during the latter part of his life, a literary monarch, and he was a genial and kind-hearted ruler. There is a story, not quite certain to be true, that he gave the boy Pope a shilling for translating the story of Pyramus and Thisbe. Dean Lockier describes his goodnatured way of taking an interruption and correction

---

[h] Tom Brown, in ' The Reasons for Mr. Bayes changing his Religion.'
[i] Defence of the Essay on Dramatic Poesy.
[k] A Satire to his Muse.
[l] Spence's Anecdotes.

from himself, a youth of seventeen, and a stranger to Dryden, while he was discoursing at Will's with authority on his own 'Mac Flecknoe.' 'If anything of mine is good,' said Dryden, 'it is my "Mac Flecknoe," and I shall value myself the more on it, because it is the first piece of ridicule written in heroics.' The boy Lockier said audibly that 'Mac Flecknoe' was a fine poem, but not the first written that way. Dryden turned to him and asked 'how long he had been a dealer in poetry?' and added smilingly, 'pray, sir, what is that you did imagine to have been writ so before?' Lockier named Boileau's 'Lutrin' and Tassoni's 'Secchia Rapita.' 'It is true,' said Dryden, 'I had forgot them': and as Dryden left the coffee-house that evening, he went up to the youth who had corrected him, and asked him to come and visit him. Dryden's kindness to younger authors is one of his distinguishing attributes, and one of several proofs of an amiable nature. It was thus that he attracted and retained the friendship of Southerne, Congreve, and many others, whose respectful attention and genial kindness solaced and softened the sorrows of his latter years.

Congreve, to whom, in lines which have been already quoted, Dryden bequeathed the care of his reputation, has left an account of Dryden's character which is true, if not complete. 'He was of a nature,' says Congreve, 'exceedingly humane and compassionate; easily forgiving injuries, and capable of a prompt and sincere reconciliation with them who had offended him. . . . . His friendship, where he professed it, went much beyond his professions, and I have been told of strong and generous instances of it, by the persons themselves who received them; though his hereditary means was little more than a bare competency. . . . . . He was of very easy, I may say of very pleasing access, but something slow, and as it were diffident in his advances to others. He had something in his nature that abhorred intrusion into any society whatsoever. . . . To the best of my knowledge and observation he was of all the men that ever I knew one of the most modest, and the most easily to be discountenanced in his approaches to his superiors or his equals.'

But Dryden's character was a mixed one, and faults must be mentioned. His indecent writing, his changes in politics and in religion, and his unscrupulousness in praise and blame, are parts of his life and character which cannot be explained away or defended. If on some occasions, after Jeremy Collier's severe rebukes, he has made in his last years some apology for indecencies in his plays, it cannot be said that he has ever expressed himself with becoming contrition. Nor is his gross writing confined to his plays. Lord Macaulay has most truly said that many of his translations, whether from Virgil or Boccaccio, are full of interpolated and exaggerated indecencies. The translations from Lucretius deserve the same reproof. In his very last work, the volume of Fables, his tale from Boccaccio of Sigismunda and Guiscardo, beautifully told in verse the most melodious, is overcharged with licentious sentiments which are not Boccaccio's, but Dryden's: and yet in the preface to these Fables he could write: 'In general, I will only say that I have written nothing which savours of immorality or profaneness, at least, I am not conscious to myself of any such intention. If there happen to be found an immoral expression or a thought too wanton, they all crept into my verses through inadvertency.' Indecent thoughts came to him naturally, and he could not restrain the prurient impulse. There are many passages of contemporary writers, more or less unfriendly, which, after due allowance for spite and exaggeration, render certain what would otherwise be probable, that Dryden's licentious writing was a sign of licentiousness of life. He knew not political consistency, and he did not regard decency in some of his transitions. His sudden change at the Restoration from flattery of the Protectorate to adulation of the Stuarts cannot possibly be explained by honest conviction. To acquiesce as a good subject in the new order of things, and make the best of the monarchy which the national will had restored, would have been becoming; but for the poetical eulogist of the Commonwealth and of Cromwell to devote himself immediately to poetical praises of Charles and Clarendon, and to laments over the Commonwealth, which but a year before he had lauded and rejoiced in, is discreditable, and must have been an interested change. Almost all his virulent abuse of Shaftesbury, the great leader of opposition in the latter years of the reign of Charles the Second, is in flagrant contradiction to his former praises of the policy of the Cabal Ministry, the war with Holland, and Clifford, Shaftesbury's colleague of the Cabal government. It would be difficult in any case to give Dryden credit for perfect sincerity and dis-interestedness in his adoption of the Roman Catholic religion, after James the Second became king; but his antecedents and general character make this altogether impossible. Dryden's temperament was by no means of that sort which engenders sudden conversions. He was not impulsive, and he had no enthusiasm. His clear sharp intellect, and his strong critical faculty, made it easy for him to see faults and flaws, and pro-tected him against all fanaticism. His 'Religio Laici' is the mature expression of a faith which is more of the head than of the heart: it is the religion of a calm and clear-sighted man, who has reasoned himself into accepting a quantum of theology, and desires as little dogma as possible. How great the leap from this philosophical religion to Romanism, when a Roman Catholic king ascended the throne!

Dryden, in his literary character, is known to the multitude chiefly as a poet, but he is to be regarded and remembered also as a prose writer, as a translator, and as the leading wit in his own age of London literary society. His place among English poets is high, if not the highest, in the second class, the first being that of Chaucer and Spenser, Shakespeare and Milton, in whom genius transcends art, and the 'faculty divine' is ever apparent above subject and execution, and whose poetry streams from a 'full-welling fountain-head' of inner imagination. In Dryden, as in Pope, we admire reason, language, argument, wit, and art. Dryden is a great master of language and of verse. He is the most vigorous and polished of satirists, combining subtle refinement with fervour; and he is unequalled as a reasoner in rhyme. 'Ab-salom and Achitophel,' superior as a poem, yet presents no samples of his satirical invective equal to 'The Medal,' and

'Mac Flecknoe.' 'Religio Laici,' 'The Hind and the Panther,' and likewise 'Absalom and Achitophel,' display his
power of arguing in verse, another fine example of which is to
be found in the theological discussion of Maximin, Apollonius,
and St. Catherine, in 'Tyrannic Love.' The fierce satirist
was an exquisite song-writer; some of the songs interspersed
in his plays are gems of art, which have been much hidden
from view by the deterring grossness of many of the plays, and
of many of the songs themselves, which has prevented them
from being separately collected. Dryden as an author would
seem to have had two natures. He could be correct and
dignified when he chose, and it was easy and seemed pleasant
to him to be gross and coarse. The polished style of most
of his Prologues and Epilogues for the academical audience
of Oxford University is in marked contrast with the prurient
indecency of the addresses which he prepared for the loose,
dissolute courtiers and vulgar cits of London. Gracefully
in one of the Oxford Prologues has he discriminated between
the University and the Town.

> 'Our poet, could he find forgiveness here,
> Would wish it rather than a plaudit there.
> He owns no crown from those Prætorian bands,
> But knows that right is in this Senate's hands.
> Kings make their poets whom themselves think fit,
> But 'tis your suffrage makes authentic wit.' [m]

The plays of Dryden, as plays, contribute little to his fame.
They were mostly hastily composed, and written as money-
making tasks. But there are scattered through them many
beautiful passages of pure and noble thought, and many lines
which fasten on the memory and are quoted from mouth to
mouth, often without its being known whence they come—
an unfailing test of poetic power. The following, which has
been often quoted, and cannot be quoted too often, is one of
many 'beauties' of 'Aurengzebe':—

[m] Prologue to the University of Oxford, 1673, p. 420 of Globe edition.

> ' When I consider life, 'tis all a cheat,
> Yet fooled with hope, men favour the deceit,
> Trust on, and think to-morrow will repay :
> To-morrow 's falser than the former day,
> Lies worse, and while it says we shall be blest
> With some new joys, cuts off what we possest.
> Strange cozenage ! none would live past years again,
> Yet all hope pleasure in what yet remain,
> And from the dregs of life think to receive
> What the first sprightly running could not give.
> I'm tired of waiting for this chymic gold,
> Which fools us young and beggars us when old.'

To one of Dryden's plays, the Second Part of 'The Conquest of Granada,' we owe—

> ' Forgiveness to the injured does belong,
> But they ne'er pardon who have done the wrong.'

To another play, 'All for Love,' we owe—

> ' Men are but children of a larger growth :
> Our appetites as apt to change as theirs,
> And full as craving too, and full as vain.'

It is Almanzor in the First Part of 'The Conquest of Granada' who exclaims, addressing the King Boabdallin—

> ' Obeyed as sovereign by thy subjects be,
> But know that I alone am king of me:
> I am as free as Nature first made man,
> Ere the base laws of servitude began,
> When wild in woods the noble savage ran.'

Candiope, in 'The Maiden Queen,' describes the retired courtier longing to return to court—

> ' Those who like you have once in courts been great,
> May think they wish, but wish not, to retreat,
> They seldom go but when they cannot stay ;
> As losing gamesters throw the dice away.
> E'en in that cell where you repose would find,
> Visions of court will haunt your restless mind ;
> And glorious dreams stand ready to restore,
> The pleasing shades of all you had before.'

Maximin says, in 'Tyrannic Love,'—

> ' Fate's dark recesses we can never find,
> But Fortune at some hours is always kind;
> The lucky have whole days, which still they choose,
> The unlucky have but hours, and these they lose.'

These are a few specimens of many passages of power and beauty in Dryden's little-read and generally inferior plays. His faculty of placing words is wonderful, and conspicuous in prose as well as in poetry. He was specially fitted for a translator. The faults of his translation of Virgil are mostly faults of haste and carelessness. Wanting money, he finished in three years what he rightly told Tonson that it would require seven years to do well.

We learn from Pope, through Dean Lockier, that Dryden made Will's coffee-house, in Russell Street, Covent Garden, the great resort of all the wits in London, and that some years after his death Addison carried the wits away from Will's to another coffee-house in the same street, and on the opposite side of it, Button's [n]. Pope, who was but twelve years old when Dryden died, had been taken once to Will's in Dryden's last year to get a sight of the poet. Addison succeeded to Dryden's critical chair, and the mantle of the poet fell in a little time on Pope, who regarded Dryden as his teacher of versification, and whose first poems, the Pastorals, were published nine years after Dryden's death.

Notices of the early editions of the poems comprised in this volume are subjoined, as important in connexion with the history of the text :—

Heroic Stanzas on Oliver Cromwell. The date on the title-page of the first edition is 1659, but it was doubtless published before the end of 1658. There are two editions of 1659. The first was probably published with two other

[n] Spence's Anecdotes, p. 113.

poems on the same subject by Waller and Sprat, the volume having the title, 'Three Poems upon the Death of his late Highness, Oliver, Lord Protector of England, Scotland, and Ireland, written by Mr. Edm. Waller, Mr. Jo. Dryden, Mr. Sprat of Oxford: London, Printed by William Wilson, and are to be sold in Well-yard, near Little St. Bartholomew's Hospital: 1659.' Dryden's poem is printed first in this collection, with the separate heading of 'Heroic Stanzas consecrated to the Glorious Memory of his Most Serene and Renowned Highness, Oliver, late Lord Protector of the Commonwealth, &c. Written after the celebration of his Funeral.' In the other edition of 1659 Dryden's poem is printed alone; it has the same publisher. There is considerable difference of spelling and punctuation between the two, but none of words. During the reigns of Charles the Second and James the Second, Dryden did not republish this poem, or include it in any list of his works; but it was reprinted in 1682 by a political foe. In the reign of William, Jacob Tonson, Dryden's publisher and friend, republished the poem in 1695 from the separate edition of 1659. It was afterwards printed in the first volume of the 'State Poems,' with several corruptions of the text; and this corrupt reprint was reproduced in the edition of the 'Miscellany Poems' in 1716. Several later editors followed this corrupt copy. The editions of 1659 contain the correct text.

Astræa Redux. This was originally published in 1660 in folio, by Henry Herringman. Dryden's name is printed *Driden* on the title-page. The poem was republished in 1688, in quarto, by Tonson, together with the Panegyric on Charles the Second at the Coronation, the Address to Lord Chancellor Clarendon on New Year's Day, 1662, and the Annus Mirabilis; and then in 1688. The spelling *Driden* was preserved on the title-page of 'Astræa Redux.' The text of the folio edition of 1660 is perfectly to be trusted.

Annus Mirabilis. The first edition of 1667 is a little volume in small octavo, 'printed by Henry Herringman at the Anchor of the Lower Walk of the New Exchange, 1667.'

Dryden, who was not in the habit of careful correction of
the press, printed a list of *errata* on this occasion, with the
following notice :—

'To the Readers.

'Notwithstanding the diligence which has been used in my absence,
some faults have escaped the press ; and I have so many of my own to
answer for, that I am not willing to be charged with those of the printer.
I have only noted the gravest of them, not such as by false stops have
confounded the sense, but such as by mistaken words have corrupted it.'

This little volume, which Sir Walter Scott does not appear
to have seen, contains the best text. Tonson's reprint, in
quarto, 1688, contains several changes of text, which are
generally changes for the worse; a few, however, may be
accepted as improvements. The text of 1688 was literally
followed in the edition of the 'Miscellany Poems' of 1716. The
poem is printed in this volume, as also in the Globe edition,
with the title-page of the first edition, which has not been
generally given by modern editors, and also with Dryden's
own marginal indications, which have been often omitted.

Absalom and Achitophel. The first edition was in folio,
published by Jacob Tonson in November 1681. A second
edition appeared in quarto before the end of December, with
several minor changes, and two considerable additions. This
second edition is authoritative for the text. Seven more
editions were published in Dryden's lifetime. That in the
folio volume of Dryden's poems, published by Tonson after
Dryden's death in 1701, is there called the tenth edition.

Religio Laici. The first edition is in quarto, published
in November 1682; there was a second edition in the same
year, and a third in 1683. The poem was not again reprinted
till it appeared in Tonson's folio edition of Dryden's poems
of 1701.

The Hind and the Panther. This poem was first published in quarto in April 1687, and a second edition was
published in the same year. The Revolution of 1688 stopped

the demand for the poem. The reprint in Tonson's folio volume of 1701 is called there the third edition. There are several errors in this last reprint; the correct text is to be sought in either of the two editions of 1687.

A bibliographical notice of the 'Miscellany Poems,' edited by Dryden, is added, much confusion arising out of the continued connexion of his name with volumes of the series and with whole collections published after his death. The first volume of 'Miscellanies' was published by Dryden in 1684; there is a second edition of this volume, 1692, and a third, 1702. There is no important difference between the first and second editions, but the third is considerably different. The second volume of Dryden's 'Miscellanies' was called 'Sylvæ,' and published in 1685. A third edition of this volume was published in 1702.   The third volume of Dryden's series of 'Miscellanies' was called 'Examen Poeticum,' and appeared in 1693; there was a second edition in 1706. The fourth and last of Dryden's volumes is called 'Annual Miscellany for the year 1694'; and there is a second edition of 1708.

After Dryden's death a fifth volume was published by Jacob Tonson in 1704, and a sixth in 1709, with neither of which Dryden had anything to do. Pope's Pastorals were first published in the sixth volume.

An edition of 'Miscellany Poems,' in six volumes, was published by Tonson in 1716. This is quite different, both by addition and omission, from the previous sets of six volumes, and has no just title to the name, by which it goes, of Dryden's Miscellany Poems. There are later reprints of these so-called Dryden's Miscellany Poems of 1716.

A POEM

UPON THE DEATH

OF HIS LATE HIGHNESS, OLIVER,

LORD PROTECTOR OF ENGLAND, SCOTLAND,

AND IRELAND,

B

HEROIC STANZAS,

CONSECRATED TO THE MEMORY OF HIS HIGHNESS

OLIVER,

LATE LORD PROTECTOR OF THIS COMMONWEALTH, &c.

WRITTEN AFTER THE CELEBRATING OF HIS FUNERAL

1

AND now 'tis time; for their officious haste
  Who would before have borne him to the sky,
Like eager Romans, ere all rites were past,
  Did let too soon the sacred eagle fly.

2

Though our best notes are treason to his fame
  Joined with the loud applause of public voice,
Since Heaven what praise we offer to his name
  . Hath rendered too authentic by its choice;

3

Though in his praise no arts can liberal be,
  Since they, whose Muses have the highest flown,
Add not to his immortal memory,
  But do an act of friendship to their own;

4

Yet 'tis our duty and our interest too
  Such monuments as we can build to raise,
Lest all the world prevent what we should do
  And claim a title in him by their praise.

5

How shall I then begin or where conclude
  To draw a fame so truly circular?
For in a round what order can be shewed,
  Where all the parts so equal-perfect are?

6

His grandeur he derived from Heaven alone,
  For he was great, ere Fortune made him so;
And wars, like mists that rise against the sun,
  Made him but greater seem, not greater grow.

7

No borrowed bays his temples did adorn,
  But to our crown he did fresh jewels bring;
Nor was his virtue poisoned, soon as born,
  With the too early thoughts of being king.

8

Fortune, that easy mistress of the young,
  But to her ancient servants coy and hard,
Him at that age her favourites ranked among
  When she her best-loved Pompey did discard.

9

He, private, marked the faults of others' sway
  And set as sea-marks for himself to shun;
Not like rash monarchs, who their youth betray
  By acts their age too late would wish undone.

10

And yet dominion was not his design;
  We owe that blessing not to him but Heaven,
Which to fair acts unsought rewards did join,
  Rewards that less to him than us were given.

11

Our former chiefs, like sticklers of the war,
  First sought to inflame the parties, then to poise,
The quarrel loved, but did the cause abhor,
  And did not strike to hurt, but make a noise.

12

War, our consumption, was their gainful trade;
  We inward bled, whilst they prolonged our pain;
He fought to end our fighting, and assayed
  To stanch the blood by breathing of the vein.

13

Swift and resistless through the land he passed,
  Like that bold Greek who did the East subdue,
And made to battles such heroic haste
  As if on wings of victory he flew.

14

He fought, secure of fortune as of fame,
  Till by new maps the Island might be shown
Of conquests, which he strewed where'er he came,
  Thick as the galaxy with stars is sown.

15

His palms, though under weights they did not stand,
  Still thrived; no winter could his laurels fade:
Heaven in his portrait showed a workman's hand
  And drew it perfect, yet without a shade.

16

Peace was the prize of all his toil and care,
  Which war had banished and did now restore:
Bologna's walls thus mounted in the air
  To seat themselves more surely than before.

17

Her safety rescued Ireland to him owes;
  And treacherous Scotland, to no interest true,
Yet blessed that fate which did his arms dispose
  Her land to civilize as to subdue.

18

Nor was he like those stars which only shine
  When to pale mariners they storms portend;
He had his calmer influence, and his mien
  Did love and majesty together blend.

19

'Tis true his countenance did imprint an awe
  And naturally all souls to his did bow,
As wands of divination downward draw
  And point to beds where sovereign gold doth grow.

20

When, past all offerings to Feretrian Jove,
  He Mars deposed and arms to gowns made yield,
Successful counsels did him soon approve
  As fit for close intrigues as open field.

21

To suppliant Holland he vouchsafed a peace,
  Our once bold rival in the British main,
Now tamely glad her unjust claim to cease
  And buy our friendship with her idol, gain.

22

Fame of the asserted sea, through Europe blown,
  Made France and Spain ambitious of his love;
Each knew that side must conquer he would own
  And for him fiercely as for empire strove.

23

No sooner was the Frenchman's cause embraced
  Than the light Monsieur the grave Don outweighed:
His fortune turned the scale where'er 'twas cast,
  Though Indian mines were in the other laid.

24

When absent, yet we conquered in his right:
  For, though some meaner artist's skill were shown
In mingling colours or in placing light,
  Yet still the fair designment was his own.

25

For from all tempers he could service draw;
  The worth of each with its alloy he knew;
And, as the confident of Nature, saw
  How she complexions did divide and brew:

26

Or he their single virtues did survey
  By intuition in his own large breast,
Where all the rich ideas of them lay
  That were the rule and measure to the rest.

27

When such heroic virtue Heaven sets out,
  The stars, like Commons, sullenly obey,
Because it drains them, when it comes about,
  And therefore is a tax they seldom pay.

28

From this high spring our foreign conquests flow
  Which yet more glorious triumphs do portend,
Since their commencement to his arms they owe,
  If springs as high as fountains may ascend.

29

He made us freemen of the Continent
  Whom nature did like captives treat before,
To nobler preys the English Lion sent,
  And taught him first in Belgian walks to roar.

30

That old unquestioned pirate of the land,
  Proud Rome, with dread the fate of Dunkirk heard,
And trembling wished behind more Alps to stand,
  Although an Alexander were her guard.

31

By his command we boldly crossed the Line,
  And bravely fought where southern stars arise ;
We traced the far-fetched gold unto the mine,
  And that which bribed our fathers made our prize.

32

Such was our Prince, yet owned a soul above
  The highest acts it could produce to show:
Thus poor mechanic arts in public move,
  Whilst the deep secrets beyond practice go.

33

Nor died he when his ebbing fame went less,
  But when fresh laurels courted him to live;
He seemed but to prevent some new success,
  As if above what triumphs earth could give.

34
His latest victories still thickest came,
  As near the centre motion does increase;
Till he, pressed down by his own weighty name,
  Did, like the Vestal, under spoils decease.

35
But first the Ocean as a tribute sent
  That giant-prince of all her watery herd;
And the Isle, when her protecting Genius went,
  Upon his obsequies loud sighs conferred.

36
No civil broils have since his death arose,
  But faction now by habit does obey;
And wars have that respect for his repose
  As winds for halcyons when they breed at sea.

37
His ashes in a peaceful urn shall rest;
  His name a great example stands to show
How strangely high endeavours may be blessed
  Where piety and valour jointly go.

ASTRÆA REDUX.

A POEM ON THE HAPPY RESTORATION AND RETURN

OF HIS SACRED MAJESTY

CHARLES THE SECOND.

'Jam redit et Virgo, redeunt Saturnia regna.'—VIRGIL, [*Eclog.* iv. 6.]

ASTRÆA REDUX.

Now with a general peace the world was blest,
While ours, a world divided from the rest,
A dreadful quiet felt, and worser far
Than arms, a sullen interval of war.
Thus, when black clouds draw down the labouring skies, 5
Ere yet abroad the winged thunder flies,
An horrid stillness first invades the ear
And in that silence we the tempest fear.
The ambitious Swede like restless billows tost,
On this hand gaining what on that he lost,　　　　10
Though in his life he blood and ruin breathed,
To his now guideless kingdom peace bequeathed;
And Heaven, that seemed regardless of our fate,
For France and Spain did miracles create
Such mortal quarrels to compose in peace　　　15
As nature bred and interest did increase.
We sighed to hear the fair Iberian bride
Must grow a lily to the Lily's side;
While our cross stars denied us Charles his bed
Whom our first flames and virgin love did wed.　　20
For his long absence Church and State did groan;
Madness the pulpit, faction seized the throne.
Experienced age in deep despair was lost
To see the rebel thrive, the loyal crost:
Youth that with joys had unacquainted been　　　25
Envied gray hairs that once good days had seen:
We thought our sires, not with their own content,
Had, ere we came to age, our portion spent.
Nor could our nobles hope their bold attempt
Who ruined crowns would coronets exempt:　　　30

For when, by their designing leaders taught
To strike at power which for themselves they sought,
The vulgar, gulled into rebellion, armed,
Their blood to action by the prize was warmed;
The sacred purple then and scarlet gown,　　　　35
Like sanguine dye to elephants, was shown.
Thus, when the bold Typhoeus scaled the sky
And forced great Jove from his own heaven to fly,
(What king, what crown from treason's reach is free,
If Jove and heaven can violated be?)　　　　40
The lesser gods that shared his prosperous state
All suffered in the exiled Thunderer's fate.
The rabble now such freedom did enjoy
As winds at sea that use it to destroy:
Blind as the Cyclops and as wild as he,　　　　45
They owned a lawless savage liberty,
Like that our painted ancestors so prized,
Ere empire's arts their breasts had civilized.
How great were then our Charles his woes who thus
Was forced to suffer for himself and us!　　　　50
He, tossed by fate and hurried up and down,
Heir to his father's sorrows with his crown,
Could taste no sweets of youth's desired age,
But found his life too true a pilgrimage.
Unconquered yet in that forlorn estate,　　　　55
His manly courage overcame his fate.
His wounds he took, like Romans, on his breast,
Which by his virtue were with laurels drest.
As souls reach Heaven, while yet in bodies pent,
So did he live above his banishment.　　　　60
That sun, which we beheld with cozened eyes
Within the water, moved along the skies.
How easy 'tis, when Destiny proves kind,
With full-spread sails to run before the wind!
But those that 'gainst stiff gales laveering go　　　　65
Must be at once resolved and skilful too.
He would not, like soft Otho, hope prevent,
But stayed and suffered fortune to repent.

These virtues Galba in a stranger sought
And Piso to adopted empire brought.　　　　　70
How shall I then my doubtful thoughts express
That must his sufferings both regret and bless?
For when his early valour Heaven had crost,
And all at Worcester but the honour lost,
Forced into exile from his rightful throne,　　　75
He made all countries where he came his own,
And, viewing monarchs' secret arts of sway,
A royal factor for their kingdoms lay.
Thus banished David spent abroad his time,
When to be God's anointed was his crime,　　　80
And, when restored, made his proud neighbours rue
Those choice remarks he from his travels drew.
Nor is he only by afflictions shown
To conquer others' realms, but rule his own;
Recovering hardly what he lost before,　　　85
His right endears it much, his purchase more.
Inured to suffer ere he came to reign,
No rash procedure will his actions stain.
To business ripened by digestive thought,
His future rule is into method brought,　　　90
As they who first proportion understand
With easy practice reach a master's hand.
Well might the ancient poets then confer
On Night the honoured name of Counseller;
Since, struck with rays of prosperous fortune blind,　　　95
We light alone in dark afflictions find.
In such adversities to sceptres trained,
The name of Great his famous grandsire gained:
Who, yet a king alone in name and right,
With hunger, cold, and angry Jove did fight;　　　100
Shocked by a covenanting League's vast powers,
As holy and as Catholic as ours:
Till Fortune's fruitless spite had made it known
Her blows not shook but riveted his throne.

　　Some lazy ages, lost in sleep and ease,　　　105
No action leave to busy chronicles:

Such, whose supine felicity but makes
In story chasms, in epoches mistakes,
O'er whom Time gently shakes his wings of down
Till with his silent sickle they are mown.　　　110
Such is not Charles his too too active age,
Which, governed by the wild distempered rage
Of some black star infecting all the skies,
Made him at his own cost, like Adam, wise.
Tremble, ye nations who, secure before,　　　115
Laughed at those arms that 'gainst our selves we bore;
Roused by the lash of his own stubborn tail,
Our Lion now will foreign foes assail.
With alga who the sacred altar strows?
To all the sea-gods Charles an offering owes,　　　120
A bull to thee, Portunus, shall be slain,
A lamb to you, the tempests of the main.
For those loud storms that did against him roar
Have cast his shipwracked vessel on the shore.
Yet, as wise artists mix their colours so　　　125
That by degrees they from each other go,
Black steals unheeded from the neighbouring white
Without offending the well-cozened sight,
So on us stole our blessed change, while we
The effect did feel but scarce the manner see.　　　130
Frosts that constrain the ground and birth deny
To flowers that in its womb expecting lie
Do seldom their usurping power withdraw,
But raging floods pursue their hasty thaw:
Our thaw was mild, the cold not chased away,　　　135
But lost in kindly heat of lengthened day.
Heaven would no bargain for its blessings drive,
But what we could not pay for freely give.
The Prince of Peace would, like himself, confer
A gift unhoped without the price of war:　　　140
Yet, as He knew His blessing's worth, took care
That we should know it by repeated prayer,
Which stormed the skies and ravished Charles from thence,
As Heaven it self is took by violence.

Booth's forward valour only served to show   145
He durst that duty pay we all did owe;
The attempt was fair, but Heaven's prefixed hour
Not come: so, like the watchful travellour
That by the moon's mistaken light did rise,
Lay down again and closed his weary eyes.   150
'Twas Monk, whom Providence designed to loose
Those real bonds false freedom did impose.
The blessèd saints that watched this turning scene
Did from their stars with joyful wonder lean
To see small clues draw vastest weights along,   155
Not in their bulk but in their order strong.
Thus pencils can by one slight touch restore
Smiles to that changed face that wept before.
With ease such fond chimeras we pursue
As Fancy frames for Fancy to subdue;   160
But when ourselves to action we betake,
It shuns the mint, like gold that chymists make.
How hard was then his task, at once to be
What in the body natural we see
Man's architect distinctly did ordain   165
The charge of muscles, nerves, and of the brain,
Through viewless conduits spirits to dispense,
The springs of motion from the seat of sense.
'Twas not the hasty product of a day,
But the well-ripened fruit of wise delay.   170
He, like a patient angler, ere he strook,
Would let them play a while upon the hook.
Our healthful food the stomach labours thus,
At first embracing what it straight doth crush.
Wise leeches will not vain receipts obtrude,   175
While growing pains pronounce the humours crude;
Deaf to complaints, they wait upon the ill,
Till some safe crisis authorize their skill.
Nor could his acts too close a vizard wear
To scape their eyes whom guilt had taught to fear,   180
And guard with caution that polluted nest
Whence Legion twice before was dispossest:

Once sacred House, which when they entered in,
They thought the place could sanctify a sin;
Like those that vainly hoped kind Heaven would wink, 185
While to excess on martyrs' tombs they drink.
And as devouter Turks first warn their souls
To part, before they taste forbidden bowls,
So these, when their black crimes they went about,
First timely charmed their useless conscience out. 190
Religion's name against it self was made;
The shadow served the substance to invade.
Like zealous Missions, they did care pretend
Of souls in show, but made the gold their end.
The incensed powers beheld with scorn from high 195
An heaven so far distant from the sky,
Which durst with horses' hoofs that beat the ground
And martial brass belie the thunder's sound.
'Twas hence at length just vengeance thought it fit
To speed their ruin by their impious wit; 200
Thus Sforza, cursed with a too fertile brain,
Lost by his wiles the power his wit did gain.
Henceforth their fogue must spend at lesser rate
Than in its flames to wrap a nation's fate.
Suffered to live, they are like Helots set 205
A virtuous shame within us to beget;
For by example most we sinned before
And glass-like clearness mixed with frailty bore.
But since, reformed by what we did amiss,
We by our sufferings learn to prize our bliss; 210
Like early lovers, whose unpractised hearts
Were long the May-game of malicious arts,
When once they find their jealousies were vain,
With double heat renew their fires again.
'Twas this produced the joy that hurried o'er 215
Such swarms of English to the neighbouring shore
To fetch that prize by which Batavia made
So rich amends for our impoverished trade.
Oh, had you seen from Scheveline's barren shore,
Crowded with troops and barren now no more, 220

Afflicted Holland to his farewell bring
True sorrow, Holland to regret a king;
While waiting him his royal fleet did ride,
And willing winds to their lowered sails denied,
The wavering streamers, flags, and Standard out,   225
The merry seamen's rude but cheerful shout,
And last the cannons' voice that shook the skies,
And, as it fares in sudden ecstasies,
At once bereft us both of ears and eyes.
The Naseby, now no longer England's shame,   230
But better to be lost in Charles his name,
Like some unequal bride in nobler sheets,
Receives her lord; the joyful London meets
The princely York, himself alone a freight;
The Swiftsure groans beneath great Gloucester's weight: 235
Secure as when the halcyon breeds, with these
He that was born to drown might cross the seas.
Heaven could not own a Providence, and take
The v   lth three nations ventured at a stake.
The same indulgence Charles his voyage blessed   240
Which in his right had miracles confessed.
The winds that never moderation knew,
Afraid to blow too much, too faintly blew;
Or out of breath with joy could not enlarge
Their straightened lungs, or conscious of their charge. 245
The British Amphitrite, smooth and clear,
In richer azure never did appear,
Proud her returning Prince to entertain
With the submitted fasces of the main.

And welcome now, great Monarch, to your own!   250
Behold the approaching cliffs of Albion.
It is no longer motion cheats your view;
As you meet it, the land approacheth you.
The land returns, and in the white it wears
The marks of penitence and sorrow bears.   255
But you, whose goodness your descent doth show,
Your heavenly parentage and earthly too,

C

By that same mildness which your father's crown
Before did ravish shall secure your own.
Not tied to rules of policy, you find   260
Revenge less sweet than a forgiving mind.
Thus, when the Almighty would to Moses give
A. sight of all he could behold and live,
A voice before His entry did proclaim
Long-suffering, goodness, mercy, in His name.   265
Your power to justice doth submit your cause,
Your goodness only is above the laws,
Whose rigid letter, while pronounced by you,
Is softer made. So winds that tempests brew,
When through Arabian groves they take their flight,   270
Made wanton with rich odours, lose their spite.
And as those lees that trouble it refine
The agitated soul of generous wine,
So tears of joy, for your returning spilt,
Work out and expiate our former guilt.   275
Methinks I see those crowds on Dover's strand,
Who in their haste to welcome you to land
Choked up the beach with their still growing store
And made a wilder torrent on the shore:
While, spurred with eager thoughts of past delight,   280
Those who had seen you court a second sight,
Preventing still your steps and making haste
To meet you often wheresoe'er you past.
How shall I speak of that triumphant day,
When you renewed the expiring pomp of May!   285
A month that owns an interest in your name;
You and the flowers are its peculiar claim.
That star, that at your birth shone out so bright
It stained the duller sun's meridian light,
Did once again its potent fires renew,   290
Guiding our eyes to find and worship you.
    And now Time's whiter series is begun,
Which in soft centuries shall smoothly run;
Those clouds that overcast your morn shall fly,
Dispelled to farthest corners of the sky.   295

Our nation, with united interest blest,
Not now content to poise, shall sway the rest.
Abroad your empire shall no limits know,
But, like the sea, in boundless circles flow;
Your much-loved fleet shall with a wide command   300
Besiege the petty monarchs of the land;
And as old Time his offspring swallowed down,
Our ocean in its depths all seas shall drown.
Their wealthy trade from pirates' rapine free,
Our merchants shall no more adventurers be;   305
Nor in the farthest East those dangers fear
Which humble Holland must dissemble here.
Spain to your gift alone her Indies owes,
For what the powerful takes not he bestows;
And France that did an exile's presence fear   310
May justly apprehend you still too near.
At home the hateful names of parties cease,
And factious souls are wearied into peace.
The discontented now are only they
Whose crimes before did your just cause betray: 315
Of those your edicts some reclaim from sins,
But most your life and blest example wins.
Oh happy Prince, whom Heaven hath taught the way
By paying vows to have more vows to pay!
Oh happy age! Oh times like those alone   320
By fate reserved for great Augustus' throne,
When the joint growth of arms and hearts foreshew
The world a Monarch, and that Monarch you!

ANNUS MIRABILIS:

THE YEAR OF WONDERS, 1666.

AN HISTORICAL POEM;

CONTAINING

THE PROGRESS AND VARIOUS SUCCESSES OF OUR NAVAL WAR WITH HOLLAND

UNDER THE CONDUCT OF HIS HIGHNESS PRINCE RUPERT AND HIS GRACE THE DUKE OF ALBEMARLE,

AND DESCRIBING THE FIRE OF LONDON.

'Multum interest res poscat, an homines latius imperare velint.'
Trajan Imperator ad Plin. [PLIN. *Epist.* x. 33.]

'Urbs antiqua ruit, multos dominata per annos.'—VIRG. [*Æn.* ii. 363.]

TO THE METROPOLIS OF GREAT BRITAIN,

THE MOST RENOWNED AND LATE FLOURISHING CITY OF LONDON, IN ITS
REPRESENTATIVES THE LORD MAYOR AND COURT OF ALDERMEN,
THE SHERIFFS AND COMMON COUNCIL OF IT.

As perhaps I am the first who ever presented a work of this 5
nature to the metropolis of any nation, so is it likewise con-
sonant to justice, that he who was to give the first example
of such a dedication should begin it with that City which has
set a pattern to all others of true loyalty, invincible courage,
and unshaken constancy. Other cities have been praised 10
for the same virtues, but I am much deceived if any have
so dearly purchased their reputation: their fame has been
won them by cheaper trials than an expensive though necessary war, a consuming pestilence, and a more consuming fire.
To submit your selves with that humility to the judgments 15
of Heaven, and at the same time to raise your selves with
that vigour above all human enemies; to be combated at
once from above and from below; to be struck down and
to triumph: I know not whether such trials have been ever
paralleled in any nation, the resolution and successes of them 20
never can be. Never had prince or people more mutual
reason to love each other, if suffering for each other can
endear affection. You have come together a pair of matchless lovers, through many difficulties; he, through a long
exile, various traverses of fortune, and the interposition of 25
many rivals, who violently ravished and withheld you from
him; and certainly you have had your share in sufferings.
But Providence has cast upon you want of trade, that you
might appear bountiful to your country's necessities; and
the rest of your afflictions are not more the effects of God's 30
displeasure (frequent examples of them having been in the
reign of the most excellent princes) than occasions for the

manifesting of your Christian and civil virtues. To you,
therefore, this Year of Wonders is justly dedicated, because
you have made it so: you, who are to stand a wonder to
all years and ages, and who have built your selves an immortal
5 monument on your own ruins. You are now a phœnix in
her ashes, and, as far as humanity can approach, a great
emblem of the suffering. Deity. But Heaven never made
so much piety and virtue to leave it miserable. I have
heard indeed of some virtuous persons who have ended
10 unfortunately, but never of any virtuous nation. Providence
is engaged too deeply, when the cause becomes so general;
and I cannot imagine it has resolved the ruin of that people
at home, which it has blessed abroad with such successes.
I am, therefore, to conclude that your sufferings are at an
15 end, and that one part of my poem has not been more an
history of your destruction, than the other a prophecy of
your restoration. The accomplishment of which happiness,
as it is the wish of all true Englishmen, so is by none
more passionately desired than by

20   The greatest of your admirers

        and most humble of your servants,

            JOHN DRYDEN.

AN ACCOUNT OF THE ENSUING POEM,

Sir,

I am so many ways obliged to you and so little able
to return your favours that, like those who owe too much, 5
I can only live by getting farther into your debt. You
have not only been careful of my fortune, which was the
effect of your nobleness, but you have been solicitous of
my reputation, which is that of your kindness. It is not
long since I gave you the trouble of perusing a play for me; 10
and now, instead of an acknowledgment, I have given you
a greater in the correction of a poem. But since you are
to bear this persecution, I will at least give you the encouragement of a martyr; you could never suffer in a nobler
cause. For I have chosen the most heroic subject which 15
any poet could desire: I have taken upon me to describe
the motives, the beginning, progress, and successes of a most
just and necessary war; in it the care, management, and
prudence of our King; the conduct and valour of a royal
Admiral and of two incomparable Generals; the invincible 20
courage of our captains and seamen, and three glorious
victories, the result of all. After this, I have in the fire
the most deplorable, but withal the greatest argument that
can be imagined; the destruction being so swift, so sudden,
so vast and miserable, as nothing can parallel in story. The 25
former part of this poem, relating to the war, is but a due
expiation for my not serving my King and country in it.
All gentlemen are almost obliged to it: and I know no
reason we should give that advantage to the commonalty
of England, to be foremost in brave actions, which the 30
noblesse of France would never suffer in their peasants. I
should not have written this but to a person who has been
ever forward to appear in all employments, whither his honour

and generosity have called him.   The latter part of my poem,
which describes the fire, I owe, first, to the piety and fatherly
affection of our Monarch to his suffering subjects; and, in
the second place, to the courage, loyalty, and magnanimity
5 of the City; both which were so conspicuous that I have
wanted words to celebrate them as they deserve. I have
called my poem historical, not epic, though both the actions
and actors are as much heroic as any poem can contain.
But since the action is not properly one, nor that accom-
10 plished in the last successes, I have judged it too bold a
title for a few stanzas, which are little more in number than
a single Iliad or the longest of the Æneids. For this reason
(I mean not of length, but broken action, tied too severely
to the laws of history) I am apt to agree with those who
15 rank Lucan rather among historians in verse than epic poets;
in whose room, if I am not deceived, Silius Italicus, though
a worse writer, may more justly be admitted. I have chosen
to write my poem in quatrains or stanzas of four in alternate
rhyme, because I have ever judged them more noble and of
20 greater dignity both for the sound and number than any
other verse in use amongst us; in which I am sure I have
your approbation. The learned languages have certainly a
great advantage of us in not being tied to the slavery of
any rhyme, and were less constrained in the quantity of
25 every syllable, which they might vary with spondees or
dactyls, besides so many other helps of grammatical figures
for the lengthening or abbreviation of them, than the modern
are in the close of that one syllable, which often confines,
and more often corrupts, the sense of all the rest. But in
30 this necessity of our rhymes, I have always found the couplet
verse most easy (though not so proper for this occasion),
for there the work is sooner at an end, every two lines concluding the labour of the poet; but in quatrains he is to
carry it farther on, and not only so, but to bear along in his
35 head the troublesome sense of four lines together. For
those who write correctly in this kind must needs acknowledge that the last line of the stanza is to be considered in
the composition of the first. Neither can we give ourselves

the liberty of making any part of a verse for the sake of rhyme, or concluding with a word which is not current English, or using the variety of female rhymes; all which our fathers practised. And for the female rhymes, they are still in use amongst other nations: with the Italian in every 5 line, with the Spaniard promiscuously, with the French alternately, as those who have read the Alaric, the Pucelle, or any of their latter poems, will agree with me. And besides this, they write in Alexandrines or verses of six feet, such as, amongst us, is the old translation of Homer by Chapman; 10 all which by lengthening of their chain makes the sphere of their activity the larger. I have dwelt too long upon the choice of my stanza, which you may remember is much better defended in the Preface to Gondibert; and therefore I will hasten to acquaint you with my endeavours in the 15 writing. In general I will only say I have never yet seen the description of any naval fight in the proper terms which are used at sea; and if there be any such in another language, as that of Lucan in the third of his Pharsalia, yet I could not prevail myself of it in the English; the terms of arts 20 in every tongue bearing more of the idiom of it than any other words. We hear, indeed, among our poets, of the thundering of guns, the smoke, the disorder and the slaughter; but all these are common notions. And certainly as those who in a logical dispute keep in general terms would hide 25 a fallacy, so those who do it in any poetical description would . veil their ignorance.

> ‘ Descriptas servare vices operumque colores
> Cur ego, si nequeo ignoroque, poeta salutor ?’

For my own part, if I had little knowledge of the sea, yet 30 I have thought it no shame to learn; and if I have made some few mistakes, it is only, as you can bear me witness, because I have wanted opportunity to correct them, the whole poem being first written, and now sent you from a place where I have not so much as the converse of any 35 seaman. Yet though the trouble I had in writing it was great, it was more than recompensed by the pleasure; I

found myself so warm in celebrating the praises of military
men, two such especially as the Prince and General, that
it is no wonder if they inspired me with thoughts above
my ordinary level. And I am well satisfied, that as they
5 are incomparably the best subject I have ever had, excepting
only the royal family, so also that this I have written of them
is much better than what I have performed on any other.
I have been forced to help out other arguments; but this
has been bountiful to me: they have been low and barren
10 of praise, and I have exalted them and made them fruitful; but
here—*Omnia sponte sua reddit justissima tellus.* I have had a
large, a fair, and a pleasant field; so fertile, that, without my
cultivating, it has given me two harvests in a summer, and in
both oppressed the reaper. All other greatness in subjects is
15 only counterfeit, it will not endure the test of danger; the
greatness of arms is only real. Other greatness burdens a
nation with its weight; this supports it with its strength.
And as it is the happiness of the age, so is it the peculiar
goodness of the best of kings, that we may praise his subjects
20 without offending him. Doubtless it proceeds from a just
confidence of his own virtue, which the lustre of no other
can be so great as to darken in him; for the good or the
valiant are never safely praised under a bad or a degenerate
prince. But to return from this digression to a farther
25 account of my poem: I must crave leave to tell you, that,
as I have endeavoured to adorn it with noble thoughts, so
much more to express those thoughts with elocution. The
composition of all poems is or ought to be of wit; and wit
in the poet, or wit-writing (if you will give me leave to use a
30 school-distinction), is no other than the faculty of imagination
in the writer; which, like a nimble spaniel, beats over and
ranges through the field of memory, till it springs the quarry
it hunted after: or, without metaphor, which searches over
all the memory for the species or ideas of those things which
35 it designs to represent. Wit written is that which is well de-
fined the happy result of thought, or product of that imagination. But to proceed from wit in the general notion of it
to the proper wit of an heroic or historical poem, I judge

it chiefly to consist . in the delightful imaging of persons,
actions, passions, or things. 'Tis not the jerk or sting of
an epigram, nor the seeming contradiction of a poor antithesis
(the delight of an ill-judging audience in a play of rhyme),
nor the jingle of a more poor paronomasia; neither is it so much 5
the morality of a grave sentence, affected by Lucan, but
more sparingly used by Virgil; but it is some lively and apt
description, dressed in such colours of speech, that it sets
before your eyes the absent object as perfectly and more
delightfully than nature. So then the first happiness of the 10
poet's imagination is properly invention, or finding of the
thought; the second is fancy, or the variation, driving, or
moulding of that thought as the judgment represents it
proper to the subject; the third is elocution, or the art of
clothing and adorning that thought so found and varied, in 15
apt, significant, and sounding words. The quickness of the
imagination is seen in the invention, the fertility in the
fancy, and the accuracy in the expression. For the two
first of these Ovid is famous amongst the poets; for the
latter, Virgil. Ovid images more often the movements and 20
affections of the mind, either combating between two contrary
passions, or extremely discomposed by one; his words, therefore, are the least part of his care; for he pictures nature
in disorder, with which the study and choice of words is
inconsistent. This is the proper wit of dialogue or discourse, 25
and consequently of the drama, where all that is said is to
be supposed the effect of sudden thought; which, though
it excludes not the quickness of wit in repartees, yet admits
not a too curious election of words, too frequent allusions
or use of tropes, or in fine anything that shows remoteness 30
of thought or labour in the writer. On the other side, Virgil
speaks not so often to us in the person of another, like Ovid,
but in his own: he relates almost all things as from himself,
and thereby gains more liberty than the other to express his
thoughts with all the graces of elocution, to write more 35
figuratively, and to confess as well the labour as the force
of his imagination. Though he describes his Dido well and
naturally, in the violence of her passions, yet he must yield

in that to the Myrrha, the Byblis, the Althæa of Ovid. For
as great an admirer of him as I am, I must acknowledge
that, if I see not more of their souls than I see of Dido's, at
least I have a greater concernment for them: and that con-
5 vinces me that Ovid has touched those tender strokes more
delicately than Virgil could. But when action or persons
are to be described, when any such image is to be set before
us, how bold, how masterly are the strokes of Virgil! We see
the objects he represents us within their native figures, in
10 their proper motions; but we so see them as our own eyes
could never have beheld them, so beautiful in themselves.
We see the soul of the poet, like that universal one of which
he speaks, informing and moving through all his pictures:

'Totamque infusa per artus
15 Mens agitat molem et magno se corpore miscet.'

We behold him embellishing his images, as he makes Venus
breathing beauty upon her son Æneas:

'Lumenque juventæ
Purpureum et lætos oculis afflarat honores:
20 Quale manus addunt ebori decus, aut ubi flavo
Argentum Pariusve lapis circumdatur auro.'

See his Tempest, his Funeral Sports, his Combat of Turnus
and Æneas, and in his Georgics, which I esteem the divinest
part of all his writings, the Plague, the Country, the Battle
25 of Bulls, the Labour of the Bees, and those many other
excellent images of nature, most of which are neither great
in themselves nor have any natural ornament to bear them
up; but the words wherewith he describes them are so
excellent, that it might be well applied to him which was
30 said by Ovid, *Materiam superabat opus:* the very sound of
his words has often somewhat that is connatural to the
subject; and while we read him, we sit, as in a play, behold-
ing the scenes of what he represents. To perform this, he
made frequent use of tropes, which you know change the
35 nature of a known word by applying it to some other signi-

fication; and this is it which Horace means in his Epistle to
the Pisos:

> ‘Dixeris egregie, notum si callida verbum
> Reddiderit junctura novum.’

But I am sensible I have presumed too far to entertain you
with a rude discourse of that art which you both know so
well, and put into practice with so much happiness. Yet
before I leave Virgil, I must own the vanity to tell you,
and by you the world, that he has been my master in this
poem: I have followed him everywhere, I know not with
what success, but I am sure with diligence enough: my
images are many of them copied from him, and the rest
are imitations of him. My expressions also are as near as
the idioms of the two languages would admit of in translation.
And this, Sir, I have done with that boldness for which I
will stand accountable to any of our little critics, who,
perhaps, are not better acquainted with him than I am.
Upon your first perusal of this poem, you have taken notice
of some words which I have innovated (if it be too bold for
me to say refined) upon his Latin; which, as I offer not
to introduce into English prose, so I hope they are neither
improper nor altogether unelegant in verse; and in this
Horace will again defend me:

> ‘Et nova fictaque nuper habebunt verba fidem si
> Græco fonte cadent parce detorta.’

The inference is exceeding plain; for if a Roman poet
might have liberty to coin a word, supposing only that it
was derived from the Greek, was put into a Latin termination, and that he used this liberty but seldom and with
modesty; how much more justly may I challenge that privilege to do it with the same pre-requisites, from the best
and most judicious of Latin writers? In some places, where
either the fancy or the words were his or any other’s, I have
noted it in the margin, that I might not seem a plagiary;
in others I have neglected it, to avoid as well tediousness
as the affectation of doing it too often. Such descriptions
or images, well wrought, which I promise not for mine,

are, as I have said, the adequate delight of heroic poesy;
for they beget admiration, which is its proper object; as
the images of the burlesque, which is contrary to this, by
the same reason beget laughter; for the one shows nature
5 beautified, as in the picture of a fair woman, which we all
admire; the other shows her deformed, as in that of a
lazar, or of a fool with distorted face and antic gestures, at
which we cannot forbear to laugh, because it is a deviation
from nature. But though the same images serve equally
10 for the epic poesy, and for the historic and panegyric, which
are branches of it, yet a several sort of sculpture is to be
used in them. If some of them are to be like those of
Juvenal, *Stantes in curribus Æmiliani,* heroes drawn in their
triumphal chariots and in their full proportion; others are
15 to be like that of Virgil, *Spirantia mollius æra:* there is somewhat more of softness and tenderness to be shown in them.
You will soon find I write not this without concern. Some,
who have seen a paper of verses which I wrote last year
to her Highness the Duchess, have accused them of that
20 only thing I could defend in them. They have said, I did
humi serpere, that I wanted not only height of fancy, but
dignity of words to set it off. I might well answer with
that of Horace, *Nunc non erat his locus;* I knew I addressed
them to a lady, and accordingly I affected the softness of
25 expression and the smoothness of measure, rather than the
height of thought; and in what I did endeavour, it is no
vanity to say I have succeeded. I detest arrogance; but
there is some difference betwixt that and a just defence.
But I will not farther bribe your candour, or the reader's.
30 I leave them to speak for me; and, if they can, to make
out that character, not pretending to a greater, which I have
given them.

VERSES TO HER ROYAL HIGHNESS THE DUCHESS,

On the Memorable Victory gained by the Duke against the Hollanders, June 3, 1665, and on her Journey afterwards into the North.

MADAM,   5
WHEN for our sakes your hero you resigned
To swelling seas and every faithless wind,
When you released his courage and set free
A valour fatal to the enemy,
You lodged your country's cares within your breast,   10
The mansion where soft love should only rest,
And, ere our foes abroad were overcome,
The noblest conquest you had gained at home.
Ah, what concerns did both your souls divide!
Your honour gave us what your love denied: 15
And 'twas for him much easier to subdue
Those foes he fought with than to part from you.
That glorious day, which two such navies saw
As each unmatched might to the world give law,
Neptune, yet doubtful whom he should obey,   20
Held to them both the trident of the sea:
The winds were hushed, the waves in ranks were cast
As awfully as when God's people past,
Those yet uncertain on whose sails to blow,
These where the wealth of nations ought to flow.
Then with the Duke your Highness ruled the day;   25
While all the brave did his command obey,
The fair and pious under you did pray.
How powerful are chaste vows! the wind and tide
You bribed to combat on the English side.
Thus to your much-loved lord you did convey   30
An unknown succour, sent the nearest way;
New vigour to his wearied arms you brought,
(So Moses was upheld while Israel fought,)
While from afar we heard the cannon play,   25
Like distant thunder on a shiny day.

D

For absent friends we were ashamed to fear
When we considered what you ventured there.
Ships, men, and arms our country might restore,
But such a leader could supply no more. ·
5 With generous thoughts of conquest he did burn,
Yet fought not more to vanquish than return.
Fortune and victory he did pursue
To bring them as his slaves to wait on you:
Thus beauty ravished the rewards of fame
10 And the fair triumphed when the brave o'ercame.
Then, as you meant to spread another way
By land your conquests far as his by sea,
Leaving our southern clime, you marched along
The stubborn North, ten thousand Cupids strong.
15 Like Commons, the nobility resort
In crowding heaps to fill your moving court:
To welcome your approach the vulgar run,
Like some new envoy from the distant sun,
And country beauties by their lovers go,
20 Blessing themselves and wondering at the show.
So, when the new-born phœnix first is seen,
Her feathered subjects all adore their queen,
And while she makes her progress through the East,
From every grove her numerous train's increast;
25 Each poet of the air her glory sings,
And round him the pleased audience clap their wings.

And now, Sir, 'tis time I should relieve you from the
tedious length of this account. You have better and more
profitable employment for your hours, and I wrong the
30 public to detain you longer. In conclusion, I must leave
my poem to you with all its faults, which I hope to find
fewer in the printing by your emendations. I know you
are not of the number of those, of whom the younger Pliny
speaks; *Nec sunt parum multi, qui carpere amicos suos judicium
35 vocant:* I am rather too secure of you on that side. Your
candour in pardoning my errors may make you more remiss
in correcting them; if you will not withal consider that they

come into the world with your approbation, and through
your hands. I beg from you the greatest favour you can
confer upon an absent person, since I repose upon your
management what is dearest to me, my fame and reputation;
and, therefore, I hope it will stir you up to make my poem 5
fairer by many of your blots. If not, you know the story
of the.gamester who married the rich man's daughter and,
when her father denied the portion, christened all the children
by his surname, that, if in conclusion they. must beg, they
should do so by one name as well as by the other. But 10
since the reproach of my faults will light on you, 'tis but
reason I should do you that justice to the readers to let
them know, that, if there be anything tolerable in this poem,
they owe the argument to your choice, the writing to your
encouragement, the correction to your judgment, and the 15
care of it to your friendship, to which he must ever acknowledge himself to owe all things who is,

Sir,

The most obedient

and most faithful of your servants,

JOHN DRYDEN.

From Charlton, in Wiltshire,
   Nov. 10, 1666.

ANNUS MIRABILIS:

THE YEAR OF WONDERS, 1666.

1

In thriving arts long time had Holland grown,
    Crouching at home and cruel when abroad;
Scarce leaving us the means to claim our own,
    Our King they courted and our merchants awed.

2

Trade, which like blood should circularly flow,
    Stopped in their channels, found its freedom lost:
Thither the wealth of all the world did go,
    And seemed but shipwracked on so base a coast.

3

For them alone the heavens had kindly heat,
    In eastern quarries[a] ripening precious dew;
For them the Idumæan balm did sweat
    And in hot Ceylon spicy forests grew.

4

The sun but seemed the labourer of their year;
    Each wexing moon[b] supplied her watery store
To swell those tides which from the Line did bear
    Their brim-full vessels to the Belgian shore.

5

Thus mighty in her ships stood Carthage long
    And swept the riches of the world from far,
Yet stooped to Rome, less wealthy but more strong;
    And this may prove our second Punic war.

[a] *In eastern quarries.* Precious stones at first are dew condensed, and hardened by the warmth of the sun or subterranean fires.

[b] *Each wexing moon.* According to their opinions who think that great heap of the waters under the Line is depressed into tides by the moon toward the poles.

6

What peace can be, where both to one pretend,
  But they more diligent and we more strong?
Or if a peace, it soon must have an end,
  For they would grow too powerful, were it long.

7

Behold two nations then engaged so far
  That each seven years the fit must shake each land;
Where France will side to weaken us by war
  Who only can his vast designs withstand.

8

See how he feeds the Iberian[c] with delays
  To render us his timely friendship vain;
And while his secret soul on Flanders preys,
  He rocks the cradle of the babe of Spain.

9

Such deep designs of empire does he lay
  O'er them whose cause he seems to take in hand,
And prudently would make them lords at sea
  To whom with ease he can give laws by land.

10

This saw our King, and long within his breast
  His pensive counsels balanced to and fro;
He grieved the land he freed should be opprest
  And he less for it than usurpers do.

11

His generous mind the fair ideas drew
  Of fame and honour, which in dangers lay;
Where wealth, like fruit on precipices, grew,
  Not to be gathered but by birds of prey.

12

The loss and gain each fatally were great,
  And still his subjects called aloud for war:
But peaceful kings, o'er martial people set,
  Each other's poise and counterbalance are.

[c] *The Iberian.* The Spaniard.

13

He first surveyed the charge with careful eyes,
  Which none but mighty monarchs could maintain;
Yet judged, like vapours that from limbecs rise,
  It would in richer showers descend again.

14

At length resolved to assert the watery ball,
  He in himself did whole armados bring;
Him aged seamen might their master call
  And choose for General, were he not their King.

15

It seems as every ship their Sovereign knows,
  His awful summons they so soon obey;
So hear the scaly herd when Proteus blows[d],
  And so to pasture follow through the sea.

16

To see this fleet upon the ocean move
  Angels drew wide the curtains of the skies;
And Heaven, as if there wanted lights above,
  For tapers made two glaring comets rise;

17

Whether they unctuous exhalations are
  Fired by the sun, or seeming so alone,
Or each some more remote and slippery star
  Which loses footing when to mortals shown;

[d] *When Proteus blows,* or—
    'Cæruleus Proteus immania ponti
      Armenta, et magnas pascit sub gurgite phocas.'—VIRG.
[Not quoted exactly by Dryden:
      'Cæruleus Proteus, magnum qui piscibus æquor
      Et juncto bipedum curru metitur equorum.

      .   .   .   .

      Quippe ita Neptuno visum est; immania cujus
      Armenta et turpes pascit sub gurgite phocas.'
                    VIRG. *Georg.* iv. 388.]

18

Or one that bright companion of the sun,
  Whose glorious aspect sealed our new-born King,
And now, a round of greater years begun,
  New influence from his walks of light did bring.

19

Victorious York did first with famed success
  To his known valour make the Dutch give place;
Thus Heaven our Monarch's fortune did confess,
  Beginning conquest from his royal race.

20

But since it was decreed, auspicious King,
  In Britain's right that thou shouldst wed the main,
Heaven as a gage would cast some precious thing,
  And therefore doomed that Lawson should be slain.

21

Lawson amongst the foremost met his fate,
  Whom sea-green Sirens from the rocks lament;
Thus, as an offering for the Grecian state,
  He first was killed who first to battle went.

22

Their chief[e] blown up, in air, not waves expired
  To which his pride presumed to give the law;
The Dutch confessed Heaven present and retired,
  And all was Britain the wide ocean saw.

23

To nearest ports their shattered ships repair,
  Where by our dreadful cannon they lay awed;
So reverently men quit the open air
  Where thunder speaks the angry gods abroad.

24

The attempt at Berghen. And now approached their fleet from India, fraught
  With all the riches of the rising sun,
And precious sand from southern climates[f] brought,
  The fatal regions where the war begun.

---

[e] The Admiral of Holland.   [f] *Southern climates.* Guinea.

25

Like hunted castors conscious of their store,
   Their way-laid wealth to Norway's coasts they bring;
There first the North's cold bosom spices bore,
   And winter brooded on the eastern spring.

26

By the rich scent we found our perfumed prey,
   Which, flanked with rocks, did close in covert lie;
And round about their murdering cannon lay,
   At once to threaten and invite the eye.

27

Fiercer than cannon and than rocks more hard,
   The English undertake the unequal war:
Seven ships alone, by which the port is barred,
   Besiege the Indies and all Denmark dare.

28

These fight like husbands, but like lovers those;
   These fain would keep and those more fain enjoy;
And to such height their frantic passion grows
   That what both love both hazard to destroy.

29

Amidst whole heaps of spices lights a ball,
   And now their odours armed against them fly:
Some preciously by shattered porcelain fall
   And some by aromatic splinters die.

30

And though by tempests of the prize bereft,
   In Heaven's inclemency some ease we find;
Our foes we vanquished by our valour left,
   And only yielded to the seas and wind.

31

Nor wholly lost we so deserved a prey,
   For storms repenting part of it restored,
Which as a tribute from the Baltic sea
   The British ocean sent her mighty lord.

32

Go, mortals, now and vex yourselves in vain
  For wealth, which so uncertainly must come;
When what was brought so far and with such pain
  Was only kept to lose it nearer home.

33

The son who, twice three months on the ocean tost,
  Prepared to tell what he had passed before,
Now sees in English ships the Holland coast
  And parents' arms in vain stretched from the shore.

34

This careful husband had been long away
  Whom his chaste wife and little children mourn,
Who on their fingers learned to tell the day
  On which their father promised to return.

35

Such are the proud designs of human kind*s*,
  And so we suffer shipwrack everywhere!
Alas, what port can such a pilot find
  Who in the night of Fate must blindly steer!

36

The undistinguished seeds of good and ill
  Heaven in his bosom from our knowledge hides,
And draws them in contempt of human skill,
  .Which oft for friends mistaken foes provides.

37

Let Munster's prelate ever be accurst,
  In whom we seek the German faith[h] in vain;
Alas, that he should teach the English first
  That fraud and avarice in the Church could reign!

s Such are, &c. From Petronius: 'Si bene calculum ponas,
ubique fit naufragium.' [*Satyr.* c. 115.]
  h *The German faith.* Tacitus saith of them: ' Nullos mortalium armis aut fide ante Germanos esse.' [Said of the Germans,
according to Tacitus, by two Germans. *Ann.* xiii. 45.]

38

Happy who never trust a stranger's will
  Whose friendship's in his interest understood;
Since money given but tempts him to be ill,
  When power is too remote to make him good.

39

Till now, alone the mighty nations strove;
  The rest at gaze without the lists did stand;
And threatening France, placed like a painted Jove,
  Kept idle thunder in his lifted hand.

*War declared
by France.*

40

That eunuch guardian of rich Holland's trade
  Who envies us what he wants power to enjoy,
Whose noiseful valour does no foe invade
  And weak assistance will his friends destroy;

41

Offended that we fought without his leave,
  He takes this time his secret hate to show;
Which Charles does with a mind so calm receive
  As one that neither seeks nor shuns his foe.

42

With France to aid the Dutch the Danes unite;
  France as their tyrant, Denmark as their slave;
But when with one three nations join to fight,
  They silently confess that one more brave.

43

Lewis had chased the English from his shore,
  But Charles the French as subjects does invite;
Would Heaven for each some Solomon restore,
  Who by their mercy may decide their right!

44

Were subjects so but only by their choice
  And not from birth did forced dominion take,
Our Prince alone would have the public voice
  And all his neighbours' realms would deserts make.

45

He without fear a dangerous war pursues,
   Which without rashness he began before:
As honour made him first the danger choose,
   So still he makes it good on virtue's score.

46

The doubled charge his subjects' love supplies,
   Who in that bounty to themselves are kind:
So glad Egyptians see their Nilus rise
   And in his plenty their abundance find.

47

Prince Rupert and Duke of Albemarle sent to sea. With equal power he does two chiefs create,
   Two such as each seemed worthiest when alone;
Each able to sustain a nation's fate,
   Since both had found a greater in their own.

48

Both great in courage, conduct, and in fame,
   Yet neither envious of the other's praise;
Their duty, faith, and interest too the same,
   Like mighty partners, equally they raise.

49

The Prince long time had courted Fortune's love,
   But once possessed did absolutely reign:
Thus with their Amazons the heroes strove,
   And conquered first those beauties they would gain.

50

The Duke beheld, like Scipio, with disdain
   That Carthage which he ruined rise once more,
And shook aloft the fasces of the main
   To fright those slaves with what they felt before.

51

Together to the watery camp they haste,
   Whom matrons passing to their children show;
Infants' first vows for them to Heaven are cast,
   And future people bless them as they go[1].

[1] *Future people.* 'Examina infantium futurusque populus.'—
PLIN. *jun. in Pan. ad Traj.* [c. 26.]

52

With them no riotous pomp nor Asian train
  To infect a navy with their gaudy fears,
To make slow fights and victories but vain;
  But war severely like itself appears.

53

Diffusive of themselves, where'er they pass,
  They make that warmth in others they expect;
Their valour works like bodies on a glass
  And does its image on their men project.

54

Our fleet divides, and straight the Dutch appear,   *Duke of*
  In number and a famed commander bold: *Albemarle's*
The narrow seas can scarce their navy bear   *battle,*
  Or crowded vessels can their soldiers hold.   *first day.*

55

The Duke, less numerous, but in courage more,
  On wings of all the winds to combat flies;
His murdering guns a loud defiance roar
  And bloody crosses on his flag-staffs rise.

56

Both furl their sails and strip them for the fight;
  Their folded sheets dismiss the useless air;
The Elean plains[k] could boast no nobler sight,
  When struggling champions did their bodies bare.

57

Borne each by other in a distant line,
  The sea-built forts in dreadful order move;
So vast the noise, as if not fleets did join,
  But lands unfixed and floating nations strove[l].

[k] *The Elean, &c.* Where the Olympic games were celebrated.
[l] From Virgil: 'Credas innare revulsas Cycladas,' &c.—[*Æn.*
viii. 691.]

58

Now passed, on either side they nimbly tack;
  Both strive to intercept and guide the wind:
And in its eye more closely they come back
  To finish all the deaths they left behind.

59

On high-raised decks the haughty Belgians ride,
  Beneath whose shade our humble frigates go;
Such port the elephant bears, and so defied
  By the rhinoceros, her unequal foe.

60

And as the build, so different is the fight;
  Their mounting shot is on our sails designed:
Deep in their hulls our deadly bullets light
  And through the yielding planks a passage find.

61

Our dreaded Admiral from far they threat,
  Whose battered rigging their whole war receives;
All bare, like some old oak which tempests beat,
  He stands, and sees below his scattered leaves.

62

Heroes of old when wounded shelter sought;
  But he, who meets all danger with disdain,
Even in their face his ship to anchor brought
  And steeple-high stood propped upon the main.

63

At this excess of courage all-amazed,
  The foremost of his foes a while withdraw;
With such respect in entered Rome they gazed
  Who on high chairs the god-like fathers saw.

64

And now as, where Patroclus' body lay,
  Here Trojan chiefs advanced and there the Greek,
Ours o'er the Duke their pious wings display
  And theirs the noblest spoils of Britain seek.

65

Meantime his busy mariners he hastes
  His shattered sails with rigging to restore;
And willing pines ascend his broken masts,
  Whose lofty heads rise higher than before.

66

Straight to the Dutch he turns his dreadful prow,
  More fierce the important quarrel to decide:
Like swans in long array his vessels show,
  Whose crests advancing do the waves divide.

67

They charge, recharge, and all along the sea
  They drive and squander the huge Belgian fleet;
Berkeley alone, who nearest danger lay,
  Did a like fate with lost Creusa meet.

68

The night comes on, we eager to pursue
  The combat still and they ashamed to leave:
Till the last streaks of dying day withdrew
  And doubtful moonlight did our rage deceive.

69

In the English fleet each ship resounds with joy
  And loud applause of their great leader's fame;
In fiery dreams the Dutch they still destroy,
  And slumbering smile at the imagined flame.

70

Not so the Holland fleet, who, tired and done,
  Stretched on their decks like weary oxen lie;
Faint sweats all down their mighty members run,
  Vast bulks, which little souls but ill supply.

71

In dreams they fearful precipices tread,
  Or shipwracked labour to some distant shore,
Or in dark churches walk among the dead;
  They wake with horror and dare sleep no more.

72

Second day's battle.

The morn they look on with unwilling eyes,
 Till from their maintop joyful news they hear
Of ships which by their mould bring new supplies
 And in their colours Belgian lions bear.

73

Our watchful General had discerned from far
 This mighty succour, which made glad the foe;
He sighed, but, like a father of the war,
 His face spake hope, while deep his sorrows flow[m].

74

His wounded men he first sends off to shore,
 Never till now unwilling to obey:
They not their wounds but want of strength deplore
 And think them happy who with him can stay.

75

Then to the rest, 'Rejoice,' said he, 'to-day!
 'In you the fortune of Great Britain lies;
'Among so brave a people you are they
 'Whom Heaven has chose to fight for such a prize.

76

'If number English courages could quell,
 'We should at first have shunned, not met our foes,
'Whose numerous sails the fearful only tell;
 'Courage from hearts and not from numbers grows.'

77

He said, nor needed more to say: with haste
 To their known stations cheerfully they go;
And all at once, disdaining to be last,
 Solicit every gale to meet the foe.

78

Nor did the encouraged Belgians long delay,
 But bold in others, not themselves, they stood:
So thick, our navy scarce could sheer their way,
 But seemed to wander in a moving wood.

[m] 'Spem vultu simulat, premit altum corde dolorem.'
           VIRG. [*Æn.* ii. 213.]

79

Our little fleet was now engaged so far
  That like the sword-fish in the whale they fought;
The combat only seemed a civil war,
  Till through their bowels we our passage wrought.

80

Never had valour, no, not ours before
  Done aught like this upon the land or main;
Where not to be o'ercome was to do more
  Than all the conquests former Kings did gain.

81

The mighty ghosts of our great Harrys rose,
  And armed Edwards looked with anxious eyes,
To see this fleet among unequal foes,
  By which Fate promised them their Charles should
    rise.

82

Meantime the Belgians tack upon our rear,
  And raking chase-guns through our sterns they
    send;
Close by, their fire-ships like jackals appear
  Who on their lions for the prey attend.

83

Silent in smoke of cannon they come on:
  Such vapours once did fiery Cacus hide[n]:
In these the height of pleased revenge is shown
  Who burn contented by another's side.

84

Sometimes from fighting squadrons of each fleet,
  Deceived themselves or to preserve some friend,
Two grappling Ætnas on the ocean meet
  And English fires with Belgian flames contend.

[n] ' Ille autem.' [Virg. *Æn.* viii. 251.]

85

Now at each tack our little fleet grows less;
  And, like maimed fowl, swim lagging on the main;
Their greater loss their numbers scarce confess,
  While they lose cheaper than the English gain.

86

Have you not seen when, whistled from the fist,
  Some falcon stoops at what her eye designed,
And, with her eagerness the quarry missed,
  Straight flies at check and clips it down the wind;

87

The dastard crow, that to the wood made wing
  And sees the groves no shelter can afford,
With her loud caws her craven kind does bring,
  Who, safe in numbers, cuff the noble bird.

88

Among the Dutch thus Albemarle did fare:
  He could not conquer and disdained to fly:
Past hope of safety, 'twas his latest care,
  Like falling Cæsar, decently to die.

89

Yet pity did his manly spirit move,
  To see those perish who so well had fought;
And generously with his despair he strove,
  Resolved to live till he their safety wrought.

90

Let other muses write his prosperous fate,
  Of conquered nations tell and kings restored;
But mine shall sing of his eclipsed estate,
  Which, like the sun's, more wonders does afford.

91

He drew his mighty frigates all before,
  On which the foe his fruitless force employs;
His weak ones deep into his rear he bore
  Remote from guns, as sick men from the noise.

92

His fiery cannon did their passage guide,
  And following smoke obscured them from the foe ;
Thus Israel safe from the Egyptian's pride
  By flaming pillars and by clouds did go.

93

Elsewhere the Belgian force we did defeat,
  But here our courages did theirs subdue ;
So Xenophon once led that famed retreat
  Which first the Asian empire overthrew.

94

The foe approached ; and one for his bold sin
  Was sunk, as he that touched the Ark was slain :
The wild waves mastered him and sucked him in,
  And smiling eddies dimpled on the main.

95

This seen, the rest at awful distance stood :
  As if they had been there as servants set
To stay or to go on, as he thought good,
  And not pursue, but wait on his retreat.

96

So Libyan huntsmen on some sandy plain,
  From shady coverts roused, the lion chase :
The kingly beast roars out with loud disdain,
  And slowly moves, unknowing to give place [o].

97

But if some one approach to dare his force,
  He swings his tail and swiftly turns him round,
With one paw seizes on his trembling horse,
  And with the other tears him to the ground.

[o] The simile is Virgil's : ' Vestigia retro improperata refert.'
[More fully and correctly :—
      ' Haud aliter retro dubius vestigia Turnus
      Improperata refert, et mens exæstuat ira.'
                              Æn. ix. 797.].

98

Amidst these toils succeeds the balmy night;
  Now hissing waters the quenched guns restore:
And weary waves P, withdrawing from the fight,
  Lie lulled and panting on the silent shore.

99

The moon shone clear on the becalmed flood,
  Where, while her beams like glittering silver play,
Upon the deck our careful General stood,
  And deeply mused on the succeeding day q.

100

'That happy sun,' said he, 'will rise again,
  Who twice victorious did our navy see,
And I alone must view him rise in vain,
  Without one ray of all his star for me.

101

'Yet like an English general will I die,
  And all the ocean make my spacious grave:
Women and cowards on the land may lie;
  The sea's a tomb that's proper for the brave.'

102

Restless he passed the remnants of the night,
  Till the fresh air proclaimed the morning nigh;
And burning ships, the martyrs of the fight,
  With paler fires beheld the eastern sky.

103

Third day. But now, his stores of ammunition spent,
  His naked valour is his only guard;
Rare thunders are from his dumb cannon sent
  And solitary guns are scarcely heard.

P *Weary waves*, from Statius:
    'Nec trucibus fluviis idem sonus: occidit horror
    Æquoris, et terris maria acclinata quiescunt.'
                     [*Sylv.* v. 4, 5.]
q The 3rd of June, famous for two former victories.

104

Thus far had Fortune power, here forced to stay;
  Nor longer durst with virtue be at strife;
This as a ransom Albemarle did pay
  For all the glories of so great a life.

105

For now brave Rupert from afar appears,
  Whose waving streamers the glad General knows;
With full-spread sails his eager navy steers,
  And every ship in swift proportion grows.

106

The anxious Prince had heard the cannon long
  And from that length of time dire omens drew
Of English overmatched, and Dutch too strong
  Who never fought three days but to pursue.

107

Then, as an eagle, who with pious care
  Was beating widely on the wing for prey,
To her now silent eyry does repair,
  And finds her callow infants forced away;

108

Stung with her love, she stoops upon the plain,
  The broken air loud whistling as she flies;
She stops and listens and shoots forth again
  And guides her pinions by her young ones' cries:

109

With such kind passion hastes the Prince to fight
  And spreads his flying canvas to the sound;
Him whom no danger, were he there, could fright,
  Now absent, every little noise can wound.

110

As in a drought the thirsty creatures cry
  And gape upon the gathered clouds for rain,
And first the martlet meets it in the sky,
  And with wet wings joys all the feathered train;

111

With such glad hearts did our despairing men
   Salute the appearance of the Prince's fleet,
And each ambitiously would claim the ken
   That with first eyes did distant safety meet.

112

The Dutch, who came like greedy hinds before
   To reap the harvest their ripe ears did yield,
Now look like those, when rolling thunders roar
   And sheets of lightning blast the standing field.

113

Full in the Prince's passage, hills of sand
   And dangerous flats in secret ambush lay,
Where the false tides skim o'er the covered land
   And seamen with dissembled depths betray.

114

The wily Dutch, who, like fallen angels, feared
   This new Messiah's coming, there did wait,
And round the verge their braving vessels steered
   To tempt his courage with so fair a bait.

115

But he unmoved contemns their idle threat,
   Secure of fame whene'er he please to fight;
His cold experience tempers all his heat,
   And inbred worth does boasting valour slight.

116

Heroic virtue did his actions guide,
   And he the substance, not the appearance, chose;
To rescue one such friend he took more pride
   Than to destroy whole thousands of such foes.

117

But when approached, in strict embraces bound
   Rupert and Albemarle together grow;
He joys to have his friend in safety found,
   Which he to none but to that friend would owe.

118

The cheerful soldiers, with new stores supplied,
  Now long to execute their spleenful will;
And in revenge for those three days they tried
  Wish one like Joshua's, when the sun stood still.

119

Thus reinforced, against the adverse fleet,   *Fourth day's battle.*
  Still doubling ours, brave Rupert leads the way;
With the first blushes of the morn they meet
  And bring night back upon the new-born day.

120

His presence soon blows up the kindling fight,
  And his loud guns speak thick like angry men;
It seemed as slaughter had been breathed all night
  And Death new pointed his dull dart again.

121

The Dutch too well his mighty conduct know
  And matchless courage, since the former fight;
Whose navy like a stiff stretched cord did show,
  Till he bore in and bent them into flight.

122

The wind he shares, while half their fleet offends
  His open side and high above him shows;
Upon the rest at pleasure he descends
  And doubly harmed he double harms bestows.

123

Behind, the General mends his weary pace
  And sullenly to his revenge he sails;
So glides[r] some trodden serpent on the grass
  And long behind his wounded volume trails.

[r] *So glides*, &c. From Virgil:
    ' Quum medii nexus extremæque agmina caudæ
    Solvuntur, tardosque trahit sinus ultimus orbes,' &c.
                    [*Georg.* iii. 423.]

124

The increasing sound is borne to either shore
  And for their stakes the throwing nations fear,
Their passion double with the cannons' roar,
  And with warm wishes each man combats there.

125

Plied thick and close as when the fight begun,
  Their huge unwieldy navy wastes away:
So sicken waning moons too near the sun
  And blunt their crescents on the edge of day.

126

And now, reduced on equal terms to fight,
  Their ships like wasted patrimonies show,
Where the thin scattering trees admit the light
  And shun each other's shadows as they grow.

127

The warlike Prince had severed from the rest
  Two giant ships, the pride of all the main:
Which with his one so vigorously he pressed
  And flew so home they could not rise again.

128

Already battered by his lee they lay;
  In vain upon the passing winds they call;
The passing winds through their torn canvas play
  And flagging sails on heartless sailors fall.

129

Their opened sides receive a gloomy light,
  Dreadful as day let in to shades below;
Without, grim Death rides barefaced in their sight
  And urges entering billows as they flow.

130

When one dire shot, the last they could supply,
  Close by the board the Prince's main-mast bore:
All three now helpless by each other lie,
  And this offends not and those fear no more.

131

So have I seen some fearful hare maintain
　A course, till tired before the dog she lay,
Who, stretched behind her, pants upon the plain,
　Past power to kill as she to get away:

132

With his lolled tongue he faintly licks his prey;
　His warm breath blows her flix up as she lies;
She, trembling, creeps upon the ground away
　And looks back to him with beseeching eyes.

133

The Prince unjustly does his stars accuse,
　Which hindered him to push his fortune on;
For what they to his courage did refuse
　By mortal valour never must be done.

134

This lucky hour the wise Batavian takes
　And warns his tattered fleet to follow home;
Proud to have so got off with equal stakes,
　Where 'twas a triumph not to be o'ercome[a].

135

The General's force, as kept alive by fight,
　Now, not opposed, no longer can pursue;
Lasting till Heaven had done its courage right,
　When he had conquered he his weakness knew.

136

He casts a frown on the departing foe
　And sighs to see him quit the watery field;
His stern fixed eyes no satisfaction show
　For all the glories which the fight did yield.

[a] From Horace:

> 'Quos opimus
> Fallere et effugere est triumphus.'
> [4 *Od.* iv. 51.]

137

Though, as when fiends did miracles avow,
  He stands confessed even by the boastful Dutch;
He only does his conquest disavow
  And thinks too little what they found too much.

138

Returned, he with the fleet resolved to stay;
  No tender thoughts of home his heart divide;
Domestic joys and cares he puts away,
  For realms are households which the great must
    guide.

139

As those who unripe veins in mines explore
  On the rich bed again the warm turf lay,
Till time digests the yet imperfect ore,
  And know it will be gold another day;

140

So looks our Monarch on this early fight,
  The essay and rudiments of great success,
Which all-maturing time must bring to light,
  While he, like Heaven, does each day's labour bless.

141

Heaven ended not the first or second day,
  Yet each was perfect to the work designed:
God and kings work, when they their work survey,
  And passive aptness in all subjects find.

142

His Majesty repairs the fleet.

In burdened vessels first with speedy care
  His plenteous stores do seasoned timber send;
Thither the brawny carpenters repair
  And as the surgeons of maimed ships attend.

143

With cord and canvas from rich Hamburg sent
  His navy's moulted wings he imps once more;
Tall Norway fir their masts in battle spent,
  And English oak sprung leaks and planks restore.

144

All hands employed, the royal work grows warm[t];
   Like labouring bees on a long summer's day,
Some sound the trumpet for the rest to swarm
   And some on bells of tasted lilies play;

145

With glewy wax some new foundation lay
   Of virgin-combs, which from the roof are hung;
Some armed within doors upon duty stay
   Or tend the sick or educate the young:

146

So here some pick out bullets from the side,
   Some drive old oakum through each seam and rift:
Their left hand does the caulking-iron guide,
   The rattling mallet with the right they lift.

147

With boiling pitch another near at hand,
   From friendly Sweden brought, the seams instops,
Which well paid o'er the salt sea waves withstand
   And shake them from the rising beak in drops.

148

Some the galled ropes with dauby marling bind
   Or sear-cloth masts with strong tarpauling coats:
To try new shrouds one mounts into the wind
   And one below their ease or stiffness notes.

149

Our careful Monarch stands in person by
   His new cast cannons' firmness to explore,
The strength of big-corned powder loves to try
   And ball and cartridge sorts for every bore.

150

Each day brings fresh supplies of arms and men
   And ships which all last winter were abroad,
And such as fitted since the fight had been
   Or new from stocks were fallen into road.

   t 'Fervet opus:' the same similitude in Virgil. [*Georg.* iv.

151

The goodly London in her gallant trim,
    The phœnix-daughter of the vanished old,
Like a rich bride does to the ocean swim
    And on her shadow rides in floating gold.

152

Her flag aloft, spread ruffling to the wind,
    And sanguine streamers seem the flood to fire;
The weaver, charmed with what his loom designed,
    Goes on to sea and knows not to retire.

153

With roomy decks, her guns of mighty strength,
    Whose low-laid mouths each mounting billow laves,
Deep in her draught and warlike in her length,
    She seems a sea wasp flying on the waves.

154

This martial present, piously designed,
    The loyal City give their best-loved King:
And, with a bounty ample as the wind,
    Built, fitted, and maintained, to him did bring.

155

By viewing nature Nature's handmaid, Art,
    Makes mighty things from small beginnings grow:
Thus fishes first to shipping did impart
    Their tail the rudder and their head the prow.

156

Some log perhaps upon the waters swam,
    An useless drift, which, rudely cut within
And hollowed, first a floating trough became
    And cross some rivulet passage did begin.

157

In shipping such as this the Irish kern
    And untaught Indian on the stream did glide,
Ere sharp-keeled boats to stem the flood did learn,
    Or fin-like oars did spread from either side.

158

Add but a sail, and Saturn so appeared,
  When from lost empire he to exile went,
And with the golden age to Tiber steered,
  Where coin and first commerce he did invent.

159

Rude as their ships was navigation then,
  No useful compass or meridian known;
Coasting, they kept the land within their ken,
  And knew no North but when the pole-star shone.

160

Of all who since have used the open sea
  Than the bold English none more fame have won;
Beyond the year and out of Heaven's high way [u]
  They make discoveries where they see no sun.

161

But what so long in vain, and yet unknown,
  By poor mankind's benighted wit is sought,
Shall in this age to Britain first be shown
  And hence be to admiring nations taught.

162

The ebbs of tides and their mysterious flow
  We, as art's elements, shall understand,
And as by line upon the ocean go
  Whose paths shall be familiar as the land.

163

Instructed ships shall sail to quick commerce [x],
  By which remotest regions are allied;
Which makes one city of the universe,
  Where some may gain and all may be supplied.

164

Then we upon our globe's last verge shall go
  And view the ocean leaning on the sky:
From thence our rolling neighbours we shall know
  And on the lunar world securely pry.

u ' Extra anni solisque vias.'—VIRG. [*Æn*. vi. 797.]
x By a more exact knowledge of longitude.

165

This I foretell, from your auspicious care
  Who great in search of God and Nature grow;
Who best your wise Creator's praise declare,
  Since best to praise His works is best to know.

166

O, truly Royal! who behold the law
  And rule of beings in your Maker's mind,
And thence, like limbecs, rich ideas draw
  To fit the levelled use of human kind.

167

But first the toils of war we must endure
  And from the injurious Dutch redeem the seas;
War makes the valiant of his right secure
  And gives up fraud to be chastised with ease.

168

Already were the Belgians on our coast,
  Whose fleet more mighty every day became
By late success, which they did falsely boast,
  And now by first appearing seemed to claim.

169

Designing, subtle, diligent, and close,
  They knew to manage war with wise delay:
Yet all those arts their vanity did cross
  And by their pride their prudence did betray.

170

Nor stayed the English long; but, well supplied,
  Appear as numerous as the insulting foe;
The combat now by courage must be tried
  And the success the braver nation show.

171

There was the Plymouth squadron new come in,
  Which in the Straits last winter was abroad,
Which twice on Biscay's working bay had been
  And on the midland sea the French had awed.

172

Old expert Allen, loyal all along,
  Famed for his action on the Smyrna fleet;
And Holmes, whose name shall live in epic song,
  While music numbers, or while verse has feet;

173

Holmes, the Achates of the Generals' fight,
  Who first bewitched our eyes with Guinea gold,
As once old Cato in the Romans' sight
  The tempting fruits of Afric did unfold.

174

With him went Spragge, as bountiful as brave,
  Whom his high courage to command had brought;
Harman, who did the twice-fired Harry save
  And in his burning ship undaunted fought.

175

Young Hollis, on a Muse by Mars begot,
  Born, Cæsar-like, to write and act great deeds,
Impatient to revenge his fatal shot,
  His right hand doubly to his left succeeds.

176

Thousands were there in darker fame that dwell,
  Whose deeds some nobler poem shall adorn;
And though to me unknown, they sure fought well
  Whom Rupert led and who were British born.

177

Of every size an hundred fighting sail;
  So vast the navy now at anchor rides
That underneath it the pressed waters fail
  And with its weight it shoulders off the tides.

178

Now, anchors weighed, the seamen shout so shrill
  That heaven and earth and the wide ocean rings:
A breeze from westward waits their sails to fill
  And rests in those high beds his downy wings.

179

The wary Dutch this gathering storm foresaw
And durst not bide it on the English coast;
Behind their treacherous shallows they withdraw
And there lay snares to catch the British host.

180

So the false spider, when her nets are spread,
Deep ambushed in her silent den does lie,
And feels far off the trembling of her thread,
Whose filmy cord should bind the struggling fly;

181

Then, if at last she find him fast beset,
She issues forth and runs along her loom:
She joys to touch the captive in her net
And drags the little wretch in triumph home.

182

The Belgians hoped that with disordered haste
Our deep-cut keels upon the sands might run,
Or, if with caution leisurely were past,
Their numerous gross might charge us one by one.

183

But, with a fore-wind pushing them above
And swelling tide that heaved them from below,
O'er the blind flats our warlike squadrons move
And with spread sails to welcome battle go.

184

It seemed as there the British Neptune stood,
With all his host of waters at command,
Beneath them to submit the officious flood,
And with his trident shoved them off the sand 7.

185

To the pale foes they suddenly draw near
And summon them to unexpected fight:
They start, like murderers when ghosts appear
And draw their curtains in the dead of night.

7 'Levat ipse tridenti et vastas aperit syrtes,' &c.

Virg. [*Æn.* i. 145.]

186

Now van to van the foremost squadrons meet,   *Second battle.*
  The midmost battles hasting up behind,
Who view far off the storm of falling sleet
  And hear their thunder rattling in the wind.

187

At length the adverse Admirals appear, ·
  The two bold champions of each country's right;
Their eyes describe the lists as they come near
  And draw the lines of death before they fight.

188

The distance judged for shot of every size,
  The linstocks touch, the ponderous ball expires:
The vigorous seaman every porthole plies
  And adds his heart to every gun he fires.

189

Fierce was the fight on the proud Belgians' side
  For honour, which they seldom sought before;
But now they by their own vain boasts were tied
  And forced at least in show to prize it more.

190

But sharp remembrance on the English part
  And shame of being matched by such a foe
Rouse conscious virtue up in every heart,
  And seeming to be stronger makes them so [z].

191

Nor long the Belgians could that fleet sustain
  Which did two Generals' fates and Cæsar's bear;
Each several ship a victory did gain,
  As Rupert or as Albemarle were there.

192

Their battered Admiral too soon withdrew,
  Unthanked by ours for his unfinished fight;
But he the minds of his Dutch masters knew
  Who called that providence which we called flight.

---

[z] 'Possunt quia posse videntur.'—VIRG. [*Æn.* v. 23.]

193

Never did men more joyfully obey
  Or sooner understood the sign to fly;
With such alacrity they bore away
  As if to praise them all the States stood by.

194

O famous leader of the Belgian fleet!
  Thy monument inscribed such praise shall wear
As Varro, timely flying, once did meet,
  Because he did not of his Rome despair.

195

Behold that navy, which a while before
  Provoked the tardy English close to fight,
Now draw their beaten vessels close to shore,
  As larks lie dared to shun the hobby's flight.

196

Whoe'er would English monuments survey
  In other records may our courage know;
But let them hide the story of this day,
  Whose fame was blemished by too base a foe.

197

Or if too busily they will inquire
  Into a victory which we disdain,
Then let them know the Belgians did retire
  Before the patron saint [a] of injured Spain.

198

Repenting England, this revengeful day,
  To Philip's manes [b] did an offering bring,
England, which first by leading them astray
  Hatched up rebellion to destroy her King.

  [a] *Patron saint*; St. James, on whose day this victory was
gained.
  [b] *Philip's manes*; Philip II. of Spain, against whom the Hollanders rebelling were aided by Queen Elizabeth.

199

Our fathers bent their baneful industry
  To check a monarchy that slowly grew,
But did not France or Holland's fate foresee,
  Whose rising power to swift dominion flew.

200

In Fortune's empire blindly thus we go
  And wander after pathless destiny;
Whose dark resorts since prudence cannot know,
  In vain it would provide for what shall be.

201

But whate'er English to the blessed shall go,
  And the fourth Harry or first Orange meet,
Find him disowning of a Bourbon foe
  And him detesting a Batavian fleet.

202

Now on their coasts our conquering navy rides,
  Waylays their merchants and their land besets;
Each day new wealth without their care provides;
  They lie asleep with prizes in their nets.

203

So close behind some promontory lie
  The huge leviathans to attend their prey,
And give no chase, but swallow in the fry,
  Which through their gaping jaws mistake the way.

204

Nor was this all; in ports and roads remote
  Destructive fires among whole fleets we send;
Triumphant flames upon the water float
  And out-bound ships at home their voyage end.

Burning of the fleet in the Uly by Sir Robert Holmes.

205

Those various squadrons, variously designed,
  Each vessel freighted with a several load,
Each squadron waiting for a several wind,
  All find but one, to burn them in the road.

206

Some bound for Guinea golden sand to find
  Bore all the gauds the simple natives wear;
Some for the pride of Turkish courts designed
  For folded turbans finest holland bear;

207

Some English wool, vexed in a Belgian loom
  And into cloth of spungy softness made,
Did into France or colder Denmark doom,
  To ruin with worse ware our staple trade.

208

Our greedy seamen rummage every hold,
  Smile on the booty of each wealthier chest,
And, as the priests who with their gods make bold,
  Take what they like and sacrifice the rest.

209

Transition to the Fire of London. But, ah! how unsincere are all our joys,
  Which sent from Heaven, like lightning, make no
    stay!
Their palling taste the journey's length destroys,
  Or grief sent post o'ertakes them on the way.

210

Swelled with our late successes on the foe,
  Which France and Holland wanted power to cross,
We urge an unseen fate to lay us low
  And feed their envious eyes with English loss.

211

Each element His dread command obeys
  Who makes or ruins with a smile or frown;
Who as by one He did our nation raise,
  So now He with another pulls us down.

212

Yet, London, empress of the northern clime,
  By an high fate thou greatly didst expire;

Great as the world's, which at the death of time
  Must fall and rise a nobler frame by fire [c].

213

As when some dire usurper Heaven provides
  To scourge his country with a lawless sway;
His birth perhaps some petty village hides
  And sets his cradle out of Fortune's way;

214

Till, fully ripe, his swelling fate breaks out
  And hurries him to mighty mischiefs on;
His Prince, surprised, at first no ill could doubt,
  And wants the power to meet it when 'tis known.

215

Such was the rise of this prodigious fire,
  Which, in mean buildings first obscurely bred,
From thence did soon to open streets aspire
  And straight to palaces and temples spread.

216

The diligence of trades, and noiseful gain,
  And luxury, more late, asleep were laid;
All was the Night's, and in her silent reign
  No sound the rest of Nature did invade.

217

In this deep quiet, from what source unknown,
  Those seeds of fire their fatal birth disclose;
And first few scattering sparks about were blown,
  Big with the flames that to our ruin rose.

218

Then in some close-pent room it crept along
  And, smouldering as it went, in silence fed;
Till the infant monster, with devouring strong,
  Walked boldly upright with exalted head.

[c] 'Quum mare, quum tellus, correptaque regia cœli ardeat,' &c.
[Not quite correctly quoted by Dryden:
    'Esse quoque in fatis reminiscitur, affore tempus
    Quo mare, quo tellus correptaque regia cœli
    Ardeat, et mundi moles operosa laboret.'
              OVID, *Metam.* vii. 453.]

219

Now, like some rich or mighty murderer,
  Too great for prison which he breaks with gold,
Who fresher for new mischiefs does appear
  And dares the world to tax him with the old,

220

So scapes the insulting fire his narrow jail
  And makes small outlets into open air;
There the fierce winds his tender force assail
  And beat him downward to his first repair.

221

The winds, like crafty courtesans, withheld
  His flames from burning but to blow them more:
And, every fresh attempt, he is repelled
  With faint denials, weaker than before [d].

222

And now, no longer letted of his prey,
  He leaps up at it with enraged desire,
O'erlooks the neighbours with a wide survey,
  And nods at every house his threatening fire.

223

The ghosts of traitors from the Bridge descend,
  With bold fanatic spectres to rejoice;
About the fire into a dance they bend
  And sing their sabbath notes with feeble voice.

224

Our guardian angel saw them where they sate,
  Above the palace of our slumbering King;
He sighed, abandoning his charge to Fate,
  And drooping oft looked back upon the wing.

[d] *Like crafty, &c.* 'Hæc arte tractabat cupidum virum ut illius animum inopia accenderet.' [Incorrectly quoted by Dryden from Terence:

  'Hæc arte tractabat virum
  Ut illius animum cupidum inopia accenderet.'
                    Heautontim. ii. 3. 106.]

225

At length the crackling noise and dreadful blaze
  Called up some waking lover to the sight;
And long it was ere he the rest could raise,
  Whose heavy eyelids yet were full of night.

226

The next to danger, hot pursued by fate,
  Half-clothed, half-naked, hastily retire;
And frighted mothers strike their breasts too late
  For helpless infants left amidst the fire.

227

Their cries soon waken all the dwellers near;
  Now murmuring noises rise in every street;
The more remote run stumbling with their fear,
  And in the dark men justle as they. meet.

228

So weary bees in little cells repose;
  But if night-robbers lift the well-stored hive,
An humming through their waxen city grows,
  And out upon each other's wings they drive.

229

Now streets grow thronged and busy as by day;
  Some run for buckets to the hallowed quire;
Some cut the pipes, and some the engines play,
  And some more bold mount ladders to the fire.

230

In vain; for from the east a Belgian wind
  His hostile breath through the dry rafters sent;
The flames impelled soon left their foes behind
  And forward with a wanton fury went.

231

A key of fire ran all along the shore
  And lighted all the river with a blaze[e];
The wakened tides began again to roar,
  And wondering fish in shining waters gaze.

[e] 'Sigæa igni freta lata relucent.'—VIRG. [*Æn.* ii. 312.]

232

Old Father Thames raised up his reverend head,
    But feared the fate of Simois would return;
Deep in his ooze he sought his sedgy bed
    And shrank his waters back into his urn.

233

The fire meantime walks in a broader gross;
    To either hand his wings he opens wide;
He wades the streets, and straight he reaches cross
    And plays his longing flames on the other side.

234

At first they warm, then scorch, and then they take;
    Now with long necks from side to side they feed;
At length, grown strong, their mother-fire forsake,
    And a new colony of flames succeed.

235

To every nobler portion of the town
    The curling billows roll their restless tide;
In parties now they straggle up and down,
    As armies unopposed for prey divide.

236

One mighty squadron, with a sidewind sped,
    Through narrow lanes his cumbered fire does haste,
By powerful charms of gold and silver led
    The Lombard bankers and the Change to waste.

237

Another backward to the Tower would go
    And slowly eats his way against the wind;
But the main body of the marching foe
    Against the imperial palace is designed.

238

Now day appears; and with the day the King,
    Whose early care had robbed him of his rest;
Far off the cracks of falling houses ring
    And shrieks of subjects pierce his tender breast.

239

Near as he draws, thick harbingers of smoke
  With gloomy pillars cover all the place;
Whose little intervals of night are broke
  By sparks that drive against his sacred face.

240

More than his guards his sorrows made him known
  And pious tears which down his cheeks did shower;
The wretched in his grief forgot their own;
  So much the pity of a king has power.

241

He wept the flames of what he loved so well
  And what so well had merited his love;
For never prince in grace did more excel
  Or royal city more in duty strove.

242

Nor with an idle care did he behold:
  Subjects may grieve, but monarchs must redress;
He cheers the fearful and commends the bold
  And makes despairers hope for good success.

243

Himself directs what first is to be done
  And orders all the succours which they bring;
The helpful and the good about him run
  And form an army worthy such a King.

244

He sees the dire contagion spread so fast
  That, where it seizes, all relief is vain,
And therefore must unwillingly lay waste
  That country which would else the foe maintain.

245

The powder blows up all before the fire;
  The amazed flames stand gathered on a heap,
And from the precipice's brink retire,
  Afraid to venture on so large a leap.

246

Thus fighting fires a while themselves consume,
  But straight, like Turks forced on to win or die,
They first lay tender bridges of their fume
  And o'er the breach in unctuous vapours fly.

247

Part stays for passage, till a gust of wind
  Ships o'er their forces in a shining sheet;
Part, creeping under ground, their journey blind
  And, climbing from below, their fellows meet.

248

Thus to some desert plain or old wood-side
  Dire night-hags come from far to dance their
      round,
And o'er broad rivers on their fiends they ride
  Or sweep in clouds above the blasted ground.

249

No help avails: for, hydra-like, the fire
  Lifts up his hundred heads to aim his way;
And scarce the wealthy can one half retire
  Before he rushes in to share the prey.

250

The rich grow suppliant and the poor grow proud:
  Those offer mighty gain and these ask more;
So void of pity is the ignoble crowd,
  When others' ruin may increase their store.

251

As those who live by shores with joy behold
  Some wealthy vessel split or stranded nigh,
And from the rocks leap down for shipwracked gold
  And seek the tempest which the others fly:

252

So these but wait the owners' last despair
  And what's permitted to the flames invade;
Even from their jaws they hungry morsels tear
  And on their backs the spoils of Vulcan lade.

253

The days were all in this lost labour spent;
  And when the weary King gave place to night,
His beams he to his royal brother lent,
  And so shone still in his reflective light.

254

Night came, but without darkness or repose,
  A dismal picture of the general doom;
Where souls distracted, when the trumpet blows,
  And half unready with their bodies come.

255

Those who have homes, when home they do repair,
  To a last lodging call their wandering friends;
Their short uneasy sleeps are broke with care,
  To look how near their own destruction tends:

256

Those who have none sit round where once it was
  And with full eyes each wonted room require,
Haunting the yet warm ashes of the place,
  As murdered men walk where they did expire.

257

Some stir up coals and watch the vestal fire,
  Others in vain from sight of ruin run
And, while through burning labyrinths they retire,
  With loathing eyes repeat what they would shun.

258

The most in fields like herded beasts lie down,
  To dews obnoxious on the grassy floor;
And while their babes in sleep their sorrows drown,
  Sad parents watch the remnants of their store.

259

While by the motion of the flames they guess
  What streets are burning now, and what are near,
An infant, waking, to the paps would press
  And meets instead of milk a falling tear.

260

No thought can ease them but their Sovereign's care,
  Whose praise the afflicted as their comfort sing;
Even those whom want might drive to just despair
  Think life a blessing under such a King.

261

Meantime he sadly suffers in their grief,
  Outweeps an hermit and outprays a saint;
All the long night he studies their relief,
  How they may be supplied and he may want.

262

King's prayer. 'O God,' said he, 'Thou patron of my days,
  Guide of my youth in exile and distress!
Who me unfriended broughtst by wondrous ways,
  The kingdom of my fathers to possess:

263

'Be Thou my judge, with what unwearied care
  I since have laboured for my people's good,
To bind the bruises of a civil war
  And stop the issues of their wasting blood.

264

'Thou who hast taught me to forgive the ill
  And recompense as friends the good misled,
If mercy be a precept of Thy will,
  Return that mercy on Thy servant's head.

265

'Or if my heedless youth has stepped astray,
  Too soon forgetful of Thy gracious hand,
On me alone Thy just displeasure lay,
  But take Thy judgments from this mourning land.

266

'We all have sinned, and Thou hast laid us low
  As humble earth from whence at first we came;
Like flying shades before the clouds we show,
  And shrink like parchment in consuming flame.

267

'O let it be enough what Thou hast done,
   When spotted deaths ran armed through every
      street,
With poisoned darts, which not the good could shun,
   The speedy could outfly or valiant meet.

268

'The living few and frequent funerals then
   Proclaimed Thy wrath on this forsaken place;
And now those few, who are returned again,
   Thy searching judgments to their dwellings trace.

269

'O pass not, Lord, an absolute decree
   Or bind Thy sentence unconditional,
But in Thy sentence our remorse foresee
   And in that foresight this Thy doom recall.

270

'Thy threatenings, Lord, as Thine Thou mayest re-
     voke:
But if immutable and fixed they stand,
Continue still Thyself to give the stroke,
   And let not foreign foes oppress Thy land.'

271

The Eternal heard, and from the heavenly quire
   Chose out the cherub with the flaming sword,
And bad him swiftly drive the approaching fire
   From where our naval magazines were stored.

272

The blessed minister his wings displayed,
   And like a shooting star he cleft the night;
He charged the flames, and those that disobeyed
   He lashed to duty with his sword of light.

273

The fugitive flames, chastised, went forth to prey
   On pious structures by our fathers reared;
By which to Heaven they did affect the way,
   Ere faith in churchmen without works was heard.

274

The wanting orphans saw with watery eyes
   Their founders' charity in dust laid low,
And sent to God their ever-answered cries;
   For he protects the poor who made them so.

275

Nor could thy fabric, Paul's, defend thee long,
   Though thou wert sacred to thy Maker's praise,
Though made immortal by a poet's song,
   And poets' songs the Theban walls could raise.

276

The daring flames peeped in and saw from far
   The awful beauties of the sacred quire;
But, since it was profaned by civil war,
   Heaven thought it fit to have it purged by fire.

277

Now down the narrow streets it swiftly came
   And, widely opening, did on both sides prey;
This benefit we sadly owe the flame,
   If only ruin must enlarge our way.

278

And now four days the Sun had seen our woes,
   Four nights the Moon beheld the incessant fire;
It seemed as if the stars more sickly rose
   And farther from the feverish North retire.

279

In the empyrean Heaven, the blessed abode,
   The thrones and the dominions prostrate lie,
Not daring to behold their angry God;
   And a hushed silence damps the tuneful sky.

280

At length the Almighty cast a pitying eye,
   And mercy softly touched His melting breast;
He saw the town's one half in rubbish lie
   And eager flames give on to storm the rest.

281

An hollow crystal pyramid he takes, .
   In firmamental waters dipped above;
Of it a broad extinguisher he makes,
   And hoods the flames that to their quarry strove.

282

The vanquished fires withdraw from every place
   Or, full with feeding, sink into a sleep:
Each household Genius shows again his face
   And from the hearths the little Lares creep.

283

Our King this more than natural change beholds,
   With sober joy his heart and eyes abound;
To the All-good his lifted hands he folds,
   And thanks him low on his redeemed ground.

284

As, when sharp frosts had long constrained the earth,
   A kindly thaw unlocks it with mild rain,
And first the tender blade peeps up to birth,
   And straight the green fields laugh with promised
      grain':

285

By such degrees the spreading gladness grew
   In every heart which fear had froze before;
The standing streets with so much joy they view
   That with less grief the perished they deplore.

286

The father of the people opened wide
   His stores, and all the poor with plenty fed:
Thus God's anointed God's own place supplied
   And filled the empty with his daily bread.

287

This royal bounty brought its own reward
   And in their minds so deep did print the sense,
That, if their ruins sadly they regard,
   'Tis but with fear the sight might drive him thence.

288

But so may he live long that town to sway
    Which by his auspice they will nobler make,
As he will hatch their ashes by his stay
    And not their humble ruins now forsake.

289

They have not lost their loyalty by fire;
    Nor is their courage or their wealth so low,
That from his wars they poorly would retire
    Or beg the pity of a vanquished foe.

290

Not with more constancy the Jews of old,
    By Cyrus from rewarded exile sent,
Their royal city did in dust behold
    Or with more vigour to rebuild it went.

291

The utmost malice of their stars is past,
    And two dire comets which have scourged the town
In their own plague and fire have breathed their last,
    Or dimly in their sinking sockets frown.

292

Now frequent trines the happier lights among,
    And high-raised Jove from his dark prison freed,
Those weights took off that on his planet hung,
    Will gloriously the new-laid work succeed.

293

Methinks already from this chymic flame
    I see a city of more precious mould,
Rich as the town which gives the Indies name,
    With silver paved and all divine with gold*f*.

294

Already, labouring with a mighty fate,
    She shakes the rubbish from her mounting brow
And seems to have renewed her charter's date
    Which Heaven will to the death of time allow.

f Mexico.

295

More great than human now and more August [g],
  New deified she from her fires does rise:
Her widening streets on new foundations trust,
  And, opening, into larger parts she flies.

296

Before, she like some shepherdess did show
  Who sate to bathe her by a river's side,
Not answering to her fame, but rude and low,
  Nor taught the beauteous arts of modern pride.

297

Now like a maiden queen she will behold
  From her high turrets hourly suitors come;
The East with incense and the West with gold
  Will stand like suppliants to receive her doom.

298

The silver Thames, her own domestic flood,
  Shall bear her vessels like a sweeping train,
And often wind, as of his mistress proud,
  With longing eyes to meet her face again.

299

The wealthy Tagus and the wealthier Rhine
  The glory of their towns no more shall boast,
And Seine, that would with Belgian rivers join,
  Shall find her lustre stained and traffic lost.

300

The venturous merchant who designed more far
  And touches on our hospitable shore,
Charmed with the splendour of this northern star
  Shall here unlade him and depart no more.

301

Our powerful navy shall no longer meet
  The wealth of France or Holland to invade;
The beauty of this town without a fleet
  From all the world shall vindicate her trade.

[g] Augusta, the old name of London.

G

302

And while this famed emporium we prepare,
  The British ocean shall such triumphs boast,
That those who now disdain our trade to share
  Shall rob like pirates on our wealthy coast.

303

Already we have conquered half the war,
  And the less dangerous part is left behind;
Our trouble now is but to make them dare
  And not so great to vanquish as to find.

304

Thus to the Eastern wealth through storms we go,
  But now, the Cape once doubled, fear no more;
A constant trade-wind will securely blow
  And gently lay us on the spicy shore.

ABSALOM AND ACHITOPHEL.

A POEM.

'Si propius stes
Te capiat magis.'
[HORACE, *Ars Poet.* 361.]

TO THE READER.

'TIS not my intention to make an apology for my poem:
some will think it needs no excuse, and others will receive
none. The design, I am sure, is honest; but he who draws
his pen for one party must expect to make enemies of the
other. For wit and fool are consequents of Whig and Tory; 5
and every man is a knave or an ass to the contrary side.
There's a treasury of merits in the Fanatic church as well
as in the Papist, and a pennyworth to be had of saintship,
honesty, and poetry, for the lewd, the factious, and the
blockheads; but the longest chapter in Deuteronomy has not 10
curses enough for an Anti-Bromingham. My comfort is,
their manifest prejudice to my cause will render their judgment of less authority against me. Yet if a poem have a
genius, it will force its own reception in the world; for there
is a sweetness in good verse, which tickles even while it hurts; 15
and no man can be heartily angry with him who pleases him
against his will. The commendation of adversaries is the
greatest triumph of a writer, because it never comes unless
extorted. But I can be satisfied on more easy terms: if I
happen to please the more moderate sort, I shall be sure 20
of an honest party and, in all probability, of the best judges;
for the least concerned are commonly the least corrupt. And
I confess I have laid in for those, by rebating the satire,
where justice would allow it, from carrying too sharp an
edge. They who can criticize so weakly as to imagine I have 25
done my worst, may be convinced at their own cost that I
can write severely with more ease than I can gently. I have
but laughed at some men's follies, when I could have de-
claimed against their vices; and other men's virtues I have
commended as freely as I have taxed their crimes. And now, 30
if you are a malicious reader, I expect you should return

upon me that I affect to be thought more impartial than I am; but if men are not to be judged by their professions, God forgive you commonwealth's-men for professing so plausibly for the government. You cannot be so unconscionable as to charge me for not subscribing of my name; for that would reflect too grossly upon your own party, who never dare, though they have the advantage of a jury to secure them. If you like not my poem, the fault may possibly be in my writing, though 'tis hard for an author to judge against himself; but more probably 'tis in your morals, which cannot bear the truth of it. The violent on both sides will condemn the character of Absalom, as either too favourably or too hardly drawn; but they are not the violent whom I desire to please. The fault on the right hand is to extenuate, palliate, and indulge; and, to confess freely, I have endeavoured to commit it. Besides the respect which I owe his birth, I have a greater for his heroic virtues; and David himself could not be more tender of the young man's life, than I would be of his reputation. But since the most excellent natures are always the most easy and, as being such, are the soonest perverted by ill counsels, especially when baited with fame and glory, it is no more a wonder that he withstood not the temptations of Achitophel than it was for Adam not to have resisted the two devils, the serpent and the woman. The conclusion of the story I purposely forbore to prosecute, because I could not obtain from myself to show Absalom unfortunate. The frame of it was cut out but for a picture to the waist; and if the draught be so far true, it is as much as I designed.

Were I the inventor, who am only the historian, I should certainly conclude the piece with the reconcilement of Absalom to David. And who knows but this may come to pass? Things were not brought to an extremity where I left the story: there seems yet to be room left for a composure; hereafter there may only be for pity. I have not so much as an uncharitable wish against Achitophel, but am content to be accused of a good-natured error, and to hope with Origen, that the Devil himself may at last be saved. For which reason, in this poem, he is neither brought to set his house in order, nor to dispose of his person afterwards as he in wisdom shall think fit. God is infinitely merciful ; and his vicegerent is only not so, because he is not infinite.

The true end of satire is the amendment of vices by correction. And he who writes honestly is no more an enemy to the offender than the physician to the patient, when he prescribes harsh remedies to an inveterate disease ; for those are only in order to prevent the chirurgeon's work of an *Ense rescindendum,* which I wish not to my very enemies. To conclude all; if the body politic have any analogy to the natural, in my weak judgment, an act of oblivion were as necessary in a hot distempered state as an opiate would be in a raging fever.

ABSALOM AND ACHITOPHEL.

In pious times, ere priestcraft did begin,
Before polygamy was made a sin,
When man on many multiplied his kind,
Ere one to one was cursedly confined,
When nature prompted and no law denied   5
Promiscuous use of concubine and bride,
Then Israel's monarch after Heaven's own heart
His vigorous warmth did variously impart
To wives and slaves, and, wide as his command,
Scattered his Maker's image through the land.   10
Michal, of royal blood, the crown did wear,
A soil ungrateful to the tiller's care:
Not so the rest; for several mothers bore
To god-like David several sons before.
But since like slaves his bed they did ascend,   15
No true succession could their seed attend.
Of all this numerous progeny was none
So beautiful, so brave, as Absalon:
Whether, inspired by some diviner lust,
His father got him with a greater gust,   20
Or that his conscious destiny made way
By manly beauty to imperial sway.
Early in foreign fields he won renown
With kings and states allied to Israel's crown;
In peace the thoughts of war he could remove   25
And seemed as he were only born for love.
Whate'er he did was done with so much ease,
In him alone 'twas natural to please;

His motions all accompanied with grace,
And Paradise was opened in his face.   30
With secret joy indulgent David viewed
His youthful image in his son renewed;
To all his wishes nothing he denied
And made the charming Annabel his bride.
What faults he had (for who from faults is free?)   35
His father could not or he would not see.
Some warm excesses, which the law forbore,
Were construed youth that purged by boiling o'er;
And Amnon's murder by a specious name
Was called a just revenge for injured fame.   40
Thus praised and loved, the noble youth remained,
While David undisturbed in Sion reigned.
But life can never be sincerely blest;
Heaven punishes the bad, and proves the best.
The Jews, a headstrong, moody, murmuring race   45
As ever tried the extent and stretch of grace;
God's pampered people, whom, debauched with ease,
No king could govern nor no God could please;
Gods they had tried of every shape and size
That godsmiths could produce or priests devise;   50
These Adam-wits, too fortunately free,
Began to dream they wanted liberty;
And when no rule, no precedent was found
Of men by laws less circumscribed and bound,
They led their wild desires to woods and caves   55
And thought that all but savages were slaves.
They who, when Saul was dead, without a blow
Made foolish Ishbosheth the crown forego;
Who banished David did from Hebron bring,
And with a general shout proclaimed him King;   60
Those very Jews who at their very best
Their humour more than loyalty exprest,
Now wondered why so long they had obeyed
An idol monarch which their hands had made;
Thought they might ruin him they could create   65
Or melt him to that golden calf, a State.

But these were random bolts; no formed design
Nor interest made the factious crowd to join:
The sober part of Israel, free from stain,
Well knew the value of a peaceful reign;   70
And looking backward with a wise affright
Saw seams of wounds dishonest to the sight,
In contemplation of whose ugly scars
They cursed the memory of civil wars.
The moderate sort of men, thus qualified,   75
Inclined the balance to the better side;
And David's mildness managed it so well,
The bad found no occasion to rebel.
But when to sin our biassed nature leans,
The careful Devil is still at hand with means   80
And providently pimps for ill desires;
The good old cause, revived, a plot requires.
Plots true or false are necessary things,
To raise up commonwealths and ruin kings.

The inhabitants of old Jerusalem   85
Were Jebusites; the town so called from them,
And theirs the native right.
But when the chosen people grew more strong,
The rightful cause at length became the wrong;
And every loss the men of Jebus bore,   90
They still were thought God's enemies the more.
Thus worn and weakened, well or ill content,
Submit they must to David's government:
Impoverished and deprived of all command,
Their taxes doubled as they lost their land;   95
And, what was harder yet to flesh and blood,
Their gods disgraced, and burnt like common wood.
This set the heathen priesthood in a flame,
For priests of all religions are the same.
Of whatsoe'er descent their godhead be,   100
Stock, stone, or other homely pedigree,
In his defence his servants are as bold,
As if he had been born of beaten gold.

The Jewish Rabbins, though their enemies,
In this conclude them honest men and wise: 105
For 'twas their duty, all the learned think,
To espouse his cause by whom they eat and drink.
From hence began that Plot, the nation's curse,
Bad in itself, but represented worse,
Raised in extremes, and in extremes decried,   110
With oaths affirmed, with dying vows denied,
Not weighed or winnowed by the multitude,
But swallowed in the mass, unchewed and crude.
Some truth there was, but dashed and brewed with lies
To please the fools and puzzle all the wise: 115
Succeeding times did equal folly call
Believing nothing or believing all.
The Egyptian rites the Jebusites embraced,
Where gods were recommended by their taste;
Such savoury deities must needs be good   120
As served at once for worship and for food.
By force they could not introduce these gods,
For ten to one in former days was odds:
So fraud was used, the sacrificer's trade;
Fools are more hard to conquer than persuade.   125
Their busy teachers mingled with the Jews
And raked for converts even the court and stews:
Which Hebrew priests the more unkindly took,
Because the fleece accompanies the flock.
Some thought they God's anointed meant to slay   130
By guns, invented since full many a day:
Our author swears it not; but who can know
How far the Devil and Jebusites may go?
This plot, which failed for want of common sense,
Had yet a deep and dangerous consequence;   135
For as, when raging fevers boil the blood,
The standing lake soon floats into a flood,
And every hostile humour which before
Slept quiet in its channels bubbles o'er;
So several factions from this first ferment   140
Work up to foam and threat the government.

Some by their friends, more by themselves thought wise,
Opposed the power to which they could not rise.
Some had in courts been great and, thrown from thence,
Like fiends were hardened in impenitence. 145
Some by their Monarch's fatal mercy grown
From pardoned rebels kinsmen to the throne
Were raised in power and public office high;
Strong bands, if bands ungrateful men could tie.
Of these the false Achitophel was first, 150
A name to all succeeding ages curst:
For close designs and crooked counsels fit,
Sagacious, bold, and turbulent of wit,
Restless, unfixed in principles and place,
In power unpleased, impatient of disgrace; 155
A fiery soul, which, working out its way,
Fretted the pigmy body to decay
And o'er-informed the tenement of clay.
A daring pilot in extremity,
Pleased with the danger, when the waves went high, 160
He sought the storms; but, for a calm unfit,
Would steer too nigh the sands to boast his wit.
Great wits are sure to madness near allied,
And thin partitions do their bounds divide;
Else, why should he, with wealth and honour blest, 165
Refuse his age the needful hours of rest?
Punish a body which he could not please,
Bankrupt of life, yet prodigal of ease?
And all to leave what with his toil he won
To that unfeathered two-legged thing, a son, 170
Got, while his soul did huddled notions try,
And born a shapeless lump, like anarchy.
In friendship false, implacable in hate,
Resolved to ruin or to rule the state;
To compass this the triple bond he broke,— 175
The pillars of the public safety shook,
And fitted Israel for a foreign yoke;
Then, seized with fear, yet still affecting fame,
Usurped a patriot's all-atoning name.

So easy still it proves in factious times   180
With public zeal to cancel private crimes.
How safe is treason and how sacred ill,
Where none can sin against the people's will,
Where crowds can wink and no offence be known,
Since in another's guilt they find their own!   185
Yet fame deserved no enemy can grudge;
The statesman we abhor, but praise the judge.
In Israel's courts ne'er sat an Abbethdin
With more discerning eyes or hands more clean,
Unbribed, unsought, the wretched to redress,   190
Swift of despatch and easy of access.
Oh! had he been content to serve the crown
With virtues only proper to the gown,
Or had the rankness of the soil been freed
From cockle that oppressed the noble seed,   195
David for him his tuneful harp had strung
And Heaven had wanted one immortal song.
But wild ambition loves to slide, not stand,
And fortune's ice prefers to virtue's land.
Achitophel, grown weary to possess   200
A lawful fame and lazy happiness,
Disdained the golden fruit to gather free
And lent the crowd his arm to shake the tree.
Now, manifest of crimes contrived long since,
He stood at bold defiance with his Prince,   205
Held up the buckler of the people's cause
Against the crown, and skulked behind the laws.
The wished occasion of the Plot he takes;
Some circumstances finds, but more he makes;
By buzzing emissaries fills the ears   210
Of listening crowds with jealousies and fears
Of arbitrary counsels brought to light,
And proves the King himself a Jebusite.
Weak arguments! which yet he knew full well
Were strong with people easy to rebel.   215
For governed by the moon, the giddy Jews
Tread the same track when she the prime renews:

And once in twenty years their scribes record,
By natural instinct they change their lord.
Achitophel still wants a chief, and none   220
Was found so fit as warlike Absalon.
Not that he wished his greatness to create,
For politicians neither love nor hate;
But, for he knew his title not allowed
Would keep him still depending on the crowd, 225
That kingly power, thus ebbing out, might be
Drawn to the dregs of a democracy.
Him he attempts with studied arts to please
And sheds his venom in such words as these:

'Auspicious prince, at whose nativity   230
Some royal planet ruled the southern sky,
Thy longing country's darling and desire,
Their cloudy pillar and their guardian fire,
Their second Moses, whose extended wand
Divides the seas and shows the promised land, 235
Whose dawning day in every distant age
Has exercised the sacred prophet's rage,
The people's prayer, the glad diviner's theme,
The young men's vision and the old men's dream,
Thee Saviour, thee the nation's vows confess, 240
And never satisfied with seeing bless:
Swift unbespoken pomps thy steps proclaim,
And stammering babes are taught to lisp thy name.
How long wilt thou the general joy detain,
Starve and defraud the people of thy reign? 245
Content ingloriously to pass thy days,
Like one of virtue's fools that feeds on praise;
Till thy fresh glories, which now shine so bright,
Grow stale and tarnish with our daily sight.
Believe me, royal youth, thy fruit must be 250
Or gathered ripe, or rot upon the tree.
Heaven has to all allotted, soon or late,
Some lucky revolution of their fate:
Whose motions if we watch and guide with skill,

(For human good depends on human will,) 255
Our fortune rolls as from a smooth descent
And from the first impression takes the bent;
But, if unseized, she glides away like wind
And leaves repenting folly far behind.
Now, now she meets you with a glorious prize 260
And spreads her locks before her as she flies.
Had thus old David, from whose loins you spring,
Not dared, when fortune called him to be King,
At Gath an exile he might still remain,
And Heaven's anointing oil had been in vain. 265
Let his successful youth your hopes engage,
But shun the example of declining age.
Behold him setting in his western skies,
The shadows lengthening as the vapours rise;
He is not now, as when, on Jordan's sand, 270
The joyful people thronged to see him land,
Covering the beach and blackening all the strand,
But like the Prince of Angels, from his height
Comes tumbling downward with diminished light:
Betrayed by one poor plot to public scorn, 275
(Our only blessing since his curst return,)
Those heaps of people, which one sheaf did bind,
Blown off and scattered by a puff of wind.
What strength can he to your designs oppose,
Naked of friends, and round beset with foes? 280
If Pharaoh's doubtful succour he should use,
A foreign aid would more incense the Jews;
Proud Egypt would dissembled friendship bring,
Foment the war, but not support the King;
Nor would the royal party e'er unite 285
With Pharaoh's arms to assist the Jebusite;
Or, if they should, their interest soon would break
And with such odious aid make David weak.
All sorts of men, by my successful arts
Abhorring kings, estrange their altered hearts 290
From David's rule: and 'tis the general cry,
Religion, commonwealth, and liberty.

If you, as champion of the public good,
Add to their arms a chief of royal blood,
What may not Israel hope, and what applause   295
Might such a general gain by such a cause?
Not barren praise alone, that gaudy flower,
Fair only to the sight, but solid power;
And nobler is a limited command,
Given by the love of all your native land,   300
Than a successive title, long and dark,
Drawn from the mouldy rolls of Noah's ark.'

What cannot praise effect in mighty minds,
When flattery soothes and when ambition blinds?
Desire of power, on earth a vicious weed,   305
Yet sprung from high is of celestial seed;
In God 'tis glory, and when men aspire,
'Tis but a spark too much of heavenly fire.
The ambitious youth, too covetous of fame,
Too full of angel's metal in his frame,   310
Unwarily was led from virtue's ways,
Made drunk with honour and debauched with praise.
Half loth and half consenting to the ill,
For loyal blood within him struggled still,
He thus replied: 'And what pretence have I   315
To take up arms for public liberty?
My father governs with unquestioned right,
The faith's defender and mankind's delight,
Good, gracious, just, observant of the laws;
And Heaven by wonders has espoused his cause.   320
Whom has he wronged in all his peaceful reign?
Who sues for justice to his throne in vain?
What millions has he pardoned of his foes
Whom just revenge did to his wrath expose?
Mild, easy, humble, studious of our good,   325
Inclined to mercy and averse from blood.
If mildness ill with stubborn Israel suit,
His crime is God's beloved attribute.
What could he gain his people to betray

Or change his right for arbitrary sway?   330
Let haughty Pharaoh curse with such a reign
His fruitful Nile, and yoke a servile train.
If David's rule Jerusalem displease,
The dog-star heats their brains to this disease.
Why then should I, encouraging the bad,   335
Turn rebel and run popularly mad?
Were he a tyrant, who by lawless might
Oppressed the Jews and raised the Jebusite,
Well might I mourn; but nature's holy bands
Would curb my spirits and restrain my hands;   340
The people might assert their liberty,
But what was right in them were crime in me.
His favour leaves me nothing to require,
Prevents my wishes and outruns desire;
What more can I expect while David lives?   345
All but his kingly diadem he gives:
And that'—But there he paused, then sighing said,
'Is justly destined for a worthier head;
For when my father from his toils shall rest
And late augment the number of the blest,   350
His lawful issue shall the throne ascend,
Or the collateral line, where that shall end.
His brother, though oppressed with vulgar spite,
Yet dauntless and secure of native right,
Of every royal virtue stands possest,   355
Still dear to all the bravest and the best.
His courage foes, his friends his truth proclaim,
His loyalty the King, the world his fame.
His mercy even the offending crowd will find,
For sure he comes of a forgiving kind.   360
Why should I then repine at Heaven's decree
Which gives me no pretence to royalty?
Yet oh that Fate, propitiously inclined,
Had raised my birth or had debased my mind,
To my large soul not all her treasure lent,   365
And then betrayed it to a mean descent!
I find, I find my mounting spirits bold,

And David's part disdains my mother's mould.
Why am I scanted by a niggard birth?
My soul disclaims the kindred of her earth,   370
And, made for empire, whispers me within,
Desire of greatness is a god-like sin.'

   Him staggering so when Hell's dire agent found,
While fainting virtue scarce maintained her ground,
He pours fresh forces in, and thus replies: 375
'The eternal God, supremely good and wise,
Imparts not these prodigious gifts in vain.
What wonders are reserved to bless your reign!
Against your will your arguments have shown,
Such virtue's only given to guide a throne.   380
Not that your father's mildness I contemn,
But manly force becomes the diadem.
'Tis true he grants the people all they crave,
And more perhaps than subjects ought to have:
For lavish grants suppose a monarch tame   385
And more his goodness than his wit proclaim.
But when should people strive their bonds to break,
If not when kings are negligent or weak?
Let him give on till he can give no more,
The thrifty Sanhedrin shall keep him poor;   390
And every shekel which he can receive
Shall cost a limb of his prerogative.
To ply him with new plots shall be my care,
Or plunge him deep in some expensive war;
Which when his treasure can no more supply,   395
He must with the remains of kingship buy.
His faithful friends our jealousies and fears
Call Jebusites and Pharaoh's pensioners,
Whom when our fury from his aid has torn,
He shall be naked left to public scorn.   400
The next successor, whom I fear and hate,
My arts have made obnoxious to the State,
Turned all his virtues to his overthrow,
And gained our elders to pronounce a foe.

His right for sums of necessary gold   405
Shall first be pawned, and afterwards be sold;
Till time shall ever-wanting David draw
To pass your doubtful title into law.
If not, the people have a right supreme
To make their kings, for kings are made for them.   410
All empire is no more than power in trust,
Which, when resumed, can be no longer just.
Succession, for the general good designed,
In its own wrong a nation cannot bind:
If altering that the people can relieve,   415
Better one suffer than a nation grieve.
The Jews well know their power: ere Saul they chose
God was their King, and God they durst depose.
Urge now your piety, your filial name,
A father's right and fear of future fame,   420
The public good, that universal call,
To which even Heaven submitted, answers all.
Nor let his love enchant your generous mind;
'Tis Nature's trick to propagate her kind.
Our fond begetters, who would never die,   425
Love but themselves in their posterity.
Or let his kindness by the effects be tried,
Or let him lay his vain pretence aside.
God said, He loved your father; could He bring
A better proof than to anoint him King?   430
It surely showed, He loved the shepherd well
Who gave so fair a flock as Israel.
Would David have you thought his darling son?
What means he then to alienate the crown?
The name of godly he may blush to bear;   435
'Tis after God's own heart to cheat his heir.
He to his brother gives supreme command,
To you a legacy of barren land,
Perhaps the old harp on which he thrums his lays
Or some dull Hebrew ballad in your praise.   440
Then the next heir, a prince severe and wise,
Already looks on you with jealous eyes,

Sees through the thin disguises of your arts,
And marks your progress in the people's hearts;
Though now his mighty soul its grief contains,   445
He meditates revenge who least complains;
And like a lion, slumbering in the way
Or sleep dissembling, while he waits his prey,
His fearless foes within his distance draws,
Constrains his roaring and contracts his paws,   450
Till at the last, his time for fury found,
He shoots with sudden vengeance from the ground,
The prostrate vulgar passes o'er and spares,
But with a lordly rage his hunters tears;
Your case no tame expedients will afford,   455
Resolve on death or conquest by the sword,
Which for no less a stake than life you draw,
And self-defence is Nature's eldest law.
Leave the warm people no considering time,
For then rebellion may be thought a crime.   460
Prevail yourself of what occasion gives,
But try your title while your father lives;
And, that your arms may have. a fair pretence,
Proclaim you take them in the King's defence;
Whose sacred life each minute would expose   465
To plots from seeming friends and secret foes.
And who can sound the depth of David's soul?
Perhaps his fear his kindness may control:
He fears his brother, though he loves his son,
For plighted vows too late to be undone.   470
If so, by force he wishes to be gained,
Like women's lechery to seem constrained.
Doubt not: but, when he most affects the frown,
Commit a pleasing rape upon the crown.
Secure his person to secure your cause: 473
They who possess the Prince possess the laws.'

He said, and this advice above the rest
With Absalom's mild nature suited best;
Unblamed of life (ambition set aside),

Not stained with cruelty nor puffed with pride, 480
How happy had he been, if Destiny
Had higher placed his birth or not so high!
His kingly virtues might have claimed a throne
And blessed all other countries but his own;
But charming greatness since so few refuse, 485
'Tis juster to lament him than accuse.
Strong were his hopes a rival to remove,
With blandishments to gain the public love,
To head the faction while their zeal was hot,
And popularly prosecute the plot. 490
To further this, Achitophel unites
The malcontents of all the Israelites,
Whose differing parties he could wisely join
For several ends to serve the same design:
The best, (and of the princes some were such,) 495
Who thought the power of monarchy too much,
Mistaken men and patriots in their hearts,
Not wicked, but seduced by impious arts;
By these the springs of property were bent
And wound so high they cracked the government. 500
The next for interest sought to embroil the state,
To sell their duty at a dearer rate,
And make their Jewish markets of the throne,
Pretending public good to serve their own.
Others thought kings an useless heavy load, 505
Who cost too much and did too little good.
These were for laying honest David by
On principles of pure good husbandry.
With them joined all the haranguers of the throng
That thought to get preferment by the tongue. 510
Who follow next a double danger bring,
Not only hating David, but the King;
The Solymæan rout, well versed of old
In godly faction and in treason bold,
Cowering and quaking at a conqueror's sword, 515
But lofty to a lawful prince restored,
Saw with disdain an Ethnic plot begun

And scorned by Jebusites to be outdone.
Hot Levites headed these; who pulled before
From the ark, which in the Judges' days they bore,   520
Resumed their cant, and with a zealous cry
Pursued their old beloved theocracy,
Where Sanhedrin and priest enslaved the nation
And justified their spoils by inspiration;
For who so fit for reign as Aaron's race,   525
If once dominion they could found in grace?
These led the pack; though not of surest scent,
Yet deepest mouthed against the government.
A numerous host of dreaming saints succeed
Of the true old enthusiastic breed: 530
'Gainst form and order they their power employ,
Nothing to build and all things to destroy.
But far more numerous was the herd of such
Who think too little and who talk too much.
These out of mere instinct, they knew not why,   535
Adored their fathers' God and property,
And by the same blind benefit of Fate
The Devil and the Jebusite did hate:
Born to be saved even in their own despite,
Because they could not help believing right.   540
Such were the tools; but a whole Hydra more
Remains of sprouting heads too long to score.
Some of their chiefs were princes of the land;
In the first rank of these did Zimri stand,
A man so various that he seemed to be   545
Not one, but all mankind's epitome:
Stiff in opinions, always in the wrong,
Was everything by starts and nothing long;
But in the course of one revolving moon
Was chymist, fiddler, statesman, and buffoon;   550
Then all for women, painting, rhyming, drinking,
Besides ten thousand freaks that died in thinking.
Blest madman, who could every hour employ
With something new to wish or to enjoy!
Railing and praising were his usual themes,   555

And both, to show his judgment, in extremes:
So over-violent or over-civil
That every man with him was God or Devil.
In squandering wealth was his peculiar art;
Nothing went unrewarded but desert.   560
Beggared by fools whom still he found too late,
He had his jest, and they had his estate..
He laughed himself from Court; then sought relief
By forming parties, but could ne'er be chief:
For spite of him, the weight of business fell   565
On Absalom and wise Achitophel;
Thus wicked but in will, of means bereft,
He left not faction, but of that was left.
   Titles and names 'twere tedious to rehearse
Of lords below the dignity of verse.   570
Wits, warriors, commonwealth's-men were the best;
Kind husbands and mere nobles all the rest.
And therefore in the name of dulness be
The well-hung Balaam and cold Caleb free;
And canting Nadab let oblivion damn   575
Who made new porridge for the paschal lamb.
Let friendship's holy band some names assure,
Some their own worth, and some let scorn secure.
Nor shall the rascal rabble here have place
Whom kings no titles gave, and God no grace: 580
Not bull-faced Jonas, who could statutes draw
To mean rebellion and make treason law.
But he, though bad, is followed by a worse,
The wretch who Heaven's anointed dared to curse;
Shimei, whose youth did early promise bring   585
Of zeal to God and hatred to his King,
Did wisely from expensive sins refrain
And never broke the Sabbath but for gain:
Nor ever was he known an oath to vent
Or curse, unless against the government.   590
Thus heaping wealth by the most ready way
Among the Jews, which was to cheat and pray,
The City, to reward his pious hate

Against his master, chose him magistrate.
His hand a vare of justice did uphold,   595
His neck was loaded with a chain of gold.
During his office treason was no crime,
The sons of Belial had a glorious time;
For Shimei, though not prodigal of pelf,
Yet loved his wicked neighbour as himself.   600
When two or three were gathered to declaim
Against the monarch of Jerusalem,
Shimei was always in the midst of them:
And, if they cursed the King when he was by,
Would rather curse than break good company.   605
If any durst his factious friends accuse,
He packed a jury of dissenting Jews;
Whose fellow-feeling in the godly cause
Would free the suffering saint from human laws:
For laws are only made to punish those   610
Who serve the King, and to protect his foes.
If any leisure time he had from power,
Because 'tis sin to misemploy an hour,
His business was by writing to persuade
That kings were useless and a clog to trade: 615
And that his noble style he might refine,
No Rechabite more shunned the fumes of wine.
Chaste were his cellars, and his shrieval board
The grossness of a city feast abhorred:
His cooks with long disuse their trade forgot;   620
Cool was his kitchen, though his brains were hot.
Such frugal virtue malice may accuse;
But sure 'twas necessary to the Jews:
For towns once burnt such magistrates require
As dare not tempt God's providence by fire.   625
With spiritual food he fed his servants well,
But free from flesh that made the Jews rebel:
And Moses' laws he held in more account
For forty days of fasting in the mount.
To speak the rest, who better are forgot,   630
Would tire a well-breathed witness of the plot.

Yet, Corah, thou shalt from oblivion pass;
Erect thyself, thou monumental brass,
High as the serpent of thy metal made,
While nations stand secure beneath thy shade.   635
What though his birth were base, yet comets rise
From earthy vapours, ere they shine in skies.
Prodigious actions may as well be done
By weaver's issue as by prince's son.
This arch-attester for the public good   640
By that one deed ennobles all his blood.
Who ever asked the witnesses' high race
Whose oath with martyrdom did Stephen grace?
Ours was a Levite, and as times went then,
His tribe were God Almighty's gentlemen.   645
Sunk were his eyes, his voice was harsh and loud,
Sure signs he neither choleric was nor proud:
His long chin proved his wit, his saint-like grace
A church vermilion and a Moses' face.
His memory, miraculously great,   650
Could plots exceeding man's belief repeat;
Which therefore cannot be accounted lies,
For human wit could never such devise.
Some future truths are mingled in his book,
But where the witness failed, the prophet spoke: 655
Some things like visionary flights appear;
The spirit caught him up, the Lord knows where;
And gave him his Rabbinical degree
Unknown to foreign University.
His judgment yet his memory did excel,   660
Which pieced his wondrous evidence so well
And suited to the temper of the times,
Then groaning under Jebusitic crimes.
Let Israel's foes suspect his heavenly call
And rashly judge his writ apocryphal;   665
Our laws for such affronts have forfeits made,
He takes his life who takes away his trade.
Were I myself in witness Corah's place,
The wretch who did me such a dire disgrace

Should whet my memory, though once forgot,   670
To make him an appendix of my plot.
His zeal to Heaven made him his Prince despise,
And load his person with indignities.
But zeal peculiar privilege affords,
Indulging latitude to deeds and words: 675
And Corah might for Agag's murder call,
In terms as coarse as Samuel used to Saul.
What others in his evidence did join,
The best that could be had for love or coin,
In Corah's own predicament will fall,   680
For Witness is a common name to all.

Surrounded thus with friends of every sort,
Deluded Absalom forsakes the court;
Impatient of high hopes, urged with renown,
And fired with near possession of a crown.   685
The admiring crowd are dazzled with surprise
And on his goodly person feed their eyes.
His joy concealed, he sets himself to show,
On each side bowing popularly low,
His looks, his gestures, and his words he frames   690
And with familiar ease repeats their names.
Thus formed by nature, furnished out with arts,
He glides unfelt into their secret hearts.
Then with a kind compassionating look,
And sighs, bespeaking pity ere he spoke,   695
Few words he said, but easy those and fit,
More slow than Hybla-drops and far more sweet.
'I mourn, my countrymen, your lost estate,
Though far unable to prevent your fate:
Behold a banished man, for your dear cause   700
Exposed a prey to arbitrary laws!
Yet oh that I alone could be undone,
Cut off from empire, and no more a son!
Now all your liberties a spoil are made,
Egypt and Tyrus intercept your trade,   705
And Jebusites your sacred rites invade.

My father, whom with reverence yet I name,
Charmed into ease, is careless of his fame,
And, bribed with petty sums of foreign gold,
Is grown in Bathsheba's embraces old;   710
Exalts his enemies, his friends destroys,
And all his power against himself employs.
He gives, and let him give, my right away;
But why should he his own and yours betray?
He, only he can make the nation bleed,   715
And he alone from my revenge is freed.
Take then my tears (with that he wiped his eyes),
'Tis all the aid my present power supplies:
No court-informer can these arms accuse;
These arms may sons against their fathers use.   720
And 'tis my wish, the next successor's reign
May make no other Israelite complain.'

Youth, beauty, graceful action seldom fail,
But common interest always will prevail;
And pity never ceases to be shown   725
To him who makes the people's wrongs his own.
The crowd that still believe their kings oppress
With lifted hands their young Messiah bless:
Who now begins his progress to ordain
With chariots, horsemen, and a numerous train;   730
From east to west his glories he displays
And, like the sun, the promised land surveys.
Fame runs before him as the morning star,
And shouts of joy salute him from afar;
Each house receives him as a guardian god   735
And consecrates the place of his abode.
But hospitable treats did most commend
Wise Issachar, his wealthy western friend.
This moving court that caught the people's eyes,
And seemed but pomp, did other ends disguise;   740
Achitophel had formed it, with intent
To sound the depths and fathom, where it went,
The people's hearts, distinguish friends from foes,

And try their strength before they came to blows.
Yet all was coloured with a smooth pretence   745
Of specious love and duty to their prince.
Religion and redress of grievances,
Two names that always cheat and always please,
Are often urged; and good king David's life
Endangered by a brother and a wife.   750
Thus in a pageant show a plot is made,
And peace itself is war in masquerade.
Oh foolish Israel! never warned by ill!
Still the same bait, and circumvented still!
Did ever men forsake their present ease,   755
In midst of health imagine a disease,
Take pains contingent mischiefs to foresee,
Make heirs for monarchs, and for God decree?
What shall we think? Can people give away
Both for themselves and sons their native sway?   760
Then they are left defenceless to the sword
Of each unbounded, arbitrary lord;
And laws are vain by which we right enjoy,
If kings unquestioned can those laws destroy.
Yet if the crowd be judge of fit and just,   765
And kings are only officers in trust,
Then this resuming covenant was declared
When kings were made, or is for ever barred.
If those who gave the sceptre could not tie
By their own deed their own posterity,   .   770
How then could Adam bind his future race?
How could his forfeit on mankind take place?
Or how could heavenly justice damn us all
Who ne'er consented to our father's fall?
Then kings are slaves to those whom they command   775
And tenants to their people's pleasure stand.
Add that the power, for property allowed,
Is mischievously seated in the crowd;
For who can be secure of private right,
If sovereign sway may be dissolved by might?   780
Nor is the people's judgment always true:

The most may err as grossly as the few,
And faultless kings run down by common cry
For vice, oppression, and for tyranny.
What standard is there in a fickle rout,   785
Which, flowing to the mark, runs faster out?
Nor only crowds but Sanhedrins may be
Infected with this public lunacy,
And share the madness of rebellious times,
To murder monarchs for imagined crimes.   790
If they may give and take whene'er they please,
Not kings alone, the Godhead's images,
But government itself at length must fall
To nature's state, where all have right to all.
Yet grant our lords, the people, kings can make,   795
What prudent men a settled throne would shake?
For whatsoe'er their sufferings were before,
That change they covet makes them suffer more.
All other errors but disturb a state,
But innovation is the blow of fate.   800
If ancient fabrics nod and threat to fall,
To patch the flaws and buttress up the wall,
Thus far 'tis duty: but here fix the mark;
For all beyond it is to touch our ark.
To change foundations, cast the frame anew,   805
Is work for rebels who base ends pursue,
At once divine and human laws control,
And mend the parts by ruin of the whole.
The tampering world is subject to this curse,
To physic their disease into a worse.   810

Now what relief can righteous David bring?
How fatal 'tis to be too good a king!
Friends he has few, so high the madness grows;
Who dare be such must be the people's foes.
Yet some there were even in the worst of days;   815
Some let me name, and naming is to-praise.
In this short file Barzillai first appears,
Barzillai, crowned with honour and with years.

Long since the rising rebels he withstood
In regions waste beyond the Jordan's flood: 820
Unfortunately brave to buoy the state,
But sinking underneath his master's fate.
In exile with his godlike prince he mourned,
For him he suffered, and with him returned.
The court he practised, not the courtier's art: 825
Large was his wealth, but larger was his heart,
Which well the noblest objects knew to chuse,
The fighting warrior, and recording Muse.
His bed could once a fruitful issue boast;
Now more than half a father's name is lost.   830
His eldest hope, with every grace adorned,
By me, so Heaven will have it, always mourned
And always honoured, snatched in manhood's prime
By unequal fates and Providence's crime:
Yet not before the goal of honour won,   835
All parts fulfilled of subject and of son;
Swift was the race, but short the time to run.
Oh narrow circle, but of power divine,
Scanted in space, but perfect in thy line!
By sea, by land, thy matchless worth was known,   840
Arms thy delight, and war was all thy own:
Thy force infused the fainting Tyrians propped,
And haughty Pharaoh found his fortune stopped.
Oh ancient honour! oh unconquered hand,
Whom foes unpunished never could withstand!   845
But Israel was unworthy of thy name:
Short is the date of all immoderate fame.
It looks as Heaven our ruin had designed,
And durst not trust thy fortune and thy mind.
Now, free from earth, thy disencumbered soul   850
Mounts up, and leaves behind the clouds and starry
        pole:
From thence thy kindred legions mayest thou bring
To aid the guardian angel of thy King.
Here stop, my Muse, here cease thy painful flight;
No pinions can pursue immortal height: 855

Tell good Barzillai thou canst sing no more,
And tell thy soul she should have fled before:
Or fled she with his life, and left this verse
To hang on her departed patron's hearse?
Now take thy steepy flight from heaven, and see   860
If thou canst find on earth another he:
Another he would be too hard to find;
See then whom thou canst see not far behind.
Zadoc the priest, whom, shunning power and place,
His lowly mind advanced to David's grace.   865
With him the Sagan of Jerusalem,
Of hospitable soul and noble stem;
Him of the western dome, whose weighty sense
Flows in fit words and heavenly eloquence.
The Prophets' sons, by such example led,   870
To learning and to loyalty were bred:
For colleges on bounteous kings depend,
And never rebel was to arts a friend.
To these succeed the pillars of the laws,
Who best could plead, and best can judge a cause.   875
Next them a train of loyal peers ascend;
Sharp-judging Adriel, the Muses' friend,
Himself a Muse: in Sanhedrin's debate
True to his Prince, but not a slave of state;
Whom David's love with honours did adorn   880
That from his disobedient son were torn.
Jotham of piercing wit and pregnant thought,
Endued by nature and by learning taught
To move assemblies, who but only tried
The worse a while, then chose the better side,   885
Nor chose alone, but turned the balance too,
So much the weight of one brave man can do.
Hushai, the friend of David in distress,
In public storms of manly stedfastness;
By foreign treaties he informed his youth   890
And joined experience to his native truth.
His frugal care supplied the wanting throne,
Frugal for that, but bounteous of his own:

'Tis easy conduct when exchequers flow,
But hard the task to manage well the low.　　895
For sovereign power is too depressed or high,
When kings are forced to sell or crowds to buy.
Indulge one labour more, my weary Muse,
For Amiel: who can Amiel's praise refuse?
Of ancient race by birth, but nobler yet　　900
In his own worth and without title great:
The Sanhedrin long time as chief he ruled,
Their reason guided and their passion cooled:
So dexterous was he in the Crown's defence,
So formed to speak a loyal nation's sense,　　905
That, as their band was Israel's tribes in small,
So fit was he to represent them all.
Now rasher charioteers the seat ascend,
Whose loose careers his steady skill commend:
They, like the unequal ruler of the day,　　910
Misguide the seasons and mistake the way,
While he, withdrawn, at their mad labour smiles
And safe enjoys the sabbath of his toils.

These were the chief, a small but faithful band
Of worthies in the breach who dared to stand　　915
And tempt the united fury of the land.
With grief they viewed such powerful engines bent
To batter down the lawful government.
A numerous faction, with pretended frights,
In Sanhedrins to plume the regal rights;　　920
The true successor from the Court removed;
The plot by hireling witnesses improved.
These ills they saw, and, as their duty bound,
They showed the King the danger of the wound;
That no concessions from the throne would please,　　925
But lenitives fomented the disease;
That Absalom, ambitious of the crown,
Was made the lure to draw the people down;
That false Achitophel's pernicious hate
Had turned the plot to ruin Church and State;　　930

The council violent, the rabble worse;
That Shimei taught Jerusalem to curse.

With all these loads of injuries opprest,
And long revolving in his careful breast
The event of things, at last his patience tired,   935
Thus from his royal throne, by Heaven inspired,
The godlike David spoke; with awful fear
His train their Maker in their master hear.

'Thus long have I, by native mercy swayed,
My wrongs dissembled, my revenge delayed;   940
So willing to forgive the offending age;
So much the father did the king assuage.
But now so far my clemency they slight,
The offenders question my forgiving right.
That one was made for many, they contend;   945
But 'tis to rule, for that's a monarch's end.
They call my tenderness of blood my fear,
Though manly tempers can the longest bear.
Yet since they will divert my native course,
'Tis time to show I am not good by force.   950
Those heaped affronts that haughty subjects bring
Are burdens for a camel, not a king.
Kings are the public pillars of the State,
Born to sustain and prop the nation's weight:
If my young Samson will pretend a call   955
To shake the column, let him share the fall;
But oh that yet he would repent and live!
How easy 'tis for parents to forgive!
With how few tears a pardon might be won
From nature, pleading for a darling son!   960
Poor pitied youth, by my paternal care
Raised up to all the height his frame could bear!
Had God ordained his fate for empire born,
He would have given his soul another turn:
Gulled with a patriot's name, whose modern sense   965
Is one that would by law supplant his prince;

The people's brave, the politician's tool;
Never was patriot yet but was a fool.
Whence comes it that religion and the laws
Should more be Absalom's than David's cause?   970
His old instructor, ere he lost his place,
Was never thought endued with so much grace.
Good heavens, how faction can a patriot paint!
My rebel ever proves my people's saint.
Would they impose an heir upon the throne?   975
Let Sanhedrins be taught to give their own.
A king's at least a part of government,
And mine as requisite as their consent:
Without my leave a future king to choose
Infers a right the present to depose.   980
True, they petition me to approve their choice:
But Esau's hands suit ill with Jacob's voice.
My pious subjects for my safety pray,
Which to secure, they take my power away.
From plots and treasons Heaven preserve my years,   985
But save me most from my petitioners.
Unsatiate as the barren womb or grave,
God cannot grant so much as they can crave.
What then is left but with a jealous eye
To guard the small remains of royalty?   990
The law shall still direct my peaceful sway,
And the same law teach rebels to obey:
Votes shall no more established power control,
Such votes as make a part exceed the whole.
No groundless clamours shall my friends remove   995
Nor crowds have power to punish ere they prove;
For gods and godlike kings their care express
Still to defend their servants in distress.
Oh that my power to saving were confined!
Why am I forced, like Heaven, against my mind   1000
To make examples of another kind?
Must I at length the sword of justice draw?
Oh curst effects of necessary law!
How ill my fear they by my mercy scan!

Beware the fury of a patient man. 1005
Law they require, let Law then show her face;
They could not be content to look on Grace
Her hinder parts, but with a daring eye
To tempt the terror of her front and die.
By their own arts, 'tis righteously decreed, 1010
Those dire artificers of death shall bleed.
Against themselves their witnesses will swear
Till, viper-like, their mother-plot they tear,
And suck for nutriment that bloody gore
Which was their principle of life before. 1015
Their Belial with their Beelzebub will fight;
Thus on my foes my foes shall do me right.
Nor doubt the event; for factious crowds engage
In their first onset all their brutal rage.
Then let them take an unresisted course; 1020
Retire and traverse, and delude their force:
But when they stand all breathless, urge the fight
And rise upon them with redoubled might: -
For lawful power is still superior found, 1024
When long driven back at length it stands the ground.'

He said. The Almighty, nodding, gave consent;
And peals of thunder shook the firmament.
Henceforth a series of new time began,
The mighty years in long procession ran;
Once more the godlike David was restored, 1030
And willing nations knew their lawful lord.

RELIGIO LAICI;

OR

A LAYMAN'S FAITH.

A POEM.

'Ornari res ipsa negat, contenta doceri.'
[MANILIUS, *Astronom.* iii. 39.]

THE PREFACE.

A POEM with so bold a title, and a name prefixed from which the handling of so serious a subject would not be expected, may reasonably oblige the author to say somewhat in defence both of himself and of his undertaking. In the first place, if it be objected to me that, being a layman, I ought not to have concerned myself with speculations which belong to the profession of divinity, I could answer that perhaps laymen, with equal advantages of parts and knowledge, are not the most incompetent judges of sacred things; but in the due sense of my own weakness and want of learning I plead not this; I pretend not to make my self a judge of faith in others, but only to make a confession of my own. I lay no unhallowed hand upon the Ark, but wait on it with the reverence that becomes me at a distance. In the next place I will ingenuously confess, that the helps I have used in this small Treatise were many of them taken from the works of our own reverend divines of the Church of England; so that the weapons with which I combat irreligion are already consecrated, though I suppose they may be taken down as lawfully as the sword of Goliah was by David, when they are to be employed for the common cause against the enemies of piety. I intend not by this to entitle them to any of my errors, which yet I hope are only those of charity to mankind; and such as my own charity has caused me to commit, that of others may more easily excuse. Being naturally inclined to scepticism in philosophy, I have no reason to impose my opinions in a subject which is above it; but, whatever they are, I submit them with all reverence

to my mother Church, accounting them no farther mine, than
as they are authorized or at least uncondemned by her.
And, indeed, to secure my self on this side, I have used the
necessary precaution of showing this paper, before it was
5 published, to a judicious and learned friend, a man inde-
fatigably zealous in the service of the Church and State, and
whose writings have highly deserved of both. He was pleased
to approve the body of the discourse, and I hope he is more
my friend than to do it out of complaisance ; 'tis true he had
10 too good a taste to like it all ; and amongst some other faults
recommended to my second view what I have written perhaps
too boldly on St. Athanasius, which he advised me wholly
to omit. I am sensible enough that I had done more prudently to have followed his opinion ; but then I could not
15 have satisfied my self that I had done honestly not to have
written what was my own. It has always been my thought,
that heathens who never did, nor without miracle could, hear
of the name of Christ, were yet in a possibility of salvation.
Neither will it enter easily into my belief, that before the
20 coming of our Saviour the whole world, excepting only the
Jewish nation, should lie under the inevitable necessity of
everlasting punishment, for want of that Revelation, which
was confined to so small a spot of ground as that of Palestine.
Among the sons of Noah we read of one only who was
25 accursed ; and if a blessing in the ripeness of time was reserved for Japhet (of whose progeny we are), it seems un-
accountable to me, why so many generations of the same
offspring as preceded our Saviour in the flesh should be all
involved in one common condemnation, and yet that their
30 posterity should be entitled to the hopes of salvation: as
if a Bill of Exclusion had passed only on the fathers, which
debarred not the sons from their succession ; or that so many
ages had been delivered over to Hell, and so many reserved
for Heaven, and that the Devil had the first choice, and God
35 the next. Truly I am apt to think that the revealed religion
which was taught by Noah to all his sons might continue for
some ages in the whole posterity. That afterwards it was
included wholly in the family of Shem is manifest ; but when

the progenies of Cham and Japhet swarmed into colonies, and
those colonies were subdivided into many others, in process
of time their descendants lost by little and little the primitive
and purer rites of divine worship, retaining only the notion of
one deity; to which succeeding generations added others; 5
for men took their degrees in those ages from conquerors to
gods. Revelation being thus eclipsed to almost all mankind,
the Light of Nature, as the next in dignity, was substituted;
and that is it which St. Paul concludes to be the rule of the
heathens, and by which they are hereafter to be judged. If 10
my supposition be true, then the consequence which I have
assumed in my poem may be also true; namely, that Deism,
or the principles of natural worship, are only the faint remnants or dying flames of revealed religion in the posterity of
Noah: and that our modern philosophers, nay, and some of 15
our philosophizing divines, have too much exalted the faculties
of our souls, when they have maintained that by their force
mankind has been able to find out that there is one supreme
agent or intellectual Being which we call God; that praise
and prayer are his due worship; and the rest of those deduce- 20
ments, which I am confident are the remote effects of Revelation, and unattainable by our Discourse, I mean as simply
considered, and without the benefit of divine illumination.
So that we have not lifted up our selves to God by the weak
pinions of our Reason, but he has been pleased to descend to 25
us; and what Socrates said of him, what Plato writ, and the
rest of the heathen philosophers of several nations, is all no
more than the twilight of Revelation, after the sun of it was
set in the race of Noah. That there is something above us,
some principle of motion, our Reason can apprehend, though 30
it cannot discover what it is by its own virtue. And, indeed,
'tis very improbable that we, who by the strength of our
faculties cannot enter into the knowledge of any being, not
so much as of our own, should be able to find out by them
that supreme nature, which we cannot otherwise define than 35
by saying it is infinite; as if infinite were definable, or infinity
a subject for our narrow understanding. They who would
prove religion by reason do but weaken the cause which they

endeavour to support: 'tis to take away the pillars from our
faith, and to prop it only with a twig; 'tis to design a tower
like that of Babel, which, if it were possible (as it is not)
to reach heaven, would come to nothing by the confusion of
5 the workmen. For every man is building a several way;
impotently conceited of his own model and his own materials:
reason is always striving, and always at a loss; and of necessity
it must so come to pass, while 'tis exercised about that which
is not its proper object. Let us be content at last to know God
10 by his own methods; at least, so much of him as he is pleased
to reveal to us in the sacred Scriptures: to apprehend them to
be the word of God is all our reason has to do; for all beyond
it is the work of faith, which is the seal of Heaven impressed
upon our human understanding.
15   And now for what concerns the holy bishop Athanasius,
the Preface of whose Creed seems inconsistent with my
opinion, which is, that heathens may possibly be saved: in the
first place, I desire it may be considered that it is the Preface
only, not the Creed itself, which, till I am better informed,
20 is of too hard a digestion for my charity. It is not that I am
ignorant how many several texts of Scripture seemingly support that cause; but neither am I ignorant how all those
texts may receive a kinder and more mollified interpretation. Every man who is read in Church history knows that
25 Belief was drawn up after a long contestation with Arius
concerning the divinity of our blessed Saviour and his being.
one substance with the Father; and that, thus compiled, it
was sent abroad among the Christian churches, as a kind of
test, which whosoever took was looked on as an orthodox
30 believer. It is manifest from hence, that the heathen part of
the empire was not concerned in it; for its business was not
to distinguish betwixt Pagans and Christians, but betwixt
heretics and true believers. This, well considered, takes off
the heavy weight of censure, which I would willingly avoid
35 from so venerable a man; for if this proportion, 'whosoever
will be saved,' be restrained only to those to whom it was
intended, and for whom it was composed, I mean the Christians, then the anathema reaches not the heathens, who had

never heard of Christ and were nothing interested in that
dispute. After all, I am far from blaming even that prefatory
addition to the creed, and as far from cavilling at the con-
tinuation of it in the Liturgy of the Church, where on the
days appointed 'tis publicly read: for I suppose there is the same reason for it now in opposition to the Socinians as there
was then against the Arians; the one being a heresy, which
seems to have been refined out of the other; and with how
much more plausibility of reason it combats our religion, with
so much more caution to be avoided: and therefore the
prudence of our Church is to be commended, which has
interposed her authority for the recommendation of this
Creed. Yet to such as are grounded in the true belief,
those explanatory Creeds, the Nicene and this of Athanasius, might perhaps be spared; for what is supernatural
will always be a mystery in spite of exposition, and for
my own part, the plain Apostles' Creed is most suitable
to my weak understanding, as the simplest diet is the most
easy of digestion.

I have dwelt longer on this subject than I intended, and
longer than perhaps I ought; for having laid down, as my
foundation, that the Scripture is a rule, that in all things
needful to salvation it is clear, sufficient, and ordained by God
Almighty for that purpose, I have left my self no right to
interpret obscure places, such as concern the possibility of
eternal happiness to heathens : because whatsoever is obscure
is concluded not necessary to be known.

But by asserting the Scripture to be the canon of our faith,
I have unavoidably created to my self two sorts of enemies:
the Papists, indeed, more directly, because they have kept
the Scripture from us what they could and have reserved to
themselves a right of interpreting what they have delivered
under the pretence of infallibility: and the Fanatics more
collaterally, because they have assumed what amounts to an
infallibility in the private spirit, and have detorted those texts
of Scripture which are not necessary to salvation to the
damnable uses of sedition, disturbance, and destruction of
the civil government. To begin with the Papists, and to

speak freely, I think them the less dangerous, at least in
appearance, to our present state, for not only the penal laws
are in force against them, and their number is contemptible;
but also their peerage and commons are excluded from parlia-
5 ments, and consequently those laws in no probability of being
repealed. A general and uninterrupted plot of their clergy
ever since the Reformation I suppose all Protestants believe;
for 'tis not reasonable to think but that so many of their
orders, as were outed from their fat possessions, would en-
10 deavour a re-entrance against those whom they account
heretics. As for the late design, Mr. Coleman's letters, for
aught I know, are the best evidence; and what they discover,
without wire-drawing their sense or malicious glosses, all men
of reason conclude credible.   If there be anything more
15 than this required of me, I must believe it as well as I am
able, in spite of the witnesses, and out of a decent conformity
to the votes of Parliament; for I suppose the Fanatics will
not allow the private spirit in this case. Here the infallibility
is at least in one part of the government; and our under-
20 standings as well as our wills are represented. But to return
to the Roman Catholics, how can we be secure from the
practice of Jesuited Papists in that religion? For not two
or three of that order, as some of them would impose upon
us, but almost the whole body of them are of opinion,
25 that their infallible master has a right over kings, not only in
spirituals but temporals. Not to name Mariana, Bellarmine,
Emanuel Sa, Molina, Santarel, Simancha, and at least twenty
others of foreign countries; we can produce of our own
nation, Campian, and Doleman or Parsons : besides many
30 are named whom I have not read, who all of them attest this
doctrine, that the Pope can depose and give away the right of
any sovereign prince, *si vel paulum deflexerit*, if he shall never
so little warp : but if he once comes to be excommunicated,
then the bond of obedience is taken off from subjects; and
35 they may and ought to drive him like another Nebuchad-
nezzar, *ex hominum Christianorum dominatu*, from exercising
dominion over Christians; and to this they are bound by
virtue of divine precept, and by all the ties of conscience,

under no less penalty than damnation.   If they answer me, as
a learned priest has lately written, that this doctrine of the
Jesuits is not *de fide*, and that consequently they are not
obliged by it, they must pardon me if I think they have said
nothing to the purpose; for 'tis a maxim in their Church, 5
where points of faith are not decided, and that doctors are of
contrary opinions, they may follow which part they please;
but more safely the most received and most authorized.
And their champion Bellarmine has told the world, in his
Apology, that the King of England is a vassal to the Pope
ratione directi domini, and that he holds in villanage of his
Roman landlord.   Which is no new claim put in for England.
Our chronicles are his authentic witnesses, that King John
was deposed by the same plea, and Philip Augustus admitted
tenant.   And which makes the more for Bellarmine, the 15
French King was again ejected when our King submitted to
the Church, and the crown received under the sordid condition of a vassalage.

'Tis not sufficient for the more moderate and well-meaning
Papists (of which I doubt not there are many) to produce 20
the evidences of their loyalty to the late King, and to declare
their innocency in this Plot: I will grant their behaviour in
the first to have been as loyal and as brave as they desire, and
will be willing to hold them excused as to the second (I mean,
when it comes to my turn and after my betters, for it is a 25
madness to be sober alone, while the nation continues drunk):
but that saying of their Father Cres, is still running in my
head, that they may be dispensed with in their obedience to
an heretic prince, while the necessity of the times shall
oblige them to it; for that, as another of them tells us, is 30
only the effect of Christian prudence; but when once they
shall get power to shake him off, an heretic is no lawful king,
and consequently to rise against him is no rebellion.   I should
be glad, therefore, that they would follow the advice which
was charitably given them by a reverend prelate of our 35
Church; namely, that they would join in a public act of
disowning and detesting those Jesuitic principles, and sub-
scribe to all doctrines which deny the Pope's authority of

deposing kings, and releasing subjects from their oath of allegiance; to which I should think they might easily be induced, if it be true that this present Pope has condemned the doctrine of king-killing (a thesis of the Jesuits) 5 amongst others, *ex cathedrâ,* as they call it, or in open consistory.

Leaving them, therefore, in so fair a way (if they please themselves) of satisfying all reasonable men of their sincerity and good meaning to the government, I shall make bold to 10 consider that other extreme of our religion, I mean the Fanatics or Schismatics of the English Church. Since the Bible has been translated into our tongue, they have used it so as if their business was not to be saved, but to be damned by its contents. If we consider only them, better had it been 15 for the English nation that it had still remained in the original Greek and Hebrew, or at least in the honest Latin of St. Jerome, than that several texts in it should have been prevaricated to the destruction of that government which put it into so ungrateful hands.

20 How many heresies the first translation of Tyndal produced in few years, let my Lord Herbert's 'History of Henry the Eighth' inform you; insomuch that for the gross errors in it, and the great mischiefs it occasioned, a sentence passed on the first edition of the Bible, too shameful almost to be 25 repeated. After the short reign of Edward the Sixth, who had continued to carry on the Reformation on other principles than it was begun, every one knows that not only the chief promoters of that work, but many others, whose consciences would not dispense with Popery, were forced for fear of persecution to change climates; from whence returning at the beginning of Queen Elizabeth's reign, many of them who had been in France and at Geneva brought back the rigid opinions and imperious discipline of Calvin, to graff upon our Reformation; which, though they cunningly concealed at first, as 35 well knowing how nauseously that drug would go down in a lawful monarchy which was prescribed for a rebellious commonwealth, yet they always kept it in reserve, and were never wanting to themselves, either in court or parliament, when

either they had any prospect of a numerous party of fanatic
members in the one, or the encouragement of any favourite in
the other, whose covetousness was gaping at the patrimony
of the Church. They who will consult the works of our
venerable Hooker, or the account of his life, or more particularly the letter written to him on this subject by George
Cranmer, may see by what gradations they proceeded; from
the dislike of cap and surplice, the very next step was admonitions to the parliament against the whole government
ecclesiastical; then came out volumes in English and Latin in
defence of their tenets; and immediately practices were set
on foot to erect their discipline without authority. Those
not succeeding, satire and railing was the next; and Martin
Mar-prelate, the Marvel of those times, was the first presbyterian scribbler who sanctified libels and scurrility to the use
of the good old cause. Which was done, says my author,
upon this account: that, their serious treatises having been
fully answered and refuted, they might compass by railing
what they had lost by reasoning; and, when their cause was
sunk in court and parliament, they might at least hedge in a
stake amongst the rabble; for to their ignorance all things are
wit which are abusive; but if Church and State were made
the theme, then the doctoral degree of wit was to be taken at
Billingsgate; even the most saint-like of the party, though
they durst not excuse this contempt and vilifying of the
government, yet were pleased, and grinned at it with a
pious smile, and called it a judgment of God against the
hierarchy. Thus sectaries, we may see, were born with
teeth, foul-mouthed and scurrilous from their infancy; and
if spiritual pride, venom, violence, contempt of superiors,
and slander had been the marks of orthodox belief, the
Presbytery and the rest of our Schismatics, which are their
spawn, were always the most visible Church in the Christian world.

  'Tis true, the government was too strong at that time for a
rebellion; but to show what proficiency they had made in
Calvin's school, even then their mouths watered at it; for two
of their gifted brotherhood, Hacket and Coppinger, as the

story tells us, got up into a pease-cart and harangued the
people, to dispose them to an insurrection and to establish
their discipline by force; so that, however it comes about
that now they celebrate Queen Elizabeth's birthnight, as that
5 of their saint and patroness, yet then they were for doing the
work of the Lord by arms against her; and in all probability
they wanted but a fanatic lord-mayor and two sheriffs of
their party to have compassed it.

Our venerable Hooker, after many admonitions which he
10 had given them, towards the end of his preface breaks out
into this prophetic speech: 'There is in every one of these
considerations most just cause to fear, lest our hastiness to
embrace a thing of so perilous consequence, [meaning the
Presbyterian discipline,] should cause posterity to feel those
15 evils which as yet are more easy for us to prevent than they
would be for them to remedy.'

How fatally this Cassandra has foretold, we know too
well by sad experience: the seeds were sown in the time
of Queen Elizabeth, the bloody harvest ripened in the reign
20 of King Charles the Martyr; and, because all the sheaves
could not be carried off without shedding some of the
loose grains, another crop is too likely to follow; nay, I
fear 'tis unavoidable, if the Conventiclers be permitted still
to scatter.

25 A man may be suffered to quote an adversary to our religion, when he speaks truth. And 'tis the observation of
Maimbourg, in his 'History of Calvinism,' that, wherever
that discipline was planted and embraced, rebellion, civil war,
and misery attended it. And how, indeed, should it happen
30 otherwise? Reformation of Church and State has always
been the ground of our divisions in England. While we were
Papists, our holy Father rid us by pretending authority out of
the Scriptures to depose princes; when we shook off his
authority, the sectaries furnished themselves with the same
35 weapons, and out of the same magazine, the Bible: so that
the Scriptures, which are in themselves the greatest security
of governors, as commanding express obedience to them, are
now turned to their destruction; and never, since the Re-

formation, has there wanted a text of their interpreting to
authorize a rebel. And 'tis to be noted, by the way, that the
doctrines of king-killing and deposing, which have been taken
up only by the worst party of the Papists, the most frontless
flatterers of the Pope's authority, have been espoused, 5
defended, and are still maintained by the whole body of
Nonconformists and Republicans. 'Tis but dubbing themselves the people of God, which 'tis the interest of their
preachers to tell them they are, and their own interest to
believe; and, after that, they cannot dip into the Bible, 10
but one text or another will turn up for their purpose: if
they are under persecution, as they call it, then that is a
mark of their election; if they flourish, then God works
miracles for their deliverance, and the saints are to
possess the earth. 15

They may think themselves to be too roughly handled in
this paper; but I, who know best how far I could have gone
on this subject, must be bold to tell them they are spared:
though at the same time I am not ignorant that they interpret
the mildness of a writer to them, as they do the mercy of the 20
government; in the one they think it fear, and conclude it
weakness in the other. The best way for them to confute
me is, as I before advised the Papists, to disclaim their
principles and renounce their practices. We shall all be
glad to think them true Englishmen, when they obey the 25
King; and true Protestants, when they conform to the
Church discipline.

It remains that I acquaint the reader, that the verses were
written for an ingenious young gentleman, my friend, upon
his Translation of 'The Critical History of the Old Testa- 30
ment,' composed by the learned Father Simon: the verses
therefore are addressed to the translator of that work, and
the style of them is, what it ought to be, epistolary.

If any one be so lamentable a critic as to require the
smoothness, the numbers, and the turn of heroic poetry in 35
this poem, I must tell him, that, if he has not read Horace, I
have studied him, and hope the style of his Epistles is not ill
imitated here. The expressions of a poem designed purely

for instruction ought to be plain and natural, and yet majestic:
for here the poet is presumed to be a kind of lawgiver, and
those three qualities which I have named are proper to the
legislative style. The florid, elevated, and figurative way is
5 for the passions; for love and hatred, fear and anger, are be-
gotten in the soul by showing their objects out of their true
proportion, either greater than the life or less; but instruction is to be given by showing them what they naturally are.
A man is to be cheated into passion, but to be reasoned into
10 truth.

RELIGIO LAICI.

DIM as the borrowed beams of moon and stars
To lonely, weary, wandering travellers
Is Reason to the soul: and as on high
Those rolling fires discover but the sky,
Not light us here, so Reason's glimmering ray   5
Was lent, not to assure our doubtful way,
But guide us upward to a better day.
And as those nightly tapers disappear
When day's bright lord ascends our hemisphere,
So pale grows Reason at Religion's sight,   10
So dies, and so dissolves in supernatural light.
Some few, whose lamp shone brighter, have been led
From cause to cause to Nature's secret head,
And found that one first principle must be;
But what or who that UNIVERSAL HE;   15
Whether some soul encompassing this ball,
Unmade, unmoved, yet making, moving all,
Or various atoms' interfering dance
Leapt into form (the noble work of chance,)
Or this great All was from eternity,   20
Not even the Stagirite himself could see,
And Epicurus guessed as well as he.
As blindly groped they for a future state,
As rashly judged of Providence and Fate.
But least of all could their endeavours find   25
What most concerned the good of human kind;
For Happiness was never to be found,
But vanished from them like enchanted ground.
One thought Content the good to be enjoyed;
This every little accident destroyed.   30
The wiser madmen did for Virtue toil,

K 2

A thorny, or at best a barren soil;
In Pleasure some their glutton souls would steep,
But found their line too short, the well too deep,
And leaky vessels which no bliss could keep.   35
Thus anxious thoughts in endless circles roll,
Without a centre where to fix the soul.
In this wild maze their vain endeavours end:
How can the less the greater comprehend?
Or finite Reason reach Infinity?   40
For what could fathom GOD were more than He.

    The Deist thinks he stands on firmer ground,
Cries εὕρηκα, the mighty secret's found:
God is that spring of good, supreme and best,
We made to serve, and in that service blest;   45
If so, some rules of worship must be given,
Distributed alike to all by Heaven;
Else God were partial, and to some denied
The means His justice should for all provide.
This general worship is to PRAISE and PRAY;   50
One part to borrow blessings, one to pay;
And when frail nature slides into offence,
The sacrifice for crimes is penitence.
Yet since the effects of Providence, we find,
Are variously dispensed to human kind;   55
That vice triumphs and virtue suffers here,
(A brand that sovereign justice cannot bear:)
Our Reason prompts us to a future state,
The last appeal from Fortune and from Fate,
Where God's all-righteous ways will be declared,   60
The bad meet punishment, the good reward.

    Thus man by his own strength to Heaven would
        soar
And would not be obliged to God for more.
Vain, wretched creature, how art thou misled
To think thy wit these god-like notions bred!   65
These truths are not the product of thy mind,
But dropped from Heaven, and of a nobler kind.
Revealed Religion first Informed thy sight,

And Reason saw not till Faith sprung the light.
Hence all thy natural worship takes the source: 70
'Tis Revelation what thou thinkst Discourse.
Else how comest thou to see these truths so clear,
Which so obscure to heathens did appear?
Not Plato these, nor Aristotle found,
Nor he whose wisdom oracles renowned. 75 *Socrates.*
Hast thou a wit so deep or so sublime,
Or canst thou lower dive or higher climb?
Canst thou by reason more of Godhead know
Than Plutarch, Seneca, or Cicero?
Those giant wits, in happier ages born, 80
When arms and arts did Greece and Rome adorn,
Knew no such system; no such piles could raise
Of natural worship, built on prayer and praise
To one sole GOD:
Nor did remorse to expiate sin prescribe, 85
But slew their fellow creatures for a bribe:
The guiltless victim groaned for their offence,
And cruelty and blood was penitence.
If sheep and oxen could atone for men,
Ah! at how cheap a rate the rich might sin! 90
And great oppressors might Heaven's wrath beguile
By offering his own creatures for a spoil!
Darest thou, poor worm, offend Infinity?
And must the terms of peace be given by thee?
Then thou art Justice in the last appeal; 95
Thy easy God instructs thee to rebel,
And, like a king remote and weak, must take
What satisfaction thou art pleased to make.
But if there be a power too just and strong
To wink at crimes and bear unpunished wrong, 100
Look humbly upward, see his will disclose
The forfeit first, and then the fine impose:
A mulct thy poverty could never pay,
Had not Eternal Wisdom found the way,
And with celestial wealth supplied thy store; 105
His justice makes the fine, His mercy quits the score.

See God descending in thy human frame;
The offended suffering in the offender's name:
All thy misdeeds to Him imputed see,
And all His righteousness devolved on thee.   110
   For granting we have sinned, and that the offence
Of man is made against Omnipotence,
Some price that bears proportion must be paid,
And infinite with infinite be weighed.
See then the Deist lost: remorse for vice   115
Not paid, or paid inadequate in price:
What further means can Reason now direct,
Or what relief from human wit expect?
That shows us sick; and sadly are we sure
Still to be sick, till Heaven reveal the cure: 120
If then Heaven's will must needs be understood,
Which must, if we want cure and Heaven be good,
Let all records of will revealed be shown,
With Scripture all in equal balance thrown,
And our one Sacred Book will be that one.   125
   Proof needs not here; for whether we compare
That impious, idle, superstitious ware
Of rites, lustrations, offerings, which before,
In various ages, various countries bore,
With Christian Faith and Virtues, we shall find   130
None answering the great ends of human kind,
But this one rule of life; that shows us best
How God may be appeased and mortals blest.
Whether from length of time its worth we draw,
The world is scarce more ancient than the law: 135
Heaven's early care prescribed for every age,
First, in the soul, and after, in the page.
Or whether more abstractedly we look
Or on the writers or the written book,
Whence but from Heaven could men, unskilled in arts,
In several ages born, in several parts,   141
Weave such agreeing truths? or how or why
Should all conspire to cheat us with a lie?
Unasked their pains, ungrateful their advice,

Starving their gain and martyrdom their price. 145
  If on the Book itself we cast our view,
Concurrent heathens prove the story true:
The doctrine, miracles; which must convince,
For Heaven in them appeals to human sense;
And though they prove not, they confirm the cause, 150
When what is taught agrees with Nature's laws.
  Then for the style, majestic and divine,
It speaks no less than God in every line;
Commanding words, whose force is still the same
As the first fiat that produced our frame. 155
All faiths beside or did by arms ascend,
Or sense indulged has made mankind their friend;
This only doctrine does our lusts oppose,
Unfed by nature's soil, in which it grows,
Cross to our interests, curbing sense and sin; 160
Oppressed without and undermined within,
It thrives through pain; its own tormenters tires,
And with a stubborn patience still aspires.
To what can Reason such effects assign,
Transcending Nature, but to laws divine? 165
Which in that sacred volume are contained;
Sufficient, clear, and for that use ordained.
  But stay; the Deist here will urge anew,   *Objection of*
No supernatural worship can be true;   *the Deist.*
Because a general law is that alone 170
Which must to all and everywhere be known:
A style so large as not this Book can claim,
Nor aught that bears Revealed Religion's name.
'Tis said the sound of a Messiah's birth
Is gone through all the habitable earth; 175
But still that text must be confined alone
To what was then inhabited, and known:
And what provision could from thence accrue
To Indian souls and worlds discovered new?
In other parts it helps, that, ages past, 180
The Scriptures there were known, and were embraced,
Till Sin spread once again the shades of night:

What's that to these who never saw the light?
   Of all objections this indeed is chief
To startle reason, stagger frail belief: 185
We grant, 'tis true, that Heaven from human sense
Has hid the secret paths of Providence;
But boundless wisdom, boundless mercy may
Find even for those bewildered souls a way;
If from His nature foes may pity claim,   190
Much more may strangers who ne'er heard His name.
And though no name be for salvation known,
But that of His Eternal Son's alone;
Who knows how far transcending goodness can
Extend the merits of that Son to man?   195
Who knows what reasons may His mercy lead,
Or ignorance invincible may plead?
Not only charity bids hope the best,
But more the great Apostle has exprest:
That if the Gentiles, whom no law inspired,   200
By nature did what was by law required,
They who the written rule had never known
Were to themselves both rule and law alone,
To Nature's plain indictment they shall plead
And by their conscience be condemned or freed.   205
Most righteous doom! because a rule revealed
Is none to those from whom it was concealed.
Then those who followed Reason's dictates right,
Lived up, and lifted high their natural light,
With Socrates may see their Maker's face,   210
While thousand rubric-martyrs want a place.
   Nor does it baulk my charity to find
The Egyptian Bishop of another mind;
For, though his Creed eternal truth contains,
'Tis hard for man to doom to endless pains   215
All who believed not all his zeal required,
Unless he first could prove he was inspired.
Then let us either think he meant to say
This faith, where published, was the only way;
Or else conclude that, Arius to confute,   220

The good old man, too eager in dispute,
Flew high; and, as his Christian fury rose,
Damned all for heretics who durst oppose.
  Thus far my charity this path hath tried,
(A much unskilful, but well meaning guide;)   225
Yet what they are, even these crude thoughts were bred
By reading that which better thou hast read,
Thy matchless author's work, which thou, my friend,
By well translating better dost commend.
Those youthful hours, which of thy equals most   230
In toys have squandered or in vice have lost,
Those hours hast thou to nobler use employed,
And the severe delights of truth enjoyed.
Witness this weighty book, in which appears
The crabbed toil of many thoughtful years,   235
Spent by thy author in the sifting care
Of Rabbins' old sophisticated ware
From gold divine, which he who well can sort
May afterwards make Algebra a sport;
A treasure which, if country curates buy,   240
They Junius and Tremellius may defy,
Save pains in various readings and translations,
And without Hebrew make most learned quotations;
A work so full with various learning fraught,—
So nicely pondered, yet so strongly wrought   245
As Nature's height and Art's last hand required:
As much as man could compass, uninspired.
Where we may see what errors have been made
Both in the copier's and translator's trade:
How Jewish, Popish interests have prevailed,   250
And where Infallibility has failed.
  For some, who have his secret meaning guessed,
Have found our author not too much a priest;
For fashion-sake he seems to have recourse
To Pope and Councils and Tradition's force: 255
But he that old traditions could subdue
Could not but find the weakness of the new:
If Scripture, though derived from heavenly birth,

Has been but carelessly preserved on earth;
If God's own people, who of God before   260
Knew what we know, and had been promised more
In fuller terms of Heaven's assisting care,
And who did neither time nor study spare
To keep this Book untainted, unperplext,
Let in gross errors to corrupt the text,   265
Omitted paragraphs, embroiled the sense,
With vain traditions stopped the gaping fence,
Which every common hand pulled up with ease,
What safety from such brushwood-helps as these?
If written words from time are not secured,   270
How can we think have oral sounds endured?
Which thus transmitted, if one mouth has failed,
Immortal lies on ages are entailed;
And that some such have been, is proved too plain;
If we consider Interest, Church, and Gain.   275
    Oh, but, says one, Tradition set aside,
Where can we hope for an unerring guide?
For since the original Scripture has been lost
All copies disagreeing, maimed the most,
Or Christian faith can have no certain ground   280
Or truth in Church tradition must be found.
    Such an omniscient Church we wish indeed;
'Twere worth both Testaments, and cast in the Creed;
But if this mother be a guide so sure
As can all doubts resolve, all truth secure,   285
Then her infallibility as well
Where copies are corrupt or lame can tell;
Restore lost canon with as little pains,
As truly explicate what still remains;
Which yet no Council dare pretend to do,   290
Unless, like Esdras, they could write it new;
Strange confidence, still to interpret true,
Yet not be sure that all they have explained
Is in the blest original contained.
More safe and much more modest 'tis to say,   295
God would not leave mankind without a way:

And that the Scriptures, though not everywhere
Free from corruption, or entire, or clear,
Are uncorrupt, sufficient, clear, entire,
In all things which our needful faith require.   300
If others in the same glass better see,
'Tis for themselves they look, but not for me;
For MY salvation must its doom receive,
Not from what OTHERS, but what I believe.

    Must all tradition then be set aside?   305
This to affirm were ignorance or pride.
Are there not many points, some needful sure
To saving faith, that Scripture leaves obscure,
Which every sect will wrest a several way?
For what one sect interprets, all sects may.   310
We hold, and say we prove from Scripture plain,
That Christ is GOD; the bold Socinian
From the same Scripture urges he's but MAN.
Now what appeal can end the important suit?
Both parts talk loudly, but the rule is mute. — 315
    Shall I speak plain, and in a nation free
Assume an honest layman's liberty?
I think, according to my little skill,
To my own mother Church submitting still,
That many have been saved, and many may,   320
Who never heard this question brought in play.
The unlettered Christian, who believes in gross,
Plods on to Heaven and ne'er is at a loss;
For the strait gate would be made straiter yet,
Were none admitted there but men of wit.   325
The few by Nature formed, with learning fraught,
Born to instruct, as others to be taught,
Must study well the sacred page; and see
Which doctrine, this or that, does best agree
With the whole tenour of the work divine,   330
And plainliest points to Heaven's revealed design;
Which exposition flows from genuine sense,
And which is forced by wit and eloquence.
Not that Tradition's parts are useless here,

Objection in behalf of Tradition urged by Father Simon.

When general, old, disinteressed, and clear: 335
That ancient Fathers thus expound the page
Gives truth the reverend majesty of age,
Confirms its force by biding every test,
For best authorities, next rules, are best;
And still the nearer to the spring we go,   340
More limpid, more unsoiled, the waters flow.
Thus, first traditions were a proof alone,
Could we be certain such they were, so known:
But since some flaws in long descent may be,
They make not truth but probability.   345
Even Arius and Pelagius durst provoke
To what the centuries preceding spoke.
Such difference is there in an oft-told tale,
But truth by its own sinews will prevail.
Tradition written, therefore, more commends   350
Authority than what from voice descends:
And this, as perfect as its kind can be,
Rolls down to us the sacred history:
Which, from the Universal Church received,
Is tried, and after for its self believed.   355

The second objection. The partial Papists would infer from hence,
Their Church in last resort should judge the sense.
Answer to the objection. But first they would assume with wondrous art
Themselves to be the whole, who are but part
Of that vast frame, the Church; yet grant they were
The handers down, can they from thence infer   361
A right to interpret? or would they alone
Who brought the present claim it for their own?
The Book's a common largess to mankind,
Not more for them than every man designed;   365
The welcome news is in the letter found;
The carrier's not commissioned to expound.
It speaks its self, and what it does contain
In all things needful to be known is plain.
    In times o'ergrown with rust and ignorance   370
A gainful trade their clergy did advance;
When want of learning kept the laymen low

And none but priests were authorized to know;
When what small knowledge was in them did dwell
And he a God who could but read or spell;   375
Then Mother Church did mightily prevail;
She parcelled out the Bible by retail,
But still expounded what she sold or gave,
To keep it in her power to damn and save.
Scripture was scarce, and as the market went,   380
Poor laymen took salvation on content,
As needy men take money, good or bad;
God's word they had not, but the priest's they had.
Yet, whate'er false conveyances they made,
The lawyer still was certain to be paid.   385
In those dark times they learned their knack so well,
That by long use they grew infallible.
At last, a knowing age began to inquire
If they the Book or that did them inspire;
And making narrower search they found, though late,
That what they thought the priest's was their estate, 391
Taught by the will produced, the written word,
How long they had been cheated on record.
Then every man, who saw the title fair,
Claimed a child's part and put in for a share,   395
Consulted soberly his private good,
And saved himself as cheap as e'er he could.
   'Tis true, my friend (and far be flattery hence),
This good had full as bad a consequence;
The Book thus put in every vulgar hand,   400
Which each presumed he best could understand,
The common rule was made the common prey,
And at the mercy of the rabble lay.
The tender page with horny fists was galled,
And he was gifted most that loudest bawled;   405
The spirit gave the doctoral degree,
And every member of a Company
Was of his trade and of the Bible free.
Plain truths enough for needful use they found,
But men would still be itching to expound;   410

Each was ambitious of the obscurest place,
No measure ta'en from Knowledge, all from GRACE.
Study and pains were now no more their care,
Texts were explained by fasting and by prayer:
This was the fruit the private spirit brought,   415
Occasioned by great zeal and little thought.
While crowds unlearned, with rude devotion warm,
About the sacred viands buzz and swarm;
The fly-blown text creates a crawling brood
And turns to maggots what was meant for food. 420
A thousand daily sects rise up and die,
A thousand more the perished race supply:
So all we make of Heaven's discovered will
Is not to have it or to use it ill.
The danger's much the same, on several shelves 425
If others wreck us or we wreck ourselves.
      What then remains but, waving each extreme,
The tides of ignorance and pride to stem?
Neither so rich a treasure to forgo
Nor proudly seek beyond our power to know? 430
Faith is not built on disquisitions vain;
The things we must believe are few and plain:
But since men will believe more than they need
And every man will make himself a creed,
In doubtful questions 'tis the safest way   435
To learn what unsuspected ancients say;
For 'tis not likely we should higher soar
In search of Heaven than all the Church before;
Nor can we be deceived, unless we see
The Scripture and the Fathers disagree.   440
If after all they stand suspected still,
(For no man's faith depends upon his will,)
'Tis some relief, that points not clearly known
Without much hazard may be let alone;
And after hearing what our Church can say,   445
If still our reason runs another way,
That private reason 'tis more just to curb
Than by disputes the public peace disturb.

For points obscure are of small use to learn: }
But common quiet is mankind's concern. 450
   Thus have I made my own opinions clear,
Yet neither praise expect nor censure fear;
And this unpolished rugged verse I chose
As fittest for discourse and nearest prose;
For while from sacred truth I do not swerve, 455
Tom Sternhold's or Tom Shadwell's rhymes will serve.

THE HIND AND THE PANTHER.

A POEM.

IN THREE PARTS.

'Antiquam exquirite matrem.'
VIRG. [*Æn.* iii. 96.]

'Et vera incessu patuit Dea.'
[*Ibid.* l. 405.]

TO THE READER.

The nation is in too high a ferment for me to expect
either fair war or even so much as fair quarter from a reader
of the opposite party.   All men are engaged either on this
side or that; and though conscience is the common word 5
which is given by both, yet if a writer fall among enemies
and cannot give the marks of *their* conscience, he is knocked
down before the reasons of his own are heard.   A Preface,
therefore, which is but a bespeaking of favour, is altogether
useless.   What I desire the reader should know concerning 10
me he will find in the body of the poem, if he have but the
patience to peruse it.   Only this advertisement let him take
beforehand, which relates to the merits of the cause.   No general characters of parties (call 'em either Sects or Churches)
can be so fully and exactly drawn as to comprehend all the 15
several members of 'em; at least all such as are received
under that denomination.   For example: there are some of
the Church by law established who envy not liberty of conscience to Dissenters, as being well satisfied that, according
to their own principles, they ought not to persecute them. 20
Yet these by reason of their fewness I could not distinguish
from the numbers of the rest, with whom they are embodied
in one common name.   On the other side, there are many of
our sects, and more indeed than I could reasonably have
hoped, who have withdrawn themselves from the communion 25
of the Panther and embraced this gracious Indulgence of his
Majesty in point of toleration.   But neither to the one nor
the other of these is this Satire any way intended: 'tis aimed
only at the refractory and disobedient on either side.   For
those who have come over to the royal party are consequently 30

supposed to be out of gun-shot. Our physicians have observed, that in process of time some diseases have abated of their virulence and have in a manner worn out their malignity, so as to be no longer mortal: and why may not I suppose
5 the same concerning some of those who have formerly been enemies to kingly government as well as Catholic religion? I hope they have now another notion of both, as having found by comfortable experience that the doctrine of persecution is far from being an article of our faith.

10   'Tis not for any private man to censure the proceedings of a foreign Prince; but without suspicion of flattery I may praise our own, who has taken contrary measures, and those more suitable to the spirit of Christianity. Some of the Dissenters, in their addresses to his Majesty, have said ' that
15 he has restored God to his empire over conscience.' I confess I dare not stretch the figure to so great a boldness; but I may safely say, that conscience is the royalty and prerogative of every private man. He is absolute in his own breast, and accountable to no earthly power for that which passes only
20 betwixt God and him. Those who are driven into the fold are, generally speaking, rather made hypocrites than converts.

  This indulgence being granted to all the sects, it ought in reason to be expected that they should both receive it and receive it thankfully. For at this time of day to refuse the
25 benefit and adhere to those whom they have esteemed their persecutors, what is it else but publicly to own that they suffered not before for conscience sake, but only out of pride and obstinacy to separate from a Church for those impositions which they now judge may be lawfully obeyed? After they
30 have so long contended for their classical ordination (not to speak of rites and ceremonies), will they at length submit to an episcopal? If they can go so far out of complaisance to their old enemies, methinks a little reason should persuade 'em. to take another step, and see whither that would lead 'em.

35   Of the receiving this toleration thankfully I shall say no more than that they ought, and I doubt not they will, consider from what hands they received it. 'Tis not from a Cyrus, a heathen prince and a foreigner, but from a Christian

king, their native sovereign, who expects a return in specie from them, that the kindness which he has graciously shown them may be retaliated on those of his own persuasion.

As for the Poem in general, I will only thus far satisfy the reader, that it was neither imposed on me nor so much as the subject given me by any man. It was written during the last winter and the beginning of this spring; though with long interruptions of ill health and other hindrances. About a fortnight before I had finished it, his Majesty's Declaration for Liberty of Conscience came abroad: which if I had so soon expected, I might have spared myself the labour of writing many things which are contained in the Third Part of it. But I was always in some hope that the Church of England might have been persuaded to have taken off the Penal Laws and the Test, which was one design of the Poem when I proposed to myself the writing of it.

It is evident that some part of it was only occasional, and not first intended: I mean that defence of myself, to which every honest man is bound, when he is injuriously attacked in print: and I refer myself to the judgment of those who have read the Answer to the Defence of the late King's Papers, and that of the Duchess (in which last I was concerned), how charitably I have been represented there. I am now informed both of the author and supervisers of his pamphlet, and will reply, when I think he can affront me : for I am of Socrates's opinion, that all creatures cannot. In the mean time let him consider whether he deserved not a more severe reprehension than I gave him formerly, for using so little respect to the memory of those whom he pretended to answer; and at his leisure look out for some original Treatise of Humility, written by any Protestant in English, I believe I may say in any other tongue : for the magnified piece of Duncomb on that subject, which either he must mean or none, and with which another of his fellows has upbraided me, was translated from the Spanish of Rodriguez; though with the omission of the seventeenth, the twenty-fourth, the twenty-fifth, and the last chapter, which will be found in comparing of the books.

He would have insinuated to the world, that her late

Highness died not a Roman Catholic; he declares himself to
be now satisfied to the contrary, in which he has given up the
cause, for matter of fact was the principal debate betwixt us.
In the mean time, he would dispute the motives of her change;
5 how preposterously, let all men judge, when he seemed to
deny the subject of the controversy, the change itself. And
because I would not take up this ridiculous challenge, he tells
the world I cannot argue : but he may as well infer that a
Catholic cannot fast because he will not take up the cudgels
10 against Mrs. James to confute the Protestant religion.

I have but one word more to say concerning the Poem as
such, and abstracting from the matters, either religious or civil,
which are handled in it. The First Part, consisting most in
general characters and narration, I have endeavoured to raise,
15 and give it the majestic turn of heroic poesy. The second
being matter of dispute, and chiefly concerning Church authority, I was obliged to make as plain and perspicuous as
possibly I could; yet not wholly neglecting the numbers,
though I had not frequent occasions for the magnificence of
20 verse. The third, which has more of the nature of domestic
conversation, is or ought to be more free and familiar than
the two former.

There are in it two Episodes or Fables, which are inter-
woven with the main design ; so that they are properly parts
25 of it, though they are also distinct stories of themselves. In
both of these I have made use of the commonplaces of satire,
whether true or false, which are urged by the members of
the one Church against the other ; at which I hope no reader
of either party will be scandalized, because they are not of
30 my invention, but as old, to my knowledge, as the times of
Boccace and Chaucer on the one side and as those of. the
Reformation on the other.

THE HIND AND THE PANTHER.

A MILK-WHITE Hind, immortal and unchanged,
Fed on the lawns and in the forest ranged;
Without unspotted, innocent within,
She feared no danger, for she knew no sin.
Yet had she oft been chased with horns and hounds   5
And Scythian shafts, and many winged wounds
Aimed at her heart; was often forced to fly,
And doomed to death, though fated not to die.
  Not so her young; for their unequal line
Was hero's make, half human, half divine.   10
Their earthly mould obnoxious was to fate,
The immortal part assumed immortal state.
Of these a slaughtered army lay in blood,
Extended o'er the Caledonian wood,
Their native walk; whose vocal blood arose   15
And cried for pardon on their perjured foes.
Their fate was fruitful, and the sanguine seed,
Endued with souls, increased the sacred breed.
So captive Israel multiplied in chains,
A numerous exile, and enjoyed her pains.   20
With grief and gladness mixed, their mother viewed
Her martyred offspring and their race renewed;
Their corps to perish, but their kind to last,
So much the deathless plant the dying fruit surpassed.
  Panting and pensive now she ranged alone,   25
And wandered in the kingdoms once her own.
The common hunt, though from their rage restrained
By sovereign power, her company disdained,
Grinned as they passed, and with a glaring eye
Gave gloomy signs of secret enmity.   30

·'Tis true she bounded by and tripped so light,
They had not time to take a steady sight;
For truth has such a face and such a mien
As to be loved needs only to be seen.
The bloody Bear, an independent beast,   35
Unlicked to form, in groans her hate expressed.
Among the timorous kind the quaking Hare
Professed neutrality, but would not swear.
Next her the buffoon Ape, as atheists use,
Mimicked all sects and had his own to chuse;   40
Still when the Lion looked, his knees he bent,
And paid at church a courtier's compliment.
The bristled baptist Boar, impure as he,
But whitened with the foam of sanctity,
With fat ,pollutions filled the sacred place   ·45
And mountains levelled in his furious race:
So first rebellion founded was in grace.
But, since the mighty ravage which he made
In German forests had his guilt betrayed,
With broken tusks and with a borrowed name,   50
He shunned the vengeance and concealed the shame,
So lurked in sects unseen. With greater guile
False Reynard fed on consecrated spoil;
The graceless beast by Athanasius first
Was chased from Nice, then by Socinus nursed,   55
His impious race their blasphemy renewed,
And Nature's king through Nature's optics viewed;
Reversed they viewed him lessened to their eye,
Nor in an infant could a God descry.
New swarming sects to this obliquely tend,   60
Hence they began, and here they all will end.
What weight of ancient witness can prevail,
If private reason hold the public scale?
But, gracious God, how well dost thou provide
For erring judgments an unerring guide!   65
Thy throne is darkness in the abyss of light,
A blaze of glory that forbids the sight.
O teach me to believe Thee thus concealed,

And search no farther than Thy self revealed;
But her alone for my director take,   70
Whom Thou hast promised never to forsake!
My thoughtless youth was winged with vain desires;
My manhood, long misled by wandering fires,
Followed false lights; and when their glimpse was gone
My pride struck out new sparkles of her own.   75
Such was I, such by nature still I am;
Be Thine the glory and be mine the shame!
Good life be now my task; my doubts are done;
What more could fright my faith than Three in One?
Can I believe eternal God could lie   80
Disguised in mortal mould and infancy,
That the great Maker of the world could die?
And, after that, trust my imperfect sense
Which calls in question His omnipotence?
Can I my reason to my faith compel,   85
And shall my sight and touch and taste rebel?
Superior faculties are set aside;
Shall their subservient organs be my guide?
And let the moon usurp the rule of day,
And winking tapers show the sun his way;   90
For what my senses can themselves perceive
I need no revelation to believe.
Can they, who say the Host should be descried
By sense, define a body glorified,
Impassible, and penetrating parts?   95
Let them declare by what mysterious arts
He shot that body through the opposing might
Of bolts and bars impervious to the light,
And stood before His train confessed in open sight.
For since thus wondrously He passed, 'tis plain   100
One single place two bodies did contain,
And sure the same omnipotence as well
Can make one body in more places dwell.
Let Reason then at her own quarry fly,
But how can finite grasp infinity?   105
  'Tis urged again, that faith did first commence

By miracles, which are appeals to sense,
And thence concluded, that our sense must be
The motive still of credibility.
For latter ages must on former wait, 110
And what began belief must propagate.
   But winnow well this thought, and you shall find
'Tis light as chaff that flies before the wind.
Were all those wonders wrought by power divine
As means or ends of some more deep design? 115
Most sure as means, whose end was this alone,
To prove the Godhead of the Eternal Son.
God thus asserted: man is to believe
Beyond what Sense and Reason can conceive,
And for mysterious things of faith rely 120
On the proponent Heaven's authority.
If then our faith we for our guide admit,
Vain is the farther search of human wit;
As when the building gains a surer stay,
We take the unuseful scaffolding away. 125
Reason by sense no more can understand;
The game is played into another hand.
Why choose we then like bilanders to creep
Along the coast, and land in view to keep,
When safely we may launch into the deep? 130
In the same vessel which our Saviour bore,
Himself the pilot, let us leave the shore,
And with a better guide a better world explore.
Could He his Godhead veil with flesh and blood
And not veil these again to be our food? 135
His grace in both is equal in extent;
The first affords us life, the second nourishment.
And if He can, why all this frantic pain
To construe what his clearest words contain,
And make a riddle what He made so plain? 140
To take up half on trust and half to try,
Name it not faith, but bungling bigotry.
Both knave and fool the merchant we may call
To pay great sums and to compound the small,

For who would break with Heaven, and would not break
    for all? 145
Rest then, my soul, from endless anguish freed:
Nor sciences thy guide, nor sense thy creed.
Faith is the best insurer of thy bliss;
The bank above must fail before the venture miss.
But Heaven and heaven-born faith are far from thee, 150
Thou first apostate to divinity.
Unkennelled range in thy Polonian plains;
A fiercer foe, the insatiate Wolf remains.

  Too boastful Britain, please thyself no more
That beasts of prey are banished from thy shore; 155
The Bear, the Boar, and every savage name,
Wild in effect, though in appearance tame,
Lay waste thy woods, destroy thy blissful bower,
And, muzzled though they seem, the mutes devour.
More haughty than the rest, the wolfish race 160
Appear with belly gaunt and famished face;
Never was so deformed a beast of grace.
His ragged tail betwixt his legs he wears,
Close clapped for shame; but his rough crest he rears,
And pricks up his predestinating ears. 165
His wild disordered walk, his haggered eyes,
Did all the bestial citizens surprise;
Though feared and hated, yet he ruled a while,
As captain or companion of the spoil.
Full many a year his hateful head had been 170
For tribute paid, nor since in Cambria seen;
The last of all the litter scaped by chance,
And from Geneva first infested France.
Some authors thus his pedigree will trace,
But others write him of an upstart race; 175
Because of Wickliff's brood no mark he brings
But his innate antipathy to kings.
These last deduce him from the Helvetian kind,
Who near the Leman lake his consort lined:
That fiery Zuinglius first the affection bred, 180
And meagre Calvin blessed the nuptial bed.

In Israel some believe him whelped long since,
When the proud Sanhedrim oppressed the Prince,
Or, since he will be Jew, derive him higher,
When Corah with his brethren did conspire   185
From Moses' hand the sovereign sway to wrest,
And Aaron of his ephod to devest;
Till opening earth made way for all to pass,
And could not bear the burden of a class.
The Fox and he came shuffled in the dark,   190
If ever they were stowed in Noah's ark;
Perhaps not made; for all their barking train
The Dog (a common species) will contain;
And some wild curs, who from their masters ran,
Abhorring the supremacy of man,   195
In woods and caves the rebel-race began.
  O happy pair, how well have you increased!
What ills in Church and State have you redressed!
With teeth untried and rudiments of claws,
Your first essay was on your native laws: 200
Those having torn with ease and trampled down,
Your fangs you fastened on the mitred crown,
And freed from God and monarchy your town.
What though your native kennel still be small,
Bounded betwixt a puddle and a wall;   205
Yet your victorious colonies are sent
Where the North Ocean girds the continent.
Quickened with fire below, your monsters breed
In fenny Holland and in fruitful Tweed;
And, like the first, the last affects to be   210
Drawn to the dregs of a democracy.
As, where in fields the fairy rounds are seen,
A rank sour herbage rises on the green;
So, springing where these midnight elves advance,
Rebellion prints the footsteps of the dance.   215
Such are their doctrines, such contempt they show
To Heaven above and to their Prince below
As none but traitors and blasphemers know.
God like the tyrant of the skies is placed,

And kings, like slaves, beneath the crowd debased. 220
So fulsome is their food that flocks refuse
To bite, and only dogs for physic use.
As, where the lightning runs along the ground,
No husbandry can heal the blasting wound;
Nor bladed grass nor bearded corn succeeds, 225
But scales of scurf and putrefaction breeds:
Such wars, such waste, such fiery tracks of dearth
Their zeal has left, and such a teemless earth.
But as the poisons of the deadliest kind
Are to their own unhappy coasts confined, 230
As only Indian shades of sight deprive,
And magic plants will but in Colchos thrive,
So Presbytery and pestilential zeal
Can only flourish in a common-weal.
From Celtic woods is chased the wolfish crew; 235
But ah! some pity e'en to brutes is due:
Their native walks, methinks, they might enjoy,
Curbed of their native malice to destroy.
Of all the tyrannies on human kind
The worst is that which persecutes the mind. 240
Let us but weigh at what offence we strike;
'Tis but because we cannot think alike.
In punishing of this, we overthrow
The laws of nations and of nature too.
Beasts are the subjects of tyrannic sway, 245
Where still the stronger on the weaker prey;
Man only of a softer mould is made,
Not for his fellows' ruin, but their aid:
Created kind, beneficent and free,
The noble image of the Deity. 250
  One portion of informing fire was given
To brutes, the inferior family of Heaven:
The Smith Divine, as with a careless beat,
Struck out the mute creation at a heat;
But when arrived at last to human race, 255
The Godhead took a deep considering space,
And, to distinguish man from all the rest,

Unlocked the sacred treasures of his breast,
And mercy mixed with reason did impart,
One to his head, the other to his heart;   260
Reason to rule, but mercy to forgive,
The first is law, the last prerogative.
And like his mind his outward form appeared,
When issuing naked to the wondering herd
He charmed their eyes, and for they loved they feared.   265
Not armed with horns of arbitrary might,
Or claws to seize their furry spoils in fight,
Or with increase of feet to o'ertake them in their flight:
Of easy shape, and pliant every way,
Confessing still the softness of his clay,   270
And kind as kings upon their coronation day;
With open hands, and with extended space
Of arms to satisfy a large embrace.
Thus kneaded up with milk, the new-made man
His kingdom o'er his kindred world began;   275
Till knowledge misapplied, misunderstood,
And pride of empire scoured his balmy blood.
Then, first rebelling, his own stamp he coins;
The murderer Cain was latent in his loins;
And blood began its first and loudest cry   280
For differing worship of the Deity.
Thus persecution rose, and farther space
Produced the mighty hunter of his race.
Not so the blessed Pan his flock increased,
Content to fold them from the famished beast: 285
Mild were his laws; the Sheep and harmless Hind
Were never of the persecuting kind.
Such pity now the pious pastor shows,
Such mercy from the British Lion flows
That both provide protection for their foes.   290
    Oh happy regions, Italy and Spain,
Which never did those monsters entertain!
The Wolf, the Bear, the Boar, can there advance
No native claim of just inheritance;
And self-preserving laws, severe in show,   295

May guard their fences from the invading foe.
Where birth has placed them, let them safely share
The common benefit of vital air;
Themselves unharmful, let them live unharmed,
Their jaws disabled and their claws disarmed;   300
Here, only in nocturnal howlings bold,
They dare not seize the Hind nor leap the fold.
More powerful, and as vigilant as they,
The Lion awfully forbids the prey.
Their rage repressed, though pinched with famine sore,   305
They stand aloof, and tremble at his roar;
Much is their hunger, but their fear is more.
  These are the chief; to number o'er the rest
And stand, like Adam, naming every beast,
Were weary work; nor will the Muse describe   310
A slimy-born and sun-begotten tribe,
Who, far from steeples and their sacred sound,
In fields their sullen conventicles found.
These gross, half-animated lumps I leave,
Nor can I think what thoughts they can conceive.   315
But if they think at all, 'tis sure no higher
Than matter put in motion may aspire;
Souls that can scarce ferment their mass of clay,
So drossy, so divisible are they
As would but serve pure bodies for allay,   320
Such souls as shards produce, such beetle things
As only buzz to heaven with evening wings,
Strike in the dark, offending but by chance,
Such are the blindfold blows of ignorance.
They know not beings, and but hate a name;   325
To them the Hind and Panther are the same.
  The Panther, sure the noblest next the Hind,
And fairest creature of the spotted kind;
Oh, could her inborn stains be washed away,
She were too good to be a beast of prey!   330
How can I praise, or blame, and not offend,
Or how divide the frailty from the friend?
Her faults and virtues lie so mixed, that she

Nor wholly stands condemned nor wholly free.
Then, like her injured Lion, let me speak;   335
He cannot bend her and he would not break.
Unkind already, and estranged in part,
The Wolf begins to share her wandering heart.
Though unpolluted yet with actual ill,
She half commits who sins but in her will.   340
If, as our dreaming Platonists report,
There could be spirits of a middle sort,
Too black for heaven and yet too white for hell,
Who just dropped half-way down, nor lower fell;
So poised, so gently she descends from high,   345
It seems a soft dismission from the sky.
Her house not ancient, whatsoe'er pretence
Her clergy heralds make in her defence;
A second century not half-way run,
Since the new honours of her blood begun.   350
A Lion old, obscene, and furious made
By lust, compressed her mother in a shade;
Then by a left-hand marriage weds the dame,
Covering adultery with a specious name;
So schism begot; and sacrilege and she,   355
A well matched pair, got graceless heresy.
'God's and kings' rebels have the same good cause,
To trample down divine and human laws;
Both would be called reformers, and their hate
Alike destructive both to Church and State.   360
The fruit proclaims the plant; a lawless Prince
By luxury reformed incontinence,
By ruins charity, by riots abstinence.
Confessions, fasts, and penance set aside;
Oh with what ease we follow such a guide,   365
Where souls are starved and senses gratified!
Where marriage pleasures midnight prayer supply,
And matin bells (a melancholy cry)
Are tuned to merrier notes, *Increase and Multiply*.
Religion shows a rosy-coloured face,   370
Not hattered out with drudging works of grace:

A down-hill reformation rolls apace.
What flesh and blood would crowd the narrow gate,
Or, till they waste their pampered paunches, wait?
All would be happy at the cheapest rate.   375
  Though our lean faith these rigid laws has given,
The full-fed Mussulman goes fat to heaven;
For his Arabian prophet with delights
Of sense allured his Eastern proselytes.
The jolly Luther, reading him, began   380
To interpret Scriptures by his Alcoran;
To grub the thorns beneath our tender feet
And make the paths of Paradise more sweet,
Bethought him of a wife, ere half way gone,
For 'twas uneasy travailing alone;   385
And in this masquerade of mirth and love
Mistook the bliss of Heaven for Bacchanals above.
Sure he presumed of praise, who came to stock
The etherial pastures with so fair a flock,
Burnished and battening on their food, to show   390
The diligence of careful herds below.
  Our Panther, though like these she changed her head,
Yet, as the mistress of a monarch's bed,
Her front erect with majesty she bore,
The crosier wielded and the mitre wore.   395
Her upper part of decent discipline
Showed affectation of an ancient line;
And Fathers, Councils, Church and Church's head,
Were on her reverend phylacteries read.
But what disgraced and disavowed the rest   400
Was Calvin's brand, that stigmatised the beast.
Thus, like a creature of a double kind,
In her own labyrinth she lives confined;
To foreign lands no sound of her is come,
Humbly content to be despised at home.   405
Such is her faith, where good cannot be had,
At least she leaves the refuse of the bad.
Nice in her choice of ill, though not of best,
And least deformed, because reformed the least.

M

In doubtful points betwixt her differing friends, 410
Where one for substance, one for sign contends,
Their contradicting terms she strives to join;
Sign shall be substance, substance shall be sign.
A real presence all her sons allow,
And yet 'tis flat idolatry to bow, 415
Because the Godhead's there they know not how.
Her novices are taught that bread and wine
Are but the visible and outward sign,
Received by those who in communion join.
But the inward grace or the thing signified, 420
His blood and body who to save us died,
The faithful this thing signified receive:
What is't those faithful then partake or leave?
For what is signified and understood
Is by her own confession flesh and blood. 425
Then by the same acknowledgment we know
They take the sign and take the substance too.
The literal sense is hard to flesh and blood,
But nonsense never can be understood.

Her wild belief on every wave is tost; 430
But sure no Church can better morals boast.
True to her King her principles are found;
Oh that her practice were but half so sound!
Stedfast in various turns of state she stood,
And sealed her vowed affection with her blood: 435
Nor will I meanly tax her constancy,
That interest or obligement made the tie,
(Bound to the fate of murdered monarchy.)
Before the sounding axe so falls the vine,
Whose tender branches round the poplar twine. 440
She chose her ruin, and resigned her life,
In death undaunted as an Indian wife:
A rare example! but some souls we see
Grow hard and stiffen with adversity:
Yet these by Fortune's favours are undone; 445
Resolved, into a baser form they run,
And bore the wind, but cannot bear the sun.

Let this be nature's frailty or her fate,
Or Isgrim's counsel, her new chosen mate;
Still she's the fairest of the fallen crew;   450
No mother more indulgent but the true.
  Fierce to her foes, yet fears her force to try,
Because she wants innate auctority;
For how can she constrain them to obey
Who has herself cast off the lawful sway?   455
Rebellion equals all, and those who toil
In common theft will share the common spoil.
Let her produce the title and the right
Against her old superiors first to fight;
If she reform by text, even that's as plain   460
For her own rebels to reform again.
As long as words a different sense will bear,
And each may be his own interpreter,
Our airy faith will no foundation find:
The word's a weathercock for every wind: 465
The Bear, the Fox, the Wolf by turns prevail;
The most in power supplies the present gale.
The wretched Panther cries aloud for aid
To Church and Councils, whom she first betrayed;
No help from Fathers or Tradition's train: 470
Those ancient guides she taught us to disdain,
And by that Scripture which she once abused
To Reformation stands herself accused.
What bills for breach of laws can she prefer,
Expounding which she owns herself may err?   475
And, after all her winding ways are tried,
If doubts arise, she slips herself aside
And leaves the private conscience for the guide.
If then that conscience set the offender free,
It bars her claim to Church auctority.   480
How can she censure, or what crime pretend,
But Scripture may be construed to defend?
Even those whom for rebellion she transmits
To civil power, her doctrine first acquits;
Because no disobedience can ensue,   485

Where no submission to a judge is due;
Each judging for himself, by her consent,
Whom thus absolved she sends to punishment.
Suppose the magistrate revenge her cause,
'Tis only for transgressing human laws.   490
How answering to its end a Church is made.
Whose power is but to counsel and persuade?
Oh solid rock, on which secure she stands!
Eternal house, not built with mortal hands!
Oh sure defence against the infernal gate,   495
A patent during pleasure of the State!
  Thus is the Panther neither loved nor feared,
A mere mock queen of a divided herd;
Whom soon by lawful power she might control,
Her self a part submitted to the whole.   500
Then, as the moon who first receives the light
By which she makes our nether regions bright,
So might she shine, reflecting from afar
The rays she borrowed from a better star;
Big with the beams which from her mother flow,   505
And reigning o'er the rising tides below:
Now mixing with a savage crowd she goes,
And meanly flatters her inveterate foes,
Ruled while she rules, and losing every hour
Her wretched remnants of precarious power.   510
  One evening, while the cooler shade she sought,
Revolving many a melancholy thought,
Alone she walked, and looked around in vain
With rueful visage for her vanished train:
None of her sylvan subjects made their court;   515
Levees and couches passed without resort.
So hardly can usurpers manage well
Those whom they first instructed to rebel.
More liberty begets desire of more;
The hunger still increases with the store.   520
Without respect they brushed along the wood,
Each in his clan, and filled with loathsome food
Asked no permission to the neighbouring flood.

The Panther, full of inward discontent,
Since they would go, before them wisely went; 525
Supplying want of power by drinking first,
As if she gave them leave to quench their thirst.
Among the rest, the Hind with fearful face
Beheld from far the common watering-place,
Nor durst approach; till with an awful roar 530
The sovereign Lion bad her fear no more.
Encouraged thus, she brought her younglings nigh,
Watching the motion's of her patron's eye,
And drank a sober draught; the rest amazed
Stood mutely still and on the stranger gazed; 535
Surveyed her part by part, and sought to find
The ten-horned monster in the harmless Hind,
Such as the Wolf and Panther had designed.
They thought at first they dreamed; for 'twas offence
With them to question certitude of sense, 540
Their guide in faith: but nearer when they drew,
And had the faultless object full in view,
Lord, how they all admired her heavenly hue!
Some who before her fellowship disdained,
Scarce, and but scarce, from inborn rage restrained, 545
Now frisked about her and old kindred feigned.
Whether for love or interest, every sect
Of all the savage nation showed respect.
The viceroy Panther could not awe the herd;
The more the company, the less they feared. 550
The surly Wolf with secret envy burst,
Yet could not howl, the Hind had seen him first;
But what he durst not speak, the Panther durst.
    For when the herd suffised did late repair
To ferny heaths and to their forest lair, 555
She made a mannerly excuse to stay,
Proffering the Hind to wait her half the way;
That, since the sky was clear, an hour of talk
Might help her to beguile the tedious walk.
With much good-will the motion was embraced, 560
To chat a while on their adventures passed;

Nor had the grateful Hind so soon forgot
Her friend and fellow-sufferer in the Plot.
Yet wondering how of late she grew estranged,
Her forehead cloudy and her countenance changed,   565
She thought this hour the occasion would present
To learn her secret cause of discontent,
Which well she hoped might be with ease redressed,
Considering her a well-bred civil beast
And more a gentlewoman than the rest.   570
After some common talk what rumours ran,
The lady of the spotted muff began.

THE HIND AND THE PANTHER.

THE SECOND PART.

'DAME,' said the Panther, 'times are mended well
Since late among the Philistines you fell.
The toils were pitched, a spacious tract of ground
With expert huntsmen was encompassed round;
The enclosure narrowed; the sagacious power   5
Of hounds and death drew nearer every hour.
'Tis true, the younger Lion scaped the snare,
But all your priestly calves lay struggling there,
As sacrifices on their altars laid;
While you, their careful mother, wisely fled,   10
Not trusting destiny to save your head.
For whate'er promises you have applied
To your unfailing Church, the surer side
Is four fair legs in danger to provide;
And whate'er tales of Peter's chair you tell,   15
Yet, saving reverence of the miracle,
The better luck was yours to scape so well.'
  'As I remember,' said the sober Hind,
'Those toils were for your own dear self designed,
As well as me; and with the self-same throw   20
To catch the quarry and the vermin too,
(Forgive the slanderous tongues that called you so.)
Howe'er you take it now, the common cry
Then ran you down for your rank loyalty.
Besides, in Popery they thought you nurst,   25
As evil tongues will ever speak the worst,
Because some forms and ceremonies some
You kept, and stood in the main question dumb.

Dumb you were born indeed; but thinking long,
The Test, it seems, at last has loosed your tongue.   30
And to explain what your forefathers meant
By real presence in the Sacrament,
After long fencing pushed against a wall,
Your salvo comes, that he's not there at all:
There changed your faith, and what may change may fall.
'Who can believe what varies every day,   36
Nor ever was nor will be at a stay?'
    'Tortures may force the tongue untruths to tell,
And I ne'er owned my self infallible,'
Replied the Panther: 'grant such presence were,   40
Yet in your sense I never owned it there.
A real virtue we by faith receive,
And that we in the sacrament believe.'
    'Then,' said the Hind, 'as you the matter state,
Not only Jesuits can equivocate;   45
For *real*, as you now the word expound,
From solid substance dwindles to a sound.
Methinks an Æsop's fable you repeat;
You know who took the shadow for the meat.
Your Church's substance thus you change at will,   50
And yet retain your former figure still.
I freely grant you spoke to save your life,
For then you lay beneath the butcher's knife.
Long time you fought, redoubled battery bore,
But, after all, against your self you swore;   55
Your former self, for every hour your form
Is chopped and changed, like winds before a storm.
Thus fear and interest will prevail with some;
For all have not the gift of martyrdom.'
    The Panther grinned at this, and thus replied: 60
'That men may err was never yet denied.
But, if that common principle be true,
The cannon, dame, is levelled full at you.
But, shunning long disputes, I fain would see
That wondrous wight, Infallibility.   65
Is he from Heaven, this mighty champion, come?

Or lodged below in subterranean Rome?
First, seat him somewhere, and derive his race,
Or else conclude that nothing has no place.'
  'Suppose, (though I disown it,)' said the Hind,   70
'The certain mansion were not yet assigned:
The doubtful residence no proof can bring
Against the plain existence of the thing.
Because philosophers may disagree
If sight by emission or reception be,   75
Shall it be thence inferred I do not see?
But you require an answer positive,
Which yet, when I demand, you dare not give;
For fallacies in universals live.
I then affirm that this unfailing guide   80
In Pope and General Councils must reside;
Both lawful, both combined; what one decrees
By numerous votes, the other ratifies;
On this undoubted sense the Church relies.
'Tis true some doctors in a scantier space,   85
I mean in each apart, contract the place.
Some, who to greater length extend the line,
The Church's after acceptation join.
This last circumference appears too wide;
The Church diffused is by the Council tied;   90
As members by their representatives
Obliged to laws which Prince and Senate gives.
Thus some contract and some enlarge the space:
In Pope and Council who denies the place,
Assisted from above with God's unfailing grace?   95
Those canons all the needful points contain;
Their sense so obvious and their words so plain,
That no disputes about the doubtful text
Have hitherto the labouring world perplexed.
If any should in after times appear,   100
New Councils must be called, to make the meaning clear;
Because in them the power supreme resides,
And all the promises are to the guides.
This may be taught with sound and safe defence;

But mark how sandy is your own pretence, 105
Who, setting Councils, Pope, and Church aside,
Are every man his own presuming guide.
The Sacred Books, you say, are full and plain,
And every needful point of truth contain;
All who can read interpreters may be. 110
Thus, though your several Churches disagree,
Yet every saint has to himself alone
The secret of this philosophic stone.
These principles your jarring sects unite,
When differing doctors and disciples fight; 115
Though Luther, Zuinglius, Calvin, holy chiefs,
Have made a battle royal of beliefs,
Or, like wild horses, several ways have whirled
The tortured text about the Christian world,
Each Jehu lashing on with furious force, 120
That Turk or Jew could not have used it worse.
No matter what dissension leaders make,
Where every private man may save a stake:
Ruled by the Scripture and his own advice,
Each has a blind by-path to Paradise, 125
Where driving in a circle slow or fast
Opposing sects are sure to meet at last.
A wondrous charity you have in store
For all reformed to pass the narrow door,
So much, that Mahomet had scarcely more. 130
For he, kind prophet, was for damning none,
But Christ and Moses were to save their own;
Himself was to secure his chosen race,
Though reason good for Turks to take the place,
And he allowed to be the better man 135
In virtue of his holier Alcoran.'
   'True,' said the Panther, 'I shall ne'er deny
My brethren may be saved as well as I:
Though Huguenots contemn our ordination,
Succession, ministerial vocation, 140
And Luther, more mistaking what he read,
Misjoins the sacred body with the bread,

Yet, lady, still remember I maintain
The Word in needful points is only plain.'
'Needless or needful I not now contend,   145
For still you have a loophole for a friend,'
Rejoined the matron; 'but the rule you lay
Has led whole flocks and leads them still astray
In weighty points, and full damnation's way.
For did not Arius first, Socinus now   150
The Son's eternal Godhead disavow?
And did not these by gospel texts alone
Condemn our doctrine and maintain their own?
Have not all heretics the same pretence,
To plead the Scriptures in their own defence?   155
How did the Nicene Council then decide
That strong debate? was it by Scriptures tried?
No, sure to those the rebel would not yield;
Squadrons of texts he marshalled in the field:
That was but civil war, an equal set,   160
Where piles with piles, and eagles eagles met.
With texts point-blank and plain he faced the foe:
And did not Satan tempt our Saviour so?
The good old bishops took a simpler way;
Each asked but what he heard his father say,   165
Or how he was instructed in his youth,
And by tradition's force upheld the truth.'
The Panther smiled at this, and 'when,' said she,
'Were those first Councils disallowed by me?
Or where did I at sure tradition strike,   170
Provided still it were apostolic?'
'Friend,' said the Hind, 'you quit your former ground,
Where all your faith you did on Scripture found:
Now, 'tis tradition joined with Holy Writ;
But thus your memory betrays your wit.'   175
'No,' said the Panther, 'for in that I view
When your tradition's forged, and when 'tis true.
I set them by the rule, and as they square
Or deviate from undoubted doctrine there,
This oral fiction, that old faith declare.'   180

(*Hind.*) 'The Council steered, it seems, a different course;
They tried the Scripture by tradition's force;
But you tradition by the Scripture try;
Pursued by sects, from this to that you fly,
Nor dare on one foundation to rely.   185
The Word is then deposed, and in this view
You rule the Scripture, not the Scripture you.'
Thus said the dame, and, smiling, thus pursued:
'I see tradition then is disallowed,
When not evinced by Scripture to be true,   190
And Scripture as interpreted by you.
But here you tread upon unfaithful ground,
Unless you could infallibly expound;
Which you reject as odious Popery,
And throw that doctrine back with scorn on me.   195
Suppose we on things traditive divide,
And both appeal to Scripture to decide;
By various texts we both uphold our claim,
Nay, often ground our titles on the same:
After long labour lost and time's expense,   200
Both grant the words and quarrel for the sense.
Thus all disputes for ever must depend,
For no dumb rule can controversies end.
Thus, when you said tradition must be tried
By Sacred Writ, whose sense your selves decide,   205
You said no more but that your selves must be
The judges of the Scripture sense, not we.
Against our Church-tradition you declare,
And yet your clerks would sit in Moses' chair;
At least 'tis proved against your argument,   210
The rule is far from plain, where all dissent.'
    'If not by Scriptures, how can we be sure,'
Replied the Panther, 'what tradition's pure?
For you may palm upon us new for old;
All, as they say, that glitters is not gold.'   215
    'How but by following her,' replied the dame,
'To whom derived from sire to son they came;
Where every age does on another move,

And trusts no farther than the next above;
Where all the rounds like Jacob's ladder rise,   220
The lowest hid in earth, the topmost in the skies?'
  Sternly the savage did her answer mark,
Her glowing eye-balls glittering in the dark,
And said but this:—'Since lucre was your trade,
Succeeding times such dreadful gaps have made,   225
'Tis dangerous climbing: to your sons and you
I leave the ladder, and its' omen too.'
  (*Hind.*) 'The Panther's breath was ever famed for sweet,
But from the Wolf such wishes oft I meet;
You learned this language from the blatant beast,   230
Or rather did not speak, but were possessed.
As for your answer, 'tis but barely urged:
You must evince tradition to be forged,
Produce plain proofs, unblemished authors use,
As ancient as those ages they accuse;   235
Till when, 'tis not sufficient to defame;
An old possession stands till elder quits the claim.
Then for our interest, which is named alone
To load with envy, we retort your own;
For, when traditions in your faces fly,   240
Resolving not to yield, you must decry.
As when the cause goes hard, the guilty man
Excepts, and thins his jury all he can;
So when you stand of other aid bereft,
You to the twelve Apostles would be left.   245
Your friend the Wolf did with more craft provide
To set those toys, traditions, quite aside;
And Fathers too, unless when, reason spent,
He cites them but sometimes for ornament.
But, madam Panther, you, though more sincere,   250
Are not so wise as your adulterer;
The private spirit is a better blind
Than all the dodging tricks your authors find.
For they who left the Scripture to the crowd,
Each for his own peculiar judge allowed;   255
The way to please them was to make them proud.

Thus with full sails they ran upon the shelf;
Who could suspect a cozenage from himself?
On his own reason safer 'tis to stand
Than be deceived and damned at second hand. 260
But you who Fathers and traditions take
And garble some, and some you quite forsake,
Pretending Church auctority to fix,
And yet some grains of private spirit mix,
Are like a mule made up of differing seed, 265
And that's the reason why you never breed,
At least, not propagate your kind abroad,
For home-dissenters are by statutes awed.
And yet they grow upon you every day,
While you, to speak the best, are at a stay, 270
For sects that are extremes abhor a middle way.
Like tricks of state to stop a raging flood
Or mollify a mad-brained senate's mood,
Of all expedients never one was good.
Well may they argue, (nor can you deny,) 275
If we must fix on Church-auctority,
Best on the best, the fountain, not the flood;
That must be better still, if this be good.
Shall she command who has herself rebelled?
Is Antichrist by Antichrist expelled? 280
Did we a lawful tyranny displace,
To set aloft a bastard of the race?
Why all these wars to win the Book, if we
Must not interpret for ourselves, but she?
Either be wholly slaves or wholly free. 285
For purging fires traditions must not fight;
But they must prove episcopacy's right.
Thus, those led horses are from service freed;
You never mount them but in time of need.
Like mercenaries, hired for home defence, 290
They will not serve against their native Prince.
Against domestic foes of hierarchy
These are drawn forth, to make fanatics fly;
But, when they see their countrymen at hand,

Marching against them under Church command,   295
Straight they forsake their colours and disband.'
    Thus she ; nor could the Panther well enlarge
With weak defence against so strong a charge ;
But said, 'For what did Christ his word provide,
If still his Church must want a living guide ?   300
And if all saving doctrines are not there,
Or sacred penmen could not make them clear,
From after ages we should hope in vain
For truths, which men inspired could not explain.'
    'Before the Word was written,' said the Hind,   305
'Our Saviour preached his faith to human kind:
From his Apostles the first age received
Eternal truth, and what they taught believed.
Thus by tradition faith was planted first ;
Succeeding flocks succeeding pastors nursed.   310
This was the way our wise Redeemer chose,
Who sure could all things for the best dispose,
To fence his fold from their encroaching foes.
He could have writ himself, but well foresaw
The event would be like that of Moses' law ;   315
Some difference would arise, some doubts remain,
Like those which yet the jarring Jews maintain.
No written laws can be so plain, so pure,
But wit may gloss and malice may obscure ;
Not those indited by his first command,   320
A prophet graved the text, an angel held his hand.
Thus faith was ere the written Word appeared,
And men believed, not what they read, but heard.
But since the Apostles could not be confined
To these or those, but severally designed   325
Their large commission round the world to blow,
To spread their faith, they spread their labours too.
Yet still their absent flock their pains did share ;
They hearkened still, for love produces care.
And as mistakes arose or discords fell,   330
Or bold seducers taught them to rebel,
As charity grew cold or faction hot,

Or long neglect their lessons had forgot,
For all their wants they wisely did provide,
And preaching by Epistles was supplied :   335
So, great physicians cannot all attend,
But some they visit and to some they send.
Yet all those letters were not writ to all,
Nor first intended, but occasional
Their absent sermons; nor, if they contain   340
All needful doctrines, are those doctrines plain.
Clearness by frequent preaching must be wrought;
They writ but seldom, but they daily taught;
And what one saint has said of holy Paul,
He darkly writ, is true applied to all.   345
For this obscurity could Heaven provide
More prudently than by a living guide,
As doubts arose, the difference to decide?
A guide was therefore needful, therefore made;
And, if appointed, sure to be obeyed.   350
Thus, with due reverence to the Apostles' writ,
By which my sons are taught, to which submit,
I think those truths their sacred works contain
The Church alone can certainly explain;
That following ages, leaning on the past,   355
May rest upon the primitive at last.
Nor would I thence the Word no rule infer,
But none without the Church-interpreter;
Because, as I have urged before, 'tis mute,
And is it self the subject of dispute.   360
But what the Apostles their successors taught,
They to the next, from them to us is brought,
The undoubted sense which is in Scripture sought.
From hence the Church is armed, when errors rise
To stop their entrance and prevent surprise,   365
And, safe entrenched within, her foes without defies.
By these all-festering sores her councils heal,
Which time or has disclosed or shall reveal;
For discord cannot end without a last appeal.
Nor can a council national decide,   370

But with subordination to her guide,
(I wish the cause were on that issue tried;)
Much less the Scripture; for suppose debate
Betwixt pretenders to a fair estate,
Bequeathed by some legator's last intent,   375
(Such is our dying Saviour's Testament;)
The will is proved, is opened, and is read,
The doubtful heirs their differing titles plead;
All vouch the words their interest to maintain,
And each pretends by those his cause is plain.   380
Shall then the testament award the right?
No, that's the Hungary for which they fight,
The field of battle, subject of debate,
The thing contended for, the fair estate.
The sense is intricate, 'tis only clear   385
What vowels and what consonants are there.
Therefore 'tis plain, its meaning must be tried
Before some judge appointed to decide.'
    'Suppose,' the fair apostate said, 'I grant,
The faithful flock some living guide should want,   390
Your arguments an endless chase pursue:
Produce this vaunted leader to our view,
This mighty Moses of the chosen crew.'
    The dame, who saw her fainting foe retired,
With force renewed, to victory aspired;   395
And, looking upward to her kindred sky,
As once our Saviour owned his Deity,
Pronounced His words—*She whom ye seek am I.*
Nor less amazed this voice the Panther heard
Than were those Jews to hear a God declared.   400
Then thus the matron modestly renewed:
'Let all your prophets and their sects be viewed,
And see to which of them your selves think fit
The conduct of your conscience to submit;
Each proselyte would vote his doctor best,   405
With absolute exclusion to the rest:
Thus would your Polish Diet disagree,
And end, as it began, in anarchy;

Your self the fairest for election stand,
Because you seem crown-general of the land :   410
But soon against your superstitious lawn
Some Presbyterian sabre would be drawn ;
In your established laws of sovereignty
The rest some fundamental flaw would see,
And call rebellion gospel-liberty.   415
To Church-decrees your articles require
Submission modified, if not entire.
Homage denied, to censures you proceed :
But when Curtana will not do the deed,
You lay that pointless clergy-weapon by,   420
And to the laws, your sword of justice, fly.
Now this your sects the more unkindly take,
(Those prying varlets hit the blots you make,)
Because some ancient friends of yours declare
Your only rule of faith the Scriptures are,   425
Interpreted by men of judgment sound,
Which every sect will for themselves expound,
Nor think less reverence to their doctors due
For sound interpretation, than to you.
If then by able heads are understood   430
Your brother prophets, who reformed abroad ;
Those able heads expound a wiser way,
That their own sheep their shepherd should obey.
But if you mean your selves are only sound,
That doctrine turns the Reformation round,   435
And all the rest are false reformers found ;
Because in sundry points you stand alone,
Not in communion joined with any one,
And therefore must be all the Church, or none.
Then, till you have agreed whose judge is best,   440
Against this forced submission they protest ;
While sound and sound a different sense explains,
Both play at hard-head till they break their brains ;
And from their chairs each other's force defy,
While unregarded thunders vainly fly.   445
I pass the rest, because your Church alone

Of all usurpers best could fill the throne.
But neither you nor any sect beside
For this high office can be qualified
With necessary gifts required in such a guide.   450
For that which must direct the whole must be
Bound in one bond of faith and unity;
But all your several Churches disagree.
The consubstantiating Church and priest
Refuse communion to the Calvinist;   455
The French reformed from preaching you restrain,
Because you judge their ordination vain;
And so they judge of yours, but donors must ordain.
In short, in doctrine or in discipline
Not one reformed can with another join: 460
But all from each, as from damnation, fly:
No union they pretend, but in Non-Popery.
Nor, should their members in a synod meet,
Could any Church presume to mount the seat
Above the rest, their discords to decide;   465
None would obey, but each would be the guide;
And face to face dissensions would increase,
For only distance now preserves the peace.
All in their turns accusers and accused,
Babel was never half so much confused.   470
What one can plead the rest can plead as well,
For amongst equals lies no last appeal,
And all confess themselves are fallible.
Now, since you grant some necessary guide,
All who can err are justly laid aside,   475
Because a trust so sacred to confer
Shows want of such a sure interpreter,
And how can he be needful who can err?
Then, granting that unerring guide we want,
That such there is you stand obliged to grant;   480
Our Saviour else were wanting to supply
Our needs and obviate that necessity.
It then remains, that Church can only be
The guide which owns unfailing certainty;

'Or else you slip your hold and change your side,   485
,Relapsing from a necessary guide.
[But this annexed condition of the crown,
{Immunity from errors, you disown;
'Here then you shrink, and lay your weak pretensions dowr.
For petty royalties you raise debate,   490
But this unfailing universal State
You shun, nor dare succeed to such a glorious weight;
And for that cause those promises .detest
With which our Saviour did his Church invest;
But strive to evade, and fear to find them true,   495
As conscious they were never meant to you;
All which the Mother-Church asserts her own,
And with unrivalled claim ascends the throne.
So, when of old the Almighty Father sate
In council to redeem our ruined state,   500
Millions of millions, at a distance round,
Silent the sacred consistory crowned,
To hear what mercy mixed with justice could propound;
All prompt with eager pity to fulfil
The full extent of their Creator's will.   505
But when the stern conditions were declared,
A mournful whisper through the host was heard,
And the whole hierarchy with heads hung down
Submissively declined the ponderous proffered crown.
Then, not till then, the eternal Son from high   510
Rose in the strength of all the Deity;
Stood forth to accept the terms, and underwent
A weight which all the frame of heaven had bent,
Nor he himself could bear, but as omnipotent.
Now, to remove the least remaining doubt,   515
That even the blear-eyed sects may find her out,
Behold what heavenly rays adorn her brows,
What from his wardrobe her beloved allows
To deck the wedding-day of his unspotted spouse.
Behold what marks of majesty she brings,   520
Richer than ancient heirs of Eastern kings!
Her right hand holds the sceptre and the keys,

To show whom she commands, and who obeys:
With these to bind or set the sinner free,
With that to assert spiritual royalty.   525
  'One in herself, not rent by schism, but sound,
Entire, one solid shining diamond,
Not sparkles shattered into sects like you:
One is the Church, and must be to be true,
One central principle of unity.   530
As undivided, so from errors free;
As one in faith, so one in sanctity.
Thus she, and none but she, the insulting rage
Of heretics opposed from age to age;
Still when the giant-brood invades her throne,   535
She stoops from heaven and meets them half way down,
And with paternal thunder vindicates her crown.
But like Egyptian sorcerers you stand,
And vainly lift aloft your magic wand
To sweep away the swarms of vermin from the land.   540
You could like them, with like infernal force,
Produce the plague, but not arrest the course.
But when the boils and botches with disgrace
And public scandal sat upon the face,
Themselves attacked, the Magi strove no more,   545
They saw God's finger, and their fate deplore;
Themselves they could not cure of the dishonest sore.
  'Thus one, thus pure, behold her largely spread,
Like the fair ocean from her mother-bed;
From east to west triumphantly she rides,   550
All shores are watered by her wealthy tides.
The gospel-sound, diffused from pole to pole,
Where winds can carry and where waves can roll,
The self same doctrine of the sacred page
Conveyed to every clime, in every age.   555
  'Here let my sorrow give my satire place,
To raise new blushes on my British race.
Our sailing ships like common shores we use,
And through our distant colonies diffuse
The draughts of dungeons and the stench of stews,   560

Marks of the
Catholic
Church from
the Nicene
Creed.

Whom, when their home-bred honesty is lost,
We disembogue on some far Indian coast;
Thieves, pandars, palliards, sins of every sort;
Those are the manufactures we export,
And these the missioners our zeal has made;   565
For, with my country's pardon be it said,
Religion is the least of all our trade.
  ' Yet some improve their traffic more than we;
For they on gain, their only god, rely,
And set a public price on piety.   570
Industrious of the needle and the chart,
They run full sail to their Japonian mart;
Prevention fear, and prodigal of fame,
Sell all of Christian to the very name,
Nor leave enough of that to hide their naked shame. 575
  ' Thus of three marks, which in the creed we view,
Not one of all can be applied to you;
Much less the fourth. In vain, alas! you seek
The ambitious title of Apostolic:
God-like descent! 'tis well your blood can be   580
Proved noble in the third or fourth degree;
For all of ancient that you had before,
(I mean what is not borrowed from our store,)
Was error fulminated o'er and o'er;
Old heresies condemned in ages past,   585
By care and time recovered from the blast.
  ' 'Tis said with ease, but never can be proved,
The Church her old foundations has removed,
And built new doctrines on unstable sands:
Judge that, ye winds and rains! you proved her, yet she stands.
Those ancient doctrines charged on her for new,   591
Show when, and how, and from what hands they grew.
We claim no power, when heresies grow bold,
To coin new faith, but still declare the old.
How else could that obscene disease be purged,   595
When controverted texts are vainly urged?
To prove tradition new, there's somewhat more
Required, than saying, 'Twas not used before.

Those monumental arms are never stirred,
Till schism or heresy call down Goliath's sword.   600
  'Thus what you call corruptions are in truth
The first plantations of the gospel's youth,
Old standard faith; but cast your eyes again,
And view those errors which new sects maintain,
Or which of old disturbed the Church's peaceful reign;   605
And we can point each period of the time,
When they began, and who begot the crime;
Can calculate how long the eclipse endured,
Who interposed, what digits were obscured:
Of all which are already passed away,   610
We know the rise, the progress, and decay.
  'Despair at our foundations then to strike,
Till you can prove your faith Apostolic,
A limpid stream drawn from the native source,
Succession lawful in a lineal course.   615
Prove any Church, opposed to this our head,
So one, so pure, so unconfinedly spread
Under one chief of the spiritual state,
The members all combined, and all subordinate.
Show such a seamless coat, from schism so free,   620
In no communion joined with heresy.
If such a one you find, let truth prevail;
Till when, your weights will in the balance fail;
A Church unprincipled kicks up the scale.
  'But if you cannot think (nor sure you can   625
Suppose in God what were unjust in man)
That He, the fountain of eternal grace,
Should suffer falsehood, for so long a space,
To banish truth and to usurp her place;
That seven successive ages should be lost,   630
And preach damnation at their proper cost;
That all your erring ancestors should die
Drowned in the abyss of deep idolatry;
If piety forbid such thoughts to rise,
Awake, and open your unwilling eyes: 635
God hath left nothing for each age undone,

From this to that wherein he sent his Son;
Then think but well of Him, and half your work is done.
  'See how his Church, adorned with every grace,
With open arms, a kind forgiving face,   640
Stands ready to prevent her long-lost son's embrace!
Not more did Joseph o'er his brethren weep,
Nor less himself could from discovery keep,
When in the crowd of suppliants they were seen,
And in their crew his best-beloved Benjamin.   645

The renuncia- That pious Joseph in the Church behold,
ion of the
Benedictines to To feed your famine and refuse your gold;
he Abbey
ands. The Joseph you exiled, the Joseph whom you sold.'
  Thus, while with heavenly charity she spoke,
A streaming blaze the silent shadows broke;   650
Shot from the skies a cheerful azure light;
The birds obscene to forests winged their flight,
And gaping graves received the wandering guilty spright.
  Such were the pleasing triumphs of the sky
For James his late nocturnal victory;   655

'oeta loquitur. The pledge of his Almighty Patron's love,
The fireworks which his angels made above.
I saw my self the lambent easy light
Gild the brown horror and dispel the night:
The messenger with speed the tidings bore,   660
News which three labouring nations did restore;
But Heaven's own Nuncius was arrived before.
  By this the Hind had reached her lonely cell,
And vapours rose, and dews unwholesome fell;
When she, by frequent observation wise,   665
As one who long on heaven had fixed her eyes,
Discerned a change of weather in the skies.
The western borders were with crimson spread,
The moon descending looked all flaming red;
She thought good manners bound her to invite   670
The stranger dame to be her guest that night.
'Tis true, coarse diet and a short repast,
She said, were weak inducements to the taste
Of one so nicely bred and so unused to fast;.

But what plain fare her cottage could afford,   675
A hearty welcome at a homely board
Was freely hers; and to supply the rest,
An honest meaning and an open breast.
Last, with content of mind, the poor man's wealth,
A grace-cup to their common patron's health.   680
This she desired her to accept, and stay,
For fear she might be wildered in her way,
Because she wanted an unerring guide;
And then the dew-drops on her silken hide
Her tender constitution did declare   685
Too lady-like a long fatigue to bear,
And rough inclemencies of raw nocturnal air.
But most she feared that, travelling so late,
Some evil-minded beasts might lie in wait,
And without witness wreak their hidden hate.   690
   The Panther, though she lent a listening ear,
Had more of Lion in her than to fear;
Yet wisely weighing, since she had to deal
With many foes, their numbers might prevail,
Returned her all the thanks she could afford,   695
And took her friendly hostess at her word;
Who, entering first her lowly roof, a shed
With hoary moss and winding ivy spread,
Honest enough to hide an humble hermit's head,
Thus graciously bespoke her welcome guest: 700
'So might these walls, with your fair presence blest,
Become your dwelling-place of everlasting rest,
Not for a night, or quick revolving year,
Welcome an owner, not a sojourner.
This peaceful seat my poverty secures;   705
War seldom enters but where wealth allures:
Nor yet despise it, for this poor abode
Has oft received and yet receives a God;
A God victorious of the Stygian race
Here laid his sacred limbs, and sanctified the place.   710
This mean retreat did mighty Pan contain;

Be emulous of him, and pomp disdain,
And dare not to debase your soul to gain.'
   The silent stranger stood amazed to see
Contempt of wealth and wilful poverty: 715
And, though ill habits are not soon controlled,
A while suspended her desire of gold;
But civilly drew in her sharpened paws,
Not violating hospitable laws,
And pacified her tail and licked her frothy jaws.   720
   The Hind did first her country cates provide;
Then couched her self securely by her side.

THE HIND AND THE PANTHER.

THE THIRD PART.

MUCH malice mingled with a little wit
Perhaps may censure this mysterious writ,
Because the Muse has peopled Caledon
With Panthers, Bears, and Wolves, and beasts unknown,
As if we were not stocked with monsters of our own.   5
Let Æsop answer, who has set to view
Such kinds as Greece and Phrygia never knew;
And Mother Hubbard in her homely dress
Has sharply blamed a British Lioness,
That Queen, whose feast the factious rabble keep,   10
Exposed obscenely naked and asleep.
Led by those great examples, may not I
The wanted organs of their words supply?
If men transact like brutes, 'tis equal then
For brutes to claim the privilege of men.   15
　　Others our Hind of folly will indite
To entertain a dangerous guest by night.
Let those remember that she cannot die
Till rolling time is lost in round eternity;
Nor need she fear the Panther, though untamed,   20
Because the Lion's peace was now proclaimed:
The wary savage would not give offence,
To forfeit the protection of her Prince,
But watched the time her vengeance to complete,
When all her furry sons in frequent senate met;   25
Meanwhile she quenched her fury at the flood
And with a lenten salad cooled her blood.
Their commons, though but coarse, were nothing scant,
Nor did their minds an equal banquet want.

For now the Hind, whose noble nature strove   30
To express her plain simplicity of love,
Did all the honours of her house so well,
No sharp debates disturbed the friendly meal.
She turned the talk, avoiding that extreme,
To common dangers past, a sadly pleasing theme;   35
Remembering every storm which tossed the State,
When both were objects of the public hate,
And dropped a tear betwixt for her own children's fate.
  Nor failed she then a full review to make
Of what the Panther suffered for her sake: 40
Her lost esteem, her truth, her loyal care,
Her faith·unshaken to an exiled heir,
Her strength to endure, her courage to defy,
Her choice of honourable infamy.
On these prolixly thankful she enlarged;   45
Then with acknowledgments her self she charged;
For friendship, of it self an holy tie,
Is made more sacred by adversity.
Now should they part, malicious tongues would say
They met like chance companions on the way,   50
Whom mutual fear of robbers had possessed;
While danger lasted, kindness was professed;
But that once o'er, the short-lived union ends,
The road divides, and there divide the friends.
  The Panther nodded when her speech was done,   55
And thanked her coldly in a hollow tone:
But said, her gratitude had gone too far
For common offices of Christian care.
If to the lawful heir she had been true,
She paid but Cæsar what was Cæsar's due.   60
'I might,' she added, 'with like praise describe
Your suffering sons, and so return your bribe:
But incense from my hands is poorly prized,
For gifts are scorned where givers are despised.
I served a turn, and then was cast away;   65
You, like the gaudy fly, your wings display,
And sip the sweets, and bask in your great Patron's day.'

This heard, the matron was not slow to find
What sort of malady had seized her mind:
Disdain, with gnawing envy, fell despite, 70
And cankered malice stood in open sight:
Ambition, interest, pride without control,
And jealousy, the jaundice of the soul;
Revenge, the bloody minister of ill,
With all the lean tormenters of the will. 75
'Twas easy now to guess from whence arose
Her new-made union with her ancient foes,
Her forced civilities, her faint embrace,
Affected kindness with an altered face:
Yet durst she not too deeply probe the wound, 80
As hoping still the nobler parts were sound;
But strove with anodynes to assuage the smart,
And mildly thus her medicine did impart:
  'Complaints of lovers help to ease their pain;
It shows a rest of kindness to complain, 85
A friendship loth to quit its former hold;
And conscious merit may be justly bold.
But much more just your jealousy would show,
If others' good were injury to you:
Witness, ye heavens, how I rejoice to see 90
Rewarded worth and rising loyalty!
Your warrior offspring that upheld the crown,
The scarlet honours of your peaceful gown,
Are the most pleasing objects I can find,
Charms to my sight and cordials to my mind. 95
When virtue spooms before a prosperous gale,
My heaving wishes help to fill the sail;
And if my prayers for all the brave were heard,
Cæsar should still have such, and such should still reward.
  'The laboured earth your pains have sowed and tilled;
'Tis just you reap the product of the field. 101
Yours be the harvest, 'tis the beggar's gain
To glean the fallings of the loaded wain.
Such scattered ears as are not worth your care
Your charity for alms may safely spare, 105

And alms are but the vehicles of prayer.
My daily bread is literally implored;
I have no barns nor granaries to hoard.
If Cæsar to his own his hand extends,
Say which of yours his charity offends;   110
You know, he largely gives to more than are his friends.
Are you defrauded, when he feeds the poor?
Our mite decreases nothing of your store.
I am but few, and by your fare you see
My crying sins are not of luxury.   115
Some juster motive sure your mind withdraws
And makes you break our friendship's holy laws,
For barefaced envy is too base a cause.
   'Show more occasion for your discontent;
Your love, the Wolf, would help you to invent.   120
Some German quarrel, or, as times go now,
Some French, where force is uppermost, will do.
When at the fountain's head, as merit ought
To claim the place, you take a swilling draught,
How easy 'tis an envious eye to throw   125
And tax the sheep for troubling streams below;
Or call her, when no farther cause you find,
An enemy professed of all your kind!
But then, perhaps, the wicked world would think
The Wolf designed to eat as well as drink.'   130
   This last allusion galled the Panther more,
Because indeed it rubbed upon the sore;
Yet seemed she not to wince, though shrewdly pained,
But thus her passive character maintained:
   'I never grudged, whate'er my foes report,   135
Your flaunting fortune in the Lion's court.
You have your day, or you are much belied,
But I am always on the suffering side;
You know my doctrine, and I need not say
I will not, but I cannot disobey.   140
On this firm principle I ever stood:
He of my sons who fails to make it good
By one rebellious act renounces to my blood.'

'Ah!' said the Hind, 'how many sons have you
Who call you mother whom you never knew!   145
But most of them who that relation plead
Are such ungracious youths as wish you dead.
They gape at rich revenues which you hold
And fain would nibble at your grandam gold;
Inquire into your years, and laugh to find   150
Your crazy temper shows you much declined.
Were you not dim and doted, you might see
A pack of cheats that claim a pedigree,
No more of kin to you than you to me.
Do you not know that for a little coin   155
Heralds can foist a name into the line?
They ask you blessing but for what you have;
But once possessed of what with care you save,
The wanton boys would piss upon your grave.
'Your sons of latitude that court your grace,   160
Though most resembling you in form and face,
Are far the worst of your pretended race;
And, but I blush your honesty to blot,
Pray God you prove them lawfully begot:
For in some Popish libels I have read   165
The Wolf has been too busy in your bed;
At least their hinder parts, the belly-piece,
The paunch and all that Scorpio claims are his.
Their malice too a sore suspicion brings,
For though they dare not bark, they snarl at kings.   170
Nor blame them for intruding in your line;
Fat bishoprics are still of right divine.
'Think you your new French proselytes are come
To starve abroad, because they starved at home?
Your benefices twinkled from afar,   175
They found the new Messiah by the star.
Those Swisses fight on any side for pay,
And 'tis the living that conforms, not they.
Mark with what management their tribes divide,
Some stick to you, and some to t'other side,   180
That many churches may for many mouths provide.

More vacant pulpits would more converts make;
All would have latitude enough to take.
The rest unbeneficed your sects maintain,
For ordinations without cures are vain,   185
And chamber practice is a silent gain.
Your sons of breadth at home are much like these;
Their soft and yielding metals run with ease;
They melt, and take the figure of the mould,
But harden and preserve it best in gold.'   190
 'Your Delphic sword,' the Panther then replied,
'Is double-edged and cuts on either side.
Some sons of mine, who bear upon their shield
Three steeples argent in a sable field,
Have sharply taxed your converts, who unfed   195
Have followed you for miracles of bread;
Such who themselves of no religion are,
Allured with gain, for any will declare.
Bare lies with bold assertions they can face,
But dint of argument is out of place;   200
The grim logician puts them in a fright,
'Tis easier far to flourish than to fight.
Thus, our eighth Henry's marriage they defame;
They say the schism of beds began the game,
Divorcing from the Church to wed the dame;   205
Though largely proved, and by himself professed,
That conscience, conscience would not let him rest,
I mean, not till possessed of her he loved,
And old, uncharming Catherine was removed.
For sundry years before did he complain,   210
And told his ghostly confessor his pain.
With the same impudence, without a ground
They say that, look the Reformation round,
No Treatise of Humility is found.
But if none were, the Gospel does not want,   215
Our Saviour preached it, and I hope you grant
The Sermon in the Mount was Protestant.'
 'No doubt,' replied the Hind, 'as sure as all
The writings of Saint Peter and Saint Paul;

On that decision let it stand or fall. 220
Now for my converts, who, you say, unfed
Have followed me for miracles of bread.
Judge not by hearsay, but observe at least,
If since their change their loaves have been increast.
The Lion buys no converts; if he did, 225
Beasts would be sold as fast as he could bid.
Tax those of interest who conform for gain
Or stay the market of another reign :
Your broad-way sons would never be too nice
To close with Calvin, if he paid their price ; 230
But, raised three steeples higher, would change their note,
And quit the cassock for the canting-coat.
Now, if you damn this censure as too bold,
Judge by your selves, and think not others sold.
  ' Meantime my sons accused by fame's report 235
Pay small attendance at the Lion's court,
Nor rise with early crowds, nor flatter late,
(For silently they beg who daily wait.)
Preferment is bestowed that comes unsought;
Attendance is a bribe, and then 'tis bought. . 240
How they should speed, their fortune is untried;
For not to ask is not to be denied.
For what they have their God and King they bless,
And hope they should not murmur had they less.
But if reduced subsistence to implore, 245
In common prudence they would pass your door.
Unpitied Hudibras, your champion friend,
Has shown how far your charities extend.
This lasting verse shall on his tomb be read,
He shamed you living, and upbraids you dead. 250
  ' With odious atheist names you load your foes ;
Your liberal clergy why did I expose ?
It never fails in charities like those.
In climes where true religion is professed,
That imputation were no laughing jest ; 255
But *Imprimatur*, with a chaplain's name,
Is here sufficient licence to defame.

O

What wonder is't that black detraction thrives;
The homicide of names is less than lives,
And yet the perjured murderer survives.'   260
  This said, she paused a little, and suppressed
The boiling indignation of her breast.
She knew the virtue of her blade, nor would
Pollute her satire with ignoble blood;
Her panting foes she saw before her lie,   265
And back she drew the shining weapon dry.
So when the generous Lion has in sight
His equal match, he rouses for the fight;
But when his foe lies prostrate on the plain,
He sheathes his paws, uncurls his angry mane,   270
And, pleased with bloodless honours of the day,
Walks over and disdains the inglorious prey.
So James, if great with less we may compare,
Arrests his rolling thunder-bolts in air;
And grants ungrateful friends a lengthened space   275
To implore the remnants of long-suffering grace.
  This breathing-time the matron took; and then
Resumed the thrid of her discourse again.
'Be vengeance wholly left to powers divine,
And let Heaven judge betwixt your sons and mine: 280
If joys hereafter must be purchased here
With loss of all that mortals hold so dear,
Then welcome infamy and public shame,
And last, a long farewell to worldly fame.
'Tis said with ease, but oh, how hardly tried   285
By haughty souls to human honour tied!
O sharp convulsive pangs of agonizing pride!
Down then, thou rebel, never more to rise;
And what thou didst and dost so dearly prize,
That fame, that darling fame, make that thy sacrifice. 290
'Tis nothing thou hast given; then add thy tears
For a long race of unrepenting years:
'Tis nothing yet, yet all thou hast to give:
Then add those may-be years thou hast to live:
Yet nothing still: then poor and naked come,   295

Thy Father will receive his unthrift home,
And thy blest Saviour's blood discharge the mighty sum.'
  'Thus,' she pursued, 'I discipline a son,
Whose unchecked fury to revenge would run;
He champs the bit, impatient of his loss,   300
And starts aside and flounders at the Cross.
Instruct him better, gracious God, to know
As Thine is vengeance, so forgiveness too;
That, suffering from ill tongues, he bears no more
Than what his Sovereign bears and what his Saviour bore.
  'It now remains for you to school your child,   306
And ask why God's anointed he reviled;
A King and Princess dead! did Shimei worse?
The curser's punishment should fright the curse;
Your son was warned, and wisely gave it o'er,   310
But he who counselled him has paid the score;
The heavy malice could no higher tend,
But woe to him on whom the weights descend.
So to permitted ills the dæmon flies;
His rage is aimed at him who rules the skies: 315
Constrained to quit his cause, no succour found,
The foe discharges every tire around,
In clouds of smoke abandoning the fight;
But his own thundering peals proclaim his flight.
  'In Henry's change his charge as ill succeeds;   320
To that long story little answer needs:
Confront but Henry's words with Henry's deeds.
Were space allowed, with ease it might be proved,
What springs his blessed reformation moved.
The dire effects appeared in open sight,   325
Which from the cause he calls a distant flight,
And yet no larger leap than from the sun to light.
  'Now last, your sons a double pæan sound,
A Treatise of Humility is found.
'Tis found, but better had it ne'er been sought   330
Than thus in Protestant procession brought.
The famed original through Spain is known,
Rodriguez' work, my celebrated son,

Which yours by ill-translating made his own;
Concealed its author, and usurped the name,   335
The basest and ignoblest theft of fame.
My altars kindled first that living coal;
Restore, or practise better what you stole;
That virtue could this humble verse inspire,
'Tis all the restitution I require.'   340
  Glad was the Panther that the charge was closed,
And none of all her favourite sons exposed;
For laws of arms permit each injured man
To make himself a saver where he can.
Perhaps the plundered merchant cannot tell   345
The names of pirates in whose hands he fell;
But at the den of thieves he justly flies,
And every Algerine is lawful prize.
No private person in the foe's estate
Can plead exemption from the public fate.   350
Yet Christian laws allow not such redress;
Then let the greater supersede the less:
But let the abettors of the Panther's crime
Learn to make fairer wars another time.
Some characters may sure be found to write   355
Among her sons; for 'tis no common sight,
A spotted dam, and all her offspring white.
  The savage, though she saw her plea controlled,
Yet would not wholly seem to quit her hold,
But offered fairly to compound the strife   360
And judge conversion by the convert's life.
' 'Tis true,' she said, ' I think it somewhat strange
So few should follow profitable change;
For present joys are more to flesh and blood
Than a dull prospect of a distant good.   365
'Twas well alluded by a son of mine,
(I hope to quote him is not to purloin,)
Two magnets, heaven and earth, allure to bliss;
The larger loadstone that, the nearer this:
The weak attraction of the greater fails;   370
We nod awhile, but neighbourhood prevails;

But when the greater proves the nearer too,
I wonder more your converts come so slow.
Methinks in those who firm with me remain,
It shows a nobler principle than gain.'   375
  'Your inference would be strong,' the Hind replied,
'If yours were in effect the suffering side;
Your clergy-sons their own in peace possess,
Nor are their prospects in reversion less.
My proselytes are struck with awful dread,   380
Your bloody comet-laws hang blazing o'er their head;
The respite they enjoy but only lent,
The best they have to hope, protracted punishment.
Be judge your self, if interest may prevail,
Which motives, yours or mine, will turn the scale.   385
While pride and pomp allure, and plenteous ease,
That is, till man's predominant passions cease,
Admire no longer at my slow increase.
  'By education most have been misled;
So they believe, because they so were bred.   390
The priest continues what the nurse began,
And thus the child imposes on the man.
The rest I named before, nor need repeat;
But interest is the most prevailing cheat,
The sly seducer both of age and youth;   395
They study that, and think they study truth.
When interest fortifies an argument,
Weak reason serves to gain the will's assent;
For souls already warped receive an easy bent.
  'Add long prescription of established laws,   400
And pique of honour to maintain a cause,
And shame of change, and fear of future ill,
And zeal, the blind conductor of the will;
And chief among the still-mistaking crowd,
The fame of teachers obstinate and proud;   405
And, more than all, the private judge allowed;
Disdain of Fathers which the dance began,
And last, uncertain whose the narrower span,
The clown unread and half-read gentleman.'

To this the Panther, with a scornful smile: 410
'Yet still you travail with unwearied toil,
And range around the realm without control,
Among my sons for proselytes to prowl,
And here and there you snap some silly soul.
You hinted fears of future change in state;   415
Pray Heaven you did not prophesy your fate!
Perhaps, you think your time of triumph near,
But may mistake the season of the year;
The Swallows' fortune gives you cause to fear.'
  'For charity,' replied the matron, 'tell   420
What sad mischance those pretty birds befel.'
  'Nay, no mischance,' the savage dame replied,
'But want of wit in their unerring guide,
And eager haste and gaudy hopes and giddy pride.
Yet, wishing timely warning may prevail,   425
Make you the moral, and I'll tell the tale.
  'The Swallow, privileged above the rest
Of all the birds as man's familiar guest,
Pursues the sun in summer, brisk and bold,
But wisely shuns the persecuting cold;   430
Is well to chancels and to chimneys known,
Though 'tis not thought she feeds on smoke alone.
From hence she has been held of heavenly line,
Endued with particles of soul divine.
This merry chorister had long possessed   435
Her summer seat, and feathered well her nest;
Till frowning skies began to change their cheer,
And time turned up the wrong side of the year;
The shedding trees began the ground to strow
With yellow leaves, and bitter blasts to blow.   440
Sad auguries of winter thence she drew,
Which by instinct or prophecy she knew:
When prudence warned her to remove betimes,
And seek a better heaven and warmer climes.
  'Her sons were summoned on a steeple's height,   445
And, called in common council, vote a flight;

The day was named, the next that should be fair;
All to the general rendezvous repair,
They try their fluttering wings and trust themselves in air.
But whether upward to the moon they go,   450
Or dream the winter out in caves below,
Or hawk at flies elsewhere, concerns not us to know.
  'Southwards, you may be sure, they bent their flight,
And harboured in a hollow rock at night;
Next morn they rose, and set up every sail;   455
The wind was fair, but blew a mackrel gale:
The sickly young sat shivering on the shore,
Abhorred salt-water never seen before,
And prayed their tender mothers to delay
The passage, and expect a fairer day.   460
  'With these the Martin readily concurred,
A church-begot and church-believing bird;
Of little body, but of lofty mind,
Round bellied, for a dignity designed,
And much a dunce, as Martins are by kind;   465
Yet often quoted Canon-laws and Code
And Fathers which he never understood;
But little learning needs in noble blood.
For, sooth to say, the Swallow brought him in
Her household chaplain and her next of kin: 470
In superstition silly to excess,
And casting schemes by planetary guess;
In fine, short-winged, unfit himself to fly,
His fear foretold foul weather in the sky.
  'Besides, a Raven from a withered oak   475
Left of their lodging was observed to croak.
That omen liked him not; so his advice
Was present safety, bought at any price;
A seeming pious care that covered cowardice.
To strengthen this, he told a boding dream,   480
Of rising waters and a troubled stream,
Sure signs of anguish, dangers, and distress,
With something more not lawful to express:
By which he slyly seemed to intimate

Some secret revelation of their fate.   485
For he concluded, once upon a time,
He found a leaf inscribed with sacred rhyme,
Whose antique characters did well denote
The Sibyl's hand of the Cumæan grot:
The mad divineress had plainly writ,   490
A time should come (but many ages yet)
In which sinister destinies ordain
A dame should drown with all her feathered train,
And seas from thence be called the Chelidonian main.
At this, some shook for fear; the more devout   495
Arose, and blessed themselves from head to foot.
  ''Tis true, some stagers of the wiser sort
Made all these idle wonderments their sport:
They said, their only danger was delay,
And he who heard what every fool could say   500
Would never fix his thoughts, but trim his time away.
The passage yet was good; the wind, 'tis true,
Was somewhat high, but that was nothing new,
Nor more than usual equinoxes blew.
The sun, already from the Scales declined,   505
Gave little hopes of better days behind,
But change from bad to worse of weather and of wind.
Nor need they fear the dampness of the sky
Should flag their wings, and hinder them to fly;
'Twas only water thrown on sails too dry.   510
But, least of all, philosophy presumes
Of truth in dreams from melancholy fumes;
Perhaps the Martin, housed in holy ground,
Might think of ghosts that walk their midnight round,
Till grosser atoms tumbling in the stream   515
Of fancy madly met and clubbed into a dream:
As little weight his vain presages bear,
Of ill effect to such alone who fear;
Most prophecies are of a piece with these,
Each Nostradamus can foretell with ease: 520
Not naming persons, and confounding times,
One casual truth supports a thousand lying rhymes.

'The advice was true; but fear had seized the most,
And all good counsel is on cowards lost.
The question crudely put to shun delay,   525
'Twas carried by the major part to stay.
'His point thus gained, Sir Martin dated thence
His power, and from a priest became a prince.
He ordered all things with a busy care,
And cells and refectories did prepare,   530
And large provisions laid of winter fare;
But now and then let fall a word or two,
Of hope, that Heaven some miracle might show,
And for their sakes the sun should backward go,
Against the laws of nature upward climb,   535
And, mounted on the Ram, renew the prime;
For which two proofs in sacred story lay,
Of Ahaz' dial and of Joshua's day.
In expectation of such times as these,
A chapel housed them, truly called of ease;   540
For Martin much devotion did not ask;
They prayed sometimes, and that was all their task.
'It happened (as beyond the reach of wit
Blind prophecies may have a lucky hit)
That this accomplished, or at least in part,   545
Gave great repute to their new Merlin's art.
Some Swifts, the giants of the Swallow kind,
Large-limbed, stout-hearted, but of stupid mind,
(For Swisses or for Gibeonites designed,)
These lubbers, peeping through a broken pane   550
To suck fresh air, surveyed the neighbouring plain,
And saw (but scarcely could believe their eyes)
New blossoms flourish and new flowers arise,
As God had been abroad, and walking there
Had left his footsteps and reformed the year.   555
The sunny hills from far were seen to glow
With glittering beams, and in the meads below
The burnished brooks appeared with liquid gold to flow.
At last they heard the foolish Cuckoo sing,
Whose note proclaimed the holy-day of spring.   560

'No longer doubting, all prepare to fly
And repossess their patrimonial sky.
The priest before them did his wings display;
And that good omens might attend their way,
As luck would have it, 'twas St. Martin's day.   565
  'Who but the Swallow now triumphs alone?
The canopy of heaven is all her own;
Her youthful offspring to their haunts repair,
And glide along in glades, and skim in air,
And dip for insects in the purling springs,   570
And stoop on rivers to refresh their wings.
Their mothers think a fair provision made,
That every son can live upon his trade,
And, now the careful charge is off their hands,
Look out for husbands and new nuptial bands.   575
The youthful widow longs to be supplied;
But first the lover is by lawyers tied
To settle jointure-chimneys on the bride.
So thick they couple, in so short a space,
That Martin's marriage-offerings rise apace;   580
Their ancient houses, running to decay,
Are furbished up and cemented with clay.
They teem already; stores of eggs are laid,
And brooding mothers call Lucina's aid.
Fame spreads the news, and foreign fowls appear   585
In flocks to greet the new returning year,
To bless the founder and partake the cheer.
  'And now 'twas time (so fast their numbers rise)
To plant abroad, and people colonies.   ·
The youth drawn forth, as Martin had desired   590
(For so their cruel destiny required),
Were sent far off on an ill-fated day;
The rest would need conduct them on their way,
And Martin went, because he feared alone to stay.
  'So long they flew with inconsiderate haste,   595
That now their afternoon began to waste;
And, what was ominous, that very morn
The Sun was entered into Capricorn:

Which, by their bad astronomers' account,
That week the Virgin balance should remount. 600
An infant moon eclipsed him in his way,
And hid the small remainders of his day.
The crowd amazed pursued no certain mark,
But birds met birds, and justled in the dark.
Few mind the public in a panic fright, 605
And fear increased the horror of the night.
Night came, but unattended with repose;
Alone she came, no sleep their eyes to close;
Alone, and black she came; no friendly stars arose.
  'What should they do, beset with dangers round, 610
No neighbouring dorp, no lodging to be found,
But bleaky plains, and bare unhospitable ground?
The latter brood, who just began to fly,
Sick-feathered and unpractised in the sky,
For succour to their helpless mother call: 615
She spread her wings; some few beneath them crawl;
She spread them wider yet, but could not cover all.
To augment their woes, the winds began to move
Debate in air for empty fields above,
Till Boreas got the skies, and poured amain 620
His rattling hailstones mixed with snow and rain.
  'The joyless morning late arose, and found
A dreadful desolation reign around,
Some buried in the snow, some frozen to the ground.
The rest were struggling still with death, and lay 625
The Crows' and Ravens' rights, an undefended prey,
Excepting Martin's race; for they and he
Had gained the shelter of a hollow tree:
But soon discovered by a sturdy clown,
He headed all the rabble of a town, 630
And finished them with bats, or polled them down.
Martin himself was caught alive, and tried
For treasonous crimes, because the laws provide
No Martin there in winter shall abide.
High on an oak which never leaf shall bear, 635
He breathed his last, exposed to open air;

And there his corps, unblessed, is hanging still,
To show the change of winds with his prophetic bill.'
  The patience of the Hind did almost fail,
For well she marked the malice of the tale;   640
Which ribald art their Church to Luther owes;
In malice it began, by malice grows;
He sowed the serpent's teeth, an iron-harvest rose.
But most in Martin's character and fate
She saw her slandered sons, the Panther's hate,   645
The people's rage, the persecuting State:
Then said, 'I take the advice in friendly part;
You clear your conscience, or at least your heart.
Perhaps you failed in your foreseeing skill,
For Swallows are unlucky birds to kill: 650
As for my sons, the family is blessed
Whose every child is equal to the rest;
No church reformed can boast a blameless line,
Such Martins build in yours, and more than mine;
Or else an old fanatic author lies,   655
Who summed their scandals up by centuries.
But through your parable I plainly see
The bloody laws, the crowd's barbarity;
The sunshine that offends the purblind sight,
Had some their wishes, it would soon be night.   660
Mistake me not; the charge concerns not you;
Your sons are malcontents, but yet are true,
As far as non-resistance makes them so;
But that's a word of neutral sense, you know,
A passive term, which no relief will bring,   665
But trims betwixt a rebel and a king.'
  'Rest well assured,' the Pardalis replied,
'My sons would all support the regal side,
Though Heaven forbid the cause by battle should be tried.'
  The matron answered with a loud 'Amen!'   670
And thus pursued her argument again:
'If, as you say, and as I hope no less,
Your sons will practise what your self profess,
What angry power prevents our present peace?

The Lion, studious of our common good,   675
Desires (and kings' desires are ill withstood)
To join our nations in a lasting love;
The bars betwixt are easy to remove,
For sanguinary laws were never made above.
If you condemn that Prince of tyranny,   680
Whose mandate forced your Gallic friends to fly,
Make not a worse example of your own;
Or cease to rail at causeless rigour shown,
And let the guiltless person throw the stone.
His blunted sword your suffering brotherhood   685
Have seldom felt; he stops it short of blood:
But you have ground the persecuting knife
And set it to a razor edge on life.
Cursed be the wit which cruelty refines
Or to his father's rod the scorpion joins;   690
Your finger is more gross than the great monarch's loins.
But you perhaps remove that bloody note
And stick it on the first Reformers' coat.
Oh, let their crime in long oblivion sleep;
'Twas theirs indeed to make, 'tis yours to keep.   695
Unjust or just is all the question now;
'Tis plain that, not repealing, you allow.
  'To name the Test would put you in a rage;
You charge not that on any former age,
But smile to think how innocent you stand,   700
Armed by a weapon put into your hand.
Yet still remember that you wield a sword
Forged by your foes against your sovereign lord;
Designed to hew the imperial cedar down,
Defraud succession and disheir the crown.   705
To abhor the makers and their laws approve
Is to hate traitors and the treason love:
What means it else, which now your children say,
We made it not, nor will we take away?
  'Suppose some great oppressor had by slight   710
Of law disseised your brother of his right,
Your common sire surrendering in a fright;

Would you to that unrighteous title stand,
Left by the villain's will to heir the land?
More just was Judas, who his Saviour sold;   715
The sacrilegious bribe he could not hold,
Nor hang in peace, before he rendered back the gold.
What more could you have done than now you do,
Had Oates and Bedlow and their Plot been true?
Some specious reasons for those wrongs were found; 720
The dire magicians threw their mists around,
And wise men walked as on enchanted ground.
But now, when Time has made the imposture plain
(Late though he followed truth, and limping held her train),
What new delusion charms your cheated eyes again? 725
The painted harlot might a while bewitch,
But why the hag uncased and all obscene with itch?
  ' The first Reformers were a modest race;
Our peers possessed in peace their native place,
And when rebellious arms o'erturned the State   730
They suffered only in the common fate;
But now the Sovereign mounts the regal chair,
And mitred seats are full, yet David's bench is bare.
Your answer is, they were not dispossessed;
They need but rub their metal on the Test   735
To prove their ore; 'twere well if gold alone
Were touched and tried on your discerning stone,
But that unfaithful Test unfound will pass
The dross of atheists and sectarian brass;
As if the experiment were made to hold   740
For base productions, and reject the gold.
Thus men ungodded may to places rise,
And sects may be preferred without disguise;
No danger to the Church or State from these;
The Papist only has his writ of ease.   745
No gainful office gives him the pretence
To grind the subject or defraud the prince,
Wrong conscience or no conscience may deserve
To thrive, but ours alone is privileged to sterve.
  ' Still thank your selves, you cry; your noble race 750

We banish not, but they forsake the place:
Our doors are open. True, but ere they come,
You toss your censing Test and fume the room;
As if 'twere Toby's rival to expel,
And fright the fiend who could not bear the smell.'   755
  To this the Panther sharply had replied;
But, having gained a verdict on her side,
She wisely gave the loser leave to chide;
Well satisfied to have the butt and peace,
And for the plaintiff's cause she cared the less,   760
Because she sued *in forma pauperis;*
Yet thought it decent something should be said,
For secret guilt by silence is betrayed.
So neither granted all, nor much denied,
But answered with a yawning kind of pride: 765
  'Methinks such terms of proferred peace you bring,
As once Æneas to the Italian king.
By long possession all the land is mine;
You strangers come with your intruding line
To share my sceptre, which you call to join.   770
You plead like him an ancient pedigree
And claim a peaceful seat by Fate's decree:
In ready pomp your sacrificer stands,
To unite the Trojan and the Latin bands:
And, that the league more firmly may be tied,   775
Demand the fair Lavinia for your bride.
Thus plausibly you veil the intended wrong,
But still you bring your exiled gods along;
And will endeavour, in succeeding space,
Those household poppits on our hearths to place.   780
Perhaps some barbarous laws have been preferred;
I spake against the Test, but was not heard.
These to rescind and peerage to restore
My gracious Sovereign would my vote implore;
I owe him much, but owe my conscience more.'   785
  'Conscience is then your plea,' replied the dame,
'Which, well-informed, will ever be the same.
But yours is much of the cameleon hue,

To change the dye with every different view.
When first the Lion sat with awful sway,   790
Your conscience taught you duty to obey;
He might have had your statutes and your Test;
No conscience but of subjects was professed.
He found your temper, and no farther tried,
But on that broken reed, your Church, relied.   795
In vain the sects assayed their utmost art,
With offered treasure to espouse their part;
Their treasures were a bribe too mean to move his heart.
But when, by long experience, you had proved
How far he could forgive, how well he loved;   800
A goodness that excelled his godlike race,
And only short of Heaven's unbounded grace;
A flood of mercy that o'erflowed our isle,
Calm in the rise, and fruitful as the Nile;
Forgetting whence your Egypt was supplied,   805
You thought your Sovereign bound to send the tide;
Nor upward looked on that immortal spring,
But vainly deemed he durst not be a king:
Then Conscience, unrestrained by fear, began
To stretch her limits, and extend the span;   810
Did his indulgence as her gift dispose,
And made a wise alliance with her foes.
Can Conscience own the associating name,
And raise no blushes to conceal her shame?
For sure she has been thought a bashful dame.   815
But if the cause by battle should be tried,
You grant she must espouse the regal side;
O Proteus Conscience, never to be tied!
What Phœbus from the tripod shall disclose
Which are in last resort your friends or focs?   820
Homer, who learned the language of the sky,
The seeming Gordian knot would soon untie;
Immortal powers the term of Conscience know,
But Interest is her name with men below.'

  'Conscience or Interest be it, or both in one,'   825
The Panther answered in a surly tone;

'The first commands me to maintain the crown,
The last forbids to throw my barriers down.
Our penal laws no sons of yours admit,
Our Test excludes your tribe from benefit.   830
These are my banks your ocean to withstand,
Which proudly rising overlooks the land,
And, once let in, with unresisted sway
Would sweep the pastors and their flocks away.
Think not my judgment leads me to comply   835
With laws unjust, but hard necessity:
Imperious need, which cannot be withstood,
Makes ill authentic for a greater good,
Possess your soul with patience, and attend;
A more auspicious planet may ascend;   840
Good fortune may present some happier time,
With means to cancel my unwilling crime;
(Unwilling, witness all ye Powers above!)
To mend my errors and redeem your love:
That little space you safely may allow;   845
Your all-dispensing power protects you now.'
  'Hold,' said the Hind, ''tis needless to explain;
You would postpone me to another reign;
Till when, you are content to be unjust:
Your part is to possess, and mine to trust.   850
A fair exchange proposed of future chance
For present profit and inheritance.
Few words will serve to finish our dispute;
Who will not now repeal would persecute.
To ripen green revenge your hopes attend,   855
Wishing that happier planet would ascend.
For shame, let conscience be your plea no more;
To will hereafter proves she might before;
But she's a bawd to gain, and holds the door.
  'Your care about your banks infers a fear   860
Of threatening floods and inundations near;
If so, a just reprise would only be
Of what the land usurped upon the sea;
And all your jealousies but serve to show

P

Your ground is, like your neighbour-nation, low.   865
To entrench in what you grant unrighteous laws
Is to distrust the justice of your cause,
And argues, that the true religion lies
In those weak adversaries you despise.
  ' Tyrannic force is that which least you fear;   870
The sound is frightful in a Christian's ear:
Avert it, Heaven! nor let that plague be sent
To us from the dispeopled continent.
  ' But piety commands me to refrain;
Those prayers are needless in this Monarch's reign.   875
Behold how he protects your friends opprest,
Receives the banished, succours the distressed!
Behold, for you may read an honest open breast.
He stands in daylight, and disdains to hide
An act to which by honour he is tied,   880
A generous, laudable, and kingly pride.
Your Test he would repeal, his peers restore;
This when he says he means, he means no more.'
  'Well,' said the Panther, 'I believe him just,
And yet——'
                  ' And yet, 'tis but because you must;   885
You would be trusted, but you would not trust.'
The Hind thus briefly; and disdained to enlarge
On power of kings and their superior charge,
As Heaven's trustees before the people's choice,
Though sure the Panther did not much rejoice   890
To hear those echoes given of her once loyal voice.
  ' The matron wooed her kindness to the last,
But could not win; her hour of grace was past.
Whom thus persisting when she could not bring
To leave the Wolf and to believe her King,   895
She gave her up, and fairly wished her joy
Of her late treaty with her new ally:
Which well she hoped would more successful prove
Than was the Pigeon's and the Buzzard's love.
The Panther asked what concord there could be   900
Betwixt two kinds whose natures disagree?'

The dame replied: ''Tis sung in every street,
The common chat of gossips when they meet;
But, since unheard by you, 'tis worth your while
To take a wholesome tale, though told in homely style.

'A plain good man, whose name is understood,   906
(So few deserve the name of plain and good,)
Of three fair lineal lordships stood possessed,
And lived, as reason was, upon the best.
Inured to hardships from his early youth,   910
Much had he done and suffered for his truth:
At land and sea, in many a doubtful fight,
Was never known a more adventurous knight,
Who oftener drew his sword, and always for the right.

'As Fortune would, (his fortune came though late,) 915
He took possession of his just estate;
Nor racked his tenants with increase of rent,
Nor lived too sparing, nor too largely spent;
But overlooked his hinds; their pay was just
And ready, for he scorned to go on trust: 920
Slow to resolve, but in performance quick,
So true that he was awkward at a trick.
For little souls on little shifts rely
And coward arts of mean expedients try;
The noble mind will dare do anything but lie.   925
False friends (his deadliest foes) could find no way
But shows of honest bluntness, to betray;
That unsuspected plainness he believed;
He looked into himself, and was deceived.
Some lucky planet sure attends his birth   930
Or Heaven would make a miracle on earth,
For prosperous honesty is seldom seen
To bear so dead a weight, and yet to win;
It looks as Fate with Nature's law would strive
To show plain-dealing once an age may thrive;   935
And, when so tough a frame she could not bend,
Exceeded her commission to befriend.

'This grateful man, as Heaven increased his store,
Gave God again, and daily fed his poor.

His house with all convenience was purveyed;   940
The rest he found, but raised the fabric where he prayed;
And in that sacred place his beauteous wife
Employed her happiest hours of holy life.
  'Nor did their alms extend to those alone
Whom common faith more strictly made their own;   945
A sort of Doves were housed too near their hall,
Who cross the proverb, and abound with gall.
Though some, 'tis true, are passively inclined,
The greater part degenerate from their kind;
Voracious birds, that hotly bill and breed,   950
And largely drink, because on salt they feed.
Small gain from them their bounteous owner draws,
Yet, bound by promise, he supports their cause,
As corporations privileged by laws.
  'That house, which harbour to their kind affords,   955
Was built long since, God knows, for better birds;
But fluttering there, they nestle near the throne,
And lodge in habitations not their own,
By their high crops and corny gizzards known.
Like harpies, they could scent a plenteous board;   960
Then, to be sure, they never failed their lord:
The rest was form, and bare attendance paid;
They drunk, and eat, and grudgingly obeyed.
The more they fed, they ravened still for more;
They drained from Dan, and left Beersheba poor.   965
All this they had by law, and none repined;
The preference was but due to Levi's kind:
But when some lay-preferment fell by chance,
The gourmands made it their inheritance.
When once possessed, they never quit their claim,   970
For then 'tis sanctified to Heaven's high name;
And, hallowed thus, they cannot give consent
The gifts should be profaned by worldly management.
  'Their flesh was never to the table served;
Though 'tis not thence inferred the birds were starved;
But that their master did not like the food,   976
As rank, and breeding melancholy blood.

Nor did it with his gracious nature suit,
Even though they were not Doves, to persecute :
Yet he refused (nor could they take offence) 980
Their glutton kind should teach him abstinence.
Nor consecrated grain their wheat he thought,
Which, new from treading, in their bills they brought :
But left his hinds each in his private power,
That those who like the bran might leave the flour. 985
He for himself, and not for others, chose,
Nor would he be imposed on, nor impose;
But in their faces his devotion paid,
And sacrifice with solemn rites was made,
And sacred incense on his altars laid. 990
  ' Besides these jolly birds, whose crops impure
Repaid their commons with their salt manure,
Another farm he had behind his house,
Not overstocked, but barely for his use ;
Wherein his poor domestic poultry fed 995
And from his pious hands received their bread.
Our pampered Pigeons with malignant eyes
Beheld these inmates and their nurseries ;
Though hard their fare, at evening and at morn,
A cruise of water and an ear of corn, 1000
Yet still they grudged that modicum, and thought
A sheaf in every single grain was brought.
Fain would they filch that little food away,
While unrestrained those happy gluttons prey.
And much they grieved to see so nigh their hall 1005
The bird that warned St. Peter of his fall ;
That he should raise his mitred crest on high,
And clap his wings and call his family
To sacred rites; and vex the etherial powers
With midnight matins at uncivil hours ; 1010
Nay more, his quiet neighbours should molest,
Just in the sweetness of their morning rest.
  ' Beast of a bird, supinely when he might
Lie snug and sleep, to rise above the light !
What if his dull forefathers used that cry, 1015

Could he not let a bad example die?
The world was fallen into an easier way;
This age knew better than to fast and pray.
Good sense in sacred worship would appear
So to begin as they might end the year.   1020
Such feats in former times had wrought the falls
Of crowing Chanticleers in cloistered walls.
Expelled for this and for their lands, they fled,
And sister Partlet, with her hooded head,
Was hooted hence, because she would not pray a-bed.
The way to win the restiff world to God   1026
Was to lay by the disciplining rod,
Unnatural fasts, and foreign forms of prayer:
Religion frights us with a mien severe.
'Tis prudence to reform her into ease,   1030
And put her in undress, to make her please;
A lively faith will bear aloft the mind
And leave the luggage of good works behind.
  ' Such doctrines in the Pigeon-house were taught;
You need not ask how wondrously they wrought;   1035
But sure the common cry was all for these,
Whose life and precepts both encouraged ease.
Yet fearing those alluring baits might fail,
And holy deeds o'er all their arts prevail,
(For vice, though frontless and of hardened face,   1040
Is daunted at the sight of awful grace,)
An hideous figure of their foes they drew,
Nor lines, nor looks, nor shades, nor colours true;
And this grotesque design exposed to public view.
One would have thought it an Egyptian piece,   1045
With garden-gods, and barking deities,
More thick than Ptolemy has stuck the skies.
All so perverse a draught, so far unlike,
It was no libel where it meant to strike.
Yet still the daubing pleased, and great and small   1050
To view the monster crowded Pigeon-hall.
There Chanticleer was drawn upon his knees,
Adoring shrines and stocks of sainted trees;

And by him a misshapen ugly race;
'The curse of God was seen on every face.   1055
No Holland emblem could that malice mend,
But still the worse the look the fitter for a fiend.
  'The master of the farm, displeased to find
So much of rancour in so mild a kind,
Inquired into the cause, and came to know   1060
The passive Church had struck the foremost blow;
With groundless fears and jealousies possest,
As if this troublesome intruding guest
Would drive the birds of Venus from their nest:
A deed his inborn equity abhorred;   1065
But Interest will not trust, though God should plight his word.
  'A law, the source of many future harms,
Had banished all the poultry from the farms,
With loss of life, if any should be found
To crow or peck on this forbidden ground.   1070
That bloody statute chiefly was designed
For Chanticleer the white, of clergy kind;
But after-malice did not long forget
The lay that wore the robe and coronet.
For them, for their inferiors and allies,   1075
Their foes a deadly Shibboleth devise:
By which unrighteously it was decreed,
That none to trust or profit should succeed,
Who would not swallow first a poisonous wicked weed;
Or that to which old Socrates was curst,   1080
Or henbane juice to swell them till they burst.
The patron, as in reason, thought it hard
To see this inquisition in his yard,
By which the Sovereign was of subjects' use debarred.
  'All gentle means he tried, which might withdraw 1085
The effects of so unnatural a law:
But still the Dove-house obstinately stood
Deaf to their own and to their neighbours' good;
And which was worse, if any worse could be,
Repented of their boasted loyalty;   1090
Now made the champions of a cruel cause,

And drunk with fumes of popular applause:
For those whom God to ruin has designed,
He fits for fate, and first destroys their mind.
  'New doubts indeed they daily strove to raise,   1095
Suggested dangers, interposed delays;
And emissary Pigeons had in store,
Such as the Meccan prophet used of yore,
To whisper counsels in their patron's ear;
And veiled their false advice with zealous fear.   1100
The master smiled to see them work in vain,
To wear him out and make an idle reign:
He saw, but suffered their protractive arts,
And strove by mildness to reduce their hearts;
But they abused that grace to make allies   1105
And fondly closed with former enemies;
For fools are double fools, endeavouring to be wise.
  After a grave consult what course were best,
One, more mature in folly than the rest,
Stood up, and told them with his head aside,   1110
That desperate curcs must be to desperate ills applied:
And therefore, since their main impending fear
Was from the increasing race of Chanticleer,
Some potent bird of prey they ought to find,
A foe professed to him and all his kind: 1115
Some haggared Hawk, who had her eyry nigh,
Well pounced to fasten, and well winged to fly:
One they might trust their common wrongs to wreak.
The Musquet and the Coystrel were too weak;
Too fierce the Falcon; but, above the rest,   1120
The noble Buzzard ever pleased me best:
Of small renown, 'tis true; for, not to lie,
We call him but a Hawk by courtesy.
I know he haunts the Pigeon-house and farm,
And more, in time of war has done us harm: 1125
But all his hate on trivial points depends;
Give up our forms, and we shall soon be friends.
For pigeons' flesh he seems not much to care;
Crammed chickens are a more delicious fare.

On this high potentate, without delay,   1130
I wish you would confer the sovereign sway;
Petition him to accept the government,
And let a splendid embassy be sent.
  'This pithy speech prevailed; and all agreed,
Old enmities forgot, the Buzzard should succeed.   1135
  'Their welcome suit was granted soon as heard,
His lodgings furnished, and a train prepared,
With B's upon their breast, appointed for his guard.
He came, and crowned with great solemnity,
God save king Buzzard! was the general cry.   1140
  'A portly prince, and goodly to the sight,
He seemed a son of Anak for his height:
Like those whom stature did to crowns prefer;
Black-browed and bluff, like Homer's Jupiter;
Broad-backed and brawny built for love's delight,   1145
A prophet formed to make a female proselyte.
A theologue more by need than genial bent;
By breeding sharp, by nature confident,
Interest in all his actions was discerned;
More learned than honest, more a wit than learned; 1150
Or forced by fear or by his profit led,
Or both conjoined, his native clime he fled:
But brought the virtues of his heaven along;
A fair behaviour, and a fluent tongue.
And yet with all his arts he could not thrive,   1155
The most unlucky parasite alive;
Loud praises to prepare his paths he sent,
And then himself pursued his compliment;
But by reverse of fortune chased away,
His gifts no longer than their author stay;   1160
He shakes the dust against the ungrateful race,
And leaves the stench of ordures in the place.
Oft has he flattered and blasphemed the same,
For in his rage he spares no sovereign's name:
The hero and the tyrant change their style   1165
By the same measure that they frown or smile.
When well received by hospitable foes,

The kindness he returns is to expose;
For courtesies, though undeserved and great,
No gratitude in felon-minds beget;   1170
As tribute to his wit the churl receives the treat.
His praise of foes is venomously nice;
So touched, it turns a virtue to a vice:
A Greek, and bountiful, forewarns us twice.
Seven sacraments he wisely does disown,   1175
Because he knows Confession stands for one;
Where sins to sacred silence are conveyed,
And not for fear or love to be betrayed:
But he, uncalled, his patron to control,
Divulged the secret whispers of his soul;   1180
Stood forth the accusing Satan of his crimes,
And offered to the Moloch of the times.
Prompt to assail, and careless of defence,
Invulnerable in his impudence,
He dares the world and, eager of a name,   1185
He thrusts about and justles into fame.
Frontless and satire-proof, he scours the streets,
And runs an Indian muck at all he meets.
So fond of loud report, that not to miss
Of being known (his last and utmost bliss,)   1190
He rather would be known for what he is.
  'Such was and is the Captain of the Test,
Though half his virtues are not here exprest;
The modesty of fame conceals the rest.
The spleenful Pigeons never could create   1195
A prince more proper to revenge their hate;
Indeed, more proper to revenge than save;
A king whom in His wrath the Almighty gave:
For all the grace the landlord had allowed
But made the Buzzard and the Pigeons proud,   1200
Gave time to fix their friends and to seduce the crowd.
They long their fellow-subjects to enthral,
Their patron's promise into question call,
And vainly think he meant to make them lords of all.
  'False fears their leaders failed not to suggest,   1205

As if the Doves were to be dispossest;
Nor sighs nor groans nor goggling eyes did want,
For now the Pigeons too had learned to cant.
The house of prayer is stocked with large increase,
Nor doors nor windows can contain the press: 1210
For birds of every feather fill the abode;
Even Atheists out of envy own a God;
And, reeking from the stews, adulterers come,
Like Goths and Vandals to demolish Rome.
That Conscience, which to all their crimes was mute, 1215
Now calls aloud and cries to persecute:
No rigour of the laws to be released,
And much the less, because it was their Lord's request:
They thought it great their Sovereign to control,
And named their pride nobility of soul.   1220
  ' 'Tis true, the Pigeons and their prince elect
Were short of power their purpose to effect:
But with their quills did all the hurt they could
And cuffed the tender chickens from their food:
And much the Buzzard in their cause did stir,   1225
Though naming not the patron, to infer,
With all respect, he was a gross idolater.
  ' But when the imperial owner did espy
That thus they turned his grace to villany,
Not suffering wrath to discompose his mind,   1230
He strove a temper for the extremes to find,
So to be just as he might still be kind:
Then, all maturely weighed, pronounced a doom
Of sacred strength for every age to come.
By this the Doves their wealth and state possess,   1235
No rights infringed, but licence to oppress:
Such power have they as factious lawyers long
To crowns ascribed, that kings can do no wrong.
But since his own domestic birds have tried
The dire effects of their destructive pride,   1240
He deems that proof a measure to the rest,
Concluding well within his kingly breast
His fowl of nature too unjustly were oppressed.

He therefore makes all birds of every sect
Free of his farm, with promise to respect ·   1245
Their several kinds alike, and equally protect.
His gracious edict the same franchise yields
To all the wild increase of woods and fields,
And who in rocks aloof, and who in steeples builds;
To Crows the like impartial grace affords,   1250
And Choughs and Daws, and such republic birds;
Secured with ample privilege to feed,
Each has his district and his bounds decreed:
Combined in common interest with his own,
But not to pass the Pigeons' Rubicon.   1255
    ' Here ends the reign of this pretended Dove;
All prophecies accomplished from above,
For Shiloh comes the sceptre to remove.
Reduced from her imperial high abode,
Like Dionysius to a private rod,   1260
The passive Church, that with pretended grace
Did her distinctive mark in duty place,
Now touched, reviles her Maker to his face.
    ' What after happened is not hard to guess;
The small beginnings had a large increase,   1265
And arts and wealth succeed, the secret spoils of peace.
'Tis said the Doves repented, though too late
Become the smiths of their own foolish fate:
Nor did their owner hasten their ill hour,
But, sunk in credit, they decreased in power: 1270
Like snows in warmth that mildly pass away,
Dissolving in the silence of decay.   ·
    ' The Buzzard, not content with equal place,
Invites the feathered Nimrods of his race,
To hide the thinness of their flock from sight,   1275
And all together make a seeming goodly flight:
But each have separate interests of their own;
Two Czars are one too many for a throne.
Nor can the usurper long abstain from food;
Already he has tasted Pigeon's blood,   1280
And may be tempted to his former fare,

When this indulgent lord shall late to Heaven repair.
Bare benting times and moulting months may come,
When lagging late they cannot reach their home;
Or rent in schism (for so their fate decrees)   1285
Like the tumultuous College of the Bees,
They fight their quarrel, by themselves opprest;
The tyrant smiles below, and waits the falling feast.'
   Thus did the gentle Hind her fable end,
Nor would the Panther blame it nor commend;   1290
But, with affected yawnings at the close,
Seemed to require her natural repose;
For now the streaky light began to peep,
And setting stars admonished both to sleep.
The dame withdrew, and wishing to her guest   1295
The peace of Heaven, betook her self to rest.
Ten thousand angels on her slumbers wait
With glorious visions of her future state.

NOTES.

NOTES.

Stanzas on Oliver Cromwell.

Stanza 1. The death of Cromwell was on September 3, 1658; the funeral was celebrated on November 23. The meaning of this stanza is, that 'now 'tis time,' after the funeral, to write in honour of Cromwell's memory, and that those who wrote before were too hasty. The comparison with the Romans refers to the custom of letting fly an eagle at the close of the funeral ceremonies of a Roman emperor, which were his consecration or apotheosis. The eagle flying upwards symbolized the ascent of the soul of the deceased emperor to take its place among the gods. These funeral ceremonies are minutely described by Herodianus in the case of the Emperor Severus (Hist. Roman. lib. iv.). Dryden makes reference to this custom again in his play Tyrannic Love, Act iv. Sc. 2:

> 'A God indeed after the Roman style,
>> An eagle mounting from a kindled pile.'

1. line 1. *officious haste*. *officious* means 'friendly,' 'obliging.' Poem on the Coronation, 42:

> 'Officious slumbers haste your eyes to close.'

And Threnodia Augustalis, 370:

> 'The officious Muses came along.'

Compare also 'officious flood' in Annus Mirabilis, stanza 184. 'Officious' has the same meaning in Milton, Paradise Lost, viii. 99:

> 'Yet not to Earth are those bright luminaries
>> Officious, but to thee, Earth's habitant.'

2. 4. *authentic*, stamped with authority, authoritative. This is the usual meaning with Dryden and his contemporaries. Compare The Hind and the Panther, Part iii. 838. One of Dryden's Prologues to the University of Oxford (1673) ends with this couplet:

> 'Kings make their poets whom themselves think fit,
>> But 'tis your suffrage makes authentic wit.'

In his Dedication of Aurengzebe, Dryden, speaking of the King, says, 'he has made authentic my private opinion.'

4. 3. *prevent*, anticipate; the ordinary meaning with Dryden. Compare

Astræa Redux, 67 and 282; Absalom and Achitophel, 344; The Hind and the Panther, Part ii. 641. In stanza 11 of this poem, *prevent* may mean either 'anticipate' or 'hinder,' but the former is probably the meaning.

    5. 2. *circular*, perfect, completely symmetrical.

> 'A man so absolute and circular.'
>
> Massinger, Maid of Honour, Act i. Sc. 2.

> 'In this, sister, your wisdom is not circular.'
>
> Massinger, The Emperor of the East, Act iii. Sc. 2.

> 'Any attaint might disproportion her,
>   Or make her graces less than circular.'
>
> G. Chapman, Mons d'Olive.

The idea is the same in the Latin *rotundus*, as applied by Horace to a perfect man, 'teres atque rotundus' (Sat. ii. 7. 86), and by Cicero to a perfect style, 'apta et quasi rotunda constructio' (Brutus, c. 78). Dryden, in his poem Eleanora, compares the Countess of Abingdon's perfection to an orb 'truly round' (line 273); and 'round eternity' in The Hind and the Panther (Part ii. 19), is explained as Dryden here explains the circular fame of Cromwell,

> 'For in a round what order can be shewed?'

Eternity has neither beginning nor end. Cleaveland has 'Eternity's round womb' (Rupertismus, p. 58 of ed. 1659).

> 'But in his circle wit no end is found.'
>
> Elegy on Cleaveland, before Poems, &c., 1660.

    3. *shewed.* Both spellings *shew* and *show* occur in Dryden's original editions; and the spelling is adapted to the rhyme. Here *shewed* rhymes with *conclude.* In stanzas 32 and 37 *show* rhymes with *go*, and in stanzas 14 and 24 *shown* with *sown* and *own.* In the last couplet of Astræa Redux *foreshew* rhymes with *you.*

    8. 1. *of* is wrongly replaced by *to* in the edition in the State Poems; and *to* is in Scott's edition. Pompey reached the highest point of his prosperity and glory on the occasion of his splendid triumph, on his forty-fifth birthday, after his return to Rome from his great Eastern conquests, B.C. 61. After that, his rule at Rome was attended with many troubles, till at last, vanquished by Cæsar, and a fugitive, he was assassinated in Egypt, B.C. 48, September 25, the day before that which would have completed his fifty-eighth year. Cromwell, on the other hand, first came permanently into notice in the Civil War when he was forty-five; his greatness grew from that hour, and he died at the age of fifty-nine, in great fame and power.

    11. 1. *sticklers* were sidesmen in a fight, who acted as umpires, and separated the combatants when they judged right.

> 'The dragon wing of night o'erspreads the earth
>   And, stickler-like, the armies separates.'
>
> Shakespeare, Troilus and Cressida, Act v. Sc. 8.

They were called *sticklers* from their carrying sticks or staves, with which they interfered between the combatants. The verb *stickle* is used in this sense of interfering to separate combatants in Dryden's Assignation, Act i. Sc. 1 :

> 'Nay then 'tis time to stickle.'

It occurs also in Dryden's Prologue to Southerne's Disappointment, ' roar and stickle,' rhyming with 'conventicle,' which would be either pronounced *conventickle* or with the final *e* making a distinct syllable, as occurs in Dryden with *chronicles, miracles, oracles.* See note on Astræa Redux, 106. Compare also,

> 'He used to lay about and stickle,
>   Like ram or bull at conventicle.'   Hudibras, i. 2. 435.
> 'Faith, cry St. George, let them go to 't and stickle
>   Whether in conclave or in conventicle.'

>   Cleaveland, Smectymnus, p. 39 of Poems, 1659.

The 'former chiefs,' who are compared to 'sticklers,' are the Presbyterian Parliamentary generals of the beginning of the Civil War, Essex, Manchester, Waller, and others, who were thought unwilling to prosecute to the utmost advantages gained against the king, and whom the Independents got rid of through the Self-denying Ordinance and the New Model, making Fairfax commander-in-chief, and Cromwell lieutenant-general.

12. 3. *He fought to end our fighting. end our* wrongly changed to *hinder* in the edition in the State Poems, followed in a few editions.

Assayed. Dryden spells this verb in the same way in The Hind and the Panther, Part iii. 796. But he spells it *essay* in an earlier work, Threnodia Augustalis, 162, and in his latest volume, The Fables. The substantive he uniformly spells *essay.*

4. *Breathing* (sc. opening) *of the vein,* is a peculiar and favourite phrase of Dryden. He uses it in Palamon and Arcite, Bk. iii. 775 :

> 'Nor breathing veins nor cupping will prevail.'

Also in The Spanish Friar, Act v. Sc. 2 : and in translating Virgil's ' ferire venam ' (Georgics, iii. 460), and Juvenal's ' mediam pertundite venam ' (Sat. vi. 46). Dryden's

> 'Stanch the blood by breathing of the vein,'

is illustrated by a passage of Bacon : 'There is a fifth way also in use, to let blood in an adverse part for a revulsion' (Nat. Hist. cent. 1). *Stanch* is spelt *Stench* in the separate edition of this poem of 1659. When Dryden had become prominent as a court-poet in the reign of Charles II, his adversaries frequently taunted him with this ' breathing of the vein,' interpreting it as meaning the execution of Charles I. But the line does not necessarily mean so much. It may mean no more than a vigorous and thorough policy.

13. 2. *That bold Greek who did the East subdue.* Alexander the Great.

14. The meaning of the last three lines is, ' Till the Island might by new maps be shown thick of conquests, &c. as the galaxy is sown with stars.' *Thick of* is one of Dryden's frequent Gallicisms.   It occurs again in his Palamon and Arcite, Bk. i. 230 :

> ' He through a little window cast his sight,
>   Though thick of bars, that gave a scanty light.'

This stanza has puzzled some editors, who have made changes. A semicolon or colon is placed at the end of the first line, and ' Till ' at the beginning of the second is changed into ' Still,' in the edition in the State Poems, in Broughton's, the .Wartons', and Aldine editions. Scott, first edition (1808), also has a stop at the end of the first line.

15. Aulus Gellius, in the Noctes Atticae (lib. iii. c. 6), describes this quality of the palm of thriving under oppressive weights; and, quoting Plutarch, he says that this is why the palm has been chosen as the emblem of victory, ' quoniam ingenium eiusmodi ligni est, ut ingentibus opprimenti-busque non cedat.'   The palm is the date-palm of the East, and the palm of Scripture, *Phoenix dactylifera.*   ' The righteous shall flourish like the palm-tree ' (Psalm xcii. 120).

> ' Well did he know how palms by oppression speed
>   Victorious and the victor's sacred meed ;   ·
>   The burden lifts them higher.'   Cowley, Davideis, Bk. i.

16. 3. *Bologna's walls.*   Guicciardini relates that, when the French were besieged in Bologna in 1512 by the Papal, Spanish, and Venetian forces, a mine laid by the besiegers blew up a part of the walls on which stood a chapel dedicated to the Holy Virgin, and that this, after being carried up so high in air that the besiegers saw through the breach into the town, fell down again exactly into its old place, and that there was no sign of injury. (Storia d'Italia, lib. x.)   See Roscoe's Life of Leo X, ii. 101.

17. 2. *treacherous Scotland.* ' Treacherous ' on account of the rising of 1648, under the Duke of Hamilton, for Charles I, and the war afterwards carried on by the Scots for Charles II, which ended, after the defeat of Charles at Worcester, in the complete subjugation of Scotland. Eighteen months later, when Dryden suddenly transferred all his enthusiasm to Charles, Scottish ' treachery ' would be regarded by him as virtue.

18. 3. *mien,* pronounced *mine* to rhyme with *shine.* Spelt *mine* in the edition of 1659 with Waller's and Sprat's poems, and in the other spelt *mien.* It is spelt and pronounced *mine* in the following couplet of Marvell,

> ' And everything so wished and fine
>   Starts forth withal to its bonne mine.'
>   Appleton House (Works, iii. 220).

The word introduced from the French *mine* is elsewhere spelt *meen* in Dryden, in accordance with the French pronunciation. See The Hind and the Panther, Part i. 33, where it is spelt ' meen ' in the original edition, and rhymes with 'seen.' In a song in Covent Garden Drollery, 'bonne mine' is Anglicised,

> 'She will vanquish all hearts
> With her boon mean and parts.'
>
> P. 32, Second Edition, 1672.

19. 4. *sovereign*, all-powerful. 'A sovereign remedy,' in The Flower and the Leaf, 422.

> 'To me thy tears are sovereign.'
>
> Rival Ladies, Act iii. Sc. 1.

> ''Cause there are pestilent airs which kill men
> In health, must these be soveraigne as suddenly
> To cure in sickness?' Suckling, Brennoralt, p. 20, 1638.

> 'The most sovereign prescription in Galen.'
>
> Shakespeare, Coriolanus, Act ii. Sc. 1.

20. There was a temple of Jupiter Feretrius in Rome, said to have been built by Romulus, who was also said to have given that title to Jupiter in offering to him the spoils taken from Acro, King of the Caeninenses, whom he had slain in battle. Romulus is further said to have ordained that the spoils taken by a Roman general from an enemy's general whom he had slain should be given to Jupiter Feretrius: such spoils were called 'spolia opima' (Livy i. 10). In the history of Rome there were only two subsequent cases of 'spolia opima.' Dryden here seems to mean that all spoils of war were given to Jupiter Feretrius, which was not the case: and he again betrays the same idea in translating 'exuviae bellorum' of Juvenal (Sat. x. 133):

> 'The spoils of war brought to Feretrian Jove.'

Virgil, alluding to the third instance of 'spolia opima,' those gained by Marcellus, assigns the offering to Romulus (Aen. vi. 860):

> 'Tertiaque arma patri suspendet capta Quirino.'

Dryden's translation of this line gives them to Jupiter Feretrius:

> 'And the third spoils shall grace Feretrian Jove.'

21. 2. *in* is wrongly changed into *of* in the edition in the State Poems, which is followed by Scott.

25. 3. *confident* is the spelling throughout Dryden of the word now spelt *confidant*, meaning 'one confided in.'

4. *complexions*, physical temperaments or humours. Compare

> ''Tis ill; though different your complexions are,
> The family of heaven for men should war.'
>
> Palamon and Arcite, Bk. iii. 422.

> 'All dreams, as in old Galen I have read,
> Are from repletion and complexion bred.'
>
> The Cock and the Fox, 140.

See Shakespeare's Hamlet, 'the o'ergrowth of some complexion' (Act i. Sc. 4), and The Merchant of Venice, ' it is the complexion of them all to leave the dam' (Act iii. Sc. 1).

27. 2. *Commons*, the people. Compare, in the Lines addressed to the Duchess of York,

> 'Like Commons, the nobility resort
> In crowding heaps to fill your moving court.'

29. Cromwell in 1657 sent a force of six thousand men into Flanders to act with the French against the Spaniards. The Spaniards were defeated by the French and English at Dunkirk, June 17, 1658, and Dunkirk was ceded to England. The English thus became 'freemen of the Continent.' The Duke of York was with the Spanish army as a volunteer, and Dryden afterwards, with his accustomed versatility, eulogized the Duke as reflecting lustre on his country by serving against this force (Dedication of the Conquest of Granada, 1672). Dryden's lines on the British Lion are poor enough, but even their bathos is exceeded by Waller in his poem on the same occasion:

> 'Beneath the tropics is our language spoke,
> And part of Flanders has received our yoke.'

30. 4. *Alexander.* The reigning Pope was Alexander VII.

31. In this stanza Dryden has altogether departed from truth. The reference can only be to the expedition sent out by Cromwell at the end of 1654, under Penn and Venables, to attack Spain in America and the West Indies, which was a failure. The armament did not get further than the West Indies, where it was repulsed from Hispaniola or St. Domingo ; afterwards it took Jamaica, but it never crossed the Line nor reached gold-mines in South America. It is probable that Dryden wrote in ignorance as to Hispaniola and Jamaica being north of the equator. His writings contain other as great mistakes of carelessness.

34. 2. *does*, changed in the State Poems to *doth*, which has been copied in other editions, including Scott's.

4. *the Vestal.* Tarpeia, who was crushed by the shields of the Sabines, to whom she had betrayed the citadel of Rome.

35. 2. *That* was changed into *The* by Derrick, who has been followed by subsequent editors, including Scott. The change, though slight, is material. '*That* giant-prince,' &c., clearly refers to an individual, and it is most probable that the reference is to the death of Blake, the great admiral, who had died about a twelvemonth before Cromwell, and had been buried with state in Westminster Abbey, September 4, 1657. There is no means of explaining from classical mythology the words 'giant-prince of all the watery herd.' Scott has understood the whole stanza as referring to the great storm which occurred at the time of Cromwell's death. The two last lines of the stanza are doubtless a poetical reference to the storm.

36. The first two months of Richard Cromwell's reign were serene, and there was no sign of danger or trouble for him till his Parliament met,

January 27, 1659. When Dryden wrote this poem in praise of Cromwell, there was a general expectation that his son Richard would easily maintain his power. But within a few months he lost the Protectorate; in eighteen months hence Charles Stuart was restored, and then Dryden was one of the first to extol the Stuarts and the Restoration, as is to be seen in the next poem Astræa Redux.

Astræa Redux.

Line 2. Imitating Virgil:

'Penitus toto divisos orbe Britannos.'   Eclog. i. 67.

l. 3. *A dreadful quiet*, from Tacitus, 'dira quies' (Ann. i. 65).

l. 7. *An horrid stillness first invades the ear.*   This line has been much ridiculed, and, with all respect to Dr. Johnson, who has elaborately argued in favour of an invasion of the ear by stillness, the diction cannot be justified. The following, in ridicule of this line, occurs in a poem called News from' Hell, by Captain Radcliffe:

'Laureat, who was both learned and flórid,
Was damned long since for " silence horrid,"
Nor had there been such clutter made
But that this silence did invade.'
Invade! and so it might well, that's clear,
But what did it invade?—an ear!'

The line is parodied and burlesqued in Duffet's Spanish Rogue (quoted in Genest's History of the Stage, i. 162):

'A silent noise, methinks, invades my ear.'

Compare with Dryden's line one as objectionable in Cowley:

'A dreadful silence filled the hollow place.'

Davideis, Bk. i.

ll. 9–12. Charles X of Sweden died February 12, 1660. He had succeeded Queen Christina in 1654. Sweden had been, during the greater part of his reign, and was at the time of his death, at war with Poland, Russia, Austria, Denmark, and Holland. His son being a minor, Charles X appointed by will regents, and on his death-bed exhorted these to restore peace to his kingdom. Peace was concluded with Denmark and Holland by the treaty of Oliva, May 1660, and with Austria, Prussia, and Poland by the treaty of Copenhagen in July 1660.

ll. 17, 18. By the treaty of the Pyrenees, by which peace was made between France and Spain, November 1654, it was agreed that Louis XIV, king of France, should marry the Infanta Maria Theresa, eldest daughter of Philip IV, king of Spain.

l. 35. *The sacred purple* means the bishops, and *the scarlet gown* the peers.

l. 37. *Typhoeus* (Τυφωεὺs), generally incorrectly printed *Typhœus*. The Greeks also called him Τυφῶs, whence Typhon, his usual name with the English poets. 'Roaring Typhon' (Shakespeare, Troilus and Cressida, Act i. Sc. 3). Milton and Waller also call him Typhon:

> 'Typhon, whom the den
> By ancient Tarsus held.' Paradise Lost, i. 199.

> 'So Jove himself, when Typhon Heaven does brave,
> Descends to visit Vulcan's smoky cave.'
>
> Waller, To the King.

Typhoeus or Typhon, is a hundred-headed giant, of classical mythology, fabled to have once driven Jupiter and the gods from heaven. He was after-wards quelled by Jupiter with a thunderbolt, and stowed away, according to Homer, whom Milton follows, in Cilicia (Il. 783), but Virgil placed him under the islands Inarime and Prochyta, off the west coast of Italy, near Vesuvius (Aen. ix. 716).

l. 45. *Cyclops*, wrongly printed *Cyclop* in most modern editions, including Scott's. 'Cyclops' is both singular and plural with Dryden. It occurs in the plural in Threnodia Augustalis, 441:

> 'With hardening cold and forming heat,
> The Cyclops did their strokes repeat.'

It is the same with *corps*, the usual spelling in Dryden of the word now spelt *corpse*; *corps* is both singular and plural.

l. 51. *tossed by fate.* 'Jactatus fatis' (Virg. Aen. iv. 3).

l. 61. *cozened. couz'ned* in the two early editions. The change of spelling does not affect the metre, the *e* of the last syllable being elided in pronunciation. So again, 'well-couz'ned,' line 128; 'lengthned,' line 135; 'rip'ned,' line 89; and this is the usual, though not uniform, mode of printing words of this class through the early editions of all Dryden's works.

l. 65. *laveering*, tacking; a word of Dutch origin.

> 'To catch opinion as a ship the wind,
> Which blowing cross, the pilot backwards steers,
> And, shifting sails, makes way when he laveers.'
>
> Davenant, Works, p. 280, fol. 1673.

Spelt *laver* in Suckling, but the accent is on the last syllable:

> 'Can you laver against this tempest?'
>
> The Goblins, Act iv. p. 44.

> 'With as much ease as a skipper
> Would laver against the wind.' Id. Act iv. p. 40.

l. 67. *soft Otho.* The Roman Emperor Otho, who committed suicide. He became emperor on the death of Galba, January, A.D. 69; Vitellius disputed his succession; and on the first defeat of his forces by those of Vitellius, he committed suicide at Brixellum, near Parma, in April, A.D. 69. Eutropius says of him that he was 'in privata vita mollis' (Bk. viii. c. 17);

and Martial calls him 'mollis Otho,' in his epigram on his death (vi. 32). His habits were effeminate. Suetonius says of him, 'munditiarum fuit paene muliebrum.' Compare Juvenal, 'pathici gestamen Othonis' (ii. 99).

ll. 69–70. Galba, who preceded Otho as Roman Emperor, had adopted Piso as his successor on account of his virtues. This adoption of Piso led Otho to revolt against Galba, who was slain in battle ; and then came Otho's very short reign.

ll. 73–75. An ungrammatical construction; what is meant is, 'When Heaven had crost his early valour and he had lost all at Worcester, &c.' 'All but the honour lost,' is a literal adaptation of the celebrated phrase ascribed to Francis I of France, when he is said to have announced to his mother his defeat and capture at Pavia by the Imperial troops in 1525, 'Tout est perdu hors l'honneur.' It has been lately ascertained that the exact words of Francis I were, 'De toutes choses ne m'est demeuré que l'honneur et la vie qui est sauvée,' not so epigrammatic, but essentially as fine. See Fournier's L'Esprit dans l'Histoire ; Paris, 1857.

l. 78. The meaning of this line is, that Charles was, as a royal agent, on the look-out for the kingdoms of foreign monarchs. All modern editions, including Scott's, have wrongly ' his kingdoms,' instead of ' their kingdoms.'

l. 94. By *the honoured name of Counseller*, given to Night by the ancients, Dryden perhaps refers to the Greek name for night, Εὐφρόνη, which may be translated ' well-judging,' ' well-minded.' Or he may refer to ἐν νυκτὶ βουλή.

l. 98. *His famous grandsire* is Henry IV of France, maternal grandfather of Charles II.

l. 106. *chronicles* here rhymes with *ease*, and must be pronounced *chroniclees*. This ancient pronunciation and rhyme occurs in later poems of Dryden ; with *miracles*, rhyming with *these*, in Threnodia Augustalis, 414, with *articles*, rhyming with *ease*, in Letter to Sir George Etherege, 37 (written in 1687); and with *oracles*, in the Translation of the Aeneid, Bk. ix.

> 'Their feats I fear not or vain oracles,
> 'Twas given to Venus they should cross the seas.'

In lines 14 and 241, *miracles* pronounced as *miraclees*, distinctly of three syllables, improves the rhythm. In The Hind and the Panther, Part ii. 16, *miracle* rhymes with *tell* and *well*. *Oracles* rhymes with *spells* in Hudibras :

> 'And like the devil's oracles,
> Put into doggerel rhyme her spells.' Part ii. cant. 3. 374.

l. 108. *epoches*. Broughton changed this into *epochas;* Derrick into *epocha*, which has been followed in modern editions, including Scott's. The Wartons' edition has the right word, *epoches*. The line as printed in the original edition of 1661 is,

> 'In story chasmes, in epoche's mistakes.'

The apostrophe decides the plural of *epoche*, from the Greek ἐποχή.

> 'Howe'er, since we're delivered, let there be
> From this flood too another epochee.'

> > > > Cleaveland, Poems, &c., 1660, p. 20.

l. 111. *too too.* This double *too*, very common in old writers, is rare in Charles the Second's reign. It does not occur again in Dryden, but it is in Lord Mulgrave's Essay on Satire, which has been often erroneously ascribed to Dryden, said to be written in 1675:

> 'Till the shrewd fool by thriving too too fast.'

It is to be found in Hudibras:

> 'But Mart was too too politic.'   Part ii. cant. 3. 158.

It occurs in Shakespeare:

> 'What, must I hold a candle to my shames?
> They in themselves, good sooth, are too too light.'

> > > > Merchant of Venice, Act ii. Sc. 6.

l. 115. *who* is wrongly replaced by *which* in modern editions, including Scott's.

l. 119. *strows;* printed *strowes* in the edition of 1661, *strows* in that of 1668. *Strew* is a common spelling in Dryden; but *strows* rhymes with *owes*. Scott has wrongly printed *strews*. In the translation of the Sixth Aeneid *strew* rhymes with *yew:*

> 'The fabric's front with cypress twigs they strew,
> And stick the sides with boughs of baleful yew.'

There are similar variations of spelling for rhyme in Dryden, with *show* and *shew, choose* and *chuse.* See notes on Poem on Cromwell, stanza 57, and on Absalom and Achitophel, line 527.

l. 121. Portunus was the protector of harbours in Roman mythology, and was invoked always for a happy return from a voyage. Dryden introduces him also in his address to the Duchess of Ormond prefixed to Palamon and Arcite, as helping to speed the passage of the Duchess across the Channel to Ireland:

> 'Portunus took his turn, whose ample hand
> Heaved up the lightened keel aud sunk the sand.'

This is an obvious imitation of Virgil:

> 'Et pater ipse manu magna Portunus euntem
> Impulit.'   Aen. v. 241.

l. 122. *the* is wrongly replaced by *ye*, with a comma before it, in modern editions, including Scott's.

l. 144. *As Heaven it self is took by violence.* This idea is probably from St. Matthew xi. 12: 'And from the days of John the Baptist until now the kingdom of heaven suffereth violence, and the violent take it by force.' Compare Pope, Imitation of Horace, ii. 1. 240:

> 'And Heaven is won by violence of song.'

In the preceding line,

  ' Which stormed the skies and ravished Charles from thence,'
Dryden probably had in his mind also the expulsion of Jupiter and the gods
from heaven by the Titans, referred to in line 36, and again in Threnodia
Augustalis, on the subject of prayers for Charles the Second's recovery:

  'So great a throng not Heaven itself could bar,
  'Twas almost borne by force, as in the giant's war.'

l. 148. *travellour*, so spelt in first edition, rhyming with *hour;* in second
edition of 1688 spelt *travellor.* Elsewhere spelt *traveller,* as in Religio Laici,
where *traveller* rhymes with *star.* *travellour* is printed in the early editions
of Oedipus, Act iii. Sc. 1.

ll. 148–150. The construction here is ungrammatical. There is a similar
wrong construction with *like* in Palamon and Arcite, Bk. i. 339. Palamon,
speaking of himself and Arcite hopelessly striving for Emily:

  And both are mad alike, since neither can possess:
  Both hopeless to be ransomed, never more
  To see the sun but as he passes o'er;
  Like Æsop's hounds contending for the bone,
  Each pleaded right and would be lord alone;
  The fruitless fight continued all the day,
  A cur came by and snatched the prize away.'

This passage was misunderstood by John Warton, who thinks that Palamon
ceases to speak with the line ending with *o'er*, and that then Dryden begins to
speak in his own person, ' Like Æsop's hounds' &c.; and this line is wrongly
made to begin a new paragraph in the Wartons' edition, as well as in Scott.

l. 154. This idea of leaning from the stars is a favourite with Dryden:

  ' The gods came downward to behold the wars,
  Sharpening their sights and leaning from their stars.'
         Palamon and Arcite, Bk. iii. 442.

l. 162. *Like gold that chymists make.*

  ' I'm tired of waiting for this chymic gold
  Which fools us young and beggars us when old.'
         Aurengzebe, Act iv. Sc. 1.

l. 164. In most editions there is a stop at the end of this line; in Scott's,
for instance, a note of exclamation. But this is wrong. The meaning is
that Monk's task was to be what God ordained as the charge of muscles,
&c., to dispense spirits through viewless conduits.

l. 173. This simile of the stomach and the food is used again by Dryden
in his Dedication of The Rival Ladies, printed in 1664 : ' As the stomach
makes the best concoction when it strictly embraces the nourishment, and
takes account of every little particle as it passes through.'

l. 180. *scape.* It is always *scape* in the original editions from first to last,
never '*scape or escape.*

l. 182. The two occasions referred to in this line are Cromwell's ejection of the remnant of the Long Parliament in April 1659, and Lambert's violent interruption of its sitting in October, 1659, after it had been restored by the republicans and military chiefs acting together on Richard Cromwell's deposition.

ll. 195-198. These lines contain a reference to the story of Salmoneus, king of Elis, son of Aeolus, who excited the wrath of Jupiter by driving his chariot over a brazen bridge and flinging burning torches around him, to make it seem that he could make thunder and lightning, and so to induce his subjects to regard and treat him as a god. See Virgil, Aen. vi. 585 :

> ' Vidi et crudeles dantem Salmonea poenas,
> Dum flammas Jovis et sonitus imitatur Olympi.'

l. 201. Lodovico Sforza, who murdered his nephew Giovanni Galeazzo Sforza, duke of Milan, and usurped his dukedom, and, after a course of very successful intrigues, was in 1499 driven from Italy by Louis XII of France, and ultimately died a prisoner in France in 1508.

l. 203. *fogue*, from the French *fougue*, fury ; the word thus Anglicised. The editors have all printed *fougue*. Dr. Johnson has said of Dryden, ' He had a vanity, unworthy of his abilities, to show, as may be suspected, the rank of the company with whom he lived, by the use of French words, which had then crept into conversation ; such as *fraicheur* for " coolness," *fougue* for " turbulence," and a few more, none of which the language has incorporated or retained.' *Fraischeur* occurs in Dryden's Poem on the Coronation, line 102. But Johnson is probably wrong in assigning vanity as Dryden's motive : these French words which have not been retained in our language were not more strange then than others used by him, which have remained in use and do not sound strange to us.

l. 208. *And glass-like clearness mixed with frailty bore.* Scott has printed glass-like between two commas. *Glass-like* may be understood, as Scott understood it, as agreeing with *we* of the preceding line, or as agreeing with *clearness*. Shakespeare has expressed that glass is fragile as well as reflective :

> ' *Angelo.*　　　　　　　　Nay, women are frail too.
> 　*Isabel.* Ay, as the glasses where they view themselves,
> 　　　　Which are as easy broke as they make forms.'
> 　　　　　　　　　　Measure for Measure, Act ii. Sc. 4.

The sense is better if *glass-like* is understood as applying to both *clearness* and *frailty*.

l. 224. *lowered*, pronounced as of one syllable ; *lowr'd* in original editions.

l. 225. *Standard*. *Standart* in original editions. The royal standard is meant. Most editors have wrongly printed ' Standards.' Scott prints ' Standart,' following here the old spelling.

l. 230. The ship ' Naseby,' in which Charles embarked for Dover, received from him, as he was on the point of starting, the name 'Royal Charles.'

ll. 234, 235. The Duke of York, afterwards James II, came over in the 'London,' and the Duke of Gloucester in the 'Swiftsure.' The Duke of Gloucester died in September, 1660.

'The Swiftsure groans beneath great Gloucester's weight'
is an imitation of Virgil's description of the great Aeneas, ' ingens Aeneas,' in Charon's bark, Aen. vi. 412:

'Simul accipit alveo
'Ingentem Aenean. Gemuit sub pondere cymba.'

l. 249. *submitted fasces.* From Livy, 'submissis fascibus.' Publius Valerius, consul, called the Roman people together to vindicate himself from false accusations, and he made the lictors who preceded him with the fasces, the emblems of his consular rank, lower them in recognition of the people's superior power. 'Submissis fascibus in concionem escendit' (Livy, ii. 7).

ll. 261-265. See Exodus xxxiii. and xxxiv.

l. 288. A star appeared at noon on the day of Charles the Second's birth, May 29, 1630, as the king his father was proceeding to St. Paul's to give thanks to God for the event. Charles II entered London, when restored to his throne, on his birthday; and Dryden here ascribes renewed force to the star which had been observed on the day of his birth thirty years before. There is nothing to support Scott's unnecessary conjecture that the same star was again visible on May 29, 1660. Cowley and Waller both refer to the star in such a manner as to show that it is only from its appearance on the actual day of Charles's birth that good effect is inferred:

'No star amongst ye all did, I believe,
    Such vigorous assistance give
    As that which, thirty years ago,
    At Charles his birth, did, in despite
    Of the proud sun's meridian light,
His future glories and this year foreshow
    No less effects than these we may
    Be assured of from that powerful ray
Which could outface the sun and overcome the day.'

Cowley's Ode on the Restoration.

'His thoughts rise higher when he does reflect
Of what the world may from that star expect,
Which at his birth appeared to let us see
Day for his sake would with the night agree.'

Waller's Poem on St. James's Park.

Dryden refers again to this star presiding over Charles's birth in Annus Mirabilis, stanza 18. It is mentioned by Herrick in his Pastoral upon the Birth of King Charles :

> ' And that his birth should be more singular,
>   At noon of day was seen a silver star,
>   Bright as the wise men's torch, which guided them
>   To God's sweet babe, when born at Bethlehem.'

Lilly the astrologer declared the star to be the planet Venus; and he was doubtless right. Derrick mentions that Venus was similarly seen by day in 1757. It was lately so seen in May 1868.

l. 292. *Time's whiter series.* 'White' used to mean 'fortunate,' is a Latinism. The line probably is an imitation of Silius Italicus (xv. 53):

> ' Sed current albusque dies horaeque serenae.'

Herrick uses 'white' in this sense frequently in the Hesperides; as,

> ' Adversity trusts none, but only such
>   Whom whitest Fortune dandled has too much.'

and again,

> ' They were discreetly made with white success.'

l. 310. The allusion to France's fear of an exile is either to the ready acquiescence of France in Charles's departure from Paris to take up his residence at Cologne in 1656, or more probably perhaps to the dislike more recently shown by Cardinal Mazarin to Charles's visit to Fuentarabia in the autumn of 1659, when the treaty of the Pyrenees was being negotiated.

l. 317. *your life and blest example wins.* The verb is singular, following the singular number of the noun immediately before it, a common construction of the time. In Threnodia Augustalis, 189, Dryden wrote

> ' Death and despair was in their looks.'

Scott, following Derrick, has changed *wins*, and *sins* of the preceding line, which makes the rhyme, into *win* and *sin;* an unnecessary and improper change. See also The Hind and the Panther, Part ii. 92,

> ' Obliged to laws which Prince and Senate gives.'

Annus Mirabilis.

Dedication.

P. 23, l. 6. *so is it*, unnecessarily changed by most editors, including Scott, into *so it is.*

P. 24, l. 18. *so is*, changed by the editors unnecessarily into *so it is.*

Account of the Poem.

P. 25, l. 10. The play which Dryden asked Sir R. Howard to read for him was probably The Maiden Queen, which was brought out on the stage early in 1667, on the re-opening of the theatres after the Plague and Fire.

The Maiden Queen was composed during the period of closed theatres, from the middle of 1665 to the end of 1666, and during the greater part of this period Dryden was living at Charlton in Wiltshire, whence this letter is dated, the seat of the Earl of Berkshire, his father-in-law, and father of Sir R. Howard.

l. 31. *noblesse,* changed into *nobles* by all modern editors, including Scott. *Noblesse* was in common use in Dryden's time; it occurs in his Essay of Dramatic Poesy: ' But if you mean the mixed audience of the populace and the noblesse,' &c.

P. 27, l. 2. *female rhymes;* such rhymes as of words ending with *e,* as *noble, chronicle, conventicle,* the *e* being pronounced. In the note on Astræa Redux, 106, where *chronicles* rhymes with *ease,* a few other instances of singular rhyming by Dryden of words ending in *cle* are given, one as late as his translation of the Aeneid, published in 1697. See also, for *conventicle* rhyming with *stickle,* the note on Poem on Oliver Cromwell, stanza 11.

l. 7. *the Alaric, the Pucelle;* two French poems, the first by Scudery on the Conquest of Rome by Alaric, and the second by Chapelain on Joan of Arc.

l. 8. *latter,* changed unnecessarily by Scott and other editors to *later.*

l. 10. Dryden makes a mistake in saying that Chapman's translation of Homer is in Alexandrines of six feet; it is in lines of seven feet.

l. 20. *prevail myself of it.* This French idiom (*se prévaloir de*) has been lost in all modern editions, *avail* being substituted for *prevail.* The same change has been made by the editors, including Scott, in Absalom and Achitophel, line 461, where Dryden wrote

'Prevail yourself of what occasion gives.'

arts, incorrectly changed to *art* in Scott's and other editions.

l. 28. *Descriptas servare,* &c. Horace, Ars Poetica, 87.

P. 28, l. 11. *Omnia sponte sua reddit justissima tellus,* a misquotation by Dryden, who probably confused in his memory two passages of Virgil:

'Fundit humo facilem victum justissima tellus,'

Georg. iv. 460,

and 'Omnis feret omnia tellus,' Ecl. iv. 391.

Ovid also says,

'Per se dabat omnia tellus.' Metam. i. 1021.

l. 18. *is it,* changed by Scott and other edito s unnecessarily to *it is.*

l. 32. This comparison of imagination with a spaniel is again used by Dryden in his Dedication to the Earl of Orrery of the Rival Ladies (1664): ' Imagination in a poet is a faculty so wild and lawless, that, like an high-ranging spaniel, it must have clogs tied to it, lest it outrun the judgment.'

P. 29, l. 5. *paronomasia,* a pun; called in humbler language by Dryden and his contemporaries, by Pope also, a clench or clinch.

l. 12. *driving* has been changed by the editors, including Scott, into *deriving.*

P. 30, l. 8. *We see the objects he represents us within their native figures.*
The editors, not understanding *represents us*, which means of course *represents
to us*, have changed Dryden's words to *presents us with in their native figures.*

l. 14. Virgil, Aen. vi. 726.

l. 18. Aen. i. 990.

l. 24. The editors have changed *The Battle of Bulls* to *The Battle of
the Bulls.*

l. 30. *Materiam superabat opus.*   Ovid, Metam. ii. 4.

P. 31, l. 3.   Horace, Ars Poetica, 47.

l. 24. Ars Poetica, 52.

P. 32, l. 6. Compare with this passage another in Dryden's Preface to
Tyrannic Love : ' If with much pains and some success I have drawn a deformed piece, there is as much of art and as near an imitation of nature in
a lazar as in a Venus.'

l. 13. *Stantes*, &c.   Juvenal, Sat. viii. 43.

l. 15. *Spirantia*, &c.   Virgil, Aen. vi. 848.

l. 21. *humi serpere.*   Horace, Ars Poetica, 28 :
> ' Serpit humi tutus nimium timidusque procellae.'

l. 23. *Nunc non*, &c.   Horace, Ars Poetica, 19.

P. 33, l. 1. *Verses to Her Royal Highness the Duchess.*   This is the Duchess
of York, Anne Hyde, daughter of Lord Chancellor Clarendon.   These verses
to her were now for the first time printed ; they had doubtless, before, according to the custom of the time, been circulated in manuscript, and Dryden had
probably received a handsome present from the Duke in return for his complimentary poem.   War had been declared by England against the Dutch in
February, 1665.   The Duke of York, who was Lord High Admiral, took the
command of the fleet, and went to sea in the beginning of May.   On the
3rd of June he engaged with the Dutch fleet off the coast of Suffolk, near
Lowestoft, and obtained a decided victory, showing great bravery in the
battle.   The Duke of York was not permitted to go to sea again after this
victory : the command of the fleet was then given to the Earl of Sandwich.
In August the Duke was sent by the King into Yorkshire, there being fears
of a rising in the north.   His valour at sea and his victory had made him
very popular, and he and the Duchess were received throughout the journey
with great honours.

l. 21. *sea* rhymes with *obey*, and in l. 12 of p. 34 with *way.*   So in
Annus Mirabilis, stanza 9, *sea* rhymes with *lay*, and in stanza 31 with *prey.*
This pronunciation of *sea* is constant through Dryden's works.   *Key* (quay)
and *sea* both rhyme with *weigh* in one of Dryden's latest poems, Cymon and
Iphigenia, 612 :
> ' The crew with merry shouts their anchor weigh,
>   Then ply their oars, and brush the buxom sea,
>   While troops of gathered Rhodians crowd the key.'

Lea is printed *lay* and rhymes with *way* in the original edition of The Flower and the Leaf, 260 :

> 'A tuft of daisies on a flowery lea
> They saw, and thitherward they bent their way.'

The verb *flay* is spelt *flea* in Dryden and Lee's Oedipus, Act iv. Sc. 1.

l. 34. Exodus xvii. 11–13 : 'And it came to pass, when Moses held up his hand, that Israel prevailed ; and when he let down his hand Amalek prevailed. But Moses' hands were heavy : and they took a stone, and put it under him, and he sat thereon ; and Aaron and Hur stayed up his hands, the one on the one side and the other on the other side ; and his hands were steady until the going down of the sun. And Joshua discomfited Amalek and his people with the edge of the sword.' Dryden, who is wont to repeat his illustrations, refers again to this fight of Joshua and Amalek in Britannia Rediviva, 296 :

> 'Nor Amalek can rout the chosen bands,
> While Hur and Aaron hold up Moses' hands.'

l. 35. The battle of June 3 was off the coast of Suffolk, near Lowestoft, and the guns were heard in London. Dryden refers to this fact also in the opening of his Essay of Dramatic Poesy. 'The noise of the cannon from both navies reached all ears about the city, so that, all men being alarmed with it and in a dreadful suspense of the event which they knew was then deciding, every one went following the sound as his fancy led him.' A letter from Lord Arlington, Secretary of State, to the Lord Mayor, in the Public Record Office, giving the official news of the victory, mentions ' the King having been in expectation ever since the guns were heard.'

P. 34, l. 21. Dryden repeats this simile of the phœnix in the Threnodia Augustalis, 364 :

> 'As when the new-born phœnix takes his way
> His rich paternal regions to survey,
> Of airy choristers a numerous train
> Attends his wondrous progress o'er the plain.'

l. 26. Compare with this line Pope's

> 'And all the aerial audience clap their wings.'
>
> Pastorals, i. 16.

l. 29. *I wrong the public to detain you longer.* Probably in imitation of Horace :

> 'In publica commoda peccem
> Si longo sermone morer tua tempora, Caesar.'
>
> Epist. ii. 1. 2.

L 34. *nec sunt parum multi*, &c. Plin. Epist. vii. 28.

The Poem.

[The references hereafter for the poem are to the stanzas.]

Stanza 3, line 2. Dryden's explanation of the formation of precious minerals that they are dew condensed and hardened by the sun or by subterranean fires, is in accordance with the state of knowledge at the time. The idea occurs again in stanza 139, and in his King Arthur (Act v.), where Merlin, prophesying the greatness of England, says :

> ' Behold what rolling ages shall produce,
>
>   The wealth, the loves, the glories of our Isle,
>
>   Which yet, like golden ore, unripe in beds,
>
>   Expect the warm indulgency of heaven
>
>   To call them forth to light.'

And see below in note on stanza 4, line 1, Oldham's ' eastern quarries hardened pearly dew.'

3. *the Idumæan balm did sweat* is an imitation of Virgil :

> ' Odorato sudantia ligno Balsama.'   Georg. ii. 1181.

Dryden introduces the idea of sweating in translating Juvenal, where it is not in the original :

> ' His emitur quicquid graciles huc mittitis Indi.'
>
> Juvenal, Sat. vi. 466.

Translated by Dryden diffusely,

> ' For him the rich Arabia sweats her gum,
>
>   And precious oils from distant Indies come.'

4. 1. *their year.* So printed in the first edition ; in the second edition of 1688, *the year*, which is an evident corruption, but followed by Scott. Oldham has copied from this passage in his David's Lamentation for the Death of Saul and Jonathan :

> ' For you the blest Arabia's spices grew,
>
>   And eastern quarries hardened pearly dew ;
>
>   The sun himself turned labourer for you.'

2. *wexing.* The spelling *wex* is retained ; but the word is printed *waxing* in the second edition of 1688. The spelling *wex* occurs in Dryden's latest poems, as Palamon and Arcite, Bk. ii. 649, and Secular Masque, 30.

5. 4. *our second Punic war.* The first war with the Dutch in the time of the Commonwealth had been ended advantageously for England by Cromwell in 1654 ; this ' second Punic war ' ended with humiliating disasters for England, and by no means as the second Punic war ended for Rome.

8. 1. Louis XIV, who claimed the Spanish Netherlands in right of his wife (elder sister of the infant Charles II of Spain, by a previous marriage of their common father Philip IV, who had died in 1665), abstained at present from pressing his claim, and made delusive proposals to Spain to prevent her entering into engagements with England. He postponed as long as

possible declaring himself for Holland in the war with England. France at last declared war against England, January 1666.

13. 3. *limbec*, spelt *limbeck*, an abbreviation of *alembic*, a still. It occurs again in stanza 116.

> ' I feel my strength each day and hour consume
> Like lilies wasting in a limbec's heat.'
>
> Maiden Queen, Act i. Sc. 3.

Milton speaks of Proteus

> ' drained through a limbec to his native form.'
>
> Par. Lost, iii. 605.

14. 2. *armado*, the Spanish word for ' army,' now always written *armada;* the same with *junto*, a committee, now written *junta* in English.

16. 2. *Angels drew wide the curtains of the skies.* Todd compares this line with one in Sir P. Sidney's Astrophel and Stella :

> ' Phœbus drew wide the curtains of the skies.'

4. *tapers.* This word is often used by Dryden similarly, and was more dignified than it now seems. Compare Religio Laici 18, where the moon and stars are called ' nightly tapers.'

> ' The tapers of the gods,
> The sun and moon, run down like waxen globes.'
>
> Oedipus, Act ii.

The two comets referred to had been seen in the winter of 1664-65, and in the spring of 1665. See Pepys' Diary, Dec. 17, 22, 1664, and April 6, 1665, and the Index to Mrs. Green's Calendar of State Papers, 1664-65 : also the Appendix to Sherborne's Translation of Manilius.

18. On the subject of the star which had appeared on the birthday of Charles II, see note on line 288 of Astræa Redux. ' A round of greater years begun ' is an imitation of Virgil's

> ' Magnus ab integro saeclorum nascitur ordo.'
>
> Eclog. iv.

Compare the lines at the end of Absalom and Achitophel :

> ' Henceforth a series of new time began,
> The mighty years in long procession ran.'

19. 2. This refers to the battle and victory off the coast of Suffolk, June 3, 1665, celebrated in the lines addressed to the Duchess of York. War had been declared by England against the Dutch in February.

20. 4. Sir John Lawson, who had gained naval distinction in the Dutch war of the Commonwealth, was then Admiral of the Duke of York's division of the fleet in the battle of June 2, 1665; he received a shot in the knee, and died a few days after.

21. 3. *Thus, as an offering,* &c. This refers to Protesilaus, the first Greek that landed on the Trojan shore, and the first slain.

22, and Dryden's note. *The Admiral of Holland* was Opdam, who was

R 2

blown up with his flag-ship while engaged in close fight with the Duke of York in the ' Royal Charles.'

23. Compare in The Maiden Queen, Act iii. Sc. 1,

> ' When it thunders,
> Men reverently quit the open air
> Because the angry gods are then abroad.'

24. 3. The war had been preceded by depredations of De Ruyter on British ships and subjects on the coasts of Guinea, in retaliation for proceedings of Sir Robert Holmes against the Dutch near Cape Verde, and at Goree early in 1664.

30. *Our foes we vanquished by our valour left*, an obscure and bad line: the meaning is, ' We left our foes vanquished by our valour.'

' The attempt at Berghen,' described in stanzas 24–30, was altogether unfortunate. The rich Dutch merchant fleets from Smyrna and the East Indies had taken shelter in that neutral Norse harbour. The King of Denmark agreed, on condition of receiving half the profits, to connive at the capture of the fleets by the English. The Earl of Sandwich, who was now Commander-in-Chief, the Duke of York having remained on shore, was so eager for the great prize that he did not wait until the Governor of Bergen had received instructions from the King; and when the attack was made, August 3, 1665, the Danish garrison assisted the Dutch. The attempt was a failure; one English ship was lost. The Dutch fleet under De Witt, which after the engagement convoyed the merchantmen from Bergen, was encountered by a storm, and then Sandwich captured eight men-of-war and some of the richly-laden merchant vessels.

35. 1. Dryden, in his own note, refers to Petronius. The three stanzas preceding this are also in imitation of Petronius in the same chapter of his Satyricon (c. 115): ' Hunc forsitan, proclamo, in aliqua parte terrarum secura expectat uxor; forsitan ignarus tempestatis filius; aut patrem utique reliquit aliquem, cui proficiscens osculum dedit. Haec sunt consilia mortalium, haec vota magnarum cogitationum. . . . Ite nunc, mortales, et magnis cogitationibus pectora implete.' In Dryden's short quotation from Petronius, in the note, he substitutes *fit* for *est*, which is the right word.

37. 1. The Bishop of Munster, a German sovereign prince, had, on the breaking out of the Dutch war, offered to invade Holland with twenty thousand men, in consideration of a subsidy from England, and his offer was accepted and a treaty made with him. He invaded Holland, but after France joined the Dutch in the war, he drew back in fear of France, and secretly made a separate treaty of peace with Holland in April 1666. Dryden, in his own note on ' the German faith,' says that ' Tacitus saith of them, " Nullos mortalium armis aut fide ante Germanos esse." ' But this was said, according to Tacitus, by two Germans, Verritus and Malorix, chiefs of the Frisii, who went on an embassy to Nero. (Tacit. Ann. xiii. 54.)

39. 3. France declared war against England in January 1666.

42. 4. Denmark joined Holland and France in the war against England in February 1666.

43. 2. Charles, in the declaration of war against France, promised protection to all French and Dutch subjects remaining in England, or afterwards entering, who should behave dutifully and not correspond with the enemy; and he invited to come ' especially those of the reformed religion, whose interest he would always particularly adopt.' The French king made no like offer; three months were allowed the English to withdraw with their properties. The two last lines of the stanza refer to Solomon's judgment, in 1 Kings iii, between the two women claiming the child.

51. Dryden, in his own note, refers to Pliny's Panegyric addressed to Trajan, for the phrase ' future people.' The complete sentence is : ' Adventante congiarii die, observare principis egressum in publicum, insidere vias examina infantium futurusque populus solebat.' (c. 26.)

52. 1. *riotous* is pronounced as a dissyllable, *ritous*.

54. 1. Prince Rupert and the Duke of Albemarle were now joint commanders-in-chief of the English fleet. In the last days of May, on information that the Dutch fleet was not ready for sea, and that a French squadron was near the Channel on its way from the Mediterranean to join the Dutch, an order was sent by the government to Prince Rupert to proceed at once from the Downs with twenty ships to meet the French. Albemarle proceeding eastwards at the same time with fifty-four vessels, the remainder of the fleet, was surprised on June 1, by finding the Dutch fleet, under De Ruyter, numbering more than eighty, at anchor off the North Foreland. He resolved at once to fight. The English government had been altogether misinformed. The French fleet had not yet passed the Straits of Gibraltar. Prince Rupert was ordered back from St. Helen's on the 1st of June, the first day of the battle, and he joined Albemarle on the evening of June 3.

59. 1. *high-raised decks.* The Dutch vessels were high-built. Celadon, in the Maiden Queen, compares two sisters : ' Lord, who could love that walking steeple! Ha! give me my little fifth-rate, that lies so snug. She! hang her, a Dutch-built bottom : she's so tall, there's no boarding her.' (Act iv. Sc. 1.)

60. 1. *build.* Spelt *built* in Dryden's editions, and this spelling is preserved by Scott and some other editors.

63. 3. This refers to the awe inspired by the Roman senators in the minds of the invading Gauls, when they sacked Rome, B.C. 387. Livy and Florus describe the incident graphically. ' Adeo haud secus quam venerabundi intuebantur in aedium vestibulis sedentes viros, praeter ornatum habitumque humano augustiorem, majestate etiam quam vultus gravitasque oris prae se ferebat, simillimos Diis.' (Livy, v. 41.) ' Patentes passim domos adeunt; ubi sedentes in curialibus sellis praetextatos senes velut Deos geniosque

venerati, mox eosdem . . . pari vecordia mactant.   (Florus, Epit. Rer. Roman. i. 13.)

66. 3. *show* means 'seem,' 'appear.'   A common use of the verb at the time, and in Dryden.   See stanzas 121, 122, 126, 296.

67. 2. *squander* means simply 'disperse.'   Compare Shakespeare, Merchant of Venice, Act i. Sc. 3, where Shylock says of Antonio's wealth, 'I understand, moreover, upon the Rialto, he hath a third at Mexico, a fourth for England, and other ventures he hath, squandered abroad.'

3. Vice-Admiral Sir William Berkeley fought in the van desperately against superior numbers, and continued to fight after resistance of his ship was hopeless, refusing quarter.   He was at last shot in the throat with a musket-ball, and then retired to his cabin, stretched himself on a table, and there expired.   In the first edition the line was 'Berkeley alone, not making equal way.'   This was changed in that of 1688 to what is retained in the text, 'who nearest danger lay.'   The change must have been intentional: the original words were probably thought capable of being understood as reflecting on Berkeley.   But otherwise the change is not an improvement, as it affects the comparison with Creusa, who was left behind in the flight of Aeneas from Troy.

72. On the morning of June 2, the second day of the battle, the Dutch were reinforced by an accession of sixteen men-of-war to their already greatly superior number.

78. 3. *sheer*, the old spelling of *shear*, meaning 'cut.'   In the second edition of 1688, *sheer* was turned into *steer*, perhaps by a misprint, and *steer* has appeared in all subsequent editions.   *Sheer*, a Dryden word, is clearly the right word here.

> 'And through the brackish waves their passage sheer.'
>
> Spenser's Faery Queene, Bk. iii. c. 4.

83. 2, and Dryden's note.   'Ille autem' is Dryden's reference in a note to the passage in Virgil (Aen. viii. 251) describing Cacus, the son of Vulcan, pursued and attacked by Hercules, whose cattle he had stolen, and vomiting forth smoke to conceal himself.

86. 4. *flies at check.* To 'fly at check' is to fly wildly at any bird, whether game or not.   'A young woman is a hawk upon her wings, and, if she be handsome, she is the more subject to go out at check.'   (Sir John Suckling's Letters, p. 93; Works, ed. 1696.)

clips it, cuts it, flies fast.

91. 4. In the first edition this line stood,

> 'Remote from guns as sick men are from noise.'

It was changed in the edition of 1688 to what appears in the text, which seems an improvement.

94. 2. See 1 Chron. xiii. 7–10: 'And they carried the ark of God in a new cart out of the house of Abinadab: and Uzza and Ahio drave the cart.

And when they came unto the threshingfloor of Chidon, Uzza put forth his hand to hold the ark; for the oxen stumbled. And the anger of the Lord was kindled against Uzza, and he smote him, because he put his hand to the ark; and there he died before God.'

96. 4. *Unknowing to give place.* An imitation of the Latin 'cedere nescius.' (Hor. Od. i. 6. 5.) Compare 'And knows not to retire,' in stanza 152.

> 'I dared the death, unknowing how to yield.'
>
> Palamon and Arcite, Bk. iii. l. 309.

The verb *unknow* is used in Dryden and Lee's Duke of Guise, as meaning ' to be ignorant of.' ' Can I unknow it ? ' (Act v. Sc. 1.)

99. 4, and Dryden's note. The two former victories on the 3rd of June were in 1653 and in 1665, both over the Dutch. The latter was the Duke of York's victory celebrated in Dryden's Verses to the Duchess, p. 33.

102. 1. *Remnants of the night.* *Remnants* was incorrectly changed by Broughton into *remnant*, which appears also in Scott's and other editions. *Remnants* occurs again in stanza 258 : and compare ' remnants of precarious power' (Hind and Panther, i. 510), and 'remnants of long-suffering grace.' (Id. iii. 276.) The word *remainders* also occurs in Hind and Panther, iii. 602, and in the Dedication of Eleonora, where Dryden says, addressing the Earl of Abingdon, ' You may stand aside with the small remainders of the English nobility.'

104. 1. Broughton, Derrick, and others, have changed *here forced to stay* into *he forced to stay*, which is clearly wrong.

109. 3. Compare Virgil's description of the fears of Aeneas :

> 'Et me, quem dudum non ulla injecta movebant
>
> Tela, neque adverso glomerati ex agmine Graii
>
> Nunc omnes terrent aurae, sonus excitat omnis.' Aen. ii. 726.

110. 3. *martlet*, a swift or swallow. Dryden, in a note on a line in The Hind and the Panther (Part iii. line 547),

> ' Some swifts, the giants of the swallow-kind,'

says that these giant swallows are otherwise called martlets.

115. 4. *does* is the word in the first edition : it was changed to *doth* in the edition of 1688.

118. 4. See Joshua x. 13 : ' And the sun stood still, and the moon stayed, until the people had avenged themselves upon their enemies.'

120. 2. *speak thick*, speak quick. Compare Shakespeare, 2 Henry IV, Act ii. Sc. 3 :

> ' And speaking thick, which nature made his blemish,
>
> Became the accents of the valiant;
>
> For those that could speak low and tardily
>
> Would turn their own perfection to abuse,
>
> To seem like him.'

123, and Dryden's note. There is another passage in Virgil (Aen. v. 276) comparing the motion of a ship to that of a wounded snake, which Dryden might also have referred to, and which was doubtless in his mind.

> ' Nequidquam longos fugiens dat corpore tortus;
> Parte ferox, ardensque oculis, et sibila colla
> Arduus attollens, pars vulnere clauda retentat
> Nexantem nodis, seque in sua membra plicantem:
> Tali remigio navis se tarda·movebat.'

124. 3. *passion.* The two early editions have *passion*, which is very intelligible. Broughton printed *passions*, which has been copied by subsequent editors, making *double* a verb instead of an adjective.

129. 2. *let in to:* changed by Broughton to *let into*, which is followed by other editors, including Scott, and which is certainly a deterioration. Dryden doubtless had in his mind the words in Virgil's comparison of the bursting open of the cave of Cacus by Hercules with the opening to view of the shades below :

> ' Trepidentque immisso lumine Manes.'   Aen. viii. 246.

132. 2. *flix*, the fur or soft hair of a hare or other animal.   Dyer, in The Fleece (Bk. i.), speaks of sheep with flix like deer, and not woolly.

> ' No locks Cormandel's nor Malacca's tribe
> Adorn, but sleek of flix and brown like deer.'

Browning uses the word of a lady's hair, ' flix and flax.'   These two words have probably the same origin.   Mr. Halliwell mentions *flix* as a Kentish provincialism in his Dictionary of Archaic and Provincial Words.

137. 1. See St. Mark iii. 11, 12 : ' And unclean spirits, when they saw him, fell down before him, and cried, saying, Thou art the Son of God.   And he straitly charged them that they should not make him known.'

139. Compare stanza 3 and the note on the belief then in vogue of the origin of precious metals.

141. 3. This and the following line have been spoilt by editors by changing *And* at the beginning of the fourth line into *A*.   The change makes nonsense of the passage ; it first appeared in Broughton's edition, and was copied by succeeding editors, including Scott.

143. *imps.* To imp a wing is properly, and technically in falconry, to repair it by grafting new pieces on broken feathers.   Shakespeare says metaphorically in Richard II, Act ii. Sc. 1,

> ' Imp out our drooping country's broken wing.'

Milton, in his Sonnet to Fairfax, has ' imp their serpent-wings.'   Elsewhere Dryden uses the word *imp* loosely.   ' Imped with wings ' he says of young bees, in his Translation of the Fourth Georgic ; and in the play of Oedipus, Act iv. Sc. 1 :

> ' With all the wings with which revenge
> Could imp my flight.'

144. 1, and Dryden's note.   Dryden, in his note, gives only the words

'fervet opus' from Virgil's description of the labours of the bees, part of which he closely imitates.

> 'Pars intra septa domorum
> Narcissi lacrymam et lentum de cortice gluten
> Prima favis ponunt fundamina, deinde tenaces
> Suspendunt ceras: aliae spem gentis, adultos
> Educunt foetus: aliae purissima mella
> Stipant, et liquido distendunt nectare cellas.'
>
> Georg. iv. 159.

145. 1. *foundation*, the word in the first edition: *foundations* in edition of 1688 and subsequent editions.

146. 1. *sides* is printed in the two early editions. I have altered it to *side*, to rhyme with *guide*, but *sides* may still be the right word.

147. 4. *shake*. *shakes* is printed in both the early editions, but the grammar requires *shake*, to which *waves* is nominative.

148. 1. *marling*, a small line smeared with tar, used for winding round ropes and cables to prevent their being fretted by the blocks.

2. *sear-cloth* is here a verb, meaning to cover with sear-cloth, *cere-cloth*, or cloth prepared with wax. Sir Thomas Browne, in his Hydriotaphia, speaks of a dead body 'sound and handsomely cereclothed, that after seventy-eight years was found uncorrupted.' See Richardson's Dictionary, *Sear-cloth* and *Cere-cloth*.

151. The old ship the 'London,' one of the many of the Commonwealth, had been destroyed by fire, and the city of London now presented the king with a new ship, called 'The Loyal London.' This second 'London' was burnt before the end of the war, when the Dutch surprised Chatham, in 1667.

157. *Irish kern*. Irish peasant or soldier. Compare Dryden's Dedication of Palamon and Arcite to the Duchess of Ormond, where he speaks of the reverence of the Irish for her husband's family:

> 'Awed by that house accustomed to command,
> The sturdy kerns in due subjection stand,
> Nor bear the reins in any foreign hand.'

The word occurs in Shakespeare, Macbeth, Act i. Sc. 2, ' kerns and gallow-glasses,' and again, 2 Henry VI, Act iv. Sc. 9,

> 'A puissant and a mighty power
> Of gallowglasses and stout kerns.'

Kerns are light-armed soldiers, having only darts and daggers, or knives; the gallowglasses had helmet, coat of mail, long sword and axe.

4. *fin-like oars*. The same idea is in Denham's Cooper's Hill, 'oar-finned galleys;' and Herrick has 'finny oar' in the Hesperides.

158. Saturn, driven from his throne by his son Jupiter, is said to have fled to Italy, and to have been welcomed there by Janus, king of Latium, and

becoming a partner in Janus's throne, it was further fabled that he civilised the Italians, who under his reign enjoyed a golden age.

4. Derrick unjustifiably made a change in this line, in ignorance of the pronunciation of *commerce* with the accent on the last syllable, and printed the line,

> 'Where coin and commerce first he did invent.'

Derrick was followed by other editors, including Scott. It is strange that the editors did not attend to the accentuation of *commerce* in stanza 163, where it rhymes with *universe*, and where there was no possibility of changing the line. *Commerce* is invariably so pronounced in Dryden's works, and it was the pronunciation of his time as of Shakespeare's :

> 'Peaceful commerce from dividable shores.'
>
> Troilus and Cressida, i. 3.

> 'To join in marriage and commerce
> And only 'mong themselves converse.'
>
> Hudibras, Part iii. cant. 2, l. 1383.

160. 3. *out of Heaven's high way.* Dryden refers, in his note, to Virgil's 'extra anni solisque vias.' It is a favourite idea with Dryden. See the Threnodia Augustalis, line 353,

> 'Out of the solar walk and Heaven's high way.'

Again, in Britannia Rediviva, 1306,

> 'Beyond the sunny walks and circling year.'

165. Dryden was an early member of the Royal Society, founded immediately after the Restoration: he was elected November 19, 1662.

168. 1. After the engagement of the first three days of June, which ended without decisive result, the Dutch fleet was ready and again off the English coast, a fortnight before the English had completed their repairs and preparations.

171. 1. *new* is the word in the first edition; *now* in that of 1688, which has been generally followed. *Now* is no improvement, and was very likely a misprint.

172. 1. *Old expert Allen.* Sir Thomas Allen had, at the beginning of the war, attacked in the Bay of Cadiz a large Dutch merchant squadron homeward bound from Smyrna under convoy, about forty vessels altogether, while he had only seven ships; and he had routed them and made rich prizes. Sir Thomas Allen was Vice-Admiral of the White in the fleet.

173. 1. *Holmes, the Achates, &c.* Sir Robert Holmes had had a fight with the Dutch off the coast of Africa, before the war began. This may be why he is called Achates. *generals'* is here printed instead of *general's*, the usual reading, as there were two generals, Prince Rupert and the Duke of Albemarle. Holmes was Rear-Admiral of the White.

3. Cato the Censor, when he was urging the Romans, in the year before his death, to enter on the third Punic war, having lately returned from

an embassy to Carthage, drew out from under his robe, one day in the senate, some Carthaginian figs, saying that they had been gathered only three days before in Carthage, so near was the enemy to Rome. Compare, in Dryden's Prologue to Amboyna, written in 1673, during the second Dutch war:

> 'As Cato did his Afric fruits display,
> So we before your eyes their Indies lay.'

174. 1. Sir Edmund Spragge had been knighted by Charles for his bravery in the action off Lowestoft of June 3, 1665, at the beginning of the war. He was now under Sir Jeremiah Smith, Vice-Admiral of the Blue. Spragge was killed in the next Dutch war in battle, August 11, 1672.

3. Sir John Harman was captain of the 'Henry' in the battle of the first four days of June. His ship was disabled, and he refused an offer of quarter. Then three fire-ships were successively sent against his ship. She was disengaged successively from two, each of which had set fire to her, and both fires were put out. The third fire-ship was disabled by the 'Henry's' guns. Harman carried his ship off, and took her into Harwich badly damaged. A yard of one of the masts fell on him and broke his leg.

175. 1. Captain, afterwards Sir Frescheville Hollis, son of Gervase Hollis, an antiquary: and this literary character of the father probably explains the singular description of Hollis's parentage. Hollis had lost an arm in the battle of June 3, 1665. He was killed fighting against the Dutch in the next Dutch war, May 28, 1672. The phrase 'on a Muse by Mars begot,' is not happy. Buckingham parodied it against Dryden in his reply to Absalom and Achitophel:

> 'Or more to intrigue the metaphor of man,
> Got on a muse by father Publican.'

Another satirist applied the phrase to the French musical composer, Grabut, who made the music for Dryden's opera, Albion and Albanius, and whose employment by Dryden displeased the public.

> 'Grabut his yokemate ne'er shall be forgot
> Whom the god of tunes upon a Muse begot.'

176. 1. This line is an imitation of Virgil's

> 'Multi praeterea quos fama obscura recondit.'
>
> Aen. v. 302.

184. 2. *host of waters.* This is the reading of the first edition. In the second edition of 1688, it is *hosts of waters*, which is not an improvement, but which has been generally followed.

188. 2. *linstock*, a pointed stick with a fork at the end to hold a lighted match, used by gunners in firing cannon.

194. Admiral de Ruyter was the leader of the Dutch fleet. He is here compared to Terentius Varro, who commanded the Romans in the battle of Cannae, and was after defeat thanked by the Senate because he had engaged

the enemy and had not despaired for the State, ' quia de republicâ non desperasset.'

195 4. *As larks lie dared. dared* means 'thoroughly frightened,' 'scared,' and is specially applied to larks frightened by a hawk or by any object.

'Dared like a lark that, on the open plain,
Pursued and cuffed, seeks shelter now in vain.'
Conquest of Granada, Part ii. Act v. Sc. 2.

'Who leads you now then coursed like a dared lark.'   Oedipus, Act i. Sc. 1.

'Let his grace go forward
And dare us with his cap like larks.'
Shakespeare, Henry VIII, Act iii. Sc. 2.

A *hobby* is a species of hawk. Andrew Marvel, in his treatise on the Growth of Popery and Arbitrary Government, compares the English yacht firing into a Dutch fleet, when the English flag was not saluted, to a lark daring a hobby: ' which must sure,' he says, ' have appeared as ridiculous and un-natural as for a lark to dare the hobby.' (Marvel's Works, i. 474.)

197. 4, and Dryden's note. This battle was fought on July 25, St. James's Day.

201. This stanza is an extraordinary flight of imagination in Dryden, who represents the souls of Henry IV of France, and of William, the first Prince of Orange, repenting rebellion ; Henry ' disowning' hostility to Henry III, against whom he had fought to vindicate his right of succession to the throne, and William ' detesting' the Dutch navy, the strength of the nation, and the means by which the Dutch independence had been achieved.

204. Immediately after the battle of the 25th of July, the English fleet sailed for the Dutch coast, and a squadron was detached, under Sir Robert Holmes, with five ships, to attack the islands of Uly and Schelling. Holmes destroyed a very large Dutch merchant fleet off Uly, only eight or nine out of one hundred and seventy escaping destruction: and he also destroyed with fire the chief town of Schelling. It was estimated that property to the value of upwards of a million sterling was destroyed.

207. 3. *doom*, a peculiar use of the verb. *doom* here means ' send.' The word ' destine' connects the use in this passage with the usual meaning.

209. 1. *unsincere.* The use of *sincere* in the sense of ' pure,' ' unmixed,' the meaning of the Latin *sincerus*, is common with Dryden and his con-temporaries. See Absalom and Achitophel, 43.

'And none can boast sincere felicity.'
Palamon and Arcite, Bk. iii. 897.

'Nulla est sincera voluptas
Solicitumque aliquid laetis intervenit.' Ovid, Metam. vii. 453.

215. The fire broke out on the night of September 2, 1666, and raged for six days.

216. 3. *All was the Night's.* Probably an imitation of 'Omnia noctis

erant,' in a fragment of Varro, quoted by the elder Seneca in the Controversies (iii. 16):

  ' Omnia noctis erant, placida composta quiete.'

Dr. Johnson has made the mistake of attributing this line to Seneca himself.

223. 1. *the Bridge.* London Bridge; where, by old custom, the heads of those executed for treason were exhibited. There is a reference to this custom in Shakespeare's Richard III, Act iii. Sc. 2:

  ' *Catesby (to Lord Hastings).*

    The princes both make high account of you;

  (*Aside*) For they account his head upon the bridge.'

The heads of Hugh Peters and others executed after the Restoration were exhibited on London Bridge.

231. *A key of fire. Key,* the old spelling of *quay,* and pronounced as we pronounce *quay.* Compare Cymon and Iphigenia, 612; and see note at foot of p. 240.

232. 2. The river Simois flowed into the Scamander or Xanthus, which is described by Homer as burnt up by Vulcan, defending Achilles. Scamander called Simois to his aid. (Il. xxi. 307.)

238. 3. *cracks of falling houses. Crack* means the loud noise of anything falling or breaking, and is the same as *crash.*

  ' The breaking of so great a thing should make

  A greater crack.'

    Shakespeare, Antony and Cleopatra, Act v. Sc. 1.

And Shakespeare has ' the crack of doom ' (Macbeth, Act iv. Sc. 1). Addison's couplet, criticised by Pope, has brought the old poetical word *crack* into disrepute:

  ' Should the whole frame of nature round him break,

  He unconcerned would hear the mighty crack.'

' A mighty flaw ' is used by Dryden in his Threnodia Augustalis, with reference to the end of the world.

243. Dryden's account of the King's conduct on the occasion of the fire is free from flattery. Evelyn says, ' It is not indeed imaginable, how extraordinary the vigilance and activity of the King and the Duke was, even labouring in person, and being present to command, order, reward, or encourage workmen, by which he showed his affection to his people and gained them.' (Diary, September 6, 1666.)

247. 1. *Part stays.* So in the original edition. Broughton changed *stays* into *stay,* which is preserved in most following editions, including Scott's.

250. 3. *ignoble crowd.* Probably from Virgil, ' saevitque animis ignobile vulgus ' (Aen. i. 153).

251. 4. *tempest.* So in the original edition. *tempests* in edition of 1688, and in subsequent editions.

256. 2. *require*, used in the strict sense of the Latin *requirere*, ' to seek again.'

257. 4. *repeat*, used exactly in the meaning of the Latin *repetere*, ' to reseek.'   So in Dryden's play of Tyrannic Love,

> ' I'll lead you thence to melancholy groves
> And there repeat the scenes of our past loves.'   (Act iii.)
> ' The pious Trojan so,
> Neglecting for Creusa's life his own,
> Repeats the danger of the burning town.'

Waller, Battle of the Summer Islands, Cant. iii.

267. The Great Plague had destroyed a hundred thousand souls : it had begun in the summer of 1665, and was not quite extinct when the Great Fire desolated London in September 1666.

270. 1. *threatnings* is the word of the first edition, and the spelling of the time.   In the editions of 1688 *threatings* is substituted, and this occurs in most editions.   The modern spelling *threatenings* is substituted for *threatnings* in the text.

273. 3. *affect*, seek, desire.   So in Absalom and Achitophel, 178, ' affecting fame.'

> ' The name of great let other kings affect.'

Epilogue to Albion and Albanius.

' Viamque affectat Olympo' (Virg. Georg. iv. 562) is probably imitated.

274. 2. *in dust*, changed in edition of 1688 into *in the dust*, a decided deterioration.

275. 3. The poet's song here referred to is Waller's poem ' Upon His Majesty's repairing of St. Paul's.'   Denham, in Cooper's Hill, celebrated the same poem of Waller on the repairs made by Charles I.:

> ' Paul's, the late theme of such a Muse, whose flight
> Has bravely reached and soared above thy height,
> Now shalt thou stand, though sword or time or fire,
> Or zeal more fierce than they thy fall conspire ;
> Secure whilst thee the best of poets sings,
> Preserved from ruin by the best of kings.'

280. 4. *give on*.   The words of the original editions ; changed to *drive on* in the edition of 1688, which has been followed by subsequent editors.   But *give on* is much better, and is a phrase of Dryden's.   ' The enemy gives on, by fury led,' occurs in the Indian Emperor, Act ii. Sc. 3.   Waller uses the phrase in describing the Duke of York in the naval battle of June 3, 1665 :

> ' Where he gives on, disposing of their fates,
> Terror and death on his loud cannon waits.'

281. 4. *strove*.   Derrick changed this word to *drove*, and this corruption of Dryden's text has been adopted by following editors, including Scott.

284. 2. *mild rain*, the reading of the first and second editions, was changed

to *cold rain* in the republication of this poem in the Miscellany Poems, 1716, and it has been so printed always since. *Mild* is obviously the proper epithet; *cold* is inconsistent with ' kindly rain.' Scott's edition has *cold*, the wrong word.

290. See Ezra i.–iii. for the return of the Jewish tribes from Babylon after long captivity, and their setting to work to build the Temple of Jerusalem.

292. I. *frequent trines.* A trine, or conjunction of planets in the form of a triangle, was considered fortunate by astrologers: and Dryden adds to *frequent trines* another good omen, the planet Jupiter in ascension. Dryden was learned in astrology and a firm believer. He introduces *trine* as part of a happy omen in his Ode to the Memory of Mrs. Ann Killegrew :

> ' For sure the milder planets did combine
> On thy auspicious horoscope to shine,
> And even the most malicious were in trine.'

Trine appears as a verb in Palamon and Arcite, Bk. iii. l. 389, where there is a conjunction of the deities, Saturn, Venus, and Mars.

> ' By fortune he was now to Venus trined,
> And with stern Mars in Capricorn was joined.'

l. 4. *work* in original edition; *works* in that of 1688, followed by subsequent editors.

succeed. The verb has here an active meaning, ' make to succeed.' So in Dryden's State of Innocence, Act iii. Sc. I : ' Heaven your design succeed.'

295. 2. *New deified. New* is the reading of both the early editions. Derrick changed *new* into *now;* and *now* has appeared in subsequent editions, including Scott's.

299. 3. *And Seine, that would with Belgian rivers join.* This is an allusion to the designs of Louis XIV on Spanish Flanders, which soon broke out in an invasion.

303. The boastful prophecy of this stanza was soon falsified by the events of 1667, when the Dutch fleet under De Ruyter entered the Thames, ascended to Chatham, and there burnt some of our ships. The close of the war was humiliating to England: begun in hot fury in 1665, it ended amid general dissatisfaction in England. Peace was concluded at Breda, July 31, 1667.

Absalom and Achitophel.

Preface.

P. 85. l. 5. *Whig and Tory.* These two names, so familiar to us, were new when Absalom and Achitophel was written. They were first applied in 1679 in the famous controversy about the Exclusion Bill. *Whig* is a word of Scotch origin, *Tory* of Irish. *Whig* is explained in two ways: Roger North says that it meant corrupt and sour whey (Examen, p. 321); Bishop Burnet derives it from *whiggamor*, a driver, from *whiggam*, an exclamation in use in driving horses (Hist. of Own Time, l. 43). Anyhow, the name of Whigs came to be given to the Scottish Covenanters. It was first applied in 1648 in Scotland. Tories, according to Roger North, were 'the most despicable savages among the wild Irish.' Irishmen, as Roman Catholics, were generally favourable to the Duke of York; thus his friends were called Tories. The opponents of the Court were Whigs.

l. 8. When Dryden wrote *Papist*, his editors, from Broughton downward, have printed *Popish*.

l. 11. *Anti-Bromingham.* 'Bromingham' was a cant term of the time for a Whig. Birmingham was famous for base and counterfeit coinage; a 'Birmingham groat' was a current phrase for base coin. Roger North says that the Tories nicknamed their adversaries 'Birmingham Protestants, alluding to the false groats struck at that place.'

l. 13. *a genius.* Most editors, including Scott, have omitted the *a*, thus spoiling the sentence.

l. 23. *rebating the satire.* *Rebate*, an obsolete word, means to blunt.

> 'The keener edge of battle to rebate.'
>
> Palamon and Arcite, Bk. ii. l. 502.

> 'One who never feels
> The wanton stings and motions of the sense,
> But doth rebate and blunt his natural edge
> With profits of the mind, steady and just.'
>
> Shakespeare, Measure for Measure, Act i. Sc. 4.

> 'Let no defeat
> Your sprightly courage and attempts rebate.'
>
> Oldham, Satire iii.

P. 86. l. 14. *The fault on the right hand.* Compare 'an error of the better hand,' in Cymon and Iphigenia, 237.

l. 33. *composure* here means 'arrangement,' 'reconciliation.' Dryden uses *composure* for 'composition' in his poem to Sir Robert Howard:

> 'So in your verse a native sweetness dwells
> Which shames composure and its art excels.'

P. 87. l. 9. *Ense rescindendum.* Ovid has 'ense recidendum' (Metam. i. 191).

The Poem.

It will be most convenient for the reader to preface the notes to the poem with an alphabetical key to the names in the allegory. This key is part of the one published by Tonson, Dryden's publisher, as key to this poem and to the Second Part, the most of which was written by Nahum Tate in the Miscellany Poems, vol. ii. ed. 1716.

Abbethdin, Lord Chancellor.
Absalom, Duke of Monmouth.
Achitophel, Earl of Shaftesbury.
Adriel, Earl of Mulgrave.
Agag, Sir Edmund Bury Godfrey.
Amiel, Mr. (afterwards Sir Edward) Seymour.
Annabel, Duchess of Monmouth.
Balaam, Earl of Huntingdon.
Barzillai, Duke of Ormond.
Bathsheba, Duchess of Portsmouth.
Caleb, Lord Grey of Werke.
Corah, Titus Oates.
David, King Charles II.
Egypt, France.
Ethnic Plot, Popish Plot.
Hebrew Priests, Church of England clergymen.
Hebron, Scotland.
Ishbosheth, Richard Cromwell.
Israel, England.
Issachar, Thomas Thynne of Longleat.
Jebusites, Papists.
Jerusalem, London.
Jewish Rabbins, Doctors of the Church of England.
Jonas, Sir William Jones.
Jotham, Marquis of Halifax.
Michal, Queen Catharine.
Nadab, Lord Howard of Escrick.
Pharaoh, Louis XIV, King of France.
Sagan of Jerusalem, Bishop of London.
Sanhedrin, Parliament.
Saul, Oliver Cromwell.
Shimei, Slingsby Bethel.
Sion, London.
Solymean rout, the London rabble.
Tyre, Holland.
Uzza, John Hall, commonly called Jack Hall.
Western Dome, Westminster Abbey.
Zadoc, Sancroft, Archbishop of Canterbury.
Zaken, member of parliament.
Ziloah, Sir John Moore.
Zimri, Duke of Buckingham.

l. 7. Charles II, who is David in this poem, is described as 'Israel's monarch after Heaven's own heart,' as David is in Scripture. 'The Lord hath sought him a man after his own heart.' (1 Sam. xiii. 14.) 'I have found David the son of Jesse, a man after mine own heart, which shall fulfil all my will.' (Acts xiii. 22.)

l. 17. *this*, changed to *the* by Broughton, and the error copied by following editors, including Scott.

l. 18. *Absalon.* So spelt here and in line 221 for the rhyme, in the early editions; elsewhere always *Absalom*. The Duke of Monmouth, here called Absalom, was the son of Charles by Lucy Walters, and born at Rotterdam, April 9, 1649. Till lately it has been always believed that Monmouth was the eldest of Charles II's natural sons; but a recent publication at Rome from papers in the Jesuits' College there has made known, on the authority of Charles himself, that he had a son by a lady of the name of La Cloche, in Jersey, two or three years earlier, when he was sixteen or seventeen years old. This son entered the noviciate of the Jesuit Society at Rome in 1667, under the name of James La Cloche, and came secretly to England in 1668, calling himself Henri de Rohan. See Gentleman's Magazine for January 1866.

l. 19. *inspired by.* In the first edition it was *with*.

l. 30. Compare with this line Pope's

    'And Paradise was opened in the wild.' Eloisa to Abelard, 133.

l. 34. *Annabel*, Duchess of Monmouth, was Countess of Buccleuch in her own right, and was married to Monmouth in 1665. The name of Scott was afterwards given to Monmouth, and he was created Duke of Buccleuch. The Duchess of Monmouth was an early patron and constant friend of Dryden. He dedicated to her the play of The Indian Emperor, published in 1667. In the Vindication of the Duke of Guise (1683) Dryden calls her 'the patroness of my unworthy poetry'; and in his Dedication of King Arthur to Lord Halifax, in 1691, he says that the Duchess of Monmouth had read the play in manuscript and recommended it to Queen Mary; and he calls the Duchess 'my first and best patroness.'

l. 39. *Amnon's murder.* This is probably a reference to an attack, which Monmouth was believed to have instigated, on Sir John Coventry in 1670, by some officers and men of Monmouth's troop of horseguards, in revenge for a sarcasm uttered in the House of Commons about the King's amours. Coventry's nose was slit with a penknife. The House of Commons took up the affair very warmly, and a new act was passed, making it a capital felony to wound with intention to maim or disfigure, which went by the name of the Coventry Act. There was indeed no murder in this case, but Dryden probably desired to avoid precise identification.

l. 43. *sincerely blest.* See note on Annus Mirabilis, stanza 209, on this use of *sincerely*, meaning 'without alloy.'

l. 59. *Hebron.* In the second part of Absalom and Achitophel, both in Dryden's own part and in Tate's, Hebron means Scotland; and the key to this poem represents Hebron as Scotland. But in this, the only passage of the poem where Hebron occurs, Flanders would be more appropriate. Reference is perhaps made to Monk's march from Scotland to bring about the Restoration.

l. 92. *worn and weakened. and* changed by Derrick to *or;* the error copied by following editors, including Scott.

l. 112. *Not weighed or winnowed.* Derrick substituted *nor* for *or,* which has been followed by most editors, including Scott.

l. 118. *Egyptian rites.* Egypt, in this poem, stands for France, and the Egyptian rites are the Roman Catholic rites prevailing in France.

l. 121. *And* in first edition, instead of *As.*

l. 150. *Achitophel,* Anthony Ashley Cooper, Earl of Shaftesbury. Dryden's subsequent poem of The Medal, not included in this volume, should be read, for a longer and more elaborate and severe attack on Shaftesbury. He had been Lord Chancellor in 1672-73. Dismissed from the chancellorship in November 1673, he was made President of the Privy Council in April 1679, on the reorganization of that body by the King to conciliate the parliamentary opposition. He was, however, removed from that office a few months after. Shaftesbury was now in the Tower, on a charge of high treason: he was apprehended at his house in London, July 2, 1681. After many delays, his trial came on in November, a few days after the publication of this poem, and the grand jury threw out the bill.

l. 152. *counsel* in first edition, instead of *counsels.*

l. 154. *principle* in first edition, instead of *principles.*

ll. 155-157. A correspondent of Notes and Queries, December 7, 1850 (vol. i. p. 468), has supplied the two following quotations in illustration of this triplet on Shaftesbury's fiery soul fretting his pigmy body and o'er-informing the tenement of clay. 'He was one of a lean body and visage, as if his eager soul, biting for anger at the clay of his body, desired to fret a passage through it.' (Fuller's Profane State.)

> 'The purest soul that ere was sent
> Into a clayey tenement.' Carew.

l. 163. *Great wits,* &c. 'Nullum fit magnum ingenium sine mixtura dementiae.' (Seneca, De Tranq. Anim. c. xv. s. 77.)

l. 167. The same idea of ill-usage of Shaftesbury's little body by his active mind appears in a sketch of him in Mulgrave's Essay on Satire, which was erroneously ascribed to Dryden.

> 'As by our little Machiavel we find
> That nimblest creature of the busy kind:
> His legs are crippled, and his body shakes
> Yet his bold mind that all this bustle makes

No pity of its poor companion takes.
What gravity can hold from laughing out
To see that lug his feeble limbs about?
Like hounds ill-coupled, Jowler is so strong
He jades poor Trip and drags him all along.
'Tis such a cruelty as ne'er was known
To use a body thus, though 'tis one's own.'

The Essay on Satire is said to have been written in 1675: it was first circulated in manuscript in 1679. Duke, a friend and imitator of Dryden, has described Shaftesbury in his poem called 'The Review,' and some of his lines bear traces of Dryden's descriptions here and in The Medal.

'Antonius, early in rebellious race
Swiftly set out, nor slackening in his pace;
The same ambition that his youthful heat
Urged to all ills, the little daring brat,
With unabated ardour does engage
The loathsome dregs of his decrepit age.

  . . . . .

The working ferment of his active mind,
In his weak body's cask with pain confined,
Would burst the rotten vessel where 'tis pent,
But that 'tis tapt to give the treason vent.'

The last line is an unseemly allusion to an abscess from which Shaftesbury suffered, originally caused by a fall from a carriage, when he went out to meet King Charles at Breda on the eve of the Restoration. The abscess, which was internal, at one time endangered his life. A severe operation restored him to health, which was afterwards preserved by means of a silver pipe which kept the wound always open.

l. 170. *unfeathered two-legged thing.* Dryden has here appropriated for ribaldry Plato's humorous definition of man, a two-footed animal without wings, ζῶον δίπουν ἄπτερον. Shaftesbury's son was a man of no ability, but was the father of an able man, the third Earl, the metaphysician, author of the Characteristics. Shaftesbury was three times married, but had only two children, sons, by his second wife, Lady Frances Cecil, who died in 1653: one of the two died in infancy.

l. 175. *the triple bond.* The triple alliance of England, Holland, and Sweden of 1667, directed against France. In June 1670, a second treaty, of which Shaftesbury, though at the time a prominent minister, knew nothing, was made with France for war against Holland and the establishment of the Roman Catholic religion in England. The English commissioners who signed this treaty were Arlington, Clifford, Lord Arundel of Wardour, and Sir Richard Bellings; the last two were not ministers. Another treaty was afterwards concluded on December 31, in appearance solely for alliance with France and war against Holland, and this was signed by Buckingham, Shaftesbury (then Lord Ashley), and Lauderdale, together with Arlington and Clifford. But Charles's engagement about the Roman Catholic religion in the treaty of June remained binding; and that treaty was a secret from Buckingham, Shaftesbury, and Lauderdale. Shaftesbury has his share of responsibility for a treaty of alliance with France for a war against Holland. But no one was louder at the time for this war and for the French alliance than Dryden, who wrote in 1673 a bad play, Amboyna, for the express purpose of inflaming the English public against the Dutch. He there proclaimed the alliance of the two kings of England and France to be necessary to destroy the pride of Holland:

> 'Yet is their empire no true growth, but humour,
> And only two kings' touch can cure the tumour.'

These two lines are from Dryden's Epilogue to Amboyna, and the Epilogue concludes with a reference to Cato's 'Delenda est Carthago,' quoted by Shaftesbury in his speech for the King as Chancellor to Parliament in February 1673. Dryden perhaps derived the idea from Shaftesbury's famous speech,

> 'All loyal English will like him conclude,
> Let Cæsar live, and Carthage be subdued.'

The play of Amboyna was dedicated to Lord Clifford, a friend and patron of Dryden, with fulsome praises of Clifford as a statesman. Yet Dryden in 1681 could revile Shaftesbury for 'breaking the triple bond' and 'fitting Israel for a foreign yoke.' He repeats the accusation a few months after in The Medal:

> 'Thus framed for ill, he loosed our triple hold—
> Advice unsafe, precipitous, and bold.
> From hence those tears, that Ilium of our woe:
> Who helps a powerful friend forearms a-foe.
> What wonder if the waves prevail so far,
> When he cut down the banks that made the bar?
> Seas follow but their nature to invade,
> But he by art our native strength betrayed.'

This is a flagrant example of Dryden's reckless inconsistency and unscrupulousness in attack.

l. 179. *Assumed* in first edition instead of *Usurped*.

all-atoning, all-reconciling. The verb *atone* was used differently in Dryden's time from its present use. It meant to 'harmonize,' 'unite,' and was used transitively. Thus in Dryden's Poem on the Coronation, 57:

> 'He that brought peace and discord could atone,
> His name is music of itself alone.'

'To atone her anger' (Love Triumphant, Act iv. Sc. 1), 'To atone the people' (Vindication of Duke of Guise). *Atone* was also spelt *attone*, the two *t*'s coming from the old spelling of *at* with two *t*'s; the origin of the word being *at one*, ‘ to make at one.’ *Alone* is used similarly in Shakespeare : ‘ I would do much to atone them for the love I bear to Cassio ’ (Othello Act iv. Sc. 1).

> ‘ Since we cannot atone you, we shall see
> Justice design the victor's chivalry.’   .
>
> King Richard II, Act i. Sc. 1.

Elsewhere in Shakespeare *atone* is used intransitively, meaning ‘ to agree,’ as in Coriolanus :

> ‘ He and Aufidius can no more atone
> Than violentest contrariety.’

ll. 180-191. These twelve lines were added in the second edition of the poem. A very absurd story has been told, that these lines, containing high praise of Shaftesbury as a Judge, were added by Dryden in gratitude for the gift of a nomination to the Charterhouse School for his third son, Erasmus, by Shaftesbury, after the publication of Absalom and Achitophel. The story was first published in Kippis's edition of the Biographia Britannica, published in 1779. Malone took great pains to refute this very improbable story. Dryden's son Erasmus was admitted to the Charterhouse in February 1683, on a nomination from the King. The first edition of this poem appeared in November, and the second in December, 1681. The story is simply impossible. Immediately after the publication of Absalom and Achitophel, Shaftesbury could not have abased himself by offering a favour to Dryden, even if Dryden were likely to accept it ; and then in a few months, in March 1682, Dryden published The Medal, a yet more savage attack on his supposed forgiving benefactor. After all, the idea of praising Shaftesbury as a Judge is in the lines 192-7, which were in the first edition. Why so much praise was added in the second edition may be variously explained. Dryden may have thought that further explanation was necessary for connecting the passage beginning in line 192,

> ‘ Oh ! had he been content to serve the crown,’

with the preceding denunciation of Shaftesbury as a politician. Or he may have thought that higher praise of him as a Judge might increase by contrast the effect of his abuse of the statesman. Or, as Shaftesbury had in the interval been acquitted of the charge of high treason and had triumphed over his enemies, Dryden may have wished to say something conciliatory for one whom he had so fiercely attacked, and who might now again become formidable.

l. 188. *Abbethdin*, the president of the Jewish judicature. The word is compounded of *ab*, ‘ father,’ and *beth-din*, ‘ house of judgment,’ and means literally ‘ father of the house of judgment.’

l. 196. What is meant by David's tuning his harp for Achitophel if he had been other than he was, and its then resulting that ‘ Heaven had wanted one immortal song,' probably is this, that David would then have addressed a song to Achitophel instead of a lament to Heaven. I have otherwise interpreted the passage in a note in the Globe Edition, there representing the line, 'And Heaven had wanted one immortal song,' as meaning that Dryden's own poem would then have been lost to Heaven; which would be a very arrogant boast. But I believe now that this was a wrong interpretation.

l. 197. *wanted.* *want* is here used in a simple sense no longer current, except provincially, ' to be without.' It occurs in the same sense in Pope:

> ' Friend of my life, which did not you prolong,
>   The world had wanted many an idle song.'
>
> Prologue to Satires, 27.

l. 198. Lord Macaulay, in his Essay on Sir William Temple, pointed out the probable origin of this couplet, in some verses in Knolles's History of the Turks:

> 'Greatness on goodness loves to slide, not stand,
>   And leaves for Fortune's ice Virtue's firm land.'

l. 204. *manifest of crimes*, an imitation of Sallust's ' Manifestus tanti sceleris' (Jugurtha, 39). Dryden uses the same idiom in Palamon and Arcite, Bk. i. 623:

> ' Calisto there stood manifest of shame.'

l. 209. The charge against Shaftesbury of ' making circumstances' of the alleged Popish Plot is totally without proof, and against all probability. Shaftesbury entirely believed in the Plot, as did many others of calmer temperament and high character: one of these was the virtuous Lord Russell. Shaftesbury and Russell were entirely as one in the prosecution of the plot. Bishop Burnet, who disliked Shaftesbury, and blamed him for his vehemence, acquits him of invention. (Hist. of Own Time, ii. 168.)

l. 213. To prove ' the King a Jebusite' was no calumnious attempt of Shaftesbury. We now know very well that Charles was a Roman Catholic before the Restoration, and in indiscreet private talk he frequently betrayed the sentiments of his heart. Burnet and Lord Halifax (in his ' Character of Charles the Second') both assume that he was a Roman Catholic.

l. 219. The accent is on the second syllable of *instinct*, according to the pronunciation of the time. So again in line 535.

l. 227. This line is reproduced by Dryden in The Hind and the Panther, Part i. 211. In one of the poems in Lacrymae Musarum, occasioned by the death of Lord Hastings in 1649, to which collection Dryden contributed his first known poem, the following couplet occurs:

> ' It is decreed we must be drained, I see,
>   Down to the dregs of a democracy.'

The phrase was probably early impressed on Dryden from this poem.

l. 235. *Shuts up* in first edition, instead of *Divides.*

l. 247. *Like one of virtue's fools that feeds on praise.* Scott and most editors wrongly print *feed*.

l. 280. *Naked of* is a Gallicism. Dryden uses *dry* in the same way. 'Dry of pleasure' (Love Triumphant, Act iii. Sc. 1), 'Dry of those embraces' (Amphitryon, Act iii. Sc. 1.)

l. 291. *the general cry.* Scott and most editors wrongly print *their* for *the*.

l. 314. *loyal blood.* Scott and most editors wrongly print *royal* for *loyal*.

l. 318. *mankind's delight.* 'Amor atque deliciae generis humani,' said by Suetonius of the Emperor Titus.

ll. 353–360. This elaborate eulogy on Charles's brother, James Duke of York, may be compared with Dryden's characters of James in the play The Duke of Guise, produced in 1682, and in the Threnodia Augustalis, the elegy on Charles II's death. James's truthfulness is dwelt on in both characters; his merciful and forgiving disposition in the sketch of him in The Duke of Guise, where the King of France praises to the Archbishop of Lyons his ' brother of Navarre' :

> 'I know my brother's nature; 'tis sincere,
> Above deceit, no crookedness of thought;
> Says what he means, and what he says performs;
> Brave but not rash; successful but not proud;
> So much acknowledging, that he's uneasy
> Till every petty service be o'erpaid.

Archp. Some say revengeful.

King.   Some then libel him:
> But that's what both of us have learnt to bear;
> He can forgive, but you disdain forgiveness.'
>   Duke of Guise, Act v. Sc. 1.

> 'For all the changes of his doubtful state
> His truth, like Heaven's, was kept ·inviolate;
> For him to promise is to make it fate.
> His valour can triumph o'er land and main;
> With broken oaths his fame he will not stain,
> With conquest basely bought and with inglorious gain.'
>   Threnodia Augustalis, 485–490.

Compare also Dryden's character of James in The Hind and the Panther, Part iii. beginning at line 906: 'A plain good man,' &c.

l. 416. *million* in first edition, instead of *nation*.

ll. 417, 418. Dryden here describes the government of the Commonwealth before Cromwell's Protectorate as a theocracy. In line 522 he speaks of an ' old beloved theocracy.'

l. 436. This line was changed by Derrick so as to make a question:

> ' Is 't after God's own heart to cheat his heir?'

and Derrick's change has been adopted by succeeding editors, including

Scott. Dryden makes Achitophel assert it to be ' after God's own heart to cheat his heir,' i. e. to deprive the Duke of York of his succession. This is intended for the assertion of a wicked counsellor. Derrick's change spoils the sense.

l. 447. This simile of the lion is again used by Dryden in Sigismunda and Guiscardo, 241 :

> ' For malice and revenge had put him on his guard,
>> So; like a lion that unheeded lay,
>> Dissembling sleep and watchful to betray
>> With inward rage he meditates his prey?'

l. 461. *Prevail yourself. Avail* was substituted by Derrick for *prevail*, and the editors have followed Derrick. The same has happened where Dryden uses the same verb *prevail* reflectively, as in the Preface to Annus Mirabilis.

l. 519. *Levites,* priests ; the Presbyterian ministers displaced by the Act of Uniformity.

l. 525. *Aaron's race,* the clergy. *For* in this line has been carelessly changed into *To* in most editions, including Scott's.

l. 524. *Zimri,* George Villiers, second Duke of Buckingham, a poet as well as a politician, who united great talents with extreme profligacy. There is a well-known brilliant sketch of this Buckingham in Pope's Moral Essays. He ran through a very large fortune.

> ' Alas ! how changed for him
>> That life of pleasure and that soul of whim !
>> Gallant and gay in Cleveden's proud alcove,
>> The bower of wanton Shrewsbury and love ;
>> Or just as gay at council in a ring
>> Of mimicked statesmen and their merry king.
>> No wit to flatter left of all his store !
>> No fool to laugh at, which he valued more.
>> There victor of his health, of fortune, friends,
>> And fame, this lord of useless thousands ends.'

Moral Essays, iii. 309.

Buckingham, in The Rehearsal, had unsparingly ridiculed Dryden's plays, and given Dryden the nickname of Bayes. The Rehearsal was first acted in 1671. Dryden took his revenge on Buckingham now. Buckingham wrote a reply to this poem, under the title, ' Poetic Reflections on a late Poem, entitled Absalom and Achitophel, by a Person of Honour.' This reply was a very poor production, unworthy of the author of The Rehearsal.

l. 574. *Balaam,* the Earl of Huntingdon, younger brother of the Lord Hastings, whose premature death in youth was lamented by Dryden in his first known poem. Lord Huntingdon was now a very zealous member of Shaftesbury's party, bent on the exclusion of James Duke of York from succession to the throne; but he afterwards changed his politics and became a warm adherent of James.

l. 574. *Caleb*, Frederick Lord Grey of Werke, who had no children.

l. 575. *Nadab*, Lord Howard of Escrick, the third peer of that title. He had been lately a prisoner in the Tower on account of accusations made by Fitzharris, and he is accused of having taken the Sacrament when in prison, to assert his innocence, in a mixture of ale and apples called 'lamb's wool.' Lord Howard afterwards became infamous by betraying Lord Russell and Algernon Sydney.

l. 581. *Jonas*, Sir William Jones, the Attorney-General who conducted the prosecutions of the Popish Plot. Mr. Luttrell, in a manuscript note on this poem, says that Sir William Jones drew the Habeas Corpus Act.

l. 585. This line stood in the first edition,

> 'Shimei, whose early youth did promise bring.'

Shimei is Slingsby Bethel, who had been elected one of the sheriffs of London in 1680. He had been conspicuous as a republican before the Restoration, and was a member of Richard Cromwell's parliament. His stinginess was a by-word:

> 'And though you more than Buckingham has spent
> Or Cuddon got, like stingy Bethel save,
> And grudge yourself the charges of a grave.'
>
> Oldham, Imitation of Eighth Satire of Boileau.

l. 595. *vare*, a wand, from the Spanish *vara*. The word occurs in Howel's Letters (p. 161, ed. 1728): 'The proudest don of Spain, when he is prancing upon his ginet in the street, if an alguazil show him his vare, that is, a little white staff he carrieth as a badge of his office, my don will presently off his horse and yield himself his prisoner.' The word *vase* has been substituted for *vare* in some editions, including Scott's.

l. 634. An allusion to the serpent of brass made by Moses, and 'set upon a pole' by God's command, to save the Israelites from the fiery serpents which God had sent for punishment. 'And it came to pass that if a serpent had bitten any man, when he beheld the serpent of brass he lived.' (Numbers xxi. 6, 9.)

l. 637. *earthy:* incorrectly printed *earthly* in some editions.

l. 644. *Ours was a Levite.* Titus Oates had taken orders in the Church of England, and his father was a Church of England clergyman, having been before an Anabaptist minister.

l. 649. *A church vermillion and a Moses' face.* The rubicund look of a jolly churchman, and a shining face supposed to be like that of Moses, when he came down from the Mount (Exod. xxxiv. 29-35).

l. 658. *Rabbinical degree.* Oates represented that he had received the degree of Doctor of Divinity at Salamanca.

l. 665. *wit* in first edition, instead of *writ*.

l. 676. *Agag's murder.* The murder of Sir Edmund Bury Godfrey, the magistrate before whom Oates had deposed on oath his story of the Popish Plot, and who was soon after found dead near Primrose Hill. The believers in the Popish Plot charged the Roman Catholics with having murdered Godfrey in revenge. It was urged on the opposite side that Oates and his witnesses instigated the murder in order to impute it to the Roman Catholics. Sir Edmund Bury Godfrey was reputed friendly to the Roman Catholics, and was said to be unwilling to take the depositions. Dryden's meaning seems to be that Godfrey was murdered at the call of Oates, for being friendly to the Roman Catholics. See 1 Samuel xv. for Samuel's reproaches to Saul for disobeying the Lord's command and sparing Agag.

l. 688. *Dissembling joy* in first edition, instead of *His joy concealed.*

l. 700. *Behold a banished man.* Monmouth had been sent out of England by the King in September 1679, and in November he returned without permission. The King then ordered him again to quit England, and he disobeyed, whereupon he was deprived of all his offices and banished from court.

l. 738. *Wise Issachar, his wealthy western friend.* Thomas Thynne of Longleat, who on account of his wealth went by the name of Tom of Ten Thousand. Thynne was murdered in February 1682, a few months after the publication of this poem, by assassins employed by Count Konigsmark, who desired to marry Lady Ogle, a young heiress to whom Thynne was betrothed.

l. 742. *depth* in first edition, instead of *depths.*

l. 777. In the first edition this line stood,

    ' That power which is for property allowed.'

l. 802. This line has been generally printed after Derrick,

    ' To patch their flaws and buttress up the wall.'

But the change of *the* to *their* before *flaws* is not necessary, nor is it an improvement.

l. 804. Broughton changed *our ark* into *the ark*, and has been generally followed by succeeding editors. But there is no reason for the change.

l. 817. *Barzillai*, the Duke of Ormond, an old Cavalier, who was Lord Lieutenant of Ireland for Charles I at the beginning of the Civil War, and was re-appointed by Charles II to the same post after the Restoration. He was removed in 1669, but re-appointed a few years after; and he was Lord Lieutenant of Ireland at the time of the publication of this poem. The duke was one of Dryden's patrons: Carte, in his life of Ormond, mentions Dryden as one of his periodical dinner-guests. Dryden dedicated, in 1683, to the Duke of Ormond the translation of Plutarch's Lives, to which was prefixed a Life of Plutarch, by Dryden. Ormond died in 1688, before the Revolution. Dryden dedicated his Fables, published in 1699, to the duke's grandson and successor, son of the Earl of Ossory, who had died in July 1680, and who is eulogised in the lines which soon follow.

l. 825. *The court he practised. To practise the court* is a Gallicism.

l. 827. *chuse* is the spelling here to rhyme with *Muse.* Later, in line 979, it is printed *choose*, where the rhyme is with *depose.* In The Hind and the Panther, Part i. line 40, *chuse* rhymes with *use.* See note on Astræa Redux, 119, for similar variety of spelling, *strow* and *strew* to suit rhyme: and it is the same with *show* and *shew* in Dryden.

l. 834. *By unequal fates and Providence's crime.* Compare

> ' Fortunae, Ptolemaee, pudor crimenque Deorum.'
>
> Lucan, Phars. v. 59.

Unequal fates is probably Dryden's translation of Virgil's ' fata iniqua ' (Aen. ii. 257, and x. 380).

l. 858.   *And left this verse,*
> *To hang on her departed patron's hearse.*

Compare Pope,

> ' Or teach the melancholy Muse to mourn,
> Hang the sad verse on Carolina's urn.'
>
> Epilogue to the Satires, 79.

It was an old custom to hang funereal poems on the hearse.

l. 875. *Who best could plead and best can judge a cause.* Here Dryden, who never uses a word at random, speaks of judges who had been barristers, and who formerly were the best pleaders as now the best judges. Broughton, not seeing this, changed *who best could plead*, into *who best can plead:* and succeeding editors followed him. In the Preface to The State of Innocence, Dryden had written, ' He must be a lawyer before he mounts the tribunal.'

l. 877. *Adriel*, John Sheffield, Earl of Mulgrave, who was afterwards made Marquis of Normanby by King William, and Duke of Buckinghamshire by Queen Anne. Mulgrave was a poet, and a great friend of Dryden. He was the author of the Essay on Satire, which was wrongly ascribed to Dryden, and for which Dryden was cudgelled in Rose Alley, in December, 1679. Mulgrave was bountiful to Dryden after the Revolution of 1688, when he had lost the poet-laureateship. Dryden dedicated to him the Translation of the Aeneid. Mulgrave, then Duke of Buckinghamshire, erected a monument to Dryden in Westminster Abbey, in 1720, twenty years after the poet's death. Dryden in writing ' The Muses' friend ' may have had Horace's ' Musis amicus,' applied to Lamia (Od. i. 26), in his mind.

ll. 880, 881. Charles deprived Monmouth of all his offices and honours in 1679; and of these he gave the Lord Lieutenancy of the East Riding of York-shire and the government of Hull to Mulgrave.

l. 882. *Jotham*, George Savile, who inherited a baronetcy and was created by Charles II successively Viscount, Earl, and Marquis of Halifax, was a statesman of great ability and accomplishments. He held the office of Lord Privy Seal, and was one of Charles's chief advisers during the last four years of his reign. He was a ' Trimmer,' the name given to the party of moderation in the violent disputes between Charles and the opposition, headed by Shaftesbury and Russell. He wrote the 'Character of a Trimmer.' Dryden dedicated to him his play of King Arthur, produced and published in 1691; and in this dedication he says that Halifax had 'held a principal place in King Charles's esteem, and perhaps the first in his affection during his latter troubles.' Halifax took a prominent part in bringing about the Revolution of 1688.

ready stands instead of *piercing* in the first edition in line 882.

l. 888. *Hushai*, Laurence Hyde, second son of the Lord Chancellor Clarendon, created in 1680 Viscount Hyde, and in 1682 Earl of Rochester. He was appointed one of the Commissioners of the Treasury in 1679, and soon became first Commissioner and a leading minister. On the accession of James he was made Lord Treasurer. Hyde befriended Dryden. Dryden's and Lee's Duke of Guise was dedicated to Rochester in 1682, and Dryden dedicated to him in 1692 his Cleomenes. In the latter dedication Dryden refers to Rochester's kindness to him when he was powerful at the Treasury in the reigns of Charles II and James II: 'Your goodness has not been wanting to me during the reign of my two masters, and even from a bare Treasury my success has been contrary to that of Mr. Cowley, and Gideon's fleece has there been moistened, when all the ground has been dry about it.'

l. 899. *Amiel*, Edward Seymour, who had been Speaker of the House of Commons from 1673 to 1679. He succeeded to a baronetcy in 1688, and is best known as Sir Edward Seymour. He was the head of the house of Seymour, the then Duke of Somerset being of a younger branch of the family. He opposed the Bill of Exclusion; he was afterwards an eager promoter of the Revolution.

l. 910. *the unequal ruler of the day*, Phaeton. *unequal*, incompetent.

l. 920. *plume*, pluck. The regal rights are to be plucked like a bird's feathers. Elsewhere Dryden uses the word *plume* in the sense of strip or rob by plucking: 'He has left the faction as bare of arguments as Æsop's bird of feathers, and plumed them of all those fallacies and evasions which they borrowed from Jesuits and Presbyterians.' (Vindication of the Duke of Guise.)

> 'One whom, instead of banishing a day,
> You should have plumed of all his borrowed honours.'
>
> Maiden Queen, Act ii. Sc. 1.

> 'Not with more ease the falcon from above
> Trusses in middle air the trembling dove,
> Then plumes the prey.' Translation of Aeneid, xi. 1045.

l. 939. With reference to David's speech, which begins at this line, Spence says that he was told by Pope that 'King Charles obliged Dryden to put his Oxford speech into verse, and to insert it towards the close of his Absalom and Achitophel.' (Anecdotes of Men and Books, p. 112.) The Oxford speech is the speech made by Charles at the opening of the parliament at Oxford, March 21, 1681. There are some points of resemblance in the two speeches, but David's speech is certainly far from being a paraphrase of King Charles's.

ll. 957–960. These four lines about Monmouth were added in the second edition.

l. 966. *destroy* in first edition, intead of *supplant.*

l. 987. Compare Proverbs xxx. 15, 16: 'There are three things that are never satisfied, yea, four things say not, It is enough: the grave; and the barren womb; the earth that is not filled with water; and the fire that saith not, It is enough.'

ll. 1007, 8. *Grace Her hinder parts:* this means *Grace's hinder parts.* In the same way the title of one of Dryden's Fables from Boccaccio is the ' Wife of Bath her Tale.' There is a reference here, as in Astræa Redux (262–265), to the appearance of God to Moses. 'And he (the Lord) said Thou canst not see my face, for there shall no man see me and live. And the Lord said, Behold, there is a place by me, and thou shalt stand upon a rock, and it shall come to pass, while my glory passeth by, that I will put thee in the cleft of the rock, and will cover thee with my hand, while I pass by: and I will take away mine hand and thou shalt see my back parts; but my face shall not be seen.' See The Hind and the Panther, Part iii. line 1040,

> 'Vice, though frontless and of hardened face,
> Is daunted at the sight of awful grace.'

l. 1009. From Ovid; Art Amat, i. 655,

> 'Neque enim lex aequior ulla est
> Quam necis artifices arte perire sua.'

l. 1030. 'Magnus ab integro saeclorum nascitur ordo.'

> Virg. Ecl. iv. 5.

> 'Incipient magni procedere menses.' Id. 12.

And compare in Annus Mirabilis, stanza 18,

> 'And now, a round of greater years begun.'

Religio Laici.

Preface.

P. 122, l. 16. The preface of the Athanasian Creed is, 'Whosoever will be saved, before all things it is necessary that he hold the Catholic faith. Which faith except every one do keep whole and undefiled, without doubt he shall perish everlastingly.

P. 123, l. 1. *interessed.* The form of the time, and always used by Dryden. *Disinteressed* occurs in line 335 of Religio Laici. Both here and in line 335 the old form has been replaced by the editors with the modern word, *interested, disinterested;* and the change in line 335 spoils the rhythm. Dryden has *interessing* in the Preface to the State of Innocence, and *uninteressed* in the prefaces to Troilus and Cressida and Albion and Albanius.

P. 124, l. 11. *Mr. Coleman's letters.* Edward Coleman was Secretary to the Duke of York, and a very zealous Roman Catholic. He had been engaged in correspondence with Père la Chaise, Confessor to Louis XIV, with the Pope's Nuncio, and with other Roman Catholics abroad for bringing about the establishment of the Roman Catholic religion in England. He was the first of Oates's victims: he was executed December 3, 1678.

l. 26. Mariana and the others named are all Jesuit writers of the sixteenth century.

l. 28. Edmund Campian and Robert Parsons were two English Jesuits. Parsons wrote under the name of Doleman. Campian and Parsons obtained in 1580 a bull from the Pope declaring that the previous bull of Pius V deposing and excommunicating Queen Elizabeth did for ever bind the heretics, but not Roman Catholics, until a favourable opportunity arose for putting it in execution. Armed with this bull, they came into England to proclaim that the Pope had power to dethrone monarchs, and that Queen Elizabeth's subjects were freed from their allegiance. Campian was executed for preaching this doctrine in 1581. Parsons fled to Rome, where he published, under the name of N. Doleman, a work with the title 'A Conference about the Next Succession of the Crown of England.' Parsons died at Rome in 1610.

P. 125, l. 27. *Father Cres.* Serenus Cressy was originally chaplain to the Earl of Strafford, and afterwards to Lord Falkland: he subsequently became a Roman Catholic and a Benedictine monk at Douay. After the Restoration he came to England, and was chaplain to the Queen.

P. 126, l. 18. William Tyndal, a zealous Lutheran, was the first translator into English of the New Testament and the Pentateuch. His version was prohibited and publicly burnt by order of Henry VIII, who was against the Lutherans. Tyndal was seized at Brussels and strangled and burnt to death in 1536. His last words were 'Lord, open the King's eyes.'

P. 127, l. 5. Isaac Walton's Life of Hooker, which was published in 1662, is here referred to. In it is the letter of George Cranmer to Hooker here mentioned.

l. 13. *Martin Mar-prelate,* John Penry, a Welsh clergyman of the reign of Queen Elizabeth, who became an Anabaptist and a writer against Episcopacy, under the above *nom de guerre.* He was executed in 1593 for writing against the established religion.

l. 38. *Hacket* and *Coppinger*, two Calvinistic mad enthusiasts. The former proclaimed himself in 1591 in the streets of London as the Messiah, come to purify the Church of England; and Coppinger was one of his prophets. Hacket was executed; Coppinger starved himself to death in prison. A third, Arthington, recanted and was pardoned.

P. 129, l. 29. The 'ingenious young gentleman' for whom Dryden says that he wrote this poem was a Mr. Henry Dickinson, of whom nothing else is known. The name is ascertained by a poem by Duke addressed to him by name as the translator of Father Simon's work; and in the translation the initials H. D. are given as those of the translator. Derrick made a mistake, saying that the translator complimented by Dryden was Richard Hampden, grandson of the famous John Hampden. Richard Simon, the author of the Critical History of the Old Testament, was a priest of the Oratory in Paris, and a good Oriental scholar. He wrote also a Critical History of the New Testament.

The Poem.

l. 21. *the Stagirite*, Aristotle.

l. 56. *triumphs*. The accent is on the last syllable, as was the custom in Dryden's time, and as it always is in his poems. See The Hind and the Panther, Part iii. 566. In Dryden's poem to Lady Castlemaine there is the following line,

> 'Let others still triumph and gain their cause,'

which, in apparent ignorance, is silently altered in R. Bell's edition to

> 'Let others triumph still and gain their cause.'

l. 75. For the use of the verb *renown* as transitive compare Pope:

> 'The bard whom pilfered pastorals renown.'
>
> Prologue to the Satires, i. 173.

ll. 76, 77. Todd has compared the language of these lines to Zophar's in Job: 'Canst thou by searching find out God? canst thou find out the Almighty unto perfection? It is as high as heaven; what canst thou do? deeper than hell; what canst thou know?' (Job xi. 7, 8.)

l. 80. Dryden probably had in his mind Virgil's line,

> 'Magnanimi heroes, nati melioribus annis.' Aen. vi. 649.

l. 193. Scott is much troubled about the word *Son's*, which, according to present notions of correct writing, should be *Son*. What is now still a usual colloquial form of speech was in Shakespeare's and Dryden's times customary in writing:

> 'A thousand moral paintings I can show
> That shall demonstrate these quick blows of Fortune's
> More pregnantly than words.' Timon of Athens, i. 1.

l. 213. *The Egyptian Bishop*, Athanasius, Bishop of Alexandria.

l. 228. The Critical History of the Old Testament, by the Father Richard Simon, a French divine, translated by Mr. Henry Dickinson: see note to p. 129, l. 29.

l. 241. Junius and Tremellius are two Calvinist divines who translated the Scriptures, and whom Simon criticises.

l. 283. This is a clumsy line, to be read thus—

> ' 'Twere worth both Testaments and cast in th' Creed.'

The accent is on the second syllable of *testament* as of *testator*. The editors have generally followed Derrick in omitting *and* to make the line accord with the modern pronunciation of *testament*.

l. 291. *like Esdras.* ' For Esdras had very great skill, so that he omitted nothing of the law and commandments of the Lord, but taught all Israel the ordinances and judgments.' (1 Esdras vii. 7.)

l. 335. This line has been spoilt by editors, including Scott, by printing *disinterested*, instead of Dryden's word *disinteressed*. See note on p. 123, l. 1.

l. 389. A similar line occurs in The Medal (166):

> ' The text inspires not them, but they the text inspire.'

l. 420. Compare Hudibras, iii. 2. 7 :

> ' So ere the storm of war broke out,
> Religion spawned a various rout
> Of petulant capricious sects,
> The maggots of corrupted texts.'

l. 456. Tom Sternhold is the versifier of the Psalms with Hopkins. Dryden refers contemptuously to this version of the Psalms in his portion of the Second Part of Absalom and Achitophel :

> ' Poor slaves in metre, dull and addle-pated,
> Who rhyme below even David's psalms translated.'

Shadwell, whom Dryden here couples with Sternhold, was greatly Sternhold's superior in talent; his comedies have much cleverness and merit. But he was not a good poet. Dryden's Mac Flecnoe is a severe satire exclusively devoted to Shadwell, in reprisal for Shadwell's poem, The Medal of John Bayes, a reply to Dryden's Medal; and he severely attacked Shadwell again, calling him Og, in the Second Part of Absalom and Achitophel, where he couples Shadwell with Settle, who is called Doeg :

> ' And hasten Og and Doeg to rehearse,
> Two fools that crutch their feeble sense on verse,
> Who by my Muse to all succeeding times
> Shall live in spite of their own dogrel rhymes.'

And Dryden thus concludes an apostrophe to Shadwell :

> ' And for my foes may this their blessing be,
> To talk like Doeg and to write like thee.'

The Hind and the Panther.

Preface.

P. 147, l. 26. James II had issued his famous Declaration of Indulgence, suspending all penal laws against Dissenters from the Church of England and abrogating all acts which imposed a religious test for secular office, only a few days before the appearance of this poem. The Declaration is dated April 4, 1687. The Hind and the Panther was licensed April 11, and was published shortly afterwards. The tone of this Preface, conciliatory to Protestant Dissenters, is not in accord with the tone of the poem as regards them. The spirit of the poem is for union of the Church of England with the Roman Catholics in opposition to the Protestant Nonconformists: and it is to be inferred that the Declaration of Indulgence, embracing Protestant Nonconformists and Roman Catholics alike, came by surprise on Dryden when this poem was nearly concluded, and that he endeavoured to reconcile himself in the Preface with the Protestant Dissenters, whom in the poem he had treated roughly. The tactics of James at the outset of his reign were those of Dryden's poem; he found himself compelled to change them, and, in order to benefit the Roman Catholics, to grant equal indulgence to Protestant Dissenters as well.

P. 148, l. 10. This refers to the revocation of the edict of Nantes in 1685 by Louis XIV, and the persecution of the French Protestants.

P. 149, l. 22. Dryden here publishes that he had had a part in a defence of the Duchess of York's statement of her reasons for becoming a Roman Catholic in reply to Stillingfleet. James II had published the statement of the duchess, his first wife, and daughter of Lord Chancellor Clarendon, together with papers found in Charles II's strong box in favour of the Roman Catholic faith. Stillingfleet, then Dean of St. Paul's, replied to this publication. A 'Defence' was published by the King's command, in which Dryden bore a part. Stillingfleet rejoined, and treated Dryden with contemptuous asperity.

l. 35. Dryden had asserted, in his defence of the Duchess of York's paper, that he had seen or heard of no treatise on the virtue of humility written by a Protestant. Stillingfleet called this 'a barefaced assertion of a thing known to be false,' and stated that 'within a few years, besides what has been printed formerly, such a book hath been printed in London.' Dryden now asserts that the publication of Duncomb, which he presumes to be the work alluded to by Stillingfleet, was translated from the Spanish of Rodriguez.

P. 150, l. 11. *Mrs. James.* Eleanor James, the wife of a printer, had lately published 'A Vindication of the Church of England,' in answer to a pamphlet entitled 'A New Test of the Church of England's Loyalty.'

l. 23. The two Episodes or Fables are the tales of the Swallows (Roman Catholics) persuaded to defer flight, and of the Pigeons (Church clergy) who chose a Buzzard (Dr. Burnet) to be their king.

The Poem.

l. 1. *Hind.* The Hind represents the Roman Catholic Church.

l. 6. *Scythian shafts.* The Scythians were great archers, and used poisoned arrows. It is doubtful whether Dryden here uses *Scythian* merely to denote poisoned arrows, or means actually Scythian shafts, as a part of his fable. See note below on *Caledonian*, l. 14.

l. 8. The distinction between *doomed* and *fated* is that *doom* is a sentence which may remain unexecuted, while *fate* is irreversible and irresistible. The witty parodists of The Hind and the Panther overlooked this difference when they ridiculed Dryden for this line. ' Faith, Mr. Bayes, if you were *doomed* to be hanged, whatever you were *fated* to, 'twould give you but small comfort.' (The Country and the City Mouse.) In Annus Mirabilis, stanza 207, merchandise sent to a foreign country is said to be *doomed* to it.

l. 14. *Caledonian wood.* This has been generally interpreted as meaning the old Caledonian wood of Britain in the time of the Romans, and the 'slaughtered army' of the Hind's progeny, 'extended o'er the Caledonian wood,' is explained to be the Roman Catholic priests executed in Great Britain since the Reformation. The explanation is not satisfactory, and the passage is by no means clear. In Palamon and Arcite, Book ii, where the Calydonian boar is introduced, *Calydonian* is spelt *Caledonian* in the original edition; and editors down to Scott and later have continued to print *Caledonian*. I do not feel sure that it should not be *Calydonian* here, though we do not know specially of a Calydonian wood in connexion with the long hunt of the Calydonian boar. *Calydonian* would suit better with the 'Scythian shafts' of line 6. *Calydon* would do for *Caledon* in line 3 of Part iii. of the poem : indeed the sense would be better.

> ' Because the Muse has peopled Calydon
> With Panthers, Bears, and Wolves, and beasts unknown,
> As if we were not stocked with monsters of our own.'

The reading *Calydon* gives point to ' our own' monsters, comparing them with those the poet places in Calydon. Calydon was a city of Aetolia, the mountains round which were the haunt of the famous boar, killed by Meleager. Dryden was very careless in correcting his poems for the press, and classical words are frequently misspelt in the early editions; as *Pardalis*, spelt *Pardelis* in this poem, εὕρηκα spelt εὕρεκα in Religio Laici, 43; and these misspellings have been continued by editors to the last.

l. 23. *corps*, the spelling in Dryden, is used both for singular and plural; it is the same with *Cyclops*. See note on Astræa Redux, line 45.

l. 34. Compare with this couplet on virtue Pope's on vice:

> 'Vice is a monster of so frightful mien,
> As to be hated needs but to be seen.'

l. 35. *The bloody Bear*, the Independent.

l. 37. *The quaking Hare*, the Quaker.

l. 39. *The buffoon Ape*, the Free-thinker.

l. 41. *The Lion*, the King of England. Some scoffer who had conformed to the Church of England or embraced the Roman Catholic religion for royal favour is probably here struck at. It has been suggested that Sunderland, who was a sudden Roman Catholic convert, is intended; but Dryden would hardly wish to offend any Roman Catholic convert, and he was not at all likely at this time to run a risk of offending Sunderland, who was in power. He had flatteringly dedicated ' Troilus and Cressida' to Sunderland in 1679. Dryden's parodists, however, think that there is a personal allusion in this passage, for Bayes is there made to say of it, ' That galls somewhere; I' gad I can't leave it out, though I were cudgelled every day for it.'

l. 43. *The bristled baptist Boar*, the Anabaptist. This sect arose in Germany soon after the rise of Luther, about the year 1521. They invaded Saxony under the leadership of Muncer and Pfeifer; and some years afterwards John of Leyden, with a numerous following, seized Munster and held it for some time. These Anabaptists committed great cruelties, and they were in the end conquered. John of Leyden was torn to pieces with hot pincers when Munster was retaken. The name of Anabaptist was long after in great disrepute.

l. 53. *False Reynard*, the Arian.

ll. 54, 55. The doctrine of Arius, that God the Son was not coexistent, and consequently not coequal, with God the Father, was contested by Athanasius in the Council of Nice, and condemned by that council. The Arian doctrine was embraced by Laelius Socinus, a nobleman of Sienna, towards the end of the sixteenth century: this is the origin of the Socinians. The Protestants of Poland adopted the Socinian doctrine; wherefore Dryden bids the Arian fox to range unkennelled in her Polonian plains (line 152).

l. 95. *Impassible*, incapable of suffering, *impassibilis* (Latin): *impassible* is the derived French word. In most editions, including Scott's, *Impassable* is wrongly substituted.

Penetrating parts means penetrating the parts of matter, instead of separating them. This power of penetrating is a criterion of spirit as distinct from matter. Matter cannot penetrate matter.

l. 99. This passage refers to Christ's appearance among his disciples after the crucifixion, as described in St. John xx. 19, 26. ' Then the same day at evening, being the first day of the week, when the doors were shut where the disciples were assembled for fear of the Jews, came Jesus and stood in the midst, and saith unto them, Peace be unto you.' 'And after eight days again his disciples were within, and Thomas with them : then came Jesus, the doors being shut, and stood in the midst, and said, Peace be unto you.'

l. 104. *quarry*, an object aimed at. The game which a hawk flies at is its quarry. In Annus Mirabilis, stanza 231, the buildings to which the fire was directing itself in the great conflagration of 1666 are called their quarry:

'The flames that to their quarry strove.'

l. 128. *bilanders*, coasting vessels used in Holland and there so called. The French adopted the word *bilandre*, also from the Dutch.

ll. 134, 135. *Could He his Godhead veil with flesh and blood*
And not veil these again to be our food?

This pleading of Dryden in 1687 for the doctrine of Transubstantiation may be compared with his ridicule of the same doctrine in 1681, in Absalom and Achitophel, 120.

'Such savoury deities must needs be good,
As served at once for worship and for food.'

l. 153. *the insatiate Wolf*, the Presbyterian. Dryden here turns suddenly to the Presbyterian, in bidding good-bye to the Arians and Socinians, both comprehended under Reynard the Fox, now denounced by him as 'first apostate to divinity.'

l. 165. The Presbyterians in the time of the Commonwealth wore black skull-caps, which left their ears uncovered; and their hair being close cropped all round, the ears were prominent. 'The ragged tail betwixt his legs,' was the Presbyterian's Geneva cloak.

l. 166. *haggered*, a way of spelling the word *haggard*, and Dryden's usual spelling. But in Part iii. line 1166 of this poem, it is spelt *haggared*.

l. 170. Nothing can be more ribald and offensive than the account of the Presbyterians and their genealogy which follows. Scott interprets the reference to Cambria as pointing to the refusal of the ancient British Church in the seventh century, the monks of Bangor being prominently zealous, to acknowledge the supremacy of the Pope, and admit St. Augustin as metropolitan of Britain by Pope Gregory's appointment. Ethelred, the Saxon king of Northumberland, defeated the British at Chester, and cut to pieces twelve hundred of the monks of Bangor, who had come to assist their countrymen with their prayers. It is however more probable that Dryden in his vituperative vein mixes up the extinction of wolves in Wales by the tribute of wolves' heads imposed on the kings, with the history of British Presbyterians, to whom he has given the name of wolves, and then he suggests that the Presbyterians of his day are of an inferior race to 'Wickliff's brood'—the Lollards, cruelly persecuted in the reign of Henry V.

l. 180. Zuinglius began to preach the Reformation in Zurich about 1518. He was killed in battle in a war between the canton of Zurich and four Roman Catholic cantons.

l. 181. Calvin, having been expelled from France for preaching the doctrines of the Reformation, went to Geneva, where he was appointed Professor of Divinity in 1536. He afterwards left Geneva and taught a French congregation at Strasburg.

l. 183. *Sanhedrim;* spelt *Sanhedrin* by Dryden in Absalom and Achitophel. The latter spelling connects the name with the Greek συνέδριον. Dryden has a note on this line 183, 'Vide Preface to Heylyn's History of Presbyterians.' The passage of Heylyn which he refers to is the following:— 'I know that some out of pure zeal with the cause would fain entitle them [the Presbyterians] to a descent from the Jewish Sanhedrim ordained by God himself in the time of Moses. And that it might comply the better with these ends and purposes, they have endeavoured to make that famous consistory of the seventy elders not only a co-ordinate power with that of Moses, and after his decease with the kings and princes of that state in the public government, but a power paramount and supreme, from which lay no appeal to any but to God himself; a power by which they were enabled not only to control the actions of their kings and princes, but also to correct their persons.' Heylyn proceeds: 'And yet I shall not yield them an antiquity as great as that which they desire, as great as that of Moses or the Jewish Sanhedrim, from which they would so willingly derive themselves.'

l. 187. *devest,* the spelling of the time for the word *divest* now in use, which is clearly a corruption of language. The literal meaning is 'to take clothes off,' and *de* is the proper prefix.

l. 189. Korah and the sons of Levi, who rebelled and were all swallowed up in a pit which opened in the earth, are here compared to a Presbyterian 'class'; *classis*, order.

l. 190. *The Fox,* the Arian, already spoken of as 'false Reynard.'

l. 204. The 'native kennel small' and 'bounded betwixt a puddle and a wall,' is Dryden's contemptuous description of Geneva, the puddle being the great and beautiful lake Leman.

l. 211. This line occurs in Absalom and Achitophel, 227, where see the note.

l. 235. The 'wolfish crew' chased from 'Celtic woods' are the French Protestants driven from France by the revocation of the edict of Nantes in 1685. The contemptuous tone of this passage is in marked contrast with the allusion to the persecution of the French Huguenots in the Preface.

l. 284. *the blessed Pan,* Jesus Christ. In Part ii. line 711, Christ is again spoken of as 'mighty Pan.' Compare Milton's Hymn on Christ's Nativity:

> The shepherds on the lawn
> Or ere the point of dawn,
>   Sate simply chatting in a rustic row;
> Full little thought they then
> That the mighty Pan
>   Was kindly come to live with them below.'

l. 288. This and the two following lines were probably added by Dryden after the publication of the Declaration of Indulgence.

l. 290. *for their foes.* Broughton substituted *from* for *for*, thus making the line nonsense, but his mistake has been adopted by succeeding editors, including Scott.

l. 319. *divisible*, material; divisibility being a criterion of matter.

l. 322. *Such souls as shards produce.* The probable meaning of *shard* here is dung or ordure. The word does not occur again in this sense in Dryden. In his translation of the Second Epode of Horace, he uses *shard* for an edible plant:

> 'Not heathpout or the rarer bird
> Which Phasis or Ionia yields,
> More pleasing morsels would afford
> Than the fat olives of my fields;
> Than shards or mallows for the pot
> That keep the loosened body sound.'

Some are of opinion that *shard* has the meaning 'dung' in the passage in Macbeth, Act iii. Sc. 2.

> 'The shard-borne beetle with her drowsy hums.'

This word would mean in that case 'born of dung'; the spelling *born* or *borne* is immaterial. There is a beetle called the 'turd-bug' (Halliwell's Dictionary of Archaic and Provincial Words) or 'dung-beetle.' Most commentators interpret *shard-borne* as meaning borne or carried by shards, the hard wing-cases of the beetle. *Shard* or *sherd* means in old writers the hard scale of an animal; and it might mean the mail of a beetle, but there is a gap between the mail-covering of a wing and the wing itself. Gower says of a dragon that his 'scherdes shyne as the sonne' (Confessio Amantis, l. vi.), and describes a serpent,

> 'He was so sherdid all aboute
> It held all edge tools withoute.'   Id. l. v.

These passages do not explain *shard-borne*; but they may explain 'sharded beetle' in Cymbeline, Act iii. Sc. 3:

> 'And often, to our comfort, shall we find
> The sharded beetle in a safer hold
> Than is the full-winged eagle.'

Sharded may here mean 'mail-clad,' but it may also mean 'dunged' or 'dunging,' *sharded* being *sharding* (a not uncommon use in Shakespeare of the past participle termination). In Antony and Cleopatra (Act iii. Sc. 2), Lepidus is described by Ænobarbus as hovering and gloating with praise equally over Caesar and Antony.

> 'They are his shards and he their beetle.'

The meaning of 'dung' for *shard* would be very appropriate here. The commentators generally explain *shards* as the beetle's two wing-cases, but how can they be separated from the beetle? There is a fourth passage in Shakespeare where *shard* occurs, where the meaning may be different. In Hamlet (Act v. Sc. 1) the priest says that Ophelia deserved that

'Shards, flints, and pebbles should be thrown on her.'

Shards here means broken pieces or fragments of pottery: it is the word *sherd* of the translation of the Bible. 'And he shall break it as the breaking of the potters' vessel that is broken to pieces; he shall not spare: so that there shall not be found in the bursting of it a sherd to take fire from the hearth.' (Isaiah xxx. 14.) And again in Ezekiel xxiii. 34: 'Thou shalt break the sherds' of the cup. This *sherd* is preserved in *potsherd*, fragment of a pot, which occurs, so spelt, in Dryden. Here again, however, in the passage of Hamlet, *shards* might mean 'pieces of dung.' Mr. Browning has lately written in The Ring and the Book, probably following the passage of Hamlet,

'By the roadside, mid ordure, shards, and weeds.'

l. 327. *The Panther*, the Church of England.

ll. 339, 340. Compare with this couplet Juvenal, Sat. xiii. 209:

'Nam scelus intra se tacitum qui cogitat ullum,
　　Facti crimen habet.'

l. 354. 'Conjugium vocat, hoc praetexit nomine culpam.'

Virg. Aen. iv. 172.

Henry VIII's divorce from Catharine and marriage with Anne Boleyn are here referred to, as leading to the abolition of the papal authority in England.

. l. 369. Here Dryden refers to the removal of the restriction of celibacy for priests.

l. 371. *hattered out*, wearied out. The word occurs in Ogilby's translation of the Iliad, p. 500, 1669. Jamieson, in his Scottish Dictionary, quotes from Gavan and Gob, iii. 5, 'Helmys of hard steill their hatterit and heuch.'

l. 385. I have preserved here the spelling of the original edition, *travailing*. This was the common spelling for the two meanings, 'journey' (now spelt *travel*) and 'labour.' See Part iii. line 411.

l. 388. *presumed of praise*. A common Gallicism with Dryden: it occurs again in Part iii. line 511.

l. 391. This line has been spoilt by Derrick and most subsequent editors, including Scott, by changing *The* into *Their*. *herds* here means 'shepherds.'

l. 399. *phylacteries*. The accent is on the third syllable, the *e* being long in Greek, φυλακτήριον.

l. 409. Derrick and a few other editors have spoilt this line by changing *reformed* into *deformed*:

'And least deformed, because deformed the least,'

which is simple nonsense.

ll. 417-430. Dryden here criticises the Article of the Church of England on the Eucharist, Art. xxviii. 'The Supper of the Lord is not only a sign of the love that Christians ought to have amongst themselves one to another, but rather it is a sacrament of our redemption by Christ's death ; insomuch that to such as rightly, worthily, and with faith receive the same, the bread which we break is a partaking of the body of Christ. . . . . . The body of Christ is given, taken, and eaten, in the Supper only, after an heavenly and spiritual manner. And the means whereby the body of Christ is received and eaten in the Supper is faith.'

l. 446. *Resolved* here means 'dissolved.' It is similarly used in Dryden's Eleanora, 229 :

> 'Goodness resolved into necessity.'

l. 449. *Isgrim's.* Dryden has a note on this word, ' The Wolf.' It is the name given to the wolf in the old German fable of Reynard the Fox. This is ridiculed in Montague and Prior's parody. Bayes says : ' Take it from me, Mr. Smith, there is as good morality, and as sound precepts in the delectable History of Reynard the Fox, as in any book I know, except Seneca; pray tell me where, in any other author, could I have found so pretty a name for a wolf as Isgrim?' But Dryden had Beaumont and Fletcher's example :

> 'Isgrim himself in all his bloody anger
> I can beat from the bay.'   Beggar's Bush, Act iii. Sc. 4.

l. 552. There was an old superstition that the wolf's seeing the man before he saw it, or the sight of a wolf, or the wolf's look, deprived a man of the power of speech :

> ' Vox quoque Moerin
> Jam fugit ipsa : lupi Moerin videre priores.'
>   Virg. Eclogue ix. 53.

In Theocritus (Idyl xiv. 22) the mere sight of a wolf is said to take away speech. Pliny says that when a wolf sees a man before the man sees him, it is believed to have the effect of taking away the man's power of speech for the time. There is no classical authority, however, for the power which Dryden here gives the Hind of making the wolf speechless. Shirley, in the Royal Master (Act iv. Sc. 6), states it correctly : ' The fright she was in late, like a wolf that sees a man first, hath taken away her voice.'

l. 554. *suffised*, so spelt in the original ·edition, and the spelling is here retained; from the French *suffiser*.

The Hind and the Panther. Part II.

ll. 1–11. This refers to the agitation against the Roman Catholics in consequence of the so-called Popish Plot. ' The younger Lion ' is James II, then Duke of York. The Hind replies (17-27) that the prosecution was against the Church of England as well as the Roman Catholics.

l. 21. *quarry* here stands for game as distinguished from vermin.

l. 30. The Test Acts of 1673 and 1678 prescribed a declaration denying Transubstantiation; the words of both these Acts were, 'I do believe that in the Sacrament of the Lord's Supper there is not any transubstantiation of the elements of bread and wine into the body and blood of Christ at or after the consecration thereof by any person whatsoever.'

l. 63. *cannon* is in the early editions, and it is here preserved. The word is changed to *canon* in Scott's and the Wartons' editions. *cannon* seems the best sense, and Dryden may have meant a play on the word. In Part iii. line 466 *canon* is misprinted *cannon* in the first edition, and it is corrected in the second to *canon*. But in this passage *cannon* remains.

l. 67. *subterranean Rome*, 'Roma Sotteranea,' an extensive cavern near Rome, formerly inhabited, described in a work of that name published at Rome, circa 1632. Evelyn describes his visit to this cavern in his Diary, April 11, 1645.

l. 79. *For fallacies in universals live.* 'Dolus versatur in generalibus.' Compare 'As those who in a logical dispute keep in general terms would hide a fallacy.' (Preface to Annus Mirabilis, p. 27.)

l. 142. Luther's doctrine of Consubstantiation.

l. 161. An imitation of Lucan:

> 'Infestisque obvia signis
> Signa, pares aquilas, et pila minantia pilis.'
>
> Pharsalia, i. 7.

l. 227. The omen of the ladder is, it is to be presumed, the gallows.

l. 228. The sweetness of the panther's breath is an old belief. It is mentioned by Pliny (Hist. Nat. xxi. 7).

> 'Thy baths shall be the juice of July flowers,
> Spirit of roses and of violets,
> The milk of unicorns and panthers' breath,
> Gathered in bags and mixt with Cretan wines.'
>
> Ben Jonson, The Fox, Act iii. Sc. 5.

> 'And yet your grace is bound
> To have his accusation confirmed,
> Or bunt this spotted panther to his ruin,
> Whose breath is only sweet to poison virtue.'
>
> Shirley, The Royal Master, Act iii. Sc. 1.

l. 230. *the blatant beast. blatant*, 'howling,' 'barking.' Dryden here means probably the Presbyterian, the Wolf. Derrick thought it referred to the Blatant Beast of Spenser's Faery Queen, Slander; and Scott and other editors have adopted Derrick's interpretation, printing the two words with initial capitals; but they are not so printed in the original editions.

l. 268. These statutes were suspended by James's Declaration of Indulgence, issued shortly before the publication of the poem.

l. 345. *He darkly writ.* ‘As also in all his epistles, speaking in them of those things; in which are some things hard to be understood.’ (2 Peter iii. 16.)

l. 382. Hungary, then the object of contention between the Turks and Germany.

l. 398. This refers to the reply of Jesus to the Jewish officers who went with Judas to seek him. ‘As soon then as he had said unto them, I am he, they went backward, and fell to the ground.’ (St. John xviii. 6.)

l. 410. The phrase *crown-general* is ridiculed in Prior and Montagu’s parody :·

‘There’s a pretty name now for the Spotted Mouse, The Viceroy!

‘*Smith.* But pray, why d’ ye call her so?

‘*Bayes.* Why, because it sounds prettily: I’ll call her the Crown-General presently, if I have a mind to it.’

l. 419. *Curtana.* The sword of mercy, a sword without an edge, said to have belonged to Edward the Confessor, and carried before our kings at their coronation.

l. 454. *The consubstantiating Church and priest*, the Lutherans.

l. 525. Either the accent is on the second syllable of *spiritual*, and so again in line 618, or in both lines the *i* is elided. The noun used always by Dryden is *sprite* or *spright*, not *spirit*. See line 653.

‘For after death we sprites have just such natures.’
Epilogue to Tyrannic Love.

‘You groan, sir, ever since the morning light,
As something had disturbed your noble spright.’
The Cock and the Fox, 103.

l. 538. See Exodus viii. and ix. for the Egyptian magicians unable to destroy the frogs which they had brought on Egypt, or to get rid of the lice, and also covered with boils.

l. 543. Broughton changed *botches* to *blotches*, which has been printed by succeeding editors. A *botch* is a sore: ‘The Lord shall smite thee in the knees and in the legs with a sore botch that cannot be healed.’ (Deut. xxviii. 35.)

‘Young Hylas botched with stains too foul to name.’
Garth’s Dispensary, Act ii.

l. 562. *disembogue*, from the French *désemboucher*, to open out.

‘To where Fleet ditch with disemboguing streams,
Rolls the large tribute of dead dogs to Thames.’
Pope, Dunciad, ii. 271.

l. 563. *palliard*, from the French *paillard*, a lewd person.

l. 565. *missioners.* In the first edition the word was *missionaires* direct from the French. In the second edition of the poem *missioners* was substituted. Dryden uses *missioner* again in his Epistle to Sir George Etherege:

> 'Like mighty missioner you come
>   *Ad partes infidelium.'*

l. 571. *Industrious of the needle and the chart.*   A Latinism, 'Industrious of the common good.' (Dryden's Address to his cousin John Driden, 153.)

l. 575. This passage is levelled at the Dutch, whom Dryden accuses of denying their Christianity in order to trade in Japan, where Christians were forbidden to land.

l. 576. Dryden has been describing the marks of the Catholic Church from the Nicene Creed: 'And I believe in one Catholic and Apostolic Church.'   See his marginal note at line 526.   Three marks were indicated in lines 526–531.   Now he gives the fourth mark, the apostolic origin.

l. 590. In St. Matthew vii. 24, 27: 'And the rain descended, and the floods came, and the winds blew,' &c.

l. 630. In the first edition the word was *nine* instead of *seven.*

l. 646. *That pious Joseph in the Church beheld*, &c.   Dryden's marginal note explains this passage as referring to a formal renunciation recently made by the English Benedictine monks of the abbey lands which had belonged to their order before the Reformation.   This was done in order to quiet the fears of proprietors and aid in restoring the Roman Catholic Religion in England.

l. 658. From Dryden's marginal note *Poeta loquitur*, it is to be inferred that he here describes a phenomenon seen by himself.   James's 'late nocturnal victory,' must be the battle of Sedgmoor, which began soon after midnight, and was not finished till the break of day, July 7, 1685. Dryden appears to refer to an Aurora Borealis, or a display of shooting stars seen by himself on that night, but there is no other known mention of this circumstance.   Mr. Hallam has erroneously explained the passage as referring to the night of the conception of James's heir, and he supposes that Dryden means that this event was announced by a stream of light from Heaven which he saw.   But this explanation is impossible.   James's son was born on June 10, 1688, and The Hind and the Panther was published fourteen months before, in April 1687.   With line 659 compare

> 'A beam of comfort, like the moon through clouds,
>   Gilds the brown horror and directs my way.'

Love Triumphant, Act iv. Sc. 1.

l. 721. *Cates,* provisions; contracted from an old word *achates* or *acates,* the French *achats.*

The Hind and the Panther. Part III.

ll. 8–11. Spenser, in his Mother Hubbard's Tale, represented Queen Elizabeth as a Lion asleep, while the Ape and the Fox, ministers of government, usurped the functions and did mischief.

> ' The Lion sleeping lay in secret shade,
> His crown and sceptre lying down beside.
> And having doft for heat his dreadful hide.'

The anniversary of Queen Elizabeth's succession, November 17, was an annual festival at this time of great Protestant excitement, the Pope being always burned in effigy in the evening. Dryden describes the anti-Papist demonstrations of Queen Bess's night in his Prologue to Southerne's Loyal Brother (p. 453 of Globe Edition).

l. 19. *round eternity.* See note on *circular*, Poem on Cromwell, stanza 5. Cleaveland has ' eternity's round womb' (Poems 1659, p. 58).

> ' As round and full as the great circle of eternity.'
>
> Sprat's Pindaric Ode on Cowley.

l. 21. ' The lion's peace proclaimed,' is James II's Declaration of Indulgence.

l. 25. *frequent senate*, full, well-attended senate. ' Frequens senatus,' is a phrase of Cicero (Epist. Fam. x. 12). Compare Milton :

> ' The great seraphic lords and cherubim
> In close recess and secret conclave sat
> A thousand demi-gods on golden seats,
> Frequent and full.'   Paradise Lost, i. 794.

l. 42. The Panther's ' faith unshaken to an exiled heir,' is the support given by the Church of England to James when Duke of York, and forced to live away from London and threatened with exclusion from succession to the throne.

l. 85. *It shows a rest of kindness to complain.* Dryden uses the same sentiment in a letter to Dr. Busby in 1682, complaining of his treatment of his song at Westminster : ' None complain but they desire to be reconciled at the same time; there is no mild expostulation at least which does not intimate a kindness and respect in him who makes it.'

l. 96. *spooms.* To *spoom* is a nautical term applied to a ship under sail going before the wind.

l. 114. *I am but few.* Compare ' a numerous exile,' Part i. line 20.

l. 121. *A German quarrel*, from the French ' une querelle Allemande,' which means a quarrel picked without cause.

l. 143. *renounces to my blood.* Compare, in Dryden's marginal note, Part ii. line 648, ' renunciation to the abbey-lands.' This is one of Dryden's frequent Gallicisms.

l. 152. *doted*, foolish from age.

l. 160. The 'sons of latitude,' are the divines of the Church of England who were for widening its basis and for endeavouring to comprehend a large portion of the Nonconformists. Tillotson, Stillingfleet and Burnet were leaders among these. In line 187 these divines are 'sons of breadth,' and in line 229 'broad-way sons.'

l. 194. The 'three steeples argent in a sable field,' is supposed to mean plurality of preferments, and Stillingfleet, who was in controversy with Dryden about the Duchess of York's paper, is supposed to be specially aimed at by Dryden.

l. 199. *Bare lies with bold assertions they can face.* This line means 'they can cover bare lies with a facing of bold assertions.'

l. 201. *The grim logician* is a retort on Stillingfleet, who had frequently applied this phrase to Dryden in his 'Vindication of the Answer to some late Papers.' The whole of this passage, ll. 198-217, is a paraphrase of sentences and arguments in Stillingfleet's 'Vindication.' Stillingfleet had argued strongly against the imputation on the Reformation, founded on Henry VIII's divorce and marriage, and had hotly contradicted Dryden's assertion that there was no Protestant treatise on Humility. See note on Preface, l. 35 (p. 274).

l. 217. *The Sermon in the Mount.* Dryden's *in* has been changed by modern editors, including Scott, into *on*.

l. 227. *Tax those of interest.* *To tax of* is one of Dryden's many Gallicisms.

ll. 247-250. This is not the only occasion on which Dryden has denounced the neglect which the author of Hudibras experienced. In a letter written by him in 1683 to Laurence Hyde, Earl of Rochester, then First Commissioner of the Treasury, Dryden had said, in pleading for himself, ''Tis enough for one age to have neglected Mr. Cowley and starved Mr. Butler.' Sir Walter Scott justly observes in his note on this passage, that King Charles II and his government were much more to blame than the Church.

l. 256. *But Imprimatur with a chaplain's name.* Stillingfleet's pamphlets were licensed by the Archbishop of Canterbury's chaplain.

ll. 307-309. Dryden's charges against Stillingfleet of 'reviling' and 'cursing' the king are totally unfounded. Stillingfleet's two tracts contain nothing disrespectful to Charles, James, or the Duchess of York.

l. 333. *Rodriguez' work.* Alonzo Rodriguez, a Jesuit, wrote a work called 'Exerjicio de Perfection y Virtudes Cristianas,' published at Seville, 1609. This is the work which Dryden in the Preface to this poem referred to as the original of a treatise which Stillingfleet had treated as an English work on Humility: and Dryden speaks of Duncomb as the translator. The authors of the parody on The Hind and the Panther twit Dryden with inaccuracy, and say that he has mistaken Duncombe for Allen: 'There are few mistakes but one may imagine how a man fell into them, and at least what he aimed at; but what likeness is there between Duncomb and Allen? Do they as much as rhyme?' (Preface to The Hind and the Panther Transversed, &c.) Scott rather strangely thinks that 'a sort of similarity of sound may have led to Dryden's mistake.' The English translator or adapter of the work of Rodriguez is supposed to have been the Rev. Thomas Allen, rector of Kettering, Northamptonshire.

l. 427. The tale of the Swallows is a fable of the temporary prosperity of the Roman Catholics and their ultimate discomfiture here, strangely predicted by Dryden. The Swallows hold a consultation and vote a flight in view of the coming winter. The Martin joins with the young swallows in counselling the postponement of the flight, and they then resolve to stay. Scott sees in the fable a special reference to a meeting of the leading Roman Catholics in the Savoy in 1686, to consider the prospects of their religion in England, Father Petre in the chair. At this meeting the majority were for moderation, and content with security for their estates, exemption from employments, and permission for their worship in private houses. Others were for petitioning the king for leave to sell their estates and retire with their property to France. Father Petre was against all compromise. Petre is the Martin in the fable. The gleam of sunshine which gives the Swallows hope and new life is doubtless James's Declaration of Indulgence, and the Swifts who first see the coming of spring are probably the Irish Roman Catholics.

l. 437. *cheer*, face, look. Dryden uses *cheer* in this sense twice in Palamon and Arcite.

> 'And asked him why he looked so deadly wan,
> And whence and how his change of cheer began.'
>
> Book i. line 240.

> 'For Venus, like her day, will change her cheer.'
>
> Book ii. line 83.

l. 438. *And time turned up the wrong side of the year.* Dryden probably had in his mind Horace's phrase,

> 'Simul inversum contristat Aquarius annum.'
>
> Sat. i. 1. 36.

In one of Dryden's smaller poems, 'A Song to a Fair Young Lady going out of Town in the Spring,' he uses a similar expression:

> 'And winter storms invert the year.'

l. 456. *mackrel gale.* Mackerel are best caught during a fresh gale of wind, which is therefore called a mackerel gale.

l. 468. *But little learning needs in noble blood.* Father Edward Petre, who is here contemptuously described as the Martin, was of the noble family of Petre. This account of him, put into the mouth of the Panther, yet speaks Dryden's feeling. The English Roman Catholics were divided into two parties, moderate Papists and followers of the Jesuits.

l. 475. A raven on the left was regarded by the Romans as a sure prophet, and Dryden probably has Virgil in memory:

> 'Quod nisi me quacumque novas incidere lites
>   Ante sinistra cava monuisset ab ilice cornix,
>   Nec tuus hic Moeris nec viveret ipse Menalcas.'   Ecl. ix. 14.

l. 490. *mad divineress.* The ' insana vates ' of Virgil, who so describes the Sibyl of Cumae, committing her prophecies to leaves.

> 'Insanam vatem adspicies: quae rupe sub ima
>   Fata canit, foliisque notas et nomina mandat.'   Aen. iii. 443.

l. 494. χελιδὼν (Chelidon) is the Greek for a swallow.

L 520. *Nostradamus.* This general name for a prophet is derived from Michel Notre Dame, a famous French physician and prophet, who was born 1503, and died 1566.

l. 538. *Of Ahaz' dial and of Joshua's day.* For the former see 2 Kings xx., and for the latter Joshua x.

l. 547. Dryden says in a note that swifts are ' otherwise called martlets.'

l. 604. Compare with this line

> 'But gods meet gods, and justle in the dark.'
>
>   Dryden and Lee's Œdipus, Act iv.

l. 611. *dorp,* a village; a word of Dutch origin: the English form is *thorpe.*

l. 637. *And there his corps, unblessed, is hanging still.* *are* is in the early editions instead of *is,* but this must have been a mistake.

l. 638. *To show the change of winds with his prophetic bill.* Scott says, ' It is a vulgar idea that a dead swallow, suspended in the air, intimates a change of wind by turning its bill to the point from which it is to blow.'

l. 655. The ' old fanatic author ' who ' summed up the scandals ' of the Panther's Church ' by centuries,' was John White, a Puritan member of the Long Parliament, who published in 1643 a work entitled ' The First Century of Scandalous Malignant Priests made and admitted into Benefices by the Prelates.' No second part of the work appeared. White died in 1645. He acquired from this work the name of Century White.

l. 667. *Pardalis,* the Greek and Latin name for a panther, misspelt *Pardelis* in all the editions from the original one.

ll. 690, 691. Here Dryden borrows the language which the young men advised Rehoboam to use in answer to Jeroboam, and to those who asked him to lighten his father's yoke. ' Thus shalt thou say unto them, My little finger shall be thicker than my father's loins. And now whereas my father did lade you with a heavy yoke, I will add to your yoke; my father hath chastised you with whips, but I will chastise you with scorpions.' (1 Kings xii. 10, 11.)

l. 733. *Yet David's bench is bare.* This is supposed to mean the exclusion of the Roman Catholic peers from the House of Lords, effected by the Test Act of 1678.

l. 749. *sterve.* *Sterve* is retained here as printed by Dryden. But *starve* is more commonly printed in Dryden's original editions, and *starve* is printed in line 975, where it rhymes with *serve.* *Serve* and *deserve* were, however, pronounced at that time *sarve* and *desarve.* The word is printed *sterve* in one of Dryden's Prologues to the University of Oxford, 1681 (Globe Edition, p. 451):

> ‘How ill soe'er our action may deserve,
> Oxford's a place where wit can never sterve.’

ll. 754, 755. Tobias drove away the evil spirit which haunted his bride Raguel by fumigation (Tobit viii. 1–3). ‘And when they had supped, they brought Tobias in unto her. And as he went, he remembered the words of Raphael, and took the ashes of the perfumes, and put the heart and the liver of the fish thereupon, and made a smoke therewith. The which smell when the evil spirit had smelled, he fled into the utmost parts of Egypt, and the angel bound him.’

l. 759. A misprint in this line of *but* for *butt* was in the original edition, and has been perpetuated by editors, who have one after the other printed it without any attempt to explain or correct it. ‘The but and peace’ is perfectly unintelligible. ‘The butt and peace’ is a reference to Dryden's Tempest, where the butt plays a great part in a contention of Trinculo with Stephano and Ventoso. Stephano desires permission to drink from the butt before he returns to deliberate on the terms offered by Trinculo. ‘That,’ says Trinculo, ‘I refuse, till acts of hostility be ceased. Then rogues are rather spies than ambassadors. I must take heed of my butt.’ Stephano returns with his friends Ventoso and Mustacho, and the following conversation takes place :—

> ‘*Vent.* Duke Trinculo, we have considered.
> *Trin.* Peace or war?
> *Must.* Peace and the butt.’

Act iv. Sc. 3.

I am not aware of any other writer using this phrase, but Dryden treats it as if it were well known. He uses it again in his Prologues to The Mistakes (p. 473 of the Globe Edition):

> ‘Peace and the butt is all our business here.’

l. 767. This refers to Aeneas and Latinus in Book vii. of the Aeneid.

L 818. *O Proteus Conscience, never to be tied!* Compare

> ‘Quo teneam vultus mutantem Protea nodo?’

Horace, Epist. i. 1. 90.

ll. 823, 824. *Immortal powers the term of Conscience know.*
But Interest is her name with men below.

An imitation of Homer:

> Ὃν Βριάρεων καλέουσι θεοὶ, ἄνδρες δέ τε πάντες
> Αἰγαίων.’ Iliad, i. 403.

U

l. 862. *reprise*, for ' reprisal '; so used elsewhere by Dryden. But Dryden also uses *reprise* as the French *reprise:*

> ' Disease, despair, and death as three reprises bold.'
>
> Britannia Rediviva, 231.

ll. 876–880. These lines refer to James II's open support and aid given to the French Protestant refugees. Bishop Burnet thus speaks of James's decided measures and language about the persecution of the Huguenots by Louis XIV. ' Though all endeavours were used to lessen the clamour this had raised, yet the King did not stick openly to condemn it as both unchristian and unpolitic. He took pains to clear the Jesuits of it, and laid the blame of it chiefly on the King, on Madame de Maintenon, and the Archbishop of Paris. He spoke often of it with such vehemence, that there seemed to be an affectation in it. He did more. He was very kind to the refugees. He was liberal to many of them. He ordered a brief for a charitable collection over the nation for them all; upon which great sums were sent in. They were deposited in good hands, and well distributed. The King also ordered them to be denised without paying fees, and gave them great immunities. So that in all there came over, first to last, between forty and fifty thousand of that nation.' (Hist. of Own Times, i. 664.)

l. 906. Here begins the fable of the Pigeons and the Buzzard, the second episode of the poem. The Buzzard is Dr. Burnet, afterwards Bishop of Salisbury, whom the pigeons or doves, the clergy of the Church of England, choose for their king. The ' plain good man, whose name is understood,' is James II.

l. 941. *the fabric where he prayed* is James II's Roman Catholic chapel at Whitehall.

l. 946. *A sort of Doves.* *sort* means ' number.'

> ' As when a sort of wolves infect the night
>   With their wild howlings at fair Cynthia's light.'
>
> Waller's Poems, p. 314, ed. 1705.

l. 975. Here *starved* is printed in the original and early editions, though rhyming with *served.* See note on line 749, where it is *sterved*, rhyming with *deserved.*

l. 991. *crops impure.* *crops*, which is the word of the original editions, was changed by Broughton into *corps*, and this has been copied by succeeding editors, who print *corpse*, as Scott. *Corpse*, singular, is clearly inappropriate. *Crops* is evidently the right word.

l. 995. *his poor domestic poultry.* James II's Roman Catholic priests.

l. 1006. *The bird that warned St. Peter of his fall.* ' The cock,' says Scott, ' is made an emblem of the regular clergy of Rome, on account of their nocturnal devotions and matins.'

l. 1024. *And sister Partlett, with her hooded head:* this is the nun.

l. 1056. *No Holland emblem could that malice mend.* The Dutch were famous for emblems and pictures. In Prior and Montague's parody there is a reference to this hit at the Dutch. Mr. Bayes is made to boast of his drawings. ' Oh Lord! nothing at all. I could design twenty of 'em in an hour, if I had but witty fellows about me to draw 'em. I was proffered a pension to go·into Holland and continue these emblems; but hang 'em, they are dull rogues and would spoil my invention.'

l. 1064. *The birds of Venus,* the Doves; and the phrase was doubtless intended to convey a reflection on the Church of England clergy.

ll. 1093, 94. This couplet is a free translation of two Greek lines, a fragment of Euripides preserved by Athenagoras :

> Ὅταν δὲ δαίμων ἀνδρὶ πορσύνῃ κακὰ
>
> Τὸν νοῦν ἔβλαψε πρῶτον.

Translated into Latin thus,

> ' Quem Deus vult perdere prius dementat.'

l. 1119. The *musquet* is the male of the sparrow-hawk; the *coystrel* (or *kestrel*) according to Johnson, is ' a species of degenerate hawk.'

l. 1174. *A Greek, and bountiful, forewarns us twice.* Compare

> ' Timeo Danaos et dona ferentes.' Virg. Aen. ii. 49.

ll. 1179–82. This denunciation against Burnet is supposed to refer to evidence given by him in 1675, before a committee of the House of Commons, revealing private conversations of the Duke of Lauderdale with himself, to the effect that he wished the Presbyterians in Scotland would rebel, that he might bring over the French papists to cut their throats.

l. 1188. *And runs an Indian muck at all he meets.* Dryden here takes a great liberty with the phrase ' run amuck,' which is of Malay origin, and has no connexion with our word *muck.* Scott, in his note on this passage, has the following: ' To run a-muck is a phrase derived from a practice of the Malays. When one of this nation has lost his whole substance by gaming, or sustained any other great and unsupportable calamity, he intoxicates himself with opium, and having dishevelled his hair, rushes into the streets, crying *Amocca* or *Kill,* and stabbing every one whom he meets with his creeze, until he is cut down, or shot like a mad dog.'

l. 1192. *Captain of the Test.* Burnet was at this time carrying on a controversy with Parker, Bishop of Oxford, who had proposed the abrogation of the Test. This probably is why this name is given to Burnet.

ll. 1257, 58. The reference in this couplet is to Genesis xlix. 10: ' The sceptre shall not depart from Judah, nor a lawgiver from between his feet, until Shiloh come.'

l. 1260. *Like Dionysius to a private rod.* Dionysius, the tyrant of Syracuse, became, after he was deposed, a schoolmaster at Corinth.

l. 1268. *the smiths of their own foolish fate.* A translation from the Latin, in a passage quoted from Appius in a piece ascribed to Sallust,

'Epistola ad Caesarem de Republica Ordinanda,' i. 1 : 'Res docuit id verum esse quod in carminibus Appius ait, fabrum esse quemque fortunae suae.'

l. 1283. *Bare benting times*, times when the pigeons have no food but *bent*, a coarse grass.

> 'The pigeon never knoweth woe
> Until she doth a benting go.'

(Old proverb, quoted in Latham's edition of Johnson's Dictionary.) The word *bent* is rare.   Browning uses it :

> 'For the rabbit that robs scarce a blade or a bent.'

GLOSSARY.

A.

Abate, *v. i.* lessen, ' abate of virulence.'   Preface to R. L.

Abbethdin, *sb.* chief judge among the Jews.   A. A. 188.

Admire, *v. i.* wonder.   H. P. iii. 388.

Affect, *v. t.* seek, desire.   A. M. 273; A. A. 177.

Affright, *sb.* fear.   A. A. 71.

Alga, *sb.* sea-weed.   A. R. 119.

Allay, *sb.* alloy.   H. P. i. 320.

Allude, *v. i.* compare.   H. P. iii. 366.

Amain, *adv.* vehemently.   H. P. iii. 620.

Antique, *adj.* strange, grotesque.   H. P. iii. 488.

Armado, *sb.* army.   A. M. 14.

Arose, *p. p.* arisen.   O. C. 36.

Assay, *v. t.* try, essay.   O. C. 12; H. P. iii. 796.

Atone, *v. t.* reconcile, harmonise, A. A. 179: used intransitively, R. L. 89.

Auctority, *sb.* authority.   H. P. i. 453, ii. 276.   Elsewhere *authority*.

Auspice, *sb.* patronage.   A. M. 288.

Authentic, *adj.* authoritative, authorised.   O. C. 2; H. P. iii. 838; Pref. to R. L.

B.

Bad, *v.* perfect of *bid,* ordered.   H. P. i. 531.

Benting, *adj.* ' benting times,' times when pigeons feed on bent, a coarse grass.   H. P. iii. 1283.

Big-corned, *adj.* big-grained, ' big-corned powder.'   A. M. 149.

Bilander, *sb.* coasting vessel.   H. P. i. 128.

Blatant, *adj.* howling, barking.   H. P. iii. 230.

Bleaky, *adj.* bleak.   H. P. iii. 612.

Botch, *sb.* sore spot, eruption.   H. P. ii. 542.
Brave, *sb.* bravo.   A. A. 967.
Breathe, *v. t.* to open, lance; applied to opening a vein.   O. C. 12.
Brew, *v. t.* mix, make.   O. C. 25; A. R. 296.
Broke, *p. p.* broken.   A. M. 239, 255.
Build (spelt *built* in original edition), shape.   A. M. 60.

C.

Castor, *sb.* beaver.   A. M. 25.
Cates, *sb.* food.   H. P. ii. 721.
Cense, *v. i.* scatter incense.   H. P. iii. 753.
Cham, *sb.* Ham, son of Noah.   Pref. to R. L.
Check, *sb.* 'fly at check,' fly at random.   A. M. 86.
Cheer, *sb.* countenance.   H. P. iii. 437.
Chirurgeon, *sb.* surgeon.   Pref. to A. A.
Chose, *p. p.* chosen.   A. M. 75.
Circular, *adj.* complete, perfect, 'circular fame.'   O. C. 5.
Circularly, *adv.* all round, in circles.   A. M. 2.
Clip, *v. i.* fly fast, 'clips it.'   A. M. 86.
Cockle, *sb.* weed in corn.   A. A. 195.
Commonweal, *sb.* commonwealth.   H. P. i. 234.
Complexion, *sb.* physical disposition.   O. C. 25.
Composure, *sb.* reconciliation.   Pref. to A. A.
Concernment, *sb.* care, concern.   Pref. to A. M.
Confident, *sb.* a person confided in.   O. C. 25.
Connatural, *adj.* of same nature, 'connatural to.'   Pref. to A. M.
Consequent, *sb.* consequence.   Pref. to A. A.
Corps, *sb.* corpse, body, used for plural as well as singular; plural, H. P. i. 23.
Couch, *v. t.* lay down.   H. P. i. 722.
Couchee, *sb.* evening reception.   H. P. i. 516.
Courage, *sb.* used in the plural, 'courages.'   A. M. 76, 93.
Cozenage, *sb.* deception.   H. P. ii. 258.
Crack, *sb.* noise of falling, crash.   A. M. 238.
Cross, *adv.* across.   A. M. 156, 233.
Curtana, *sb.* the sword of mercy.   H. P. ii. 419.

D.

Dared, *p. p.* frightened, bewildered; applied to larks.   A. M. 195.
Dauby, *adj.* sticky.   A. M. 148.
Decease, *v. i.* die.   O. C. 34.
Deducement, *sb.* deduction.   Pref. to R. L.

Designment, *sb.* design.   O.C. 24.
Despite, *sb.* spite.   H.P. iii. 70.
Detort, *v. t.* twist.   Pref. to R.L.
Devest, *v. t.* divest.   H.P. i. 187.
Digestive, *adj.* digesting.   A.R. 89.
Dint, *sb.* force.   H.P. iii. 200.
Disembogue, *v. i.* empty out.   H.P. ii. 562.
Disheir, *v. t.* deprive of an heir.   H.P. iii. 705.
Disinteressed, *adj.* disinterested.   R.L. 335.
Dismission, *sb.* dismissal.   H.P. i. 346.
Doom, *v. t.* destine, used familiarly, 'doom wool into France.'   A.M. 207.
Dorp, *sb.* village.   H.P. iii. 611.
Doted, *adj.* doting, foolish.   H.P. iii. 152.

E.

Earthy, *adj.* of the earth.   A.A. 637.
Eiry, *sb.* nest.   A.M. 107.
Epoche, *sb.* epoch.   A.R. 108.
Essay, *sb.* first effort, trial.   A.M. 140; H.P. i. 200.
Evince, *v. t.* prove.   H.P. ii. 190, 233.
Expire, *v. i.* applied to a ball coming out of a cannon.   A.M. 188.

F.

Face, *v. t.* put on a facing.   H.P. iii. 199.
Factor, *sb.* agent.   A.R. 78.
Firmamental, *adj.* of the firmament.   A.M. 281.
Flix, *sb.* fur of the hare.   A.M. 132.
Fogue, *sb.* fury.   A.R. 203.
Forbear, *v. t.* forbear from, spare.   A.A. 37.
Forgot, *p. p.* forgotten.   H.P. ii. 333.
Fowl, *sb.* bird, birds, used in plural sense.   A.M. 85; H.P. i. 1243.
   Fowls occurs, H.P. iii. 585.
Frequent, *adj.* crowded.   H.P. iii. 25.
Fright, *v. t.* frighten.   A.M. 50, 109; H.P. i. 79.
Frontless, *adj.* shameless.   Pref. to R.L., and H.P. iii. 1040, 1187.
Froze, *p. p.* frozen.   A.M. 285.

G.

Gage, *sb.* pledge.   A.M. 20.
Galled (spelt *gauled* in original editions), *p. p.* rubbed.   A.M. 148; R.L.
   404.

Gaud, *sb.* ornament. A. M. 206.
Genius, *sb.* ' a genius,' a character of genius. Pref. to A. A.
Give on, *v. i.* proceed violently. A. M. 280.
Godsmith, *sb.* God-maker. A. A. 50.
Graff, *v. t.* graft. Pref. to R. L.
Grave, *v. t.* engrave. H. P. ii. 321.
Gross, *sb.* size, A. M. 152, 233 : ' in gross,' in the general, R. L. 322.

H.

Haggared or haggered, *adj.* haggard, wild. H.P. i. 166 : iii. 1116.
Hard-head, H.P. ii. 443.
Hatch, *v. t.* build. A. M. 198, 288.
Hattered out, *p. p.* wearied. H. P. i. 371.
He, *pron.* used as substantive, ' another he,' A. A. 861 : ' that universal
He,' R. L. 15.
Heir, *v. t.* inherit. H. P. iii. 714.
Her, *pron.* in lieu of 's for genitive. A. A. 1008.
His, *pron.* in lieu of 's for genitive. A. R. 19, 49, 111, 231 ; H. P. ii. 655.
Hobby, *sb.* hawk. A. M. 195.
Holland, *sb.* cloth from Holland. A. M. 206.

I.

Imp, *v. t.* repair ; applied to wings. A. M. 143.
Impassible, *adj.* incapable of suffering. H. P. i. 95.
Industrious, *adj.* ' industrious of.' H. P. ii. 571.
Innocency, *sb.* innocence. Pref. to R. L.
Innovate, *v. t.* introduce for the first time. Pref. to A. M.
Instop, *v. t.* fill up. A. M. 147.
Interessed, *p. p.* interested. Pref. to R. L.

J.

Joy, *v. t.* make joyful, A. M. 110 : *v. i.* rejoice, A. M. 117, 181.

K.

Ken, *sb.* sight. A. M. 111, 159.
Kern, *sb.* Irish peasant. A. M. 157.
Key, *sb.* quay. A. M. 231.

L.

Lade, *v. t.* load. A. M. 252.
Lag, *v. i.* loiter behind. A. M. 85; H. P. iii. 1284.
Laveer, *v. i.* tack about. A. R. 65.
Lazar, *sb.* a filthy deformed person. Pref. to A. M.
Leech, *sb.* doctor. A. R. 175.
Left, *sb.* 'left of,' left by. A. A. 568.
Legator, *sb.* testator. H. P. ii. 375.
Letted, *p. p.* 'letted of,' hindered from. A. M. 222.
Levee, *sb.* morning reception. H. P. i. 516.
Like, *v. t.* please. H. P. iii. 477.
Limbec (spelt *limbeck* in original editions), *sb.* alembic. A. M. 13, 166.
Linstock, *sb.* a match-holder for firing cannon. A. M. 188.
Loll, *v. t.* stretch out. A. M. 132.

M.

Mackrel, *adj.* mackerel, 'a mackrel gale.' H. P. iii. 456.
Manifest, *adj.* 'manifest of crimes.' A. A. 204.
Mannerly, *adj.* well-mannered. H. P. i. 556.
Marling, *sb.* a small tarred line for winding round ropes. A. M. 148.
Martlet, *sb.* a species of swallow. A. M. 110; and note on H. P. iii. 547.
Miss, *v. i.* 'miss of.' H. P. iii. 1189.
Missioner, *sb.* missionary. H. P. ii. 565.
Mould, *sb.* form, shape, make, A. M. 72, 293; A. A. 368: material, H. P. i. 247.
Moulted, *p. p.* afflicted by moulting. A. M. 143.
Muck, *sb.* 'an Indian muck,' H. P. iii. 1118: 'amuck,' from *amocca*, a Malay word for 'kill.'
Musquet, *sb.* a small hawk. H. P. iii. 1119.

N.

Naked, *adj.* 'naked of friends.' A. A. 280.
Name, *sb.* used as if it were the person or thing named. H. P. i. 156.
Need, *v. i.* be needed. R. L. 126; H. P. iii. 321, 1428.
Noblesse, *sb.* nobility. Pref. to A. M.
Noiseful, *adj.* noisy. A. M. 40.

O.

Obligement, *sb.* obligation. H. P. i. 437.
Obscene, *adj.* loathsome, ugly. H. P. ii. 595, 652; iii. 726.

Officious, *adj.* obliging, serviceable. O. C. 1 ; A. M. 184.
Out, *v. t.* oust. Pref. to R. L.

P.

Pain, *sb.* labour. A. M. 32.
Palliard, *sb.* a lewd person, a rascal. H. P. ii. 563.
Pardalis, *sb.* panther. H. P. iii. 667.
Paronomasia, *sb.* pun. Pref. to A. M.
Pay o'er, *v. t.* spread over. A. M. 147.
Pile, *sb.* troop. H. P. ii. 161.
Plagiary, *sb.* plagiarist. Pref. to A. M.
'Plume, *v. t.* pluck. A. A. 920.
Poll, *v. t.* cut down. H. P. iii. 631.
Poppet, *sb.* puppet. H. P. iii. 780.
Practice, *v. t.* frequent. A. A. 825.
Presume, *v. i.* ' presume of.' H. P. i. 388 ; iii. 511.
Prevail, *v.* avail, ' prevail oneself of.' Pref. to A. M. ; A. A. 461.
Prevaricated, *p. p.* made a disingenuous use of. Pref. to R. L.
Prevent, *v. t.* anticipate, go before. O. C. 41, 33 ; A. R. 282 ; A. A. 344 ;
    H. P. ii. 641.
Prime, *sb.* spring. H. P. iii. 536.
Procedure, *sb.* proceeding. A. R. 88.
Profer, *v. t.* proffer. H. P. iii. 766. Elsewhere spelt *proffer* in original
    editions.
Proponent, *sb.* a person propounding. H. P. i. 121.
Protractive, *adj.* protracting. H. P. iii. 1103.
Purchase, *sb.* acquisition. A. R. 86.

Q.

Quarry, *sb.* anything aimed at, A.M. Pref., 86, 281 ; H.P. i. 104 : game
    as distinguished from vermin, H.P. ii. 21.
Quatrain, *sb.* stanza of four lines which rhyme alternately. Pref. to A.M.

R.

Rabbin, *sb.* rabbi, doctor among the Jews. A.A. 104.
Rabbinical, *adj.* of a doctor. A.A. 658.
Raise, *v. a.* extol. A.A. 110.
Raven, *v. i.* hunger. H.P. iii. 964.
Rebate, *v. t.* blunt. Pref. to A.A.
Reflective, *adj.* reflected. A.M. 253.
Remainders, *sb.* plural of remainder, used as if singular. H.P. iii. 602.

Remnants, *sb.* used in the plural like *remainders.* A. M. 102, 258; H. P. i. 510; iii. 276.

Renounce, *v. i.* 'renounce to.' H. P. iii. 143.

Renown, *v. t.* make renowned. R. L. 75.

Renunciation, *sb.* used with *to* after, as the verb *renounce.* H. P. ii. 648 (marginal note).

Repair, *sb.* resort. A. M. 220.

Repeat, *v. t.* reseek. A. M. 257.

Repose, *v. t.* place as a trust, with *upon* after. Pref. to A. M.

Reprise, *sb.* reprisal. H. P. iii. 862.

Republic, *adj.* republican. H. P. iii. 1251.

Require, *v. t.* seek again. A. M. 256.

Resolve, *v. i.* melt, dissolve, H. P. i. 446.

Rest, *sb.* remainder. H. P. iii. 85.

Restiff, *adj.* restive. H. P. 1026.

Retire, *v. t.* draw back. A. M. 249.

Rid, *v.* perfect of ' ride.' Pref. to R. L.

S.

Scanted, *pp.* curtailed, circumscribed. A. A. 369, 839.

Scape, *v. i.* escape. A. R. 180; A. M. 220; H. P. i. 172; ii. 7.

Seal, *v. t.* used figuratively ' sealed our new-born king.' A. M. 18.

Sear-cloth, *v. t.* cover with sear-cloth (cere or wax cloth). A. M. 148.

Shard, *sb.* dung, ordure. H. P. i. 321.

Sheer, *v. t.* cut. A. M. 78.

Shipwrack, *sb.* shipwreck. A. M. 35.

Shipwracked, *p. p.* A. R. 125; A. M. 2, 71, 251.

Shore, *sb.* sewer. H. P. ii. 558.

Show, *v. i.* appear. A. M. 66, 121, 126, 296.

Sincere, *adj.* pure. H. P. ii. 250.

Sincerely, *adv.* purely, without alloy. A. A. 43.

Sort, *sb.* number, collection. H. P. iii. 946.

Sovereign, *adj.* all-powerful. O. C. 19.

Spoom, *v. i.* sail before the wind. H. P. iii. 96.

Sprite, *sb.* spirit. H. P. ii. 653.

Squander, *v. t.* disperse. A. M. 67.

Steepy, *adv.* steep. A. A. 860.

Sterve, *v. i.* starve. H. P. iii. 749.

Stickler, *sb.* sidesman or second in a fight. O. C. 11.

Strook, *v.* (*perfect*) struck. A. R. 171.

Submit, *v. t.* lower. A. R. 249.

Succeed, *v. t.* make to follow or succeed. A. M. 175, 292.

Successive, *adj.* of or by succession. A. A. 301.

Suffice, *v. t.* suffice. H. P. i. 554.
Swift, *adj.* ' swift of despatch.' A. A. 191.
Swisses, *sb.* plural of Swiss. H. P. iii. 177.

T.

Tarnish, *v. i.* become stained. A. A. 249.
Tax, *v. t.* accuse, ' tax of.' H. P. iii. 227.
Tell, *v. t.* count. A. M. 34, 76.
Theologue, *sb.* Theologian. H. P. iii. 1147.
Thick, *adv.* quickly following. A. M. 120.
Thick, *adj.* ' thick of.' O. C. 14.
Threat, *v. t.* threaten. A. M. 61 ; A. A. 141.
Timely, *adv.* in time. A. R. 190.
Tire, *sb.* row of guns. H. P. iii. 317.
Too too, *adv.* excessively. A. R. 111.
Took, *p. p.* taken. A. R. 144.
Traditive, *adj.* traditional. H. P. ii. 196.
Transact, *v. i.* act. H.P. iii. 14.
Travellour, *sb.* traveller. A. R. 148.
Treasonous, *adj.* treasonable. H.P. iii. 633.
Trine, *sb.* conjunction of three planets making a triangle. A.M. 292.
Trust, *v. i.* followed by *on.* A.M. 295.
Turbulent, *adj.* ' turbulent of evil.' A.A. 153.

U.

Unblamed, *adj.* ' unblamed of life.' A.A. 479.
Ungodded, *p. p.* having no gods. H.P. iii. 742.
Unhoped, *adj.* unexpected. A.R. 140.
Unknowing, *adj.* not knowing. A.M. 96.
Unlade, *v. t.* empty, unload. A.M. 300.
Unsatiate, *adj.* insatiable. A. A. 987.
Unsincere, *adj.* mixed, alloyed. A. M. 209.
Unthrift, *sb.* prodigal. H. P. iii. 296.

V.

Vare, *sb.* wand. A. A. 595.

W.

Wait, *v. t.* attend, accompany. H. P. i. 557.
Want, *v. t.* be without. A. A. 197.

Wanting, *adj.* needy, poor.   A. M. 274; A. A. 407, 892.
Well-breathed, *adj.* with good lungs.   A. A. 630.
Wex, *v. i.* wax, grow.   A. M. 4.
Wilder, *v. t.* bewilder.   H. P. ii. 682.
Witness, *sb.* evidence.   H. P. i. 62.
Worser, *adj.* worse.   A. R. 3.

THE END.